"YOU HAVE NOT SWORN OFF ALL MEN, HAVE YOU, MISS POTTS?"

"I am not such a wet goose, my lord," declared Minerva. "I have merely vowed to give men back as good as I have gotten."

"What does that mean?"

"Why to value in a husband what men apparently value in a wife. If I marry, the gentleman must provide me comfort and prestige and prove especially convenient, and love will have not the least thing to do with it."

Rossland's eyebrow cocked at her words and he ceased leaning against the rail, stood up straight and took one of her hands into his. "You are mad, Miss Potts," he drawled, bowing to kiss her fingertips. "Marry me. I have always been a fool for mad and formidable women."

"Nodcock," Mina giggled. "How can anyone believe you to be dangerous?"

"Oh, but I am, sweetling," responded Rossland huskily, drawing her closer to him. "I am dangerous beyond belief."

WATCH FOR THESE ZEBRA REGENCIES

A
Devilish
Dilemma
Judith A. Lansdowne

Zebra Books
Kensington Publishing Corp.

http://www.zebrabooks.com

To the memory of Isabelle C. Berg,
who came into my life with Geordan
and departed so abruptly this past January.
I miss you.

ZEBRA BOOKS are published by

Kensington Publishing Corp.
850 Third Avenue
New York, NY 10022

First Printing: January, 1998
10 9 8 7 6 5 4 3 2 1

Printed in the United States of America

One

Miss Minerva Potts, tears streaming from her lovely blue eyes despite her effort to stem them, swirled her Kutusoff mantel about her shoulders and fled out through the Gramercys' front door, down the front steps and onto the pavement. Ignoring the line of coaches parked along the thoroughfare and shrugging aside the offers of an enterprising linkboy, she totally disregarded the fact that her flimsy dancing slippers offered no protection from the distortions in the walk and she hurried onward. All of her Aunt Letitia's admonitions about the dangers that awaited a young lady who trod the London streets unescorted had fled her mind because of the great pain and anguish in her heart. Minerva sniffed plaintively and swiped at her tears with the back of a kid-gloved hand. How could she have been such an innocent? How could she have trusted so blindly? How could she have been so easily deceived?

The sound of Donald's voice still echoed in her ears. "She is an odd little thing, Redfield, but pliable and with excellent bloodlines. And her father wields a good deal of influence in political circles. Actually, I think Minerva and I shall rub along quite nicely together. Yes, most definitely! And Miss Potts is in possession of quite a respectable dowry, Redfield, and she is a country girl besides —not like to be wishing to follow me to town at the drop of a hat. No, she will remain properly in the country where she belongs and tend to the house and the kiddies and never once question what sort of business I am about in London or think to ask me how I am spending my money. Why, what more could a gentleman desire in a wife, eh?" And he had laughed! Donald had laughed quite triumphantly.

The memory of that laugh stirred the pools of grief at the very bottom of Minerva's soul. What a fool she had been to think that Lord Whithall had actually lost his heart to her! What a gudgeon to have believed his flowery phrases and to have imagined she had seen the look of love in his lying eyes! Crying energetically now and noticing nothing at all around her, Minerva began to run and came slap up against a pristine silk cravat. She gave a little yelp as a pair of strong hands clasped abruptly about her upper arms.

Chadwick Leonardo Brumfield, Earl of Rossland, held on for dear life to the chit who had come crashing into him and listened with considerable dread as his despised cane skittered off into the gutter. His dependence upon that walking stick, lowering though he found it, could nonetheless not be denied. His balance was most precarious without it and at the present moment he was inordinately apprehensive that if he let go his grasp upon the young woman who had come smashing into him, he would end by stretching his length upon the pavement. "Well," he drawled in a voice that betrayed none of his apprehension nor his considerable self-consciousness. "Well, and what is this? Tears? And not those of a serving wench either, though I could be wrong I expect."

He loosed one hand and went to fish about in his pockets until he discovered a large square of white muslin. "In my experience," he continued smoothly, slipping the handkerchief into Minerva's hand and cudgeling his brain for some method to release the girl and retrieve his walking stick without making an utter fool of himself. "In my experience, serving wenches sometimes cry in public but they rarely ever flounce about in Kutusoff mantels and silk dancing slippers. But then, gently bred young ladies seldom go running about the streets alone, so you see I cannot be certain which you are, sweetling."

Minerva wiped angrily at her nose and eyes with the handkerchief and then gave a mighty blow and one more heart-wrenching sob while the gentleman yet clung to her arm with one powerful hand. "I am n-not a serving wench," she managed soulfully.

"Then I must assume that you are a gently bred young lady and are therefore well aware that you ought not to be wandering about the streets unescorted," continued Rossland in the most intriguing tones he could muster while his eyes searched hopefully for his ebony walking stick. "And to do so at such an hour of the evening—really, sweetling—are you totally witless? What if I had been some cutthroat after your purse or your virtue? What would you have done then, eh? And do not stare so," he added, returning his gaze to Minerva. "Anyone would think there was a chip in your china."

"A—chip in my china—?" Even though her heart was breaking, Mina's lips quivered upward just the slightest bit.

"No, do not," ordered the gentleman raising one finger admonishingly before her eyes though he still clung tightly to her arm with the other hand. "Do not smile. For if once you smile, you will lose the whole feel for the thing. Cheltenham tragedies require a great deal of emotional investment and the least hint of a smile will utterly destroy their mood." The long, thin finger encased in a York tan glove dropped from its imperative position and fluttered in beneath Mina's chin, tilting it upward just the merest bit. "Blue," Rossland mumbled with a world-weary sigh. "I thought it must be so. Apparently it is my day for blue-eyed damsels in distress. You are the fourth blue-eyed damsel I have been forced to rescue from dire circumstances since breakfast and it is only now coming on to eleven."

There was a slight twitching at the corners of his mouth and a most delectable sparkle in his eyes and Mina was shocked to discover that the mere sight of a grin threatening to overtake his handsome countenance was fast driving all thought of Lord Whithall's infamy from her mind. Why, her heart did not feel near as broken as it had a moment ago.

"Perhaps it is not broken at all," grinned the gentleman. "Perhaps it is merely bruised a bit."

"What?" she asked, startled to hear him speak her own thoughts so exactly.

"Your heart, sweetling. You suspect some wretched fellow has broken it, do you not? But young ladies' hearts are much stronger than anyone imagines. It is men's hearts that break. Mine," he drawled with a sorrowful sigh though his eyes still flashed with good humor, "mine is about to break this instant because I can think of nothing better to do at the moment than to admit to you the truth of the matter."

"The truth of the matter?"

"Indeed. My cane has apparently gone scuttling off into the gutter, sweetling. And not only can I not see the dastardly thing, but I cannot think how to retrieve it even if I could see it. For if I let go your arm, I am like to go scuttling down into the gutter myself."

"Oh. Oh!" Minerva cried in sudden comprehension. That was why this most intriguing man still maintained a firm grip upon her arm. "I shall escort you to that lamppost, sir."

"Indeed. And when we reach it?"

"Why you shall hold on to it while I find your walking stick of course." Minerva, her sobs forgotten and her tears fast drying, helped the gentleman to the post and leaving him propped, smiling, against it, she began to search for his cane. She discovered it nearly in the center of the street.

"There," she said, presenting it to him with a shy smile. "And you are not to be in the least mortified, sir. A great many dandies have walking sticks."

"Yes," nodded Rossland, "but they do not generally require them in order to maintain an upright position, nor do they find themselves required to send young ladies into the road to retrieve them." He wrapped his hand about the silver wolf's-head with diamond eyes at the top of the stick and extended his other arm to Minerva. "Come. I intend to return you. You have fled from somewhere close, no doubt. You would be hobbling about from stubbed toes and bruised feet else. You will not think me forward if I ask your name, will you—now that you have utterly destroyed my handkerchief?"

"Oh!" gasped Mina gazing down at the limp, damp, twisted mess of muslin in her hand. "Oh, I am so very sorry. I shall take it home and have it washed and ironed for you."

"You certainly will," agreed the gentleman with a nod. "And I shall come to fetch it. Where shall I come?"

"I—I am Miss Minerva Potts and I reside with my Aunt Letitia Farin in Farin House in Green Street."

"Ah," nodded the gentleman leading her back in the direction of the Gramercys', his cane tapping upon the walk beside them. "Letitia Farin neé Potts! A very large sort of lady with a thunderous voice and blazing blue eyes."

"Well, she does have blue eyes, but she is quite small and speaks quite softly."

"Softly to you, perhaps, but Letitia Potts has been berating me since I was in shortcoats and has never once done so in less than a roar. Which most likely accounts for my seeing her as larger than life. A most formidable woman! I have nightmares about her at least once a month. She is always about to cut off my ears with a meat cleaver."

Mina laughed outright at the thought. "That is utter nonsense, sir. Aunt Letitia can be brusque and at times quite overwhelming but I am certain you cannot be afraid of her. You know my name," she added after a few more steps, "am I not to have the privilege of knowing yours?"

"Indeed. I am called Rossland when people wish to refer to me politely."

Mina's heart stuttered; her hand came off his arm; she took a deep breath.

Rossland chuckled. "You have heard of me I think. And now you realize, sweetling, just how very dangerous it is to run about the London streets alone. If you had had the good sense not to do so we might never have met. You would even now be perfectly safe and I might have continued on my way all unaware of your existence. Now, of course, I cannot do that. I understand there to be a ball at the Gramercys' this evening. Is that perchance where you belong?"

Minerva nodded in silence. A tiny shudder ran up her spine. Rossland! she thought. The Devil's Delight! And she took again, most hesitantly, the arm he politely offered her.

With remarkable aplomb Rossland escorted her back to the

Gramercys', up the front steps and into the main hall past a startled, stuttering butler to whom he tossed his hat.

"No, I ain't invited, Hastings, but then, I ain't staying either, so you may erase that scowl and scuttle back to your pantry, eh? No need to announce me. It will merely arouse the twits if you do. Just lay my hat on the table and I shall collect it on my way out."

Minerva noticed the panic in Hastings's usually haughty gaze and could not help but giggle the tiniest bit as Rossland escorted her up the staircase and toward the ballroom.

"No, do not laugh at him," Rossland drawled softly. "Hastings is an old fuddyduddy, I know, but it would be a great blow to his ego to think himself an object of humor."

"I am *not* laughing at him."

"No, of course not. My mistake, sweetling. That giggle, I take it, was due to your nervousness at the sad prospect of being seen upon my arm I collect."

"No."

"Well, it should be. I have not the least doubt that our entrance will create a major stir, Miss Potts. Why, the gossipmongers will bandy your name about for weeks to come. But it cannot be helped. Despite popular opinion I have not lost all sense of propriety and I intend to escort you all the way to your aunt. Letty will likely box my ears for having the audacity to do so. But there, I doubt that worries *you*. You most obviously think Letitia a pleasant sort of woman and therefore are not concerned in the least."

The mere thought of her Aunt Letty boxing a gentleman's ears—especially this particular gentleman's ears—set Minerva to giggling again though she did her best to suppress it. As they arrived at the ballroom, however, her smile was dazzling and her eyes sparkled with mirth.

Silence filtered erratically through the room as Rossland and Minerva halted beneath the entrance arch searching the gathering for sight of Lady Letitia Farin. One conversation faltered and then another as the Gramercys' guests took note of them. Young ladies just finishing a *contredanse* gaped at the unknown gentleman in Bath superfine coat and kerseymere

pantaloons whose dark eyes flashed, and whose dark hair, un-
fashionably long, curled negligently about his ears and across
his brow. And their partners inhaled, astounded, at the sight
of Miss Minerva Potts with her arm through that of The Devil's
Delight. No one, however, was more astonished than Lady Letitia Farin neé Potts who had been searching for her niece this
past quarter hour. From the far side of the room she advanced
upon the couple with angry, determined strides. The crowd
parted in tense silence before her. When at last she reached
them, she glared up at Rossland, hands upon her hips. "Release my niece this instant, Chadwick, or I shall box your ears
on the spot."

Rossland peered down at Minerva and raised an eyebrow
most expressively. The look upon his face plainly said, "I told
you so," and set Mina off into a bout of smothered laughter.

"No need for violence, Letty," he offered then, turning his
gaze back to that lady. "I ain't attacked, captured and ravished
the chit, you know. I found her running along the walk unescorted and have come like a proper gentleman to return her
to you. You ought to thank me is what I think. I do not expect
it, mind you, but I do deserve it. Why there is no telling what
might have happened to such an innocent alone on the streets
of London at such an hour. Really, Letitia, I did think better
of you. To allow an innocent in your charge to put herself into
such danger. It is the outside of enough!"

"You, Chadwick, are the outside of enough!" sputtered Lady
Letitia as she sent a most quelling glare at the grinning Minerva. "To show your face in polite company, Chadwick—and
with my niece on your arm!"

"No, no," drawled Rossland languidly, attempting to subdue
his own grin. "You assume, Letitia. Your niece ain't on my arm.
I am on hers. And we are not in polite company at all. We are
in very impolite company, if you ask me. They are downright
rude, in fact. See how they all stare at us."

"They would not be staring if you had not had the blazing
effrontery to come strutting into this ballroom. You were not
invited and you are not wanted either and well you know it."

"Had you rather I let your niece run off into the night, Letty?

I will remember that the next time and refrain from interference then. Or had you rather I had escorted her home myself and left you to wonder where she had gone? Now that I should like to have done."

"You are a wretched barbarian," mumbled Lady Letitia, her hands abandoning her hips to tug Minerva away from him and over beside herself. "You always have some answer for everything. You have not improved a bit since you were in shortcoats."

Rossland's eyes lit with pure delight. "I have improved a bit, Letty. I do not carry frogs about in my pockets anymore nor spill milk on people. Not but what you will continue to hold that milk incident against me until the day I die though I was only three, I think, at the time. But at this precise moment you would do best, my dear, to put a smile upon your face and pretend that there is nothing the least exceptional in my appearance here. Unless, of course, you *desire* all these twits to banter your niece's name about for weeks in connection with my own."

"They would not dare!"

"Well of course they will dare, Letty. They always do. The least hint of scandal and they dine out on it forever. And you must admit that scowling at me as you are doing now will provide their dismal imaginations with endless conjectures for their tongues to wag about. If I were you, my dear, I would thank me very kindly for being so considerate as to return Miss Potts to you in grand style, take the chick under my wing and strut back into the midst of those rag-mannered stiffrumps as though nothing untoward had occurred. And," he added with a glance at Minerva, "I should discover what gentleman had had the sheer audacity to bring tears to such lovely blue eyes as those and then invite some other gentleman of my acquaintance—some barbarian, I think, crippled or no—to teach the bufflehead a lasting lesson. Your servant, Letty," he added with a bow. And then he turned and left the chamber.

Minerva would have lingered to watch him as he made his way back down the corridor, but her Aunt Letty, pasting a smile upon her face, turned that young lady immediately into the room and ushered her toward a group of dowagers who were still staring at the now empty doorway. "So good of Chadwick to come to your aid, my dear," Lady Letitia said quite loudly. "Though why you should think I had gone off without you, I cannot imagine. But there, you were not feeling at all the thing and were quite bewildered."

Ordinarily Minerva would have been flustered by such a broad hint at what was expected of her, but her mind was amazingly clear. "I cannot think how it came about Aunt Letty," she replied directly. "At first I felt faint with the heat, and then my head began to ache, and when I went off to look for you I got so very muddled that I wandered right out the front door and onto the street. I vow, I had not the vaguest idea what I was doing."

"My poor darling," murmured Lady Letitia, glancing to see if the other chaperones were being at all drawn in by this little scene. "How fortuitous for us that Chadwick was there to turn you about and escort you safely back to me. And how kind of him to order up our coach so that I might take you home at once. Is your head aching dreadfully still?"

"Extremely, Aunt Letty," replied Minerva in fading tones, one hand going to her brow. "I fear I have deplorably overdone this evening."

In a few moments, with best wishes for Minerva's health from quite a number of the dowagers and chaperones, they departed the assembly. Oddly enough, their coach *was* waiting at the front of the establishment having been called up, John Coachman said, "by a reg'lar toff in prime rig sportin' a most outrageous walkin' stick and grinnin' like a lunatic."

"Chadwick," declared Lady Letitia in icy accents as she settled back against the squabs. "Now, be so good as to enlighten me, Minerva. Why were you wandering about the streets alone? You might have been pounced upon and robbed or worse. What on earth were you thinking to do such a thing?"

Mina shook her head slowly, unable to meet her aunt's eyes across the darkened coach. "I was being incredibly foolish," she replied softly. "I did not give a thought to anything at all but what I had overheard and the terrible grief in my heart."

"The terrible grief in your heart?" asked her aunt in surprise. "Good heavens, girl, has someone died?"

"Worse even than that. I overheard Donald speaking to Lord Redfield. I did not mean to overhear. I had gone out onto the balcony to catch a breath of air and there he was with Lord Redfield, only a few steps away. And—"

"And what?"

"Well, he did not notice me, you see. And he was telling Lord Redfield—oh, Aunt Letty, I am so very embarrassed! That I should give my heart to such a—a—scoundrel!"

"A scoundrel? Lord Whithall? But he is a most acceptable match, Minerva. He has title and fortune and consequence—and excellent manners."

"Yes, and he thinks himself to be impeccable. And he wishes me to be his wife so that he might possess himself of my dowry and then bury me in the country to raise his children and keep his house. Oh, Aunt Letty, he called me odd and pliable and said I had excellent bloodlines and that we would rub along well together! It sounded like he was b-buying a horse!"

The words, along with the slight quaver in her niece's voice, brought a pang to Letitia's heart. "Oh, my dearest Mina, I am certain he meant it in no such way. Gentlemen are—well, they are—concerned with such things. It does not mean, my dear, that Lord Whithall is not fond of you."

"He vowed he loved me, Aunt Letitia, he did! And he made me believe that I loved him as well. And all the while he was merely looking for some green girl to do his bidding and leave him free to carouse about London to his heart's content. I have not the least doubt that he plans to use my dowry to set up some high flyer so that he may be happy in town while I am breeding and raising an entire flock of Whithall heirs alone in the country!"

The quaver in Minerva's voice had grown stronger, and Letitia, fearing a bout of hysterics, changed her place to sit beside her niece and put an arm about her quivering shoulders. "Do not cry, my love," she murmured sympathetically. "If all of this is true and you cannot bear the thought of such a union, you shall cry off from the match and I will send the cawker running!"

"Oh! Oh!" gasped Minerva, her voice shaking not with tears but laughter. "A cawker! Yes, and so I shall call him immediately I see him again! I did think my heart was broken you know, Aunt Letitia, but—but—now I know it is not. Because no matter how sad I feel about Donald, I cannot help but laugh when I think of Lord Rossland. Oh, Aunt Letty, you should have seen your face when you spied me upon his arm! And he said you would, you know."

"He said I would what?"

"Box his ears. He expected nothing less of you! And after all he had done for me, too."

"What," asked Lady Letitia in frozen accents, "had he done for you?"

"Why, he made me see that my heart was not broken at all. How could it be when he could make me smile with nonsensical conversation and a lift of his eyebrow? And he said, Aunt Letty, that young ladies' hearts are exceedingly durable."

"Yes, and Chadwick should know," allowed Lady Letitia awfully. "You are not to be deceived by him, Minerva. I realize how engaging that scamp may be when he sets his mind to it, but it is all a sham. His head is filled with windmills and he is the veriest thatchgallows besides and anyone will tell you so. He is not called The Devil's Delight without cause. Absolutely everything he ever chooses to do delights the Devil—that is how he gained the name—and you will have nothing further to do with him. Do you understand?"

"Yes, ma'am," nodded Minerva thoughtfully. "But I will have nothing more to do with Lord Whithall either. I am determined to bring our engagement to an end."

Lady Letitia nodded understandingly. "It seemed the most terrible betrayal, I am certain, when all the time you thought Lord Whithall to be in love with you. And I will stand behind you, Minerva, if that is your decision."

And Lady Letitia did indeed stand behind her niece, going so far as to remain in the parlor the next afternoon when Whithall arrived to take Minerva driving in Hyde Park. Seated in a corner, her tambour pulled up before her, Lady Letitia listened intently to Whithall's mumblings and mutterings and excuses as Mina confronted him with what she had overheard.

And in the end it was Lady Letitia who called Battlesby, her butler, into the chamber and ordered him to escort Lord Whithall to the door and she who requested that His Lordship not show his face in Green Street ever again.

Minerva, her eyes streaming tears as much from nerves as from anger, settled down upon the green and white striped sofa after Lord Whithall had departed and stared blindly into the empty grate. What she was to do now, she could not think. Her aunt, she knew, would expect her to throw back her shoulders, paste a smile upon her face, and carry on. But Mina did not think she could do so. Despite her disenchantment and her anger and her determination to put Lord Whithall in his place, she had sincerely trusted the man and given her heart in all innocence into his keeping. And though she knew her heart was not actually broken, she could feel it was dreadfully bruised.

How could I have smiled and laughed so at Lord Rossland last evening, she wondered, when this afternoon I feel as though my life has ended? Perhaps I was hysterical? I have never been hysterical before, but perhaps that is what it was. Perhaps I was all about in my head. Well, but I am not all about in my head now. I am quite sane and sober. And I have had a good dose of reality, too! Such a good dose that I vow I will never entrust my heart to another gentleman ever again. If Donald could say all those wonderful words to me and treat me so kindly and vow he loved me, when all he wished to do was to find himself a biddable and unsuspecting wife with a respectable dowry to add to his consequence—if he could do such a thing—then so can any other gentleman. And most likely will, too! Well, I will show the lot of them. Miss Minerva Potts is no fool. They will discover that I have become as realistic and as shrewd and as unfeeling as ever any of their sex could hope to be. Never again will I be drawn in by pretty words and fairy-tale dreams. No, and I shall not ever again expect to love or be loved either. I shall put all of that nonsense right out of my mind. And if I ever do marry, I shall do so for the exact same reasons that gentlemen do—for *my* comfort and *my* prestige and *my* convenience—and my heart will *not* be involved in it!

Two

Forager stood as still as anyone could expect a five-year-old gelding to stand, a twitch of his left ear the only noticeable motion as Rossland withdrew his walking stick from the case Luke had ingeniously rigged for it and carefully descended from the saddle before a sprawling cottage of stone and timber that lay deep in the home woods of Riddle, one of his properties a few hours southeast of London. Snuggled amidst beeches and oaks and very near the Thames, the cottage had stood for well over a century. One could walk to the river from it if he wished to do so and peer out across the waters to watch the ships coming and going from the port at Gravesend.

Someday I will walk to the river again, thought Rossland. The more I walk, the more this confounded leg will continue to improve. It must. I cannot bear to be a virtual cripple for the remainder of my years. And even if I did lose my balance most lamentably last evening when Letty's chick bumped into me, I do not generally do so these days. It was more the force of Miss Potts's arrival and the surprise of it that made me feel helpless for a moment or two. I might well have gone and fetched the wretched stick myself though I would have looked a bit foxed doing so.

In his youth Rossland had been bewitched by the river and his boyhood dreams had taken him sailing off to unknown lands, his fledgling's mind relishing the possibilities of mystery, adventure and innumerable dangers which he, of course, would bravely and courageously overcome. But of late he gave the Thames only cursory notice. He had had his share of danger and adventure and it had not proved nearly as appealing as it ought to have done. And besides, he no longer had leisure for daydreams—had not had such leisure since his father's yacht had foundered and deprived him in one instant of his last remaining parent, his elder and only brother, and his nephew Jaimie.

Thrust into responsibilities for which he had never been prepared, Rossland had become acutely aware of his change in rank and fortune, but his heart had declined to enjoy it. Of a sudden he had come to possess estates in Hertfordshire and Surrey, and a small place on the outskirts of Brighton. He had found the running of them bewildering and visited each of the properties only sporadically to confer with his estate managers and caretakers and peruse the accounts.

It was to Riddle, no more than a few hours' ride from the metropolis, and to this cottage at the far edge of the estate that he came most often—came, in fact, whenever he found himself inordinately on edge. And he was inordinately on edge now—had been ever since he had departed the Gramercys' the evening before. Nothing at all had been going well and returning Letty's niece to her had only impressed upon him more heavily all the pleasures he had forsaken in the pursuit of his very personal quest. He was, in fact, on the verge of ruining his entire life. And for what? Ah, but he knew very well for what, and if only his efforts would prove more productive—if he might see some true hope shining before him—then he would not give a fig what he lost in the process. No, he would not even regret his virtual ostracism by Polite Society or the libertine tag to his name that prevented him from wooing such sweet things as Miss Potts.

He let Forager's reins dangle, and made his way to the front door. It opened to him before he knocked. A woman of some sixty years, with a deeply lined face and white hair pulled back into a knot low on her neck, welcomed him with a smile upon her lips and a glint in her clear gray eyes. "My lord," she said. "We were not expecting you."

"No, I came on a whim, Mrs. Beaman. I found I could not

abide town another moment. How is she? Will she come and visit for a while do you think?"

"Of course she will. Been in high gig, she has, these last weeks—ever since your present arrived."

"She liked it then, eh?" he asked, following the housekeeper into a long, low-ceilinged parlor and sinking down into a highly unfashionable and ancient sofa.

"Aye, my lord. Loved it, I should say. Why there is not a moment in the day they are not together. Named it Wicky, she did, after you."

Rossland grinned. "Will I never be anything but Wicky in this house?"

"No, my lord, not to her. Will you be staying? Maitland has come down from Riddle for the afternoon to work about the garden. Shall I tell him to send word to the big house to have your chambers readied?"

"Yes, I rather think so. I have nothing pressing in town and I have not spent any time at all with Liza of late."

A great scuffling and clumping interrupted further conversation and a cry of "Wicky!" followed by a gruff bark and a happy screech preceded the entrance into the parlor of a puppy the size of a small elephant and a diminutive woman no longer in the first blush of youth, but with a beautiful heart-shaped face and hair the color of midnight. "Wicky! Wicky!" she cried, bouncing down onto the sofa beside Rossland and giving his cheek a smacking kiss. "I thought never you was coming!"

"Yes, well, I can see that," chuckled Rossland. "You look the scruffiest urchin. And such a mass of hair! Where did you get it all?"

The lady giggled and throwing her arms around his neck, rested her head upon his shoulder. "I, myself, made it," she whispered shyly.

"She found the curling iron, my lord. I could not talk her out of it. Frizzed every bit of hair on her poor head."

"Curled it," nodded the lady beside him emphatically.

"Yes, you certainly did. Did you take the tongs to that beast as well, Liza?"

"Uh-uh. Wicky has already the curls. As much as you."

"Must you call that mongrel Wicky?"

"Oui."

"But how will he and I know to which of us you are speaking? When you say, 'Wicky, come'; or 'Wicky, sit'; or 'Wicky, stay'; how will we know which of us you are ordering about?"

The perplexed look upon the pretty face made him laugh. "Perhaps," he suggested after a moment, "you might call me Chad. That is the very first part of my name, you know."

"Chad," she said, apparently examining the feel of the name upon her tongue and lips.

"Yes, Chad," he repeated. "Chadwick. You were used to call me that sometimes."

She sat silent for a moment then gave a shake of the dark hair that rose like a boiling thunder cloud about her head. "Wicky," she said, decidedly. "Both."

"Peagoose," grinned Rossland. "You are incorrigible. An utter miscreant. And you do it to confound me. Shall we go for a walk, goose? You and I and the hairy Wicky? And when we return Mrs. Beaman will have tea for us and we will sit down and pretend to be quite respectable persons."

Mrs. Beaman watched them as they wandered off into the field behind the house, her charge laughing and running in the sunlight, the puppy galumphing in her wake, and Rossland making his way tentatively but determinedly along behind them. "Poor gentleman," she murmured, turning away and crossing into the kitchen. "Poor, kind, gentleman."

Rossland watched, smiling, as Liza spun herself about in a circle, her skirts flying, her cloud of midnight tresses blowing about her like a great fog and her puppy yapping happily and dodging in at her heels. She took Rossland's breath away. Even now, after all the sorrow and all the misfortune, he could not but be fascinated by her. "Liza," he called at last, "cease spinning about; you are making me dizzy. Come and we will pick some flowers, shall we? You still like flowers, I think."

She came to him almost immediately and put her hand into his. Together they wandered along the edge of the encroaching wood and he would point at a flower and she pick it. When they had gathered a good-sized bouquet of snapdragons and daffodils, jonquils and pansies, he turned back toward the cottage. Once they reached the kitchen, he put the flowers into a vase himself and she carried them carefully into the parlor, setting them upon a cricket table near one of the leaded casements.

"Pretty," she said approvingly and he escorted her to a seat at a small dining table upon which Mrs. Beaman had laid out their tea. He urged the housekeeper to join them, and once she had consented, the three and Wicky consumed an entire tray of warm buttered scones, strawberry pastries and two pots of India black. He was loath, when tea had ended and outside the sun was beginning to set, to leave them but it would be totally unacceptable for him to take up residence at the cottage. Riddle lay only a small woods and two fields away. He would, therefore, spend the week dividing his time between the main house and this more welcoming one. And on Friday he would return to London his energies replenished, his fidgets departed and the reasons for his actions, past and present, clear and vibrant in his mind.

Minerva, who had kept to her aunt's townhouse for the entire week to recover from her broken engagement, strolled into the Goodacres' soirée with head high, chin stubbornly angled, and a sapphire riband twisted tauntingly through her golden curls. She had not the least idea what to expect—pity, curiosity, perhaps even a few sardonic remarks from some other young ladies—for she had apparently tossed away a very eligible match.

With her Aunt Letty beside her she curtsied to her host and hostess, smiled prettily and pretended that however she was accepted by the other young ladies—and gentlemen—made not the least difference in the world. And when a general hubbub of whispers and glances met her arrival and a buzz fairly burst out amongst the company and all eyes fastened on her as she crossed the threshold into the Goodacre drawing room, she bit her lower lip only for an instant, then smiled and raised her chin even higher. Her closest friend, Miss Angelica Deane, fairly flew to her side and close behind her a number of gentlemen meandered in her direction, eyeing Minerva with considerable awe and whispering amongst themselves.

"Oh, Mina!" exclaimed Miss Deane, placing a daintily mittened hand upon Minerva's arm. "Is it true? Did you truly give Lord Whithall his congé because Lord Rossland has fallen head over heels in love with you and demanded that you extricate yourself from your engagement? It is all over London!"

Minerva's eyes widened.

"Everyone says The Devil's Delight has lost his heart to you and that he has pleaded with your Aunt Letty to allow him to pay you court! And that he has taken himself from town to give your aunt time to consider the matter and will not return until he has her approval."

"Pooh," mumbled Lady Letitia.

"He left town, you know, the very evening that he returned you to the Gramercys' and no one has seen or heard from him since. Oh, it is the most romantic thing I have ever heard!"

"Angelica, who? How? Who told you this?" Minerva asked.

"Why, do you know, I cannot quite remember. But everyone has been speaking of it."

"Halfwits," muttered Lady Letitia. "Gabblemongers have not a complete brain amongst 'em."

"But it must be true," replied Miss Deane sweetly, "because even the Duchess of Winecoff ponders over it and she is Lord Rossland's godmama."

Minerva, her sense of the ridiculous coming to the fore, felt a wave of laughter rising and did her best to suppress it. Over Miss Deane's shoulder she could see the gentlemen eyeing her and a number of young ladies glaring jealously in her direction.

Had I known running off into the night and being escorted back on the arm of The Devil's Delight would stir so much interest in me I would have done so sooner, Mina thought wryly. *No, I would not,* she corrected, calling herself to order. *I am being amazingly silly.* She gave Miss Deane's hand a pat and turned, her eyes filled with mirth, to look down at her Aunt Letty. "Why do you think all those gentlemen are fidgeting about there, Aunt Letty?" she asked blandly. "I have not been introduced to the half of them, though I do recall having seen their faces from time to time. They all look as if they wish to speak to me. Now why would that be?"

"Because they have swallowed all this rot about you and Chadwick," replied Lady Letitia awfully, "as you well know. Nodcocks, all of 'em. Wishing to discover what Chadwick sees in you to send him into raptures—which he is not in, mind you."

"The gentlemen have all been asking after you the entire week!" supplied Miss Deane, her eyes aglow with enthusiasm. "Why, even the Marquis of Kensington, having discovered that I am your very best friend, came knocking upon my door to request an introduction to you."

Since the Marquis of Kensington was an incredibly proud young man who looked down his nose at almost everyone and rarely sought an introduction to any young lady, the significance of this was not lost upon Minerva who had all she could do to keep from breaking out into whoops.

"Well," she managed, once she had gotten herself under control, "we shall need to quell these rumors immediately, will we not, Aunt Letitia? It would be despicable of us to mislead the entire *ton*. You will help us to do so, will you not, Angel?"

Miss Deane gave a tiny shake of her head. "No one will believe it is not true," she replied in a tiny voice. "Not unless it is Lord Rossland, himself, tells them. And even then they will think him merely attempting to depress the buzz. Besides, Mina, I think you are playing a deep game at this very moment. Can you not trust me? Can you not tell even me the truth? Your eyes are all aglow, you know. Anyone may see the joy in them. You do not look at all like a young lady who has just cried off from an engagement but more like a young lady decidedly in love."

"Well, but it is not love, you silly goose," protested Minerva. "It is laughter at the very thought of Lord Rossland wishing to have anything at all to do with me."

"Truly?" asked Miss Deane on a tiny breath.

"Yes, truly," declared Minerva with a giggle. "Angel, think. What could The Devil's Delight find the least bit attractive about me? I am a veritable dowd with a long nose and ears that stick out no matter how hard I attempt to hide them."

"Never say any such thing," responded Miss Deane loyally and at once. "You are not the least bit a dowd and never have been."

"No, but I am certainly neither exciting nor beautiful enough to attract a man about town like Lord Rossland. Even you must admit that."

And Miss Deane might have admitted it then and there and wiped all thought of an alliance between her friend and the dangerous but intriguing Lord Rossland from her mind if at that very moment Rossland had not entered the room, come to a halt, and following all the other interested gazes, stared directly at Minerva with those sparkling dark eyes of his.

Recognizing Miss Potts on the instant, and observing that she had noticed him as well, he decided it would be deucedly bad form to cut the young woman and so made his way around the group of fidgeting young gentlemen, came to halt before her, bowed, brought her hand rakishly to his lips and then stood holding it while he greeted Lady Letitia and requested an introduction to Miss Deane. He then asked politely how Minerva went on and if her heart was on the mend.

Lady Letitia snorted. Miss Deane looked to die of palpitations. But Minerva smiled at him, her eyes brimming with mirth. "You ought not keep hold of my hand, Your Lordship," she said softly. "You are unwittingly encouraging the most abominable rumor by doing so."

"I beg your pardon," replied Rossland, loosing his grip and resting both hands upon the top of his walking stick. "I do so enjoy holding young ladies' hands that it often slips my mind I ought not to do so. What rumor?"

"Why that you have lost your heart to me and demanded that I cry off from my engagement with Lord Whithall so that you might have the opportunity to woo me yourself."

Rossland's eyes widened. His lips curved most seductively upward and his eyebrow cocked.

"At this very moment our every move is being scrutinized and measured by every person in this room," added Minerva with obvious merriment. "Is it not the most diverting thing?"

"Diverting?" murmured Rossland huskily, his gaze taking in both Lady Letitia's scowl and Miss Deane's look of blatant awe. "Why, how can you say so, Miss Potts? And I standing here before you wearing my heart on my sleeve. Ah, what a trial, that I should lose my heart to such a cruel beauty!" He reached out and took Minerva by the elbow and drew her closer to him, leaning down to whisper in her ear and causing a collective gasp to flutter around the room. "I cannot help myself," he whispered, a distinct edge of laughter to his voice. "The urge to give the gabblemongers back their own is irresistible! Will you join me, Miss Potts, or are you a pudding heart?"

Minerva, the tingling warmth of his breath sending the most enticing shudder through her, grinned at him as he drew back and then she winked. Immediately she had done so, she could not believe it of herself and blushed a most becoming shade of pink. She had actually winked—and at The Devil's Delight! What had come over her? But she knew exactly what had come over her. It was a most enjoyable feeling of camaraderie with him. Apparently they shared a similar sense of humor. But he is worse than I, she thought uprighteously, because he wishes to extend this joke.

"Chadwick, scat!" commanded Lady Letitia with a frown. "I will not have you plaguing m'niece!"

"But I ain't plaguing her, Letitia," drawled Rossland, taking a step back. "I have lost my heart to the wench and seek merely a cool glance from the icy sapphires of her eyes."

"Oh, the icy sapphires of her eyes," sighed Miss Deane.

"Rubbish," growled Lady Letitia. "Go away, Chadwick."

"Very well," Rossland acquiesced, "for the moment. But I shall return, Miss Potts. You have my word on it. I find I cannot survive without your bewitching countenance before me. Cripple or not, I shall not be cast so easily aside by your old dragon."

"Thunderation!" gasped Lady Letitia as Rossland bowed

and made his way out of the Goodacres' drawing room. "I shall comb his hair for that! Old dragon indeed!"

Viscount Goodacre had been an intimate friend of Rossland's since the earl had been a mere Master Brumfield and the two had met at Harrow at the age of nine. Nothing Rossland had said or done since then had been able to lay that friendship to rest. "And there's nothing he can do," Lord Goodacre had informed Lady Goodacre immediately upon their marriage, "nothing at all that will induce me to end the connection, so you may as well accustom yourself to him, Mary. He is like to run tame about this establishment for the rest of his days."

At the moment, Lord Goodacre was handing Rossland a glass of Madeira. He then settled himself into a wing-backed chair, the twin to the one Rossland already occupied before the hearth in the Goodacres' study. "I cannot stay, Chad," he warned. "Guests, y'know. Must play the pleasant host. You have been missing all week. Thought our little evening party had slipped your mind."

"Never. I get invited to so few of late," murmured Rossland. "I tell you, Charlie, being a villain and a scoundrel and a libertine ain't all it's purported to be. Even my godmother debates whether or not to give me the cut direct. She won't though. Interminable patience, Aunt Seraphina. Always finding excuses for me."

"Bosh, as if you need excuses. Tell the truth is what I say. Who is to hold anything against you when it is all done for the most excellent of reasons, eh?"

"Well, but it ain't *all* done for the most excellent of reasons, Charlie. I am nearly certain that I shot Killibrew only because I could no longer abide his snide remarks."

"He called you out."

"Yes, but I did not need to go, Charles. I might just as easily have apologized for pouring that champagne into his lap. I *was* sorry for it, you know. It was the very last bottle I had."

"Yes. Well, you only winged him. If he had spoken to me as he did to you, I should have killed the man."

"But I could not kill him, could I? I would have been forced to flee to the Continent. What good would I be to Liza there?"

"None. And being privy to your situation, I understand it, too. But there is not another person who does. There are so many rumors flying about concerning you—why it is like an invasion of butterflies. Anyone might capture fifty with one wave of a net. And they are beginning to whisper again about murder."

Rossland's eyes darkened. "So, someone has started it all up again. Who, do you know?"

"Never any telling where these rumors begin. If you spent more time listening to them and less time causing them, you would know that."

"Yes, I expect so. Still, if we knew who had resurrected that particular spate of talk, well, it might provide us a clue."

"Have you come up empty then?"

"A wench in Seven Dials swears she knows of a tyke might be Jaimie. But the chit's mind is fuddled with blue ruin and she ain't to be depended upon to get the story straight."

"Does she give you a name?"

"Madam Pimm."

"Pimm," muttered Goodacre thoughtfully. "Are you certain that is the name?"

"No, how could I be? The wench is gin-soaked and makes no sense at all most of the time, but she is the closest I have come and I am loath to dismiss her."

"Like as not she is merely leeching your flimsies and making up the whole, Chad."

"So I thought at first, but she mentioned the scar on his palm—from when he tried to snatch one of the coals out of the fire—you remember, Charlie."

"Yes, but there are any number of boys with scarred palms."

"I know," sighed Rossland wearily. "I know. There are times, Charles, when I think I have lost my mind. Jaimie ought to be dead. The whole of England thinks him so. Why cannot I?"

"Because they never found the tyke's body. They found

Cam's and your father's but never Jaimie's. And because of the little lad's ring. The one he had from his papa."

"Which someone had the unmitigated gall to send to me."

"Indeed."

"But they might just have easily have gotten it from a dead boy's finger as from a live one's."

"Dare you take that chance?"

"No. And well they know it, too."

"Have they asked for more money?"

"Oh yes. Two thousand pounds, Charlie. The packet to be entrusted to the host at Clarendon's Hotel on the evening of the twenty-seventh, this month, with orders that he give it upon request to a Mr. Norman Tapley."

"The first time you left it at Limmer's. And the name was different."

"The name was Leslie Hartsell. And I set out to be on hand when he came to fetch the thing, too. But be damned, Charlie! I sat in that stinking place for hours and absolutely no one came and asked for the packet. Then I set Luke to hanging about the next day, and no one came then either. And then Martindale and Perkins both had a try at it, but the packet remained in Limmer's safe until at last I gave it up and called everyone home. Whoever it is, they know me and my men and will not be caught so easily."

"What you need is assistance from someone totally innocent of all previous association with you," Goodacre muttered. "Someone who would not be thought to be involved. What?" he asked, watching a light dawn in his friend's intriguing eyes.

"Miss Minerva Potts!" exclaimed Rossland.

"Who?"

"Miss Minerva Potts! Ain't you heard the rumors, Charlie? I have lost my heart to the chick and sent her fiancé packing!"

"I should like to see the day," grinned Goodacre.

"No, but think a moment, Charles. Would I endanger in any way the life of the woman I loved? Would I set her to watching for murderers? I know they murdered Papa and Cam, Charlie, just as surely as I sit here. And they know I know it, too. But would I entrust even the least knowledge of such a bizarre situation to a young lady I wished to make my wife? I think not, lest I turn her off, and the villains will think just the same."

"You cannot possibly be contemplating the involvement of Letitia Farin's niece in this business, Chad. Letitia will draw and quarter you herself."

Rossland's eyebrow cocked. "You think so?"

"Indeed."

"Then whoever is at the bottom of this will think so too, Charlie. Damnation! I shall ask Miss Potts, shall I? She appears to be an agreeable girl. I shall get to know her better and then I shall pose the problem to her and see what she says. She need only linger in the lobby of the Clarendon for a time and attempt to catch a glimpse of whoever requests the packet after all. It is not exceptionally difficult or in the least dangerous."

Lord Goodacre downed the rest of his wine, stood and tugged Rossland from his chair. "You have had too much," he drawled, taking the glass from Rossland's hand and setting it aside. "We are returning to Mary's party where I am going to play the jovial host and you are going to be one of my many unexceptionable guests. And if you have anything other than windmills in your head, Chad, you will quash all rumors concerning yourself and the little Miss Potts. Because, if you do not, you will end in a cookpot on Lady Letitia's hearth bobbing about in boiling oil and so I warn you."

Three

Minerva's gaze fell upon Rossland the instant he reentered the Goodacres' drawing room. That was not exceptional. Each and every eligible young lady's gaze lit upon him quite as instantly. Obviously it had done not the least bit of good for their mamas to hint to them of licentiousness, iniquity, or deep, dreadful scandal. Rossland's tall form, broad shoulders and narrow hips, his rebelliously long, mahogany-colored curls and finely chiseled face from which demon-dark eyes radiated an intoxicating hint of danger, all combined to make him enticing and downright seductive. His obvious need for the ebony walking stick only increased the air of mystery that simmered about him. Numerous young heartbeats increased as he parted from Lord Goodacre and glanced searchingly about the room. Numerous young minds imagined what they would do or say if the gentleman should approach them. Rossland, however, remained totally unaware of the stunning conquests he had made upon so many blushing innocents, intent only upon discovering the whereabouts of one person. When at last he spied Mina, who had halted in the midst of a conversation with Lord St. Clair, he strode determinedly in her direction.

"Miss Potts," he drawled, his dark eyes roving over and then dismissing St. Clair. "I would have a word with you, if I may. You will spare the girl for a moment, will you not, St. Clair? Of course you will. Come, Miss Potts, let us promenade about the room, eh? I shall not keep you long." He offered his arm, and Mina placed one hand upon it and paced beside him down the length of the drawing room. He said nothing until they had turned at the corner and began to cross the width of the chamber. Then he asked her in a most polite manner if she were enjoying her Season.

"Oh, yes," Mina answered, wondering if this very obvious attention to her was his idea of playing upon the rumors as he had suggested they do earlier.

"Even though your heart came near to breaking, Miss Potts?"

"I was mistaken. My heart did not come as near to breaking as I at first suspected."

"Good girl. There ain't a man in the world worth breaking your heart over."

"There ain't? I mean, there is not?"

"No. You may very well break a vase over a man, or a china shepherdess, or even a painting you are not too very fond of— over the gentleman's head, I'm suggesting—but never, never, break your heart, sweetling. We ain't one of us worth it."

They came to the next corner but instead of turning he led her out onto a tiny balcony, dropped her hand from his sleeve, and went to lean against the balcony rail facing her. "Your Aunt Letitia is glaring daggers at us," he chuckled, gazing over her shoulder. "I should think we have about three minutes before she stalks out here to retrieve you. I am a buck of the first head, you know, and she will be bound to protect you from me."

"But it is not at all a *dark* balcony," replied Minerva, looking about her playfully.

"No, and we are in full sight of everyone. But such a scoundrel and a rake as I cannot be trusted to be alone with a gently-bred young woman even in such innocent surroundings."

"Bosh," grinned Minerva, "as if I could not handle you should you misstep."

"Could you, Miss Potts?"

"Indeed. And without making any great to-do over it, either, though you should not walk comfortably for a number of days."

His eyes twinkled in the glow of the Japanese lanterns which lighted the small space to perfection and he laughed charmingly. "I do not walk comfortably now, sweetling, but I do take your meaning. You are much like your aunt, eh? I shall mind my manners then, I assure you. Tell me, when you winked at me earlier did that mean that you might enjoy leading the gabblemongers on? I thought it did, but it may only have been something in your eye."

"Is it your wish that it was something in my eye, Your Lordship?"

"Not at all. My wish is to give the gossips something to gossip about. You have not sworn off all men, have you, Miss Potts?"

"I am not such a wet goose, my lord," declared Minerva. "I have merely vowed to give men back as good as I have gotten."

"What does that mean?"

"Why to value in a husband what men apparently value in a wife. If I marry, the gentleman must provide me comfort and prestige and prove especially convenient, and love will have not the least thing to do with it."

Rossland's eyebrow cocked at her words and he ceased leaning against the rail, stood up straight and took one of her hands into his. "You are mad, Miss Potts," he drawled, bowing to kiss her fingertips. "Marry me. I have always been a fool for mad and formidable women."

"Nodcock," Mina giggled. "How can anyone believe you to be dangerous?"

"Oh, but I am, sweetling," responded Rossland huskily, drawing her closer to him. "I am dangerous beyond belief and a profligate besides and if your Aunt Letty were not already stomping in our direction, I should kiss you here and now and set every tongue in London wagging. However," he added, freeing her hand and backing up against the rail again, "I prefer not to have my hair parted with a kitchen knife. No, Letitia," he cried then in mock terror as Lady Letitia stormed up beside them, "I vow I have done nothing unseemly to your chick!"

"Oh, nothing at all," muttered Minerva's aunt angrily. "Why not kiss the gel and be done with it, Chadwick? Her name will be scandal broth regardless now that you have confirmed the rumors."

"Why, Aunt Letitia, he has not confirmed anything at all," responded Mina with mirth-filled eyes. "His Lordship did nothing more than speak to me."

"For ten whole minutes."

"No, really?"

"Yes, and all alone on the balcony for three of them!"

"Oh, but we were not alone, Aunt Letty," replied Mina quietly. "We were in your sight every moment. Lord Rossland quite properly made certain that we were."

"Indeed. And in everyone else's sight, too, so that not one of those beetlebrains could overlook the significance of it. Chadwick, I vow, if the gel suffers from this I will part your hair with a kitchen knife!"

Mina's eyes met Rossland's and they both burst into laughter.

"I have not the least idea what you find so humorous in that," declared Lady Letitia roundly, "but you shall not think it so very amusing when I do the thing, Chadwick, I promise you."

"Yes, Letitia, I know. I sincerely request that you do not do the thing, however. I shall take myself off, shall I, and give you the opportunity to repair whatever damage I may have done? Farewell, Miss Potts," he said, bending low over her hand and brushing it with his lips. "I have greatly enjoyed our conversation and look forward to another time."

"Never!" exclaimed Lady Letitia vehemently. "You take your life in your hands, Chadwick, if you come pestering around my niece ever again."

"Ah," drawled Rossland with a wry smile, "a challenge."

"I should never have said such a thing!" exclaimed Lady Letitia as she allowed Mina to help her up the staircase to her bedchamber much later that evening. "Now that he has taken it for a challenge, we shall never see the back of him. He will be constantly upon our doorstep upsetting our peace. I shall be forced to kill the wretch."

"Oh, most certainly not, Aunt," replied Mina with a gentle reassurance. "He was merely teasing you. Could you not tell?"

"Teasing?"

"Indeed. And the only reason we both laughed was because he had just said that you would part his hair with a kitchen knife and then you threatened to do exactly that."

"Well, and he knew that I would."

"Does he know you so well, then, Aunt?"

"Exceedingly well. I have known that villain since he was in leading strings, though he most likely would not tell you that we were used to be neighbors. He rarely speaks of the past, I think. Amy, go away and settle yourself for the night, gel," she ordered her abigail. "Mina will help me to bed. Will you not?" she added rather as though there might be some doubt.

"Of course," Minerva assured the older lady, undoing the long row of tiny pearl buttons down the back of Lady Letitia's gown. "You must not fret, Aunt Letitia. I did not think that a moment spent with Lord Rossland would put you into such high fidgets. I shall not speak to him again if that is your wish."

Mina helped her aunt into a robe of rose-colored silk and urged her down onto the little seat before the dressing table. Deftly she began to unpin the older woman's hair. "Lord Rossland is nothing at all to me, you know. If he had not bumped into me and returned me to the Gramercys', why I should never have noticed the gentleman."

"It was kind in him to return you," sighed Lady Letitia. "I know it was. He might have ignored you completely and gone right on walking to wherever he was bound."

"Yes, if he were not a gentleman, and kind."

"Well, and he has always been kind," responded Lady Letitia, calming perceptibly as Mina began to draw the silver-backed brush through her aunt's long, silken hair. "But he has always been thoroughly outrageous as well. And now—he is worse."

"How has he been outrageous, Aunt?"

"Why, when he was young he left Oxford in his very first year without so much as a by your leave and rented chambers in London and opened a gambling den! Of course, he did so because his father would not buy him a commission in the cavalry. Chadwick thought to make his own money and so pay for one himself, you see. But it was a decidedly indecent thing to do."

"Gracious," murmured Minerva, because she knew it was expected of her, "that was outrageous indeed."

"Yes, and his father heard of it, came directly to town and closed the thing down at once. So then Chadwick signed on with a contractor and began to drive the Royal Mail. A gentleman driving the Mail! It was the greatest scandal! Such a thing is totally unacceptable and I have no doubt his papa told him exactly that when he came personally to the yard at Brighton and pulled him down from the box before the team had even been brought to a halt. Well, everyone expected then that the old earl would give over and buy the commission. But he would do nothing of the sort. So Chadwick went off and took the king's coin—joined up as a common foot soldier."

Minerva had a difficult time imagining Lord Rossland sloshing through mud and camping out upon the ground in the wilds, but she tried to envision him doing so and found that if the story proved true, she must indeed respect him for it.

"He was away for the longest time—years. But then there was a terrible miscommunication at Talavera and Chadwick's regiment was overrun and scattered. Chadwick's father came near to apoplexy when word arrived that though our lads had triumphed, most of Chadwick's regiment had been slaughtered on the field."

"Lord Rossland was not among the slaughtered, however."

"No. And he did save a number of his comrades and has a medal for it, but he was injured in the process and came very near to losing his leg in the end. His brother, Cameron, and Lady Elizabeth had to be married at Riddle by special license and no one at all was invited because Chadwick had contracted a most serious infection in that leg and they all feared for his life."

"That is why he must use the walking stick," murmured Minerva with a nod.

"Yes, and after all of that, everyone was certain Chadwick would at last settle down. But he did not. As soon as he was capable he set himself up in London and drank a great deal and dallied openly with a series of opera dancers and never so much as attempted to make himself acceptable to Polite Society."

"Do you mean, ma'am, that he did not pay court to all the new debutantes or that he was so debauched as to be banned from people's drawing rooms?"

"No, he was not banned then. He is not entirely banned now if it comes to that for Lord and Lady Goodacre will still invite him to all of their entertainments as will the Duke and Duchess of Winecoff. And others do not invite him but will not turn him away if he should appear. Lady Richmond, for instance, thinks him the most clever conversationalist and loves to have him amidst the guests at her drawing rooms. And a great many of the lords enjoy his wit and court him at the clubs. But then, men are forgiven scandal so much more easily than women.

"But I fear Chadwick has turned truly profligate of late. He does not mourn his father's and his brother's and his nephew's passing, you know, not by so much as a black band upon his sleeve. No sooner were they in their graves than he came to London to spend all of his time in gaming hells and hedge taverns, cavorting amongst highwaymen and panderers and taking heaven knows what kind of women to his bed. Oh! I should not have said *that!*"

Minerva bent and gave the little lady a hug. "I am not in the least scandalized, Aunt, I promise you. And he sounds the most appalling person. I shall steer clear of him from this moment forward."

"Yes, if you please. But he did not murder his papa, nor Cameron, nor the little boy no matter what some people say."

Minerva started at the word 'murder' and was tempted to question her aunt further, but it was evident that the lady was exhausted and Mina held her tongue, merely tucking her aunt up into bed before she went off to seek her own rest.

But once the abigail she shared with Lady Letitia had seen her safely between the sheets and the lamp wicks had been lowered, Mina found sleep held at bay. Each time she closed her eyes, Lord Rossland's eyes appeared before her brimming with mirth. "Oh, do go away," she muttered. "I am so very tired and you are not worth a moment of my sleeping time." But for some odd reason Lord Rossland would not go away. His eyes continued to laugh at her, and then they were joined by the rest of his pleasantly handsome face which laughed as well. And then Mina's ear tickled where he had whispered into it, and her hand tickled where he had kissed it, and totally exasperated she opened her eyes and sat up in bed. "What is going on!" she grumbled, tugging at the bedcovers. "I have not the least wish to think of you, much less have you traipsing through my mind grinning that outrageous grin of yours. You are a villain and a scapegrace and a thatchgallows, and I will *not* allow you to disrupt my peace!"

* * *

Mina made her way to the breakfast parlor the next day with heavy-lidded eyes, her naturally exuberant personality considerably muffled by lack of sleep. In a gown of pretty blue sprigged muslin, she bade her aunt good morning and settled down to address herself to a cup of hot chocolate, a shirred egg, and a piece of buttered toast. She had taken only two sips of her chocolate when Battlesby appeared with a bouquet of wildflowers in a vase of cherry red Venetian glass. "I thought perhaps you might wish to have them in here, Miss Mina," the butler offered. "The sunlight is always brightest in the breakfast room."

"Oh, how lovely!" exclaimed Minerva, her lethargy abating for an instant. "They are like a living rainbow!"

"Indeed, Miss," agreed Battlesby with a slight upward tilt of his lips. "This note accompanied them, Miss," he droned, placing a folded sheet of vellum beside Mina's plate and then setting the flowers on a Sheraton table before the easterly window. With a long, admiring look at them, he turned and exited the room.

Minerva fingered the note with some trepidation. She could not think who might send her flowers. Surely Lord Whithall would not have the audacity to begin to woo her again? But what other gentleman would step up to gain her attention so shortly after she had cried off from her engagement?

To prestige, comfort and convenience, sweetling, read the note in a most precise Copperplate hand. *Drive with me this afternoon. I shall fetch you at four.*

Mina gave a tiny gasp. *Rossland* was scrawled across the bottom of the note in a wild way, quite at odds with the rest of the writing. Minerva looked up to find her aunt's questioning gaze upon her and with a shrug she pushed the note across to that lady and watched as her aunt scanned the lines.

"I shall not accompany him, of course," Minerva sighed.

"How dare that rogue address you as sweetling!" Lady Letitia said with an accusatory lift of an eyebrow.

"Apparently he thinks nothing of it, Aunt. He has called me sweetling from the first. I shall not accept his invitation."

"Invitation?" breathed Lady Letitia with suppressed rage. "Is that what you conceive this to be, Minerva? Does he invite you to accompany him? Does he query as to whether or not you would care to take a drive? Does he even so much as question what day or time would be convenient to you?"

"Well, n-no," replied Minerva, a hint of a smile playing about her lips.

"It is an outright command!" cried Lady Letitia. "Of all the audacious brats, Chadwick is the very worst! And what is this nonsense about prestige and convenience and comfort? The man is a Bedlamite!"

"Yes, Aunt Letitia," agreed Minerva hiding her smile behind her hand. She had not the least intention of explaining to her aunt that the words had been her own and Lord Rossland simply sending them back to her. "He must be a madman indeed to think to appear upon our doorstep when you have already threatened to box his ears and part his hair with a kitchen knife."

"Oh, well, he knows I will do no such thing," replied Lady Letitia a bit more composedly. "But you must turn him away, Mina, when he does appear. You must promise me to do so."

"I promise, Aunt Letty."

No sooner had the words left Minerva's mouth than Battlesby appeared for a second time. In his hands was another vase of flowers, this vase of deep blue and filled with daffodils and violets. "For you, my lady," Battlesby intoned, placing that bouquet next to the first and putting a sealed note into Lady Letitia's hand. Lady Letitia waited until Battlesby had departed and then broke the seal. She perused the missive with a scowl upon her face that gradually eased into a smile.

"Who are they from, Aunt Letty?" Minerva asked. "Have you a secret admirer?"

"Do not be a ninnyhammer, Minerva. They are from Chadwick."

"From Lord Rossland?"

"Indeed. He begs my pardon for his indiscretions at the

Goodacres' rout and wonders if I will permit him to attempt
to redeem himself in my eyes."

"And how does he propose to redeem himself?" asked Mina,
suspiciously.

"He does not say. But he does say that he will appear upon
my doorstep at a half-past three to explain. Well, I expect I
must listen to him. It would be extremely impolite to—"

"Shoot him down?" offered Minerva with a grin.

"Yes, exactly."

"Aunt Letty," queried Minerva from behind her cup of
chocolate, "are you quite certain that you detest the Earl of
Rossland?"

"Well, well, no, I should not say that I detest Chadwick exactly. It is only that—a man of his reputation—oh, dear, to
think that he should remember that violets and daffodils are
my favorites! It is most disarming. Indeed, I fear I must see
him. It would be most indelicate of me to send that scoundrel
packing without hearing him out."

Rossland appeared in Green Street at precisely half-past
three and was ushered immediately into Lady Letitia's presence. They spoke privately for an entire quarter hour at the
end of which Minerva received a message delivered by Battlesby himself that she was to accompany the earl upon a drive
and should present herself in the Gold Saloon as soon as she
had changed her morning gown for a suitable carriage dress.

"He has cajoled Aunt Letty into accepting him then, has he,
Battlesby?" Minerva asked with a grin.

"Indeed, Miss. Turned her up sweet, he has. Always could
turn my lady up sweet when he had a mind to do it."

"Did you know Lord Rossland when he was young as well?"

"Since he was in shortcoats, Miss Mina," acknowledged Battlesby. "I was footman then to your grandpapa whose land in
Hertfordshire ran with Lord Rossland's. A most endearing rascal Master Chad was when he was a mite, but forever disrupting
my lady's peace. I knew when the flowers came," he added
with a twinkle in his eyes, "how it would be, especially as they
were violets and daffodils."

Minerva donned a carriage dress of blue velvet piped in darker blue and with a matching blue hat with a small white feather that curled along her cheek. The blue of her dress matched precisely the color of her eyes and its simple lines gave a regal bearing to her well-rounded little figure. As she glanced into the looking glass she decided that although she would never be a diamond of the first water, she looked quite nice. Lord Rossland need not disdain to be seen with her. That, in fact, was precisely what she was thinking when she entered the Gold Saloon and Lord Rossland scrambled to his feet, nearly spilling the glass of port he held, and stared appreciatively at her.

"Well," he drawled, clearing his throat and setting the port aside. "Miss Potts, how wonderful you look. You will send all the belles into the shade."

"Gracious, I shall do nothing of the sort," declared Minerva in surprise, for she had never expected to see such an admiring look in this particular gentleman's eyes. "But you shall have no cause to feel shame, I think."

"Shame? To be seen with a virtual goddess? I think not, Miss Potts. I shall likely pose like a peacock upon the box beside you. I know I shall have a hard time of it to keep from crowing."

Minerva's cheeks reddened at his response. Donald had called her many things, but never a goddess, and she knew that she was nowhere near. She opened her lips to protest that such Spanish coin as Lord Rossland offered her was most unnecessary, but then she noted, quite clearly, the sincerity in his dark eyes as his gaze roamed over her from head to toe and she swallowed her protest in amazement. Apparently, he actually did think her beautiful. And that was somehow very nice indeed.

He escorted her to his curricle with Lady Letitia at their heels and, Minerva noted, bent to bestow a kiss upon her Aunt Letty's cheek. Then he assisted Mina to the box and ascended himself, sending his tiger to the rear and taking the reins into his own hands. It was a brilliantly painted little chariot—the body a cherry red with the trim picked out in white and the wheels a bright blue with white spokes.

"I know," Rossland offered as he urged his horses into the long line of traffic attempting to reach Hyde Park at the height of the Promenade, "it is a gaudy old thing. You deserve to be driven about in a white high-perch phaeton etched in gold."

"I think your curricle is beautiful," replied Minerva.

"Do you? Lord Goodacre thinks it decadent. And your Aunt Letty, I have no doubt, agrees with him. But I like bright colors. And if a man cannot have his carriage painted to please himself— Tell me, Miss Potts, did you promise your aunt never to be seen with me again?"

Minerva glanced shyly up at him and nodded, but the laughter she met in his eyes emboldened her and she turned to him fully and laughed. "You knew I would, did you not, after she told me all about you and declared you most ineligible?"

"Well, I did think you might. I gathered from the very first that you were a well-behaved girl and would not wish to give Letty palpitations. That was the reason, I thought, that you accompanied me back to the Gramercys' without the least objection."

"But whatever did you say to Aunt Letty to change her mind and almost command me to accompany you?"

"Not much, Miss Potts. I only said that I was not as great a libertine as she imagined, and that at the moment I lingered in gaming hells and hedge taverns because I had reason to believe that my nephew had not been drowned but had been kidnapped and that I was in search of information concerning him.

"And I promised to treat you with the utmost respect and thus force the gabblemongers to admit that your influence could well save me from the wretched life that I have lived up until this time. Which would make you, Miss Potts, my redemptor, and quite add to your prestige.

"And I did add that I thought I might request your aid in helping me to rescue Jaimie if he is, indeed, kidnapped and not dead for I could see that you took after Letty in every way and must therefore be courageous and most intelligent."

Minerva studied him with amazement. "Gammon!" she proclaimed at last. "I do not believe that I have ever heard such a Banbury story in my entire life! Do you mean to tell me that my Aunt Letty swallowed it?"

"Hook, line, and sinker," nodded Rossland seriously. "Hook, line, and sinker."

Four

Major Nicholas Gaffney, late of His Majesty's forces in Portugal and presently a member of the Foreign Office staff under Lord Castlereagh, wandered bemusedly down the two short steps of Skylark Cottage and then down the little cobbled path to the front gate. If he had not seen Elizabeth again with his own eyes he would never have remembered how deucedly beautiful she was. He had met the lady only once before, at Riddle, at the belated celebration held both for her wedding and the christening of her son. Belated, of course, because of Captain Brumfield's injury and illness.

Major Gaffney ran his fingers distractedly through his closely cropped auburn hair and sighed. Whoever would have thought that Chadwick Brumfield would become the Earl of Rossland— and that the captain's life would have evolved into such an horrendous tangle because of it. Well, there was no doubt at all why Rossland had hidden his sister-in-law away. The grief over the loss of her husband and son had quite obviously driven the woman into madness. And though the *ton* as individuals might well be sympathetic to Elizabeth's condition, as a group they were notoriously pitiless. And besides, the way things had been going of late, if her pathetic condition should become common knowledge all blame for it would be laid directly at Rossland's feet.

Gaffney untied his horse from the fence post, mounted and turned the animal toward London. At least Rossland had not harmed the lady. But then Gaffney had known from the first that that particular rumor had been without foundation. Still, when a gentleman's life might well depend upon proving rumors false, his friends ought to go out of their way to do it. "And I am that nodcock's friend," the major muttered, spurring his horse to a canter, "whether he chooses to think it or not. The simpleton nearly lost his life in the saving of mine. Why should he think I would balk at returning the favor."

Lord Whithall's attention was drawn to the red, white and blue curricle by a low whistle from his companion. "Never thought to see the day," drawled Redfield. "That is Rossland coming toward us, is it not? My eyes do not deceive me? And he has a beautiful young lady up beside him? By Jove, Whithall, it is your young lady!"

"You forget," muttered Whithall, "Miss Potts is not my lady any longer."

"Oh, right, dropped you like a hot coal, did she not?"

"No," protested Whithall, his angry gaze fastened upon Minerva. "We reached a mutual understanding. We both decided that we should not suit, but Miss Potts had to be the one to cry off, Redfield. I could not do so. Most ungentlemanly. Not done."

"Certainly not," nodded Redfield, not believing at all that Whithall had had a choice in the matter but willing to soothe his comrade's pride. "Still, it is early days for her to be out and about. And with Rossland yet! It does make one wonder if there is some truth to the latest gossip—that he lost his heart to her on first sight. Though even if that be true, what Lady Letitia could be thinking to allow her niece to drive in public with that rake, I cannot imagine."

The two nodded at the earl and his companion as the curricle passed but only Rossland nodded in return. "Do you realize, sweetling, that you have just cut Lord Whithall dead?" Rossland asked Minerva with the most audacious grin.

"No, have I?" Minerva might easily have taken her gaze from him and turned to look, but she found she had not the least urge to do so. "Well, but I did not see him. It was not intentional."

"No, but if you would glance about you once in a while, you might not cut anyone, sweetling. As it is I expect a great many people are thinking you most odd because you do not acknowledge them in the least. Do you intend to keep those incredibly blue eyes fastened upon me for the duration of our drive?"

"Of course. If you want everyone to believe that our attraction is mutual and that I am totally besotted with you—which I would need to be, my lord, to take on the almost impossible task of reforming you—what better way than for them to think that I am mesmerized by the very sight of you and cannot bear to glance away from your most adorable face?"

"Well, but it must be deadly dull for you, unless my adorable face changes like the scenery," chuckled Rossland.

"But it does, my lord. Your eyebrows rise and fall at the least little thing and your lips quiver and the muscles in your jaw tighten and your eyelashes dust across your cheeks in the most bewitching way when you blink."

Rossland broke out into whoops and was forced to draw his team to a halt at the side of the path or lose control over them.

Minerva, pleased that her teasing had brought him to such a standstill, joined in his laughter.

"We are making a spectacle of ourselves," the earl managed at last, swiping at tears with the back of his gloved hand. "And I promised Letitia I would allow no such thing to occur. I vow, you are the most complete hand, Miss Potts. A born minx!"

Minerva's laughter caught on a tiny gasp and she stared up at him in surprise. "I am, am I not?" she asked. "I do not know how it comes to be. I have never been a minx before."

"No?"

"Never. I have only been an unexceptionable young lady."

Rossland studied her with a look in his eyes that she could not quite understand. He moved the reins to his left hand and tilted her chin upward with his right until she was staring directly into his great dark eyes. "I do not know how it comes to be, Miss Potts," he murmured huskily, "but since first we bumped into each other, I have never thought you to be anything like an unexceptionable young lady. You have always been a minx, I think, but no one saw fit to point it out to you before. Whithall was sadly lacking not to have brought the matter immediately to your attention."

His lips as he murmured the words moved closer and closer to her own and Minerva did think The Devil's Delight might be going to kiss her. She knew she ought to be most scandalized by such a libertine action and should certainly protest immediately and vehemently, but there was something so incredibly fine about the tingling sensation that coursed through her that she did not wish at all to bring it to an end. And when the little tiger who rode behind them with his arms folded across his chest and was generally there to go to the horses' heads when the need arose gave a shrill whistle and cried, "Blimey, Gov'ner, let the gal be, can't ye? We be drawin' a reg'lar crowd o' sightseers," Minerva was not the least thankful for his interference.

Rossland's hand left her chin at once. His lips, which had nearly touched her own, moved an acceptable distance away and he looked at once to his horses, moving them with ease back into the line of carriages meandering toward the west gate. Minerva knew very well that she should feel overwhelmingly grateful to the tiger for stopping what had been like to be a most public disgrace, but she had the oddest feeling in the pit of her stomach and she was quite certain it had nothing to do with gratitude.

"I apologize, Miss Potts," Rossland said after they had gone a short way. "As you can quite plainly see, I have not completely overcome my profligate tendencies. But then, it *is* my first day of reformation. I can see that I am like to require a great deal more work on your part. I expect you shall need to drive with me several more times before I have got it right."

"Indeed," agreed Minerva with a nod which sent her golden curls bouncing beneath the delicious blue bonnet. "And undoubtedly, my lord, you shall require guidance in other areas as well. Will you not?" she added with a hopeful smile.

Rossland had all he could do to keep from laughing again at that most hopeful glance. He would be obliged to search out Charlie and thank him for inspiring him to involve himself with an innocent. He had never guessed the experience could prove to be so delightful. "Most certainly, Miss Potts," he replied. "I expect you shall need to teach me the acceptable way to become a morning caller for one thing. I ain't never done that, you see—paid a morning call upon a young lady."

"You ain't—I mean—you have not?" Mina asked in disbelief. "Never in your life?"

"Well, I did visit your Aunt Letitia from time to time when I was a child. My father would drag me along with him when he went to see the duke whether I wished to go or not. But I rather think that is not quite the same thing."

"Oh, no, certainly not. I shall be forced to give you instruction in the matter. Perhaps we could begin tomorrow?"

"Most certainly tomorrow, sweetling," grinned Rossland. "What time?"

"Well, generally Aunt Letitia and I receive morning callers from one to three."

"You may expect me," Rossland replied taking his eyes from his team to send Minerva a happy wink.

Trevor Martindale was busily putting a shine to a pair of Rossland's Hessians—because he did not at all trust the little boots to do the job properly—when John Perkins stepped into the dressing room and bade the valet join him in his apartment at the rear of the establishment. "We shall have a glass of wine and a bit of conversation, eh, Trev? 'Tis important."

Martindale set aside the boots immediately and accompanied Perkins from the chamber. "What is it, John?" he asked quietly, a worried frown eclipsing his usual smile. "Master Chad has not been injured?"

"No, no, 'tis not so simple as that."

Unlike a considerable number of London servants forced to live in abominable accommodations, Rossland's servants were housed in a well-kept addition to the original townhouse, and the upper servants enjoyed their own private apartments which included a parlor and bedchamber for each as well as a small kitchen they shared in common. This additional structure, which was connected to the townhouse by way of a glass-enclosed corridor, had been the particular notion of the present Rossland's father. The construction had completely obliterated a kitchen garden, rose garden, and a tiny fountain that had existed at the back of the townhouse for over fifty years. Even a portion of the stable which faced on the rear street had given way to the old earl's whim, forcing the present Rossland to house only one team, his curricle, and Forager on his own premises.

The *ton* had considered this queer start a most appalling waste of time and money. It was rumored that even the little tweenies and the scullery maid had their own bedchambers and a sitting room they shared amongst themselves. Even the boots boy had his own bed. It was unheard of and quite inappropriate and not a single person among them could understand the necessity for such extravagance. And what amazed them even more was that now that the old earl had been dead for an entire three months, the new Rossland had not even begun to tear the abomination down.

Perkins led the way into his parlor and crossed to a sideboard upon which rested a bottle of fine red wine from His Lordship's cellars. He poured out two glasses and handed one to Martindale, urging him into a chair.

"Well then, what is it?" Martindale queried, taking a sip of the wine. "They are not saying Master Chad has murdered someone else, are they, John?"

"Worse!" exclaimed Perkins with a scowl. "Much worse."

"What could be worse than that?" Martindale wondered aloud.

"They say Master Chad has thrown his cap over the windmill for a young lady."

"Master Chad?"

"Indeed. And not just any young lady, but Lady Letitia Farin's niece."

Martindale's face grew a shade paler and he gulped at the

wine. "Lady Letitia? The Lady Letitia who was our neighbor
in Hertfordshire?"

"Aye. They say His Lordship has fallen head over heels for
Lord Arthur's daughter. He was the youngest boy, you recall.
Well, the girl is in Lady Letitia's charge for the Season and
word is all over London that Master Chad has set his cap at
her."

"No, it cannot be," murmured Martindale after a thoughtful silence. "Where would he meet the girl? I grant you that
he does not go into proper mourning, but he does not go
about in Polite Society either. 'Tis gossip merely."

"Are you certain, Trev? His Lordship has not mentioned,
ah, anything of a romantic nature? Because you know what
could happen if the rumor is true."

"Indeed," responded the elderly valet with a despairing
shake of his greying curls. "One misstep with a niece of Lady
Letitia's and we will all suffer."

"And he will misstep, Trev. He cannot help himself, you
know. His hands wander of their own accord. And his lips are
forever brushing against some portion of a woman's anatomy.
And he is much too whimsical to avoid being caught in a com-
promising situation with a pretty girl. Wham! Before you know
it, there will be a Potts woman ruling the roost and our peace
will be cut-up no end. It will be farewell to the good days, and
that's a fact, Trev. Any niece of Lady Letitia's will never put up
with our having three entire free days a month. Nor she won't
approve of our having our own premises like we do. And like
as not, she will have Master Chad living in the country nine
months out of the year."

"I loathe the country," groaned Martindale.

"And if we live in the country for nine months out of the
year, what will happen to Betsy and Harold and Davenport and
little Charity and all the rest of 'em, eh? You cannot think that
a Potts woman will allow His Lordship to waste his blunt by
keeping a full staff at the London house as well as at the country estates, especially when they will not be in London but once
a year—if then."

"If he does misstep, Lady Letitia will be just the one to force him to marry the girl, too," muttered Martindale. "*She* will not let him off with an apology, not her. She will have him hitched to the girl in the lick of a cat's whisker. A stickler for the proprieties, is Lady Letitia. Always was, even when she was a schoolroom miss, which is why she and Master Chad never did rub along well together."

The gentleman's valet and his grim-visaged butler stared at each other in tense silence. "Well, we shall have to do something about it," Perkins sighed at last. "You will need to speak to His Lordship, Trev."

"Me?"

"Indeed. You are most familiar with his comings and goings. He does not always confide in me."

"Well, and he does not always confide in me, either, John!"

"Then you must encourage him to do so. He was used to be a most biddable little boy—mischievous, indeed—but always sweet-tempered and possessed of a thought for another's peace of mind. He has not changed, Trev. You need only give him a hint, I think, and he will come out and ask what it is you wish him to do."

"And then I shall say that I wish him to drop this Miss Potts at once?" asked Martindale with wide eyes. "Are you mad, John? Why he will tell me exactly where to go and be perfectly justified in it, too."

"No, no, you will simply ask him if the rumors are true, and if they are, offer to aid him in courting the young lady."

"And then?"

"Well, then you will advise him to do certain things that will bring a rapid end to the affair."

"Oh, I don't know, John. Master Chad is not a fool. He has windmills in his head from time to time, but he is a downy one on a fairly regular basis. And he is playing a very deep game at the moment, too," added Martindale. "Determined, he is, to discover the truth of the drownings and whether or not Master Jaimie is alive. He takes his life in his hands roaring about as he does amidst the very dregs of society. And you know well enough that he has become most suspicious of the least little thing and cannot even bring himself to trust his friends—except for Lord Goodacre. And one thing he does not need, John—he does not need to think that I, his own valet, would deceive him."

"Do you wish a niece of Letitia Potts to rule over this household?" asked Perkins with a cock of his eyebrow.

"Most certainly not!"

"Then we *will* do whatever it takes to prevent it—ourselves and the rest of the staff as well."

Minerva could not remember when she had more enjoyed a drive. Always before she had been overwhelmingly aware that those who joined the Promenade did so to see and be seen by Society. It was a matter of prestige and much gloating and a great deal of competition. One must wear one's most fashionable carriage gown. One must be seen to be accompanied by the most exquisite gentleman. And one must strive to be recognized and acknowledged by the most important members of the *haut ton*. But this afternoon she had given no more than a fleeting thought to any of this. She did not know how it could be, but in Lord Rossland's presence she had been unconcerned with anyone's notice or opinion except his.

Perhaps it is because the gentleman is so very overwhelming, she thought as she allowed Amy to help her dress for dinner. But no, that was not it, because Lord Rossland had not been in the least overwhelming. He had been very sweet and amusing, and he had not cut up stiff when she had teased him. Donald would have cut up stiff directly she had opened her mouth in such a forward manner. Or, perhaps not. One had to be fair after all. She had never thought to tease Donald, nor to accuse him of telling Banbury stories and great clankers. Donald was so very high in the instep and so deadly serious that the mere thought of teasing him had never once occurred to her. Oh, but it was so very jolly to be in Lord Rossland's company and know—absolutely know—that you were not going to be frowned upon for indulging in a bit of frivolity now and then at his expense.

With Donald she had always been very aware that she must please him and cater to his whims and be exactly the kind of woman he desired her to be. One did, after all, strive to please the man one loved. But since she knew that Lord Rossland did not love her and had not the least intention of marrying her and was not truly courting her but only leading on the gabblemongers and her Aunt Letty as well, she had not the slightest compunction to alter her responses in deference to his.

And he was not truly dangerous. Surely he could not be. The gossips whispered of despicable and unnatural acts, but that, she thought, must be as much nonsense as the rumors about his *tendre* for her. Why he was the most charming and enjoyable gentleman she had ever met and he had done not one thing to frighten her.

Rossland was dressing for dinner himself. Inexplicably, he'd discovered upon his arrival at home an invitation from Lady Goodacre to a dinner *en famille*. His eyebrows had cocked as he read the thing. Charlie had always considered him family, but Mary? No, something was peculiar about *that* invitation. "I cannot think why she should send the thing," he mumbled, struggling with his cravat. "She ain't never liked me above half. Must be Charlie's doing is all I can think. You do not expect it is an emergency of some kind, do you, Trev?"

"Surely not, sir. Lord Goodacre is hardly one to have emergencies."

"No, I am the one has emergencies. But I cannot think why else I should be asked, especially upon the heels of their soirée. What do you think, Trev?" he added innocently, studying the creases he had applied to his cravat.

"Most acceptable, my lord."

"It is meant to be a Waterfall."

"I am certain 'tis a most creditable Waterfall, my lord."

Rossland's dark curls rippled in the breeze he made as he turned swiftly from the looking glass to stare at Martindale. "A most creditable Waterfall? What is wrong with you, Trev? I have never tied a creditable Waterfall in all my life and you have never neglected to inform me of it. Are you not well, man?"

"I am fine, my lord."

"And that's another thing," drawled Rossland suspiciously. "What is all this m'lording about? I have been m'lorded from one end of this house to the other ever since I arrived home. Even Daisy m'lorded me and dropped a curtsy. I am accustomed to one or two my lords from Perkins, but a m'lord at every other word, even from a tweeny who most often don't even take note of my presence, is doing the thing up much too brown. Confess, Martindale. Something is afoot. What are the lot of you up to now?"

"Not a thing, my lord," offered Martindale with a singularly guilty look as he helped Rossland into his waistcoat and then assisted him in the struggle to don the coat of Bath superfine that fit so snugly to the broad shoulders that anyone might think it would cut off all circulation. "We have only decided, you see, to accord you the respect you deserve. We have treated you as the second son for much too long. You are the Earl of Rossland now after all. We had a meeting, we did, while you were gone and decided that we have been sadly lacking in formality and respect. We have decided to rectify the situation, my lord."

"More like some one of you has set fire to the Blue Saloon and the rest of you have sworn to distract me until that situation has been rectified. Or one of the girls has gotten herself—" Rossland's dark eyes leveled upon Martindale with such fierce intensity that the valet came near to stumbling backward from the sheer force of the look. "One of the girls has not gotten herself—?"

"Oh, no, my lord! Most assuredly not!"

"Well, if one has, Martindale, you must not fear to tell me. It is not as though I'd put her out on the street, you know."

"I know, my lord," sighed Martindale feeling only slightly less guilty than the traitor, Guy Fawkes. "You would hunt the man down who had seduced her and blacken his eyes for a starter."

"Yes, and then I'd do to him whatever she thought fitting."

"Indeed, my lord, we all know that you would. But it does not bear discussing for there is not one of the girls in trouble. 'Tis merely as I said before, my lord. We have agreed amongst us that you are deserving of a deal more respect in your own establishment."

Rossland's lips drew into a charming smile. "I ain't never been disrespected by any of you, Martindale, not in all my years. You are not going to tell me the truth of it, are you?"

"N-no, my lord," Martindale stuttered.

"Not even if I promise not to fly up into the boughs?"

"N-no, my lord."

Rossland shrugged his shoulders. "Some other time then. But I shall get to the bottom of it and so you may tell the entire staff. Do not wait up for me, Trev. I have things to do after dinner and do not expect to be back until well into the morning. And if the Blue Saloon *is* in ruins, you would be well advised to see it restored before you wake me tomorrow. Which you must do by noon, eh? I have a morning call to make."

"A—a morning call, my lord?"

"Uh-huh. Promised to drop in on a young lady. Miss Potts is her name. You will find me something presentable to wear, will you not? Cannot go looking like a veritable rake. Lady Letitia will be there and I need to impress her as an acceptable gentleman caller for her niece."

"You, sir?" gasped Martindale before he could stop himself.

"Am I sunk so low that even you cannot imagine me as an acceptable gentleman?" queried the earl.

"Oh, oh, no, my lord. But a mere Miss Potts? Why you might search far above a mere Miss Potts, my lord, for a young lady."

"I assure you, Trev, she is not a mere Miss Potts. She is a vision and a minx and an out and out charmer."

"Yes, my lord," sighed Martindale, sinking down into the wing-backed chair in the dressing room as his employer departed. So, the gossips were correct! And now he and Perkins and all the rest of them must begin to sabotage Master Chad's first true attempt at romancing an acceptable young lady. Martindale had never felt such a Judas. But his own feelings in the matter were not to be considered. The very future of the entire staff depended upon him. If he could not succeed in squelching this affair, then their very comfortable little family might all be out on the street without references, for certainly no niece of Lady Letitia would be accepting of the unfashionable and most informal relationship between the present Earl of Rossland and his servants.

Rossland, curly-brimmed beaver set upon his curls at a rakish angle, had chosen to walk the few blocks to the Goodacres'. His cane tapping more confidently than usual against the cobbles, he told himself that he certainly ought to be puzzling over such an unexpected summons, or considering how he was to go about locating this Mrs. Pimm, or keeping his eyes peeled for an urchin with a mop of dark curls, wide-set green eyes, and a scar on the palm of his left hand. But he could not seem to concentrate on any of it. A pair of deep blue eyes, a delightful smile and golden curls bouncing beneath a delicious blue bonnet pushed all other thoughts from his mind.

Miss Potts is an enormously appealing young lady, he thought with a smile flitting across his face. Not even the wariest of villains will suspect me of using such an innocent as Miss Potts for a spy if, of course, she will agree to spy for me when I ask it of her. She is enchanting. She is entertaining. And she is most intellligent, too. This afternoon both time and my troubles seemed to fly away in her company.

Rossland grinned as he recalled the number of envious glances he had gotten from some very respectable gentlemen. And well they might be envious too, he told himself. Miss Potts looked a vision in that wonderful carriage gown and that frivolous little hat. How could such an angel have gone unnoticed except by such a dull blade as Whithall? Were the other gentlemen all staring in the opposite direction when she made her come-out? Or did Letitia frighten all the others off? That, he decided on a chuckle, is the most likely scenario.

He came to a halt before the Goodacres' townhouse, climbed the steps with only a bit of a twinge in his leg and gave the door a sharp rap. It fairly flew open. "Thank goodness you have come!" cried Lady Goodacre, dashing past her butler and throwing her arms about Rossland's neck. "Oh, thank goodness, thank goodness!" she sobbed and then buried her tear-stained face in Lord Rossland's cravat.

Five

"Well, but Charles loves you with all his heart, m'dear," Rossland mumbled, dabbing at the last of Mary's tears with the one remaining dry corner of his handkerchief. "He would never think to do such a thing. The gossips have been busy is all."

"Do you truly think so?"

"Certainly I do. I have known Charlie since the age of nine and he is the most loyal man alive. He would never betray you with another woman."

Lady Goodacre, who had been sitting for the past quarter hour on the brocade sofa in her withdrawing room with her head resting upon Rossland's shoulder, thoroughly soaking his coat, straightened herself up and took his handkerchief into her own hands. She gave a delicate little sniff and then a mighty blow and then swiped at her red nose distractedly. "But—Rachel Worthington said that her husband had said that Lord Newton had said that he had *seen* Charlie going into the place—in Bennett Street—walking right in as bold as you please."

"And when Charles arrived home, did you ask him why he had chosen to enter this particular establishment?"

"But there is only one reason for a gentleman to enter a—such an establishment," sobbed Lady Goodacre, the tears mounting to her eyes once more.

"Do not cry again, Mary, or I shall take my leave on the instant," Rossland drawled, hoping the coolness of his drone might do better at drying her tears than his sympathy had done. "You did not ask Charles what business took him to the place?"

"N-not precisely," Mary admitted fighting to choke back the next bout of tears. She had never been fond of Chadwick Brumfield, but at this particular moment and in this particular situation she found him extremely comforting. And she knew one thing beyond all doubt—that if anyone could explain to her why her Charlie had seemingly abandoned her and run to the arms of another woman it would be Lord Rossland. "I—I—"

"You accused him of seeking out the company of some high flyer, did you not?" Rossland looked down upon her with what she thought were the most critical eyes. "And then without listening to a single word from him, you burst into tears."

Mary nodded sadly.

"Well, no wonder he has gone off to his club. Charlie ain't one for confronting an angry, sobbing woman not even if she is his wife. You know that, Mary. The very first argument that the two of you had, that nodcock, Charlie, ran away from you and came shouting to me. He cannot bear to see you in tears. It ties up his tongue and turns his brain to mush. But that does not mean he is in the wrong of it. Did you invite me to dinner before or after you and Charles fought?" Rossland added quietly.

"A-after," replied Mary on a tiny gasp. "I w-wanted you to come h-help me."

"Yes, no doubt. It will not do, of course. You and I cannot share a quiet dinner at home while Charles is eating elsewhere. I will tell you what, Mary. I shall take m'self off to White's, shall I? And see if Charles is there? And if he is, I shall send him home. Provided, of course, you do not intend to ring a peal over him or soak his cravat with your tears."

"You give no credence at all to what Lord Newton saw?"

"Charlie going into some pit of passion? I should think not. If he did do so, it was some mistake. He was misdirected most likely. Knowing Charles, he probably thought it was Hummer's new Museum of Egyptian Antiquities. That particular establishment opened its doors in Bennett Street last week as I recall."

"Oh, do you think so?"

"Indeed. Now, if you will excuse me, my lady, I shall see myself out or the next thing you know the deuced gab-blemongers will be asserting that you and I are having an affair behind Charlie's back."

"I would never!"

"No, and neither would I, but truth seldom floats to the surface when it is stirred in amongst the scandal broth."

Rossland retrieved his hat and gloves and stepped outside only to have Mary follow him and without the least provocation stand upon her toes and throw her arms around his neck and give him a shy little kiss upon the cheek. "Thank you so very much, Chadwick. I am certain you are correct and Charlie had no idea what sort of place it was. He is always mistaking directions. I knew you would have the answer. And I like you much better now than I ever did before."

Rossland nodded. "I know you have never held me in esteem, Mary. But then, I never seem to put myself above reproach, do I? Still, perhaps someday I shall learn to behave properly and you will like to have me as a friend."

"Good heavens, it is Rossland!" exclaimed Angelica Deane's mama from the depths of the Deane's town coach as it rolled slowly past the Goodacre residence. "And Mary kissing him upon the doorstep like a veritable trollop!"

"I am quite certain it is all most innocent, Mama," replied Miss Deane, though in the light of the lamps her most expressive countenance quite belied her words. "Why only this afternoon Lord Rossland drove Mina quite properly in Hyde Park."

"Yes, and only moments ago we passed Lord Goodacre crossing St. James's and leaving his door unguarded against that rakeshame! Well, I shall make it clear to Letitia as soon as may be that Lord Rossland is playing Lord Goodacre for a fool and undoubtedly using poor Minerva to cover his tracks like the villain he is."

"Do you think so, Mama?" asked Miss Deane aghast.

"Definitely and without a doubt! The man is without shame and deserves to be ostracized from all decent society."

Rossland, not for a moment noticing the slowly passing town coach, disentangled himself from the lady, limped down the Goodacres' front steps and took himself off in the direction of White's Club. It was nearing nine o'clock and he was sharp set. Not having had a bite since breakfast, he had been looking very much forward to dining at the Goodacres'. Now he would be forced to settle for boiled beef and potatoes while he turned Charlie up sweet and sent him home to Mary.

He discovered Lord Goodacre alone and in high dudgeon muttering to himself over a small repast at the club. Ordering up beef and potatoes for himself to be accompanied by a bottle of the club's finest claret, Rossland took a seat across from his best friend and leaned his elbows on the table. "So, Charles," he drawled, "you have had a busy day, have you?"

"Go away, Chad, do. I am not up to nacky conversation."

"No, I know you ain't. I have just come from a visit with Mary. She wants you home, you know."

"Well, of course I know, but I am not going."

"Why not? I expect it is because you no longer love the girl, eh?"

"You know I love Mary."

"I do seem to recall it having been a love match at the start, but then, love wears off, does it not, Charles?"

"No, it does not!" fumed Goodacre around a forkful of mutton pie. "And if you would take a chance and fall in love with a decent woman yourself, you would discover it does not, too. But no, not you. You cannot be bothered. Too busy cavorting about with every barque of frailty that glances at you sideways-like."

"I did not come to discuss myself and my barques, Charles," grinned Rossland. "I have come to discuss you and yours."

Goodacre sputtered but the conversation necessarily drew to a halt as Rossland's dinner was set before him. No sooner had the waiter departed, however, than Charlie erupted into speech. "It is all your fault, you know. Mary is in hysterics and my peace ripped up no end and for what? For you."

"My fault? Did you enter that wretched abbey on my behalf then, Charlie?"

"Your's and Liza's. I had it on the best authority that it was ruled over by a Mrs. Pimm. But her name turned out to be Pimberley, not Pimm. Ugliest customer I have ever met."

"No, really?" chuckled Rossland.

"Indeed. Tipped me the ugly the moment she discovered I was not looking to avail myself of her services. Threatened to have her ruffians throw me out."

"I am sorry, Charles. Did you get an opportunity to look about before she twigged to your game?"

"Indeed. No children about. A ball, though, lying beneath the piano in the drawing room. A red ball."

"Yes, well, you are not to go into any more places like that, Charlie. You are my best friend. In fact, I expect you are my only friend, and I do not want you endangering your marriage by attempting to help me."

"Yes but, suppose the madam's name is not Pimm, Chad? Suppose it is Pimberley. That ball could belong to your nevvy."

"I shall look into it, I assure you," replied Rossland. "This Mrs. Pimberley is a new arrival, I think. The house in Bennett Street was used to belong to Maria Falk. But that's neither here nor there, Charles. You have gone and made a dashed watering pot out of your wife over the thing. She cried her way right through my coat."

Lord Goodacre's fine grey eyes stared at Rossland in amazement. "Mary? My Mary has been crying upon your shoulder?"

"Literally. I am wretchedly damp. She invited me to dine."

"Mary?"

"I fail to see why you should look so devilish surprised, Charlie," drawled Rossland fighting to keep a sober look upon his countenance. "I *do* dine. And since you had departed without the least explanation—well, the meal must go to someone."

"She never—" murmured Goodacre. "Not my Mary."

"She never what? Invited me to dine? Most assuredly she did, Charles."

Goodacre's countenance began to suffuse with red. His eyebrows knit in a deep frown. His nose crinkled and his bottom lip jutted outward. "Well, of all the—"

"Kissed me on the front stoop, too," added Rossland, his dark eyes sparkling.

"K-kissed?"

"Well, you were not there, you know. And you as much as told her that you had not the least care for her anymore."

"I never! All I said was for her to cease sniveling and jawing at me or I should take myself off. And she did not, so I did! Kissed you? Mary kissed you? In public?"

"Well, she was discomposed, Charles, and in need of comfort, and grateful to have me provide it."

"Well, by gawd, I shall provide you with a facer, cripple or not!" exclaimed Goodacre, jumping up from his chair with hands clenched. "Of all the rakeshames I have ever met! To pounce upon a man's wife the moment his back is turned!"

Rossland's control deserted him at that precise moment and he broke out into whoops. "I am s-sorry, Charlie," he stuttered through his laughter. "I h-have not seen you so very angry since I set your bed afire at school. Do you remember the stink once we got it out? I thought you would murder me."

"This is not the same thing!"

"I realize. If you draw my cork, I shall need to call you out, Charles. I do have a reputation to uphold."

Goodacre's eyes nearly started from his head. "Call me out? Me? Your best friend?"

"I am s-sorry, Charlie," managed Rossland bursting into whoops again. "I c-cannot help m'self."

"Obviously," replied Lord Goodacre horribly, staring down his most aristocratic nose with loathing. "You have lost all sense of decency, Chad. It was bound to happen, of course, cavorting about with those demons in Seven Dials and Mummery Lane the way you have been of late."

"N-no. I mean I c-cannot help teasing you. You are making it much too easy."

Goodacre's left eyebrow cocked. His nose uncrinkled. His fists began to unclench. "You did not take advantage of Mary behind my back?"

"It depends upon what you consider taking advantage, Charles," Rossland grinned.

"Did you kiss her?"

"I never said I kissed her. She kissed me, Charlie, on the cheek, as if I were some elderly uncle. Nor was I so lost to propriety as to stay and dine with the lady. You might have guessed that, since I am sitting here across from you stuffing myself full of Gerald's boiled beef and potatoes."

"Then why did you let me think—?"

"Because you had the sheer audacity to presume that you might simply walk out on the lady when she did not please you and then walk back in again when she did and that nothing would have changed. A great deal could have changed, Charles, if it had been some other rake she had turned to—a rake whose reputation is not all a sham. The least you might have done would have been to put her mind at rest. You were *not* hanging out for a bit of muslin. You might at least have reassured her of *that.*"

"I cannot abide her tears."

"Learn to, Charles, or cease doing things that are like to cause them."

"I went there to help you," muttered Goodacre accusingly as the tension drained from him and he settled back into his chair.

"Yes, and I much appreciate it, Charlie. But it would have been better, I think, had you just told me about this Mrs. Pimberley and allowed me to investigate. I have no wife to hear of it, after all, and the rumormongers would only think it boring that I was seen entering such an establishment. I told Mary, by the way, that like as not you were looking for Hummer's museum and had been misdirected."

"And she believed you?"

"Um-hmmm. At least, she wanted to do so. It will depend, I expect, upon what you tell her."

"I wish I could tell her the truth," mumbled Goodacre, pouring himself another glass of claret. "She would be a good friend to you, Mary would, if she knew the truth."

* * *

It was well after midnight when Goodacre and Rossland parted ways outside White's and Rossland, his cane tapping against the cobbles, made his way to Bennett Street. When he reached number seventeen he stood beneath the lamp and studied it thoughtfully. As brothels went, number seventeen Bennett Street had always been at the upper end of the scale. Maria Falk had kept it polished and elegantly furnished and filled to overflowing with the most beautiful and compliant of cyprians. It had been a long while, however, since the earl had last entered that establishment and Charlie's news of a new madam had come as a surprise.

Rossland did not at all recognize the man who opened the door to him—a large, grizzled ruffian who looked amazingly uncomfortable in his butler's rig—but it was obvious that the personage recognized him. This, in itself, was not remarkable. In the past three months Rossland had become more notorious than ever, even among the riff-raff. And he was easily recognizable with his rebellious curls, striking countenance, and wolf's-head walking stick.

"Lord Rossland, how kind of you to visit us," Mrs. Pimberley greeted him as he was escorted into the front parlor. She offered her hand and Rossland bowed and kissed it, taking note of the large diamond that flashed upon one finger and the sapphire that glittered on the next.

"Your servant, ma'am," he murmured huskily as he straightened. "I should have come sooner had I any idea the place was in new hands. And such beautiful hands."

The lady, who was quite as tall as Rossland, met the dark sparkle of his eyes with a suspicious gleam in her own. "A very pretty compliment, my lord. Your reputation precedes you, you know, especially here."

"No, does it? You will not have me tossed out on my ear, will you?"

"Oh, la, m'lord, what a jokester you are! Of course I shan't have you thrown out into the street. You are most welcome in this establishment any evening. And if there is something in particular you desire, you need only ask."

"How kind," Rossland murmured, his handsome features assuming a singularly lecherous mien. "And if I were to ask for a portion of your own time, madame, would it be granted me?"

She truly was a beautiful woman, this Mrs. Pimberley. Rossland's eyes followed the lush curves of her body with profound delight. From her cropped red curls to the tips of her elegantly shod feet, Mrs. Pimberley's charms were undeniable, distinctly enticing, and displayed to perfection.

"You shall have to join the queue Rossland," chuckled a voice behind him.

"Indeed. And you as well, Terwilliger," laughed a heavier voice close by. "We have all of us been after Grace this month and more, but she'll not have any of us."

Rossland grinned and turned to greet a number of acquaintances who were drinking brandy and eating cakes around the piano, each with a cyprian upon his arm. "Terwilliger, Langly, Collingsworth," he nodded. "I might have known I would be far behind the lot of you."

"Aye, at the very back of the queue," nodded Terwilliger.

"But foremost in my eyes at the moment," drawled the enticing Mrs. Pimberley taking possession of the earl's arm with both hands and accompanying him toward the others. " 'Tis Mitzie's birthday, my lord, and so we are all having cakes and brandy. You will join us."

"Honored. And which of these beauties is Mitzie?" he added, releasing himself from Mrs. Pimberley's grasp and raising a quizzing glass to his eye which caused a definite flutter amongst the barques of frailty.

"Me," announced a dab of a girl Rossland judged to be no older than thirteen. She was clinging rather desperately to Lord Langly's arm, her great brown eyes wide with alarm but a smile pasted determinedly upon her brightly painted lips.

Langly patted the hand that rested in the crook of his elbow possessively and cocked an eyebrow challengingly at Rossland. Rossland merely bowed and raised the glass with which Mrs.

Pimberley had provided him. He knew Langly's predilection for uninitiated innocents and thought the man's constant scrambling about for young girls disgusting. He had, in fact, foiled Langly's lust several times in the long-ago past though he had managed to make his interference appear to be merely accidental.

This time, however, it appeared that Langly's pathetically smiling prey was beyond the earl's help. Rossland could hardly stir up a ruckus when he had just come to the place and had as yet discovered nothing about this Mrs. Pimberley or the red ball that Charlie had noticed under the piano. It was not there now. Rossland had scanned the carpeting for it as soon as he had entered the room.

"Good fortune to you, Mitzie," he drawled, raising the glass to his lips. It was excellent cognac and his tongue delighted in it. Obviously Mrs. Pimberley, like her predecessor, intended to be extravagant in the entertainment of her customers. Rossland wondered, abruptly, if his first payment to the kidnappers had paid for the excellence of the cellars and the quality of the female companionship. His eyebrows drew together for a fraction of a second and his usually sparkling eyes glazed with ice, but then they were clear again.

He could do nothing about what the funds extorted from him were used for, but perhaps there was a way to help the little Mitzie. He grinned innocently at Langly's chosen paramour. Perhaps there was a way to save the child from Langly's clutches. Of course it would depend upon what mood Collingsworth and the young Terwilliger were in. He knew them both only slightly and though he could hope they might pick up his cue—disgust for Langly being rampant among the general run of young bucks—he could not actually depend upon it.

"It is my birthday as well," Rossland drawled nonchalantly, "though there ain't no one wishes to celebrate it."

"No, is it?" asked Terwilliger with a most speaking cock of his eyebrow. "What a delightful coincidence. I say, Grace, do you not think it portentous that Rossland should make his first appearance in your parlor upon his birthday and Mitzie's as well? Almost as though they were destined to be together."

"Oh, no," growled Langly like distant thunder.

"No, but it is," Collingsworth declared with a wink in Rossland's direction. "Fate, I should say."

Just at that point Mrs. Pimberley gave Rossland's arm a squeeze and he looked to see her smiling at him. "Would you like to have Mitzie this evening, my lord?" she asked, moving against him and whispering softly in his ear. "I can see 'tis arranged without the least fuss, I assure you."

Rossland gave the slightest of nods and she was off around the piano and beside Langly in a moment. Her finely sculpted cherry-red lips moved softly against Langly's ear and the scowl on that gentleman's face was replaced by a thoughtful frown and a subtle twitching of his lower lip.

"What can I do?" Langly sighed with a shrug of his buckram-padded shoulders. "If it is fated, then it is fated. Go hang upon Rossland's arm, m'dear," he ordered Mitzie regally. "He will see you come of age properly. I have no doubt of it."

Rossland had no idea what Mrs. Pimberley had promised Langly in return for Mitzie. He judged it to be something of particular value, however, from the speed with which Langly had accepted her offer. And now, because of it, he found himself ensconced in a most attractive bedchamber with the dab of a miss trembling before him, her painted lips still cemented into a brave smile.

"You are not going to weep excessively in a moment, are you?" he asked, crossing to an exquisite mahogany bed swathed in red draperies, climbing up upon it and stretching his long legs across the counterpane. His cane he balanced quite precisely against the night stand.

"N-no," she answered in a quiet little voice.

"Good, because I have been cried upon once today and I ain't looking forward to going through it again. Come and sit beside me, m'dear. I will not hurt you. You have my word on it."

Mitzie's big brown eyes studied him shyly, but her chin had a distinctly stubborn tilt to it and though he could see that her hands trembled, she was not twisting them nervously together before her in the time-honored display of a maiden in distress.

"Well, at least you are not blonde," he grinned disarmingly. "I am growing excessively tired of rescuing blondes, though I am rather grateful for Miss Potts."

"M-miss Potts?"

"Um-hmmm. She, however, is much older than you, I think. Eighteen at the very least."

"Well, I am almost fourteen," Mitzie declared with a certain amount of pride.

"Almost fourteen? I thought today was your birthday?"

"Naw, my pa just said as it was my birthday, 'cause Miz Pimberley said as she wouldn't pay not one farthing for no child. Oh!" she squeaked. "Oh, sir, you ain't goin' to tell the old biddy, are ye? I'm a good girl, I am, an' I can work just as hard as anyone who's fourteen. My pa'll kill me if she turns me out. Honest he will. He got a whole pony for me and Miz Pimberley'll be wantin' it back like as not if I am let go."

Rossland's eyes glistened and his lips twitched and he could feel the laughter bubbling up in him, but he fought it back. "Mitzie, my dear," he murmured, "just what sort of work is it you think you are expected to do?"

"Well, as to that, sir, I ain't sure-certain. But pa said as how I'm a canny one an' I'll figger it out. I reckon as how it's got somethin' ta do with pleasing the gentlemen, on accounta Miz Pimberley, she give me this fine gown and showed me how ta make m'lips red because she said the menfolk would like 'em that way."

"But she did not tell you what was expected of you?"

"No. She said as how the gentlemen would tell me."

Rossland smiled and patted the mattress. "Very well, Mitzie. Then if you wish to please me, sit here beside me and do not be afraid."

"I ain't never afraid," Mitzie murmured with an attempt at bravado as she climbed up onto the bed beside him.

Once the parlor in Bennett Street had emptied and the gentlemen had gone up the stairs in the company of their chosen companions, Lord Langly joined Grace Pimberley before the fire in her private sitting room. "I really do think it was a great deal to ask of me, Grace," he mumbled.

"Yes, but he is apparently enamoured of my little Mitzie and will be contented with her through the night—and at this point, that is to our great advantage."

"But what brought him here is what I wish to know. I cannot conceive that he has actually come to *know* anything, can you?"

"Well, of course not. This is an abbey, Thomas—and Rossland is a rake and a libertine. Why should he not appear upon my doorstep? I am amazed it has taken him so long to do so."

"He has been otherwise occupied," chuckled Langly.

"Who has been otherwise occupied?" queried Lord Whithall, wandering into the room with a glass of cognac in hand. "Evening, Grace, Langly."

"The gentleman who stole Miss Potts from you, my dear," Grace replied with a sympathetic quirk of her luscious lips. "It really is too bad of my lord, Rossland. First he steals your fianceé and then Thomas's cyprian. The man is insatiable."

"The Devil's Delight is here?"

"Upstairs."

"But—"

"He is well-occupied, dear heart. I am certain of it," grinned Mrs. Pimberley. "His mind will not wander from such a sweet tidbit as Mitzie until the morning—if then. And if we are very lucky, he will develop a *tendre* for the chit and remain in our sights and virtually under our thumbs for some time to come."

"I should like to have Rossland under the ground, not under my thumb," grumbled Whithall. "But he will fly his true colors in Miss Potts's presence sooner or later and then I shall have the lady back again. Wait and see."

"And what exactly do you think his true colors are, Donald?" drawled Langly lazily.

"Why, the man is a rake and a reprobate and quite possibly a murderer besides," chuckled Whithall. "Do you not believe your own rumors, Langly? I most certainly believe them."

Six

Minerva could not believe her ears, and the more Angelica Deane embellished upon the scene she and her mama had witnessed, the less Mina gave it credence—especially the part in which she, herself, was destined to serve as a proper cover for The Devil's Delight and his illicit lover, Lady Goodacre.

"In the first place," Minerva began, turning Miss Deane aside into a small alcove behind a potted plant so that none of the gentlemen in the Carringtons' ballroom would be like to interrupt them. "In the first place, Angel, if they were intent upon having a secret affair, why would Lady Goodacre kiss Lord Rossland right out on the front stoop where any passersby might witness the thing? And in the second place, everyone knows that Lord Goodacre is Lord Rossland's very best friend."

"His only friend," scowled Angelica, screwing her beautiful little face into a formidable frown. "And *that* above all things goes to prove how scurvy and unprincipled The Devil's Delight truly is. To seduce his only friend's wife and think nothing of it after Lord Goodacre has stood by him through every scandal! Why, Lord Rossland would have no entrée at all into Society if it were not for the Goodacres."

"Oh, of course he would," sighed Minerva. "He is a wealthy, unmarried earl and his godmama is the Duchess of Winecoff."

"Well, but—"

"And do not keep insisting to me that he is dishonorable. I cannot for one moment believe it," added Minerva with a contemplative pout. "I do not think that he has affairs with married ladies or drinks too much or gambles his new fortune wildly away or anything else of that nature. I think it all some great pretense on his part—tales that he allows to float about for reasons of his own."

"Truly?" asked Angelica, her eyes widening. "What reasons?"

"Well, gracious, how should I know?" Minerva replied, exasperated. "I have only spoken with the man three times in my entire life, Angel! But he is pleasant and kind and not at all the sort of person one would suspect of being a libertine."

"You *are* in love with him!"

"I am *not!* And neither is he in love with me. *That* rumor I know to be nothing but gossip. He has been nothing but a complete gentleman in my presence and he has done not the least thing exceptional so long as I have known him. And to have my best friend spread lies about him is the outside of enough. It is not Lord Rossland's actions that give him such a wretched reputation, Angel, it is other people's vivid imaginations and their very large mouths!"

"Oh!" cried Angelica.

"Yes, oh, indeed. I love you dearly, Angel, but your mouth has grown quite as large as everyone else's this evening and I am sadly disappointed in you. I do think that if you are truly my friend, you ought at least attempt to help me sink this particular dreadful story because you know, yourself, that it is not true. Why, it could lead to a duel between best friends if word of it should reach Lord Goodacre's ears. And either he or Lord Rossland might die and the other be forced to flee to the continent," murmured Minerva. "What a wretched thought!"

"But he *did* kiss her—at least, she kissed him and that is very much the same thing."

"It is not at all the same thing. And besides, it does *not* signify because you did not witness a secret alliance, Angelica. There was nothing secret about it and it is much more likely that Lady Goodacre was merely grateful for some favor Lord Rossland had done her and did no more than peck him on the cheek. I am correct, am I not? It was no more than a quick kiss on the cheek? Oh, Angelica, and for you and your mama to allow it to grow to such magnificent proportions!"

The new rumors of scandal, however, would not be put to rest despite the girls' efforts. Lady Letitia, who had declared Rossland beneath contempt upon first hearing of his infamy, did do an about face when the truth of the event was made known to her and agreed to give Rossland the benefit of the doubt, but most of the ladies and gentlemen gathered at the Carringtons' ball preferred to accept the first version of the tale and continued to batter Rossland's reputation with great enthusiasm. And that very night at that very party, Lord Goodacre became an object of pity and Lady Goodacre a woman of mystery and Lord Rossland was gleefully metamorphosized from The Devil's Delight into the very Devil himself.

Lord Goodacre, after parting from Rossland, had gone straight from his club to his townhouse and thence to his lady's chamber where he sent her abigail skittering from the room, finished brushing Mary's hair himself and then swept her up into his arms. "Invite Rossland to dine, will you?" he whispered huskily, planting a kiss upon her surprised but pliant lips. "Kiss the rascal, too?" he added, kissing the pulse at the base of her throat. "Incorrigible little peagoose! Have you no shame? You rail at me like a regular banshee for innocently entering the wrong building and then go yourself and weep upon Rossland's shoulder for well onto a quarter of an hour. What would you have done if I had gone off and wept on the shoulder of one of your lady friends, eh, m'dear?"

He deposited her gently upon her bed and stretched out beside her, his arm fitting comfortably around her and his lips brushing against her cheeks, her nose, her eyelids. "What a gudgeon you are and what a brute I am. If only you had not shouted and cried, Mary, I would not have grown so very nonplussed and stormed out. I cannot bear to see you cry. You know I cannot. It turns m'mind to mush and I am bound to make a muddle of any words I offer. I am deuced sorry, you know, to have caused you such anguish, m'dear, but 'twas only a stupid mistake and nothing more. Why there is no way, Mary, that I would seek out another woman's arms. Not when I have you, m'dear. Never!''

"I know," breathed Mary, snuggling more firmly against him. "I was beyond foolish to give precedence to gossip over what I know in my heart to be true. I know that you love me and would never betray me with another woman—any other woman. I am so very sorry, Charlie. It was not you caused me anguish, but myself by listening to the gabblemongers and believing them."

Lord and Lady Goodacre then settled in most comfortably for the remainder of the night—he relieved and grateful to have her back in his arms and she relieved and grateful to be there.

Rossland, on the other hand, was not settled in comfortably at all nor was he relieved or grateful. He was, in fact, cudgeling his brain for an acceptable means of convincing Mitzie that she ought not to remain in the house in Bennett Street. Despite his reputation the earl had little stomach for the prostitution of innocents and though he had kept a high flyer or two of his own in fine style from time to time, all of them had been older than himself and not one of them had been the least bit ingenuous.

"What it is," he sighed softly with his arm firmly about Mitzie's shoulders. "Well, you may come to discover that you do not like the work above half."

"My pa says as how I'll like it just fine, Y'r Majesty, once I get used to it."

"Yes, but your father wanted the money he was paid for you, m'dear."

"Aye, an' Miz Pimberley says as how I shall be paid too, a shilling five pence a month plus all I wish to eat and a roof over m'head an' pretty gowns to wear. An' it ain't hard, sitting next to a gentleman on the bed."

Rossland chuckled in spite of himself. "But that is not all that will be expected of you, m'dear."

" 'Tis all you've asked me to do."

"Yes, but other gentlemen will ask other things of you, Mitzie. Can you not just believe me? You will not like being a cyprian above half. I know you will not. You are much too young to have developed a taste for it. And if you will come away with me tonight I, myself, will provide you with a position that pays two shillings a month and all you can eat and I shall buy you some new gowns into the bargain. Plus," added Rossland thoughtfully, "I shall buy you a bonnet as well."

"A bonnet with cherries on it?" asked Mitzie hopefully.

"Indeed," nodded Rossland. "A bonnet with any fruit on it you've a mind to have."

"Oh, Y'r Excellence!" The pure delight in Mitzie's soulful brown eyes signaled so emphatically her acceptance of his offer that Rossland discovered himself overcome with triumph and he gave her a smacking victory kiss right on her pretty red lips.

"Oh, Y'r Gov'nership!" she gasped, blushing. "Oh, I never!"

"No, I realize you never," drawled Rossland, "which is why your father is a scoundrel for bringing you to Mrs. Pimberley. But never mind that, m'dear. You shall have a position more befitting you tomorrow, and new gowns and a new bonnet to boot."

Rossland gave the thin little shoulders a reassuring squeeze and then settled back against the pillows, his smile slowly fading and his eyes taking on a grim, frozen look as he stared at the hangings at the foot of the bed. "I expect you do not know much about this house, eh, Mitzie?" he mumbled after a long silence. "Someone said it was your first evening here, did they not?"

"Uh-huh," responded Mitzie, studying him with some trepidation. "Are you feelin' queer, Y'r Earlship? You ain't smiling anymore."

"I am fine, m'dear. It is just, well, I did not stop to think before I came here."

"Think about what?"

Rossland's gaze returned to the girl who was staring worriedly up at him. "I did not think about the fact that I am dependent upon that wretched walking stick, Mitzie. I can hardly go searching secretly about a brothel in the middle of the night while it taps with my every step. Someone is certain to hear me and come running. And then I will be tossed out upon my ear, you may believe it. Have you been here all day long, Mitzie, or just this evening?"

"All day. But what would you go searchin' for?"

"Did you at any time today see a boy about? A little boy with dark hair and green eyes?"

"I seen the pot boy," replied Mitzie, screwing her eyes shut in the effort to remember any boys at all, because she could see from the gentleman's face that her answer was very important to him. "He were a little one. But he were yellow-haired."

"Oh."

"An' Miz Pimberley's nephew. He were playin' in the parlor when first I comed. He has dark hair, darker than as yer own, Y'r Lor'ship."

"Mrs. Pimberley's nephew? Was he very little, Mitzie? The child I'm seeking is merely four."

Neville Terwilliger set aside his glass of wine untouched and eased Carrie down onto the pillows. He had never drugged anyone before in his entire life and he was thoroughly amazed at how fast the drug had worked. Gently, he pulled the covers over the sleeping cyprian and then made his way quietly to the chamber door in his stockinged feet. He checked his pocket watch by the light of the candles and nodded. Past two. The house ought to have settled down by now. All he need do was avoid Mrs. Pimberley's ruffians. And he could do that. He had come to the house in Bennett Street four times in the past week, each time noting exactly how the establishment was laid out and who might be expected to be where at what hour of the evening.

With a sigh, Terwilliger sat down in the wing chair nearest the door and pulled on his boots. Best to be wearing them if something should go wrong. A gentleman could always say he was bound for the necessary if one of the ruffians did happen to spot him. Provided, of course, that he was spotted in a corridor that led toward the rear door on the ground floor. Luckily, that was exactly where Terwilliger intended to go first. To the rear door.

He peered carefully out into the hall. No one about and no sounds from any of the chambers nearby. Running his fingers through his short brown hair, he took a deep breath and stepped out into the corridor. He thought it best to walk quietly but as openly as possible down the staircase to the ground floor, depending upon such openness to support his claim to be bound for the convenience in the rear yard. What he would do if one of the ruffians on guard insisted upon accompanying him, he had no idea, but he would confront that situation if and when it arrived.

Luckily no one at all was about to take notice of him and he gave a short sigh of relief as he reached the kitchen and opened the lock on the back door. Then he lifted the latch and swung the door quietly outward. He stood for a moment gazing into the moonlit shadows and then stepped down onto a tiny cobbled path. The night air was damp, and Terwilliger, in his shirt-sleeves, shivered as he stepped from the cobbles onto the bit of grass between the kitchen garden and the house. He took only a few more steps, enough to carry him out of sight of the one small window at the back of the kitchen, and then stopped. In a moment a shadow separated from the darkness of the building and came to stand beside him.

"How many people, Neville?" whispered Major Gaffney.

"Eight cyprians and their gentlemen, four ruffians by my count, Mrs. Pimberley, the cook, the maids, and the pot boy. And there is a very little chap sleeps under the eaves. Mrs. Pimberley's nephew, I hear tell."

"And everyone is abed?"

"I encountered no one, Major, but I should think one or two of the ruffians must be awake somewhere."

"Aye, 'tis likely, Terwilliger. But they will not be standing guard on such a quiet night as this. In the cellar drinking I expect. They will not come running unless some alarm is raised. Let us be at it then. Soonest done, soonest over."

"Yes, sir, but there is something I think you should know."

"What? Does it concern this Pimberley woman?"

"No, sir, the Earl of Rossland. He is here and—"

"Rossland? Oh, confound the man! What is he doing here?"

"Well, ah, it is a brothel, Major, and The Devil's Delight, you know, has not had anyone in keeping for the longest time."

"Yes, I know it is a brothel and I know Rossland is not a saint, but why he should require the services of a cyprian on this night of all nights!"

"He is not exactly requiring her services," mumbled Terwilliger. "Well, at least, I hope he is not, sir, for Collingsworth and I went out of our ways to put Mitzie on his arm and Rossland did lie about it being his birthday."

Major Gaffney's mind balked at the density of that remark. With a sigh he put a hand on Terwilliger's shoulder and urged him back inside the building.

Rossland leaned as lightly as possible upon Mitzie as they ascended the dark and ill-kept rear staircase to the third floor. He clutched the splintered banister with one hand and Mitzie's shoulder with the other, his despised cane abandoned far behind them, still poised against the nightstand. They had listened at each door along the second-floor corridor, peered into those where no sound at all could be detected, and in the end had found only sleeping cyprians and their customers or no one at all.

"I reckon he might be up here," whispered Mitzie. "I seen him climb the stairs this af'ernoon when Miz Pimberley told him to be off. Yes, see, there be a door over acrossed the way."

Rossland squinted through the darkness. "You are not frightened, are you, Mitzie?"

"No, Y'r Eminence. Excited is what I am to think that you might be findin' yer little lost nephew!"

"Yes, well, do not be too excited, Mitzie, because perhaps he ain't my nephew. Perhaps he does belong to Mrs. Pimberley."

They listened together with ears pressed against the door under the eaves. Hearing nothing, Rossland's hand fell to the latch. "Locked," he muttered, abruptly looking down. "Oh, the key is in the latch." As quietly as he could Rossland turned the key and pushed the door inward.

At the side of the room a coal fire smouldered upon a tiny grate. Near the grate stood a lilliputian bed with a lump in the middle of it. On a wobbly table near a miniscule window, an oil lamp with wick well-lowered shed meager light upon the scene. Rossland released Mitzie's shoulder and limped toward the light. His leg screamed at the extra weight put suddenly upon it, but he ignored the pain and reaching the table, turned the wick up high. Then he limped to the side of the bed and peered down at the little form huddled beneath the quilt.

Rossland thought his heart would burst. Carefully he lowered himself to the side of the bed. His hand went out to brush the tumbled black curls from the lad's brow. "Beamer," he whispered. "You wretched little brat. How on earth do you come to be in such a place as this?"

The little lump in the middle of the bed tossed about at the sound of his voice and then one deep green eye opened and then the other and quite of a sudden Rossland's arms were filled with a wiggling four-year-old. "Uncle Chad!" cried the child, his voice muffled against Rossland's chest. "I knew you was not dead! I told Aunt Gracie so over an' over."

"Shhh, Jaimie, not so loud," warned Rossland, holding the child away from him just enough to be able to fill his eyes with the boy. "We do not want anyone to hear us."

"We does not?"

"No. We want to be very quiet."

"I shall wisker then," replied the child in a whisper that Rossland feared could be heard all the way to the ground floor.

That whisper made Mitzie giggle and restored her existence to Rossland's mind. He looked from one to the other of them and shook his head uncertainly.

"What's wrong, Y'r Majesty?" asked Mitzie coming across the room to stand beside him.

"Oh, nothing," murmured Rossland, giving the boy an energetic hug. "I am just wondering, Mitzie, now that I have found him, how I am going to get him and you and myself out of here without causing a tremendous ruckus."

"We'll sneak," offered Mitzie confidently.

"Indeed," sighed Rossland. "You may sneak out easily enough I expect, but a cripple and a four-year-old are bound to have a rougher time of it—especially having to descend from the attics all the way to the ground floor."

Neville Terwilliger stood watch at the library door as Major Gaffney, by the light of a single candle, searched hurriedly through desk drawers. Finding nothing of interest, Gaffney took the candle into his hands and wandered about the room stopping to pull one book and then another from the shelves. He stood on a chair and peered behind a landscape above the fireplace. He moved aside everything on the fireplace mantle. And then he began to probe at the white and blue tiles that outlined the hearth.

It is here somewhere, he told himself, his long fingers pushing at the tiles. If not in this room then in another. Grace Pimberley is the woman. I am positive of that. And the woman has the papers. One of the tiles wiggled beneath Gaffney's fingers and he gave a sigh of relief. He worked at the tile for all of thirty seconds before it fell off into his hand, exposing a deep opening behind it. He stuck his hand into the aperture and pulled out an oilskin-wrapped packet. With the candle on the floor beside him, he opened the packet and spread the papers it contained out upon the carpet. "Got it," he whispered triumphantly. "Got it, Neville!" With a flourish, he stuffed one of the papers into his coat pocket, replaced the rest into the packet and stowed the packet back into the hole. He took great care replacing the tile, hoping against hope that Grace Pimberley would not notice that her hiding place had been violated.

"Time to go," he whispered. "Neville? What is it?"

"Someone on the stairs, Major," hissed Terwilliger.

Gaffney joined him at the door and both pairs of eyes peered through the narrow slit into the dimly lit hallway. "Good lord," sighed Gaffney, staring up at the staircase barely twenty feet away. "What does that nodcock think he is doing? He will fall down and break his fool neck."

Terwilliger poked the major in the ribs just as Rossland, a large bundle balanced in one arm and Mitzie holding fast to the other which wielded his cane as well, ceased descending the stairs and huddled into the shadows against the staircase wall.

"Grace Pimberley's ruffians are coming up the corridor," Terwilliger whispered.

"Well, they cannot," Gaffney whispered back. "They will catch Rossland and raise the whole household and you and I will be caught as well. Pretend you are foxed, Neville, and go confront 'em. I would do it, but they expect you to be here whereas my showing myself will make them immediately suspicious. Hold 'em at bay for at least three minutes and then let 'em take you back to your room."

Terwilliger nodded and eased his way out of the library not stepping out into the middle of the hall until he was well past the next door down. Then he swung drunkenly into the light of one of several candelabras spaced along the corridor and hailed the approaching ruffians, slurring his words in good imitation of a gentleman who was chirping merry.

Gaffney watched, widening the slit in the library door until he could see Terwilliger throwing his arms about the ruffians' shoulders and turning them back toward the parlor as he bellowed cheerily about brandy and buxom flights of fancy. Then Gaffney glanced toward the staircase. "Go, Rossland," he whispered to himself. "Drop whatever it is you are making off with and go." But Rossland continued to fumble about in the shadows along the staircase going nowhere. And then Gaffney discerned that what he had thought to be a bundle of clothing was a child and he spun out into the corridor and dashed for the stairs. In a matter of moments he was taking Jaimie from Rossland's arms and urging Mitzie down the steps ahead of

him, setting Rossland free to negotiate the steep descent unencumbered.

Mitzie reached the front door first and though it was most
heavy and took a great deal of effort, she managed to throw
open the bolt in time for the man who had come to help them
to carry the child straight out into the night. She did not,
however, join him, but waited nervously until Rossland
reached the bottom of the stairs and then she seized his free
arm and hurried him outside and closed the door quietly behind them.

"Major Gaffney?" Rossland was nonplussed to say the least
and Gaffney had all he could do to keep the earl from just
stopping and staring at him.

"Not now, Rossland. I shall explain once we have found a
hackney and gotten well out of this neighborhood. Can you
walk as far as Church Street?"

"Of course I can walk as far as Church Street, but Mitzie
must be freezing. Are you freezing, Mitzie? There ain't much
to that wretched gown. Here, stop a moment and help me out
of this coat, eh? They will not be after us. They will not notice
that Beamer and you and I are missing until morning now that
we have got clean away. Who was it outflanked Mrs. Pimberley's
jolly little guards?" he asked, shifting his attention to Gaffney.
"I thought certain we were caught."

"Terwilliger," sighed Gaffney coming to a halt and allowing
Mitzie time to tug Rossland out of his coat and slip into it
herself.

"Terwilliger?" Rossland put an arm around Mitzie's shoulders and began to walk again. "Well, who would have thought.
And he always seemed such a respectable, uncomplicated lad.
Beamer," he asked after a few more steps, "are you all right
in there?"

"Uh-huh," murmured an awe-filled little voice from between the folds of the brightly-colored quilt. "I am all burlowed
in."

"Yes, well, you stay burrowed in, Beamer, until we have got you home."

"I will, Uncle Chad."

The words nearly brought Gaffney to a standstill. "Uncle Chad? Rossland, what—how—this urchin I carry is your nephew?"

"Indeed. Thought I murdered the brat, did you not?"

"Do not be absurd. I never for a moment believed any of that rot and if you had a brain in your head you would know so, too."

"Well, it was hard to tell, Gaffney. From the moment the rumors began about my having murdered my father and Cam and that little miscreant there, my friends and acquaintances did seem to become least in sight. Even before the rumors began, now that I think on it. Aside from the locals, Charlie and Mary and Uncle Henry and Aunt Seraphina and Letitia Farin were the only ones even bothered to come to the funeral."

"I am sorry, Rossland. I did not know. I thought—well, it does not matter what I thought. When I tried to call upon you a few weeks later I found myself turned away at the door."

"Yes, I told Perkins to turn you away. By that time I had decided, you see, that I would become all I was rumored to be and more and I did not want you getting in my way."

"Flinders, but it's a good thing as 'e got in our ways tonight," exclaimed Mitzie abruptly. "I thought sure-certain we was goners, 'specially when yer cane got caught in the stair carpet and set you off balance with yer arms full o' boy. I thought we was all goin' tumblin' down an' right into the arms of them men who would have come runnin' at the noise—you can bet they would have come runnin', Y'r Lor'ship."

"Oh, is that what happened?" asked Gaffney, shifting Jaimie from one arm to the other. "Your cane got caught in the stair carpet? And here I thought you froze in fear."

"I never froze in my life!" growled Rossland, and then, catching the laughter in Gaffney's eyes as they passed beneath a streetlamp, he chuckled, himself. "I thought we were goners too," he admitted. "This wretched cane is more trouble! With the Beamer on my other arm, I could not get free and bring myself totally upright and Mitzie would not go down without us. I thank you, Major, for your swift assistance."

"You are quite welcome, I'm sure."

"But I wonder," Rossland added as they reached the corner of Church Street, "exactly what you and Terwilliger were doing in Grace Pimberley's library."

Major Nicholas Gaffney mumbled something about hailing a hackney and turned away to go waving after one and left Rossland behind on the cobbles to continue wondering.

Seven

Minerva blinked in wonderment as at precisely two o'clock the Earl of Rossland entered her Aunt Letitia's drawing room close upon Battlesby's heels. He was dressed to the nines in a morning coat of deep burgundy with three brass buttons, a burgundy and white striped waistcoat, white corduroy breeches and black Hessians polished to a mirror-like shine. All of which proved to be of no consequence at all in the face of the burgundy and white striped neckerchief tied negligently around his throat where his cravat ought to have been. And that, though it stunned Minerva, fell away to nothing when Mina realized that the earl was sans his shirt collar as well. Why he ought to be ashamed to have left his home in such a state of undress, Minerva thought dazedly. And he certainly ought to know better than to appear in Aunt Letty's drawing room so. But oh, how the sight of him like that makes my heart pound!

With his dark curls askew and his dark eyes flashing, Rossland looked a veritable and most seductive dark angel and his cane became as insignificant as any other gentleman's walking stick as he crossed to her, bowed over her hand, turned it over and brushed his lips against the inside of her wrist. The intense shock that raced through her at this unexpected intimacy set Mina's teeth to chattering. She grew extraordinarily overheated and began to wave her fan with excessive energy before her reddening countenance. Why, she had allowed Lord Whithall to kiss her upon the lips when they had become engaged and she had not felt anything like the overwhelming agitation that she felt at this very moment.

"I do beg your pardon, Miss Potts," drawled the earl as he straightened. "I would not have come, but I could not think you so uppity as to deny me the pleasure of your company simply because my valet has lost his mind."

"Explain yourself at once, Chadwick," growled Lady Letitia glacially from beside Mina, though she did not speak loudly enough to be heard by their other visitors who all stared agog at the vision Rossland presented. "What makes you think it proper to come calling upon my niece looking like a—a—complete Byron, eh? Not that that pollywoggle will not get what is coming to him. And you will likely follow in his very footsteps."

"Me, Letitia? Follow in Byron's footsteps? But I can barely write my name."

"You know perfectly well that is not what I mean."

"Yes, I do. But I did promise to call upon Miss Potts. And I could not think the lack of a collar and a cravat should be enough to prevent me from keeping my word. Apparently there has been some disaster occurred in my wardrobe, Letitia. My collars have all got ink upon them and my cravats gone limp. Martindale was in a panic, near to tears and looked for all the world as though his life were over. Well, what could I do?"

"Send the man packing and stay at home until you could be made presentable!"

"Dismiss Martindale? Really, Letitia, have you no shame? Why he knew me before I was born."

"Oh," muttered Lady Letitia so lowly that even Minerva could barely hear, "that Martindale."

"Yes, m'dear, *that* Martindale and I should like to see even you send him packing when he does not wish to go. And he will never wish to go, Letitia. He has assured me of that."

Rossland's gaze turned back to Minerva and he smiled most agreeably at her. "I am being stared at, am I not?" he asked pleasantly.

"Everyone in the room is staring at you."

"I thought as much. I do not see how Byron carries it off

night after night. Perhaps it is because he pouts well. What do you think?" he asked, allowing his lower lip to protrude slightly and lowering his eyelids in the most provocative manner.

"I think you are being extremely absurd," spluttered Minerva, her cheeks, which had almost cooled, flaming again. What she truly thought was that if Lord Rossland did one more thing to increase his roguish appearance she would become overwhelmed with passion and collapse in a most unladylike fashion into his arms regardless of anything her aunt or her other guests might think.

"Absurd? No, am I?" he grinned, abandoning the pout. "Then I shall cease at once, shall I? Will you come and sit with me just there, where everyone can see how safe you are and I may have you to myself for just a moment? Or is that totally improper?"

"Oh, take her," grumbled Lady Letitia, which surprised Mina no end. And what surprised her even more was the veriest twinkle lurking in her aunt's eyes.

"You are deep in the briars, you know," Minerva stated as Rossland seated her upon a gilded loveseat and took the opposite side for himself. "The most awful rumors have been flying about since last evening. You kissed Lady Goodacre on her front stoop and now everyone thinks that you and she— that you and she—"

Rossland's lips twitched enticingly. His eyes flashed with mirth. "That she and I—" he prompted.

"Oh, you know."

"No, tell me."

"That, that, you are her paramour."

"Mary's paramour—now that is a novel idea! I wonder who thought that one up."

"Lady Deane. She and Angelica were passing as it happened."

"Oh, but it did not just happen, sweetling. It was done. Lady Goodacre did it. Kissed me right on her front stoop."

"Yes, and so I said. And there was nothing at all secret about it."

"Not a thing, but it will be all the talk, I expect, until later this afternoon when a more delicious tale about me will emerge into the sunlight. Tell me, Miss Potts, might you consider becoming my very good friend instead of merely a most delightful acquaintance?"

"Your very good friend?"

"I find I like you, Miss Potts. You are bright and charming and a minx to boot. And you do not run off and have vapours the moment a rather discomposing rumor about me surfaces. I expect it was discomposing? I expect the gabblemongers said that I was attempting to court you in order to cover my tracks with Mary, did they not?"

"That is exactly what they said!" cried Minerva, surprised that he should think of it. "And Aunt Letitia was quite put-out until I made Angelica tell the truth of what she and her mama had seen and then Aunt Letty declared it all a hum—which is the only reason Battlesby allowed you to enter the house today."

"Well, not the only reason, sweetling. Battlesby and I raise a glass now and then down at the Coach and Four."

"You—you do?"

"And I send him flowers. From one of the Rossland greenhouses. I have done so for years now, ever since I returned from the wars. Battlesby loves flowers, you know, and when my gardener has a new shoot from something particularly nice, well, he has orders to send it on to Battlesby. That man has a veritable jungle of flowers in his quarters, you may believe me. He even smuggled me in one night to join him in a glass of port and view them. And so, you see, because of our friendship, Battlesby would have helped me gain entrance somehow if the need had arisen. I came to ask if you would consider being my comrade in arms as well as the young lady to whom I have reportedly given my heart—and taken it back again if this round of gossip is to be credited. Quite soon, mind you, the gossips will be abuzz about my shocking conduct in regard to another young woman and both Mary and you will be let off the hook. Her name is Mitzie."

"Whose name is Mitzie?" Minerva asked, attempting to follow his mind as it jumped from place to place but being constantly distracted by an overwhelming desire to have him throw her across his saddle bow and carry her off into the night. It is that stupid neckerchief, she thought, and—and how very rakish he looks without his collar. And the way he looks at me with those dark, intriguing eyes.

"Mitzie is the other young woman—well, she's a child, really. Not even fourteen. I have stolen her from a brothel. Devil a bit, I should not have said brothel in your presence, should I? Well, it don't matter, for you are not such a wet goose that you do not know what a brothel is or will be put out of countenance simply by mention of the word. If you were such a missish goose, I am quite certain I would not find myself wishing to be with you all of the time. Devil a bit! I expect I should not have said that either—about wishing to be with you all of the time. Still, it is true enough. I cannot cease thinking about you, sweetling. Even in the midst of utter mayhem I find you are constantly on my mind. I spent the entire night in that brothel wishing you were there beside me."

"What a thing to say!" exclaimed Minerva, her hands flying to cover her rapidly reddening face.

"I am sorry, sweetling," Rossland chuckled, not looking sorry at all. "I have not got this morning caller conversation down as yet. I expect I shall require more practice."

"A great deal more," grinned Minerva, deciding to ignore her flaming cheeks.

"Yes, well, but what I have come to ask will not fit into polite conversation either, so now you are prepared for it."

"I am?"

"Uh-huh. I want you to hide someone for me here in Green Street. Only until I have got things straight in my mind as to what will be best to do, you understand."

"Hide someone?"

"Yes. Mitzie and a very little boy."

Minerva's jaw dropped. Her mind flashed back over their previous conversation. "I—you—are you requesting, sir, that I give sanctuary to some cyprian you stole from a brothel last evening and—and—her child?"

"Well, he ain't her child, but I am hoping you can manage

to do just that and not tell your Aunt Letitia anything about it for the present, because Letty will not be at all pleased to have me hiding a cyprian in her establishment."

"I should think not!" exclaimed Minerva.

Rossland gazed down at her, his eyes wide with innocence. "You should think not what, Miss Potts? You should think that Letitia will not be pleased? Or you should think that you will not do me this small favor?"

There was no getting around it, Minerva thought. People might call him The Devil's Delight all they wished and expound upon his multitude of sins and his singular perversions at the very top of their lungs, but when he looked at her like that, his eyes all guileless and hopeful and trusting, she could not credit anything anyone said in regard to his depravity.

"Have you nowhere else to take them?" she queried, determined not to give in to his wishes too quickly.

"Well, no. They are residing with a gentleman acquaintance of mine at the moment, but they cannot remain there and I cannot keep them at Rossland House because they will not be safe there, you see. I mean, Miss Potts, that the person I stole them from knows exactly who took them and will haunt Rossland House hoping to recover them."

"And they do not wish to be recovered?"

"No, not at all. I—they—well, I can explain everything, sweetling. Truly, I can. But it will take a great deal more time than we have at the moment. I have already monopolized you far too long. I can see it from the look on Letty's face. One more minute and she will be over here demanding that I leave."

"Very well then," nodded Minerva. "I shall attempt to work something out with the staff. Perhaps if the both of them remain belowstairs and make themselves useful Aunt Letitia will not take note of them or Battlesby may say he hired them for some particular but temporary reason."

"I knew you would!" replied Rossland smiling widely. "You are a trump, Miss Potts! And you will not need to arrange it with the staff because Battlesby has assured me that he will see to all if you are agreeable to it. No, no, sweetling," he added quickly as Minerva began to frown, "do not climb up on your high ropes now. Battlesby agreed to aid me only if I could procure your permission. I shall tell him you have given me the nod, shall I, on my way out? There is a soirée at the Stevens' tonight. Do you and Letty attend?"

"Indeed."

"Might you develop a frightful headache and seek to remain at home? Letty will go on without you, I think, because the Stevens always set up a cardroom and play whist for chicken stakes and Letty is extremely fond of that sort of thing."

"How on earth do you know that?" queried Minerva in wonder.

"You would be amazed at all I know about your Aunt Letty. She has always been one of my favorite people. Can you develop a headache this evening? I shall deliver Mitzie and the boy directly Letty leaves if you can."

Minerva could not help but grin. Truly, he was the most outrageous gentleman, but the enthusiasm in his voice and the mischief in his eyes were irresistible. "Why even now," she murmured, carrying her hand to her brow and bestowing upon him a subtle wink. "Even now I feel a headache coming on."

Major Nicholas Gaffney was devilish uneasy as he entered his office. He had known for well over three weeks that Grace Pimberley was involved in the buying and selling of secret information concerning the war effort. Last night in Bennett Street he had acquired the evidence needed to have the woman apprehended. And he would have gone directly to Castlereagh with it the first thing this morning and had the jade brought in, too, if he had not discovered Rossland at the place with his nephew in his arms. Now his course of action was clouded and he was indecisive about how to handle what could prove to be a much more sensitive and perilous matter than he had at first supposed.

Gaffney, like the rest of Society, had thought Rossland's

nephew drowned. Not that he had subscribed to the theory that Rossland had been involved in the sinking of the *Mary Jane* and so done away with father, brother and nephew in one decisive blow in a push to inherit the title. That, of course, was nonsense. Why, any gentleman who would put his own life into peril to rescue a soldier he had never before seen and whose name he did not know—which was precisely what Rossland had done for Gaffney—to drag him from the battlefield and transport him through enemy lines back into the relative safety of the British encampment, such a man would never think to murder anyone, much less members of his own family. In fact, Gaffney had been so incensed by the prevalent rumors of Rossland's infamy that he had set out on his own, whenever he had some free moments, to look into the matter and to prove to everyone's satisfaction that the foundering of the yacht had been an accident pure and simple and that all of the rumors detrimental to Rossland's reputation—especially those which insinuated that the man was a murderer—were nothing but that—unfounded rumors.

But now he knew beyond a doubt that the foundering of the *Mary Jane* had not been an accident. Last night, with Mitzie tucked up in his own bed and Jaimie asleep in his chaise longue, Gaffney had spoken with Rossland until well after daylight. And the more Gaffney had pried from the tight-lipped gentleman, the more puzzled and distraught and astonished he himself had become. Once Rossland had given in and explained his situation, Gaffney had known to a certainty that Grace Pimberley and her associates were not the paltry spies he had thought them. And it had become obvious as well that Rossland's nephew was an important pawn in some magnificently devious plot that Mrs. Pimberley and her associates had hatched among themselves.

But, thought Gaffney, the most amazing part of the whole was that Rossland actually undertook to do such a thing and keep such a secret and that his entire family and his servants kept the secret as well—for four long years and more. It was almost beyond comprehension.

Though it had taken the major forever, at the last he had

succeeded in convincing Rossland of the inherent foolishness
of thinking to handle the situation on his own and the earl
had agreed to accept his aid. But how they were to keep the
boy safe until plans could be laid to capture the villains,
Gaffney had no idea, for Grace Pimberley would know beyond
a doubt that it had been Rossland absconded with the child
and her men would be watching for an opportunity to seize
the boy back. And Rossland's own life would now be in danger,
that was clear—as clear as the fact that the child had not been
kidnapped merely to collect a ransom from his uncle.

Gaffney had suggested that Jaimie remain with him under
the care of his batman, Harris, but Rossland had declined that
idea. "You would never live through it, Major, nor your man.
A four-year-old ain't near as easy to live with as a troop of
drunken soldiers," he had observed drily. "And it would be
noticeable to everyone nearby that you had a child living with
you. You would need to begin buying milk for one thing, and
boy's clothes for another, because I did not attempt to carry
any of his apparel out with us. And who would you say he was,
eh?" And then an odd light had dawned in Rossland's dark
eyes and he had asked Gaffney to watch over both the children
until the following evening, when, he had stated with assur-
ance, he would come to carry them away to an extremely se-
cure place.

Minerva sat amongst her morning callers thoroughly distracted. She could not believe that she had actually agreed to
deceive her aunt, nor could she imagine how she was to succeed in the deception even with Battlesby's help. Surely her
Aunt Letitia would notice the addition of a girl of thirteen and
a very little boy to her household. Oh, but she would absolutely
love to have Lord Rossland before her this very moment so
that she might put her hands around his seductively kerchiefed
neck and squeeze with all her might.

Even the Marquis of Kensington, who had made his most
elegant entrance into her Aunt Letty's parlor amidst a great

number of excited feminine whispers and sighs, could not distract her from thoughts of the earl. Though she looked politely at the marquis and gave every sign of attending with great interest to his monologue, her mind insisted upon turning Lord Kensington's precisely combed honey-gold hair into unmanageable curls the color of mahogany and his sea-green eyes into eyes of the deepest, darkest brown. And most unaccountably, the marquis's steady drone subsided into an annoying buzz beneath the distinct memory of Rossland's husky voice explaining about Mitzie and the boy.

How on earth could he? Minerva wondered. How could he just up and steal a girl from a brothel? And what about the little boy? Had the child been in the brothel as well? Perhaps he was Mitzie's brother? Was one allowed to take one's brother along when one became a cyprian? Oh, how the gabblemongers would talk once it was disclosed that Rossland had done such a thing. For the life of her, she could not understand how Lord Rossland could continue to make himself grist for the gossip mill. And this time he had done so simply to rescue some wretched little chit from a life of—

Well, of course he would do that, she thought then. He is an honorable and compassionate gentleman and he could not let a child be sold into such a despicable life if he might prevent it. He would not have given the scandalmongers so much as a moment's thought because a child's future had most definitely been at stake. Lord Rossland was not such a poltroon as to let the threat of scathing rumors deter him from what he saw to be a good and necessary deed. "Of course not," Minerva mumbled aloud with a little shake of her head, bringing Kensington to a stuttering halt.

"Of course not, Miss Potts? You have no wish to join me for an evening at the theater?"

"The theater? Oh, no. I mean, yes, I should be honored, my lord. I—I am very much afraid that my mind has been wandering. It—I—Lord Rossland was here earlier and—"

"That miscreant had the nerve to present himself in your drawing room? No wonder you are discomposed, Miss Potts. Any young lady would be most upset if forced to encounter that rake's attentions. You are not to bother about him any longer. I shall see to it myself that he ceases to annoy you."

"Oh, no, my lord. That is to say, you must not concern yourself overly much. The man—he is most dangerous, is he not?"

The marquis's chest puffed out—rather like a pouter pigeon's Minerva thought—as he lifted his nose to symbolize contempt for Rossland. "You have nothing to fear on that score, m'dear. My courage in the cause of righteousness is acknowledged throughout London. I shall merely inform the rogue that he is to cease bothering you, that his attentions are unacceptable and that you are now under my protection."

"Under your protection, my lord?"

"Well, no, not exactly that, but you understand what I mean, Miss Potts. He will not dare to approach you again once it is made clear to him that you are not without—friends."

Kensington emphasized the final word with such self-righteous pride and with such a self-satisfied look upon his haughty countenance that Mina was sorely tempted to land him a facer. Her hands fisted in her lap but she restrained herself admirably and merely glanced up at him with pretended shyness.

"You are too kind, my lord. To think that you should endanger your life for a mere nobody like myself."

"Endanger my—?"

"I have heard much about Lord Rossland. My Aunt Letitia and he were neighbors, you understand. And she has seen him shoot the pips from a playing card at fifty feet—while in his cups—by the light of a single candle—with one eye closed."

Minerva had all she could do to keep a straight face as she watched the marquis grow paler with each phrase she added. How easy it is, she thought with amazement, to tell plumpers about Lord Rossland! This wretched blowhard does not doubt one word I have just said! "No," she added, enough pity for Kensington rising to the surface to offer him an honorable way out. "I cannot in good conscience permit you to confront that scoundrel. Your death would be upon my head and I could not bear it!"

"Well, well, if that is the case," responded Kensington quietly. "I would not wish to put you to undue worry, m'dear."

"Oh, thank you so much, my lord," sighed Minerva in her best imitation of Angelica Deane performing the role of grateful ingenue. "I am so very relieved. It would put me all about in my mind to think of you at the mercy of such an acknowledged villain as Lord Rossland."

Such a villain, she thought to herself. How on earth can I say that when I have seen not the least sign of villainy in him? It is unconscionable of me to sully his reputation further. But this stiff-rumped jackanapes—to think himself so superior to Lord Rossland—it is the outside of enough! And certainly Lord Rossland will not blame me for putting this pompous pouter pigeon in his place.

Kensington very properly made his exit fifteen minutes after his arrival having arranged with Lady Letitia to escort Minerva and herself to the Drury Lane theater the following Thursday. "Though why he bothers with me I cannot comprehend," sighed Minerva, as the last of their callers departed and she sank down onto the sofa beside her aunt. "Lord Kensington never did more than nod in my direction before the incredible rumor that Lord Rossland had lost his heart to me began to circulate."

"Which is precisely what brought you to the marquis's notice," replied Lady Letitia. "Men! They will villify Chadwick from one end of England to the other, but let him be seen to enjoy himself with a young woman and the other gentlemen all come knocking upon her door to see what has caught his fancy. It is one of the reasons I gave him permission to wait upon you when he requested it. I knew he would bring the others to our doorstep."

"Did Lord Rossland tell you that he wished to reform his ways, Aunt Letty?" asked Mina, stretching a skein of yarn between her hands so that Lady Letitia might roll it into a ball.

"Precisely, though I doubt he will succeed in doing so. It is inbred in him, you know. He was a thatchgallows from the very day he was born. But at least he did have the good sense to take me into his confidence concerning his nephew."

"His—his nephew?" Minerva could not at first comprehend in what direction her aunt's mind was wandering, and then she recalled the great Banbury story Rossland had laid before her on the way to Hyde Park. "Goodness, do you mean to say it is true, Aunt Letty? That you believed him?"

"Well, of course I believed him. I made sure to check his eyes, you see, as he was telling me and there was not the least hint of a squint. He always squints the slightest bit when he lies, Minerva. One eyelid—the left—lowers the tiniest dab. It has been so since he was in leading strings."

Donald, Lord Whithall hesitated before Farin House. If Rossland had gone to pay a morning call upon Minerva, he must have done so earlier in the day, for it was quite apparent that all of the young lady's visitors had departed. He had been most amazed to see Kensington depart the premises and he wondered what on earth had prodded that stiff-rumped cub to visit in Green Street. Rossland, most likely, he thought. Let The Devil's Delight smile upon a lady and apparently even the cream of the *ton's* gentlemen wished to discover what delights that lady held out to the wretch.

Which only went to prove how useless it was to attempt to sink the man. No matter what rumors circulated about Rossland he could not be placed beneath the notice of Polite Society. Everyone noticed him—constantly! "Drat the man!" mumbled Whithall. "Why did he not just lie down and die at Talavera?"

Of course, had he done that, Whithall's present opportunities for a rich and powerful future would never have materialized. "No," muttered Whithall, "that would have been most inopportune. But he might have had the consideration to stick his spoon in the wall after he had returned, ill and near death, to England. That would have been most acceptable."

Whithall shrugged his broad shoulders and sauntered off up the street. There was no use in waiting longer. The message from Langly had come too late. Either he had missed Rossland or the gentleman had gone elsewhere and not put in an appearance at Green Street at all. And besides, Whithall thought, The Devil's Delight would not be like to involve Miss Potts in this gambit in any way, because Miss Minerva Potts was a most unexceptionable young woman and would faint dead away at the mere mention of murder and kidnapping—as would any gently bred young lady of Whithall's acquaintance. Gentlewomen were not fit to deal with subterfuge and secrets and treachery. They were not even fit to deal with the mention of such things and closed their ears to them with great determination. And certainly, Miss Minerva Potts was no exception—if she had been the sort who poked her nose into everything and could not be reined in he would never have thought to offer for the chit as he had in the first place.

Eight

Martindale's conscience would not cease to prick at him. In truth, there was no ink upon His Lordship's collars and all of his cravats were perfectly cleaned and starched. The valet sank down into the chair against the back wall of Rossland's dressing room and with a groan buried his head in his hands. How could he have been so demented, so unfeeling, as to send poor Master Chad out to call upon Letitia Farin's niece in a collarless shirt with a neckerchief tied rakishly around his throat? Odds were a royal tiger to an alley cat that Lady Letitia had raked Master Chad up one side and down the other roundly and loudly in front of everyone and then sent him packing to boot. Because Battlesby would have granted His Lordship entrance into the Farin establishment. Oh, he might have looked askance at the lad's costume and raised an eyebrow in surprise, but Battlesby had always had a fondness for Master Chad and would have admitted His Lordship nonetheless.

"What have I done?" groaned Martindale. "As if the lad were not already thought disgraceful, and I to go and add to his infamy. I am a thorough scoundrel!"

"I thought as much," came a quiet voice from the doorway.

The unexpected sound of it caused Martindale to jerk upright so suddenly as to wrench his neck.

"The moment he left, I knew," continued Perkins, stepping into the room and crossing to take a seat upon the footstool before his friend. "I knew that you would be up here castigating yourself for sending him off in such unacceptable attire."

"It was more than unacceptable attire," sighed Martindale.

"It was inappropriate and scandalous attire. I am no longer fit to be called a valet. I have committed an act of sheer betrayal!"

"No, Trevor, it was not an act of betrayal," consoled Perkins. "It was an act of self-defense *and* an act of extraordinary kindness toward His Lordship. Think, man. Can you honestly believe that Master Chad would be happy leg-shackled to a niece of Lady Letitia's? It is some aberration sends him after the girl. He is not seeing her clearly. You have done him a great favor to nip the thing in the bud. Quickest ended, soonest forgotten, Martindale. He will thank you for it one day."

"He will not thank me for the peal Lady Letitia will have rung over him."

"No, he will not be grateful for that, but it is not as though she has not been ripping up at the lad for all of his life. He is not like to take that to heart, not Master Chad."

"No, perhaps not. Perhaps it was the right thing for me to do," nodded Martindale slowly. "Surely 'tis better for the young lady as well. Such a well-brought-up, proper young lady as she must be, she'd not enjoy being hitched to such a rascal as His Lordship, especially if she's a high-stickler, which she's bound to be, being as she's Lady Letitia's niece and all."

"That's the way to look at it, m'lad," smiled Perkins. "Why you've done 'em both a favor and saved the entire staff as well."

"Yes, I have."

"Most certainly."

"And she will not wish to see him ever again, so there will be no further need to deceive His Lordship, will there?"

"Most likely not, Trevor. Most likely not."

Martindale opened his mouth to thank Perkins for setting his conscience at ease only to close it directly and spring from his chair at the sound of the earl's unmistakable step ascending the staircase. Perkins gained his feet quite as quickly but had taken only a few steps toward the doorway when it was suddenly filled by Rossland. "Good, you are both here! There is a matter of extreme importance that— What is it?" he asked abruptly taking note of the peculiar look that passed between his butler and his valet. "Not a council of war, I hope?"

"War, Your Lordship?" queried Perkins, looking down his long, slender nose in a most refined and unemotional pose.

"Indeed, Perkins, and there ain't no use wasting that butter wouldn't melt in my mouth look on me, because I know better. You are up to something, the both of you, and quite possibly everyone else in this establishment. Do you not think, just for once, that you could tell me what it is you mean to have? Or would it spoil your fun to request something of me rather than to manipulate me into it? I do remember, you know, how much you enjoyed manipulating my father."

"It would spoil our fun exceedingly, my lord," droned Perkins in his coolest tone, adding to the statement with a distinct arching of his left eyebrow.

"Oh. Well, I would not wish to do that. Sit down a moment, both of you. I have something important to discuss. Perkins, have any peculiar callers appeared upon our doorstep since I left for Green Street?"

"Peculiar, my lord? No. There was a Mr. Terwilliger left his card, and a Lord Langly, and your uncle, the duke."

"You did not tell any of them where I had gone, Perkins?"

"No, my lord. You did not, you will recall, advise me of your destination."

"Quite right," nodded Rossland. "Nor until further notice, Perkins, will you ever admit to knowing precisely where I have gone. Unless, of course, it is Lord Goodacre who asks, or a Major Gaffney."

"Major Gaffney, my lord? The Major Gaffney of Talavera?"

"You know him, Perkins?"

"Indeed, my lord. Lady Liza had to hide away when he first came to Riddle to bestow his thanks upon you, though you were quite feverish and likely do not recall his visit. And he attended the fete. And he came here once as well, though you had me send him off directly."

"I was not that feverish, Perkins. Of course I remember his coming to Riddle to thank me," replied Rossland with a distinct squinting of his left eye which told both Perkins and Martindale that he did not remember the incident at all. That particular involuntary squint had given him away since childhood, though no one, not even his father or his brother, had ever seen fit to explain to him how everyone, including cook and the neighbors, knew when he was telling a bouncer. "You will recognize the major if he should turn up, then."

"Indeed, my lord."

"Good. Because we have got to be careful for awhile, all of us. Gaffney thinks I should not even trust the two of you, but he does not know you as I do and his suspicions on that count are to be forgiven him."

"Not trust us?" asked Martindale, his guilt over the collars and neckcloths becoming a considerable lump in his throat. "Whyever would you not trust us, Your Lordship?"

"I do trust you, Trev. It is Gaffney has qualms, but I truly feel I must overlook them because you ought to be warned and in no uncertain terms either. There are like to be some most disreputable people lounging about keeping an eye on the house. Leaning against the lampposts, I should think, or pausing to read a paper upon the bench beneath the statue in the green across the street. Or perhaps posing as pedlars."

John Perkins glanced amazedly at Martindale and received an equally amazed glance in return. "But why, Your Lordship? What could such people possibly hope to gain by—"

"They hope to discover where I have stowed Jaimie," declared Rossland with a wide grin.

"Jaimie?" gasped Perkins and Martindale in unison.

"You have found Master Jaimie?" Martindale asked excitedly. "And I knew you could do it, too!"

"Well of course we knew he could do it!" exclaimed Perkins. "Have we not been depending upon him to do so since that first awful message arrived? And is the child all right, my lord? He is not harmed in anyway?"

"He is fine. He was sleeping when I left him but I expect he will wake to be the handful he has always been."

"When you left him, Master Chad?" asked Martindale. "But where have you left him? Why did you not bring him directly home? Oh, because you fear the villains will attempt to seize him again. But they most certainly will not. They will not be given such an opportunity. We shall arouse the staff and stand guard over the little fellow every minute of the day."

"No, no," sighed Rossland as he noted the martial light rise in both sets of elderly eyes. "It is not only Jaimie's safety forestalls his coming home. I fear for all of you as well. I will not have some ruffians taking one of your lives in order to get their hands upon the boy again, and they will, Trev.

"I truly thought our secret was safe, but obviously it ain't. Jaimie was not picked up along the shore by some villains who saw an opportunity to make some blunt knocking. From what Gaffney has told me combined with what I knew already, it is certain that I was right all along. The *Mary Jane* did not founder accidentally. She was scuttled and Father and Cameron murdered in a most bizarre quest to seize the Beamer. So now we must do the best we can to discover who it is did the thing and see them apprehended before Jaimie may come home to us."

"But where do you mean to hide him?" asked Perkins with a perplexed frown. "If someone seeks him you cannot possibly take him to Riddle or Skylark Cottage or even into Hertfordshire or to Brighton. And where have you left him? Is he safely stowed now?"

"Well, he is stowed, John, but he cannot stay where he is. He will stick out like an ostrich plume on a beaver because Gaffney has him. But this evening I will hide him away more safely. I do not expect that you have gotten any of my collars clean as yet, have you, Trev? Or one neckcloth starched? I am almost positive that I ought not to appear in Miss Potts's presence again in this attire. She was a dear about it, but I think it overset her just a bit to see me looking like Byron. She kept changing color, you know, and fanning herself, and looking most uncomfortable."

Minerva listened to the sound of her aunt's carriage fading into the distance and heaved a great sigh. It was almost nine o'clock and she had had a good six hours in which to ponder over and worry about her decision to aid Lord Rossland. Not that she would even think to withdraw her aid now for she had given him her word to hide the children and her word was as precious to her as was any gentleman's word to himself. Still, she could not quite bring herself to suppose that she and Battlesby would not be found out by her Aunt Letitia and most quickly too, for how on earth were they to introduce into her aunt's household two urchins without her aunt noticing? No, it would never work. By tomorrow afternoon the children would both be turned out and Lord Rossland barred from Green Street forever and herself likely on her way back to Hertfordshire accompanied by a most scathing letter to her father. And Battlesby, poor dear Battlesby! After all his years of service, Battlesby would quite likely be out on the street and without references too!

"It was unconscionable of him to request it of us," Mina mumbled to herself as she wandered aimlessly about the parlor waiting for Rossland's knock upon the door. "He ought never to have asked either Battlesby or me to deceive Aunt Letitia. I am quite certain he will not suffer for it if we are discovered because he does not give the veriest lick for anything Aunt Letitia can say or do to him. But Battlesby and I shall certainly suffer. I expect Lord Rossland does not care a groat for that."

"I do believe, Miss, that he cares a good deal more than a groat," offered Battlesby as he wandered into the parlor and set a large silver tray on a table before the fire.

"Oh, Battlesby! I did not expect you to be here. That is—"

"You did not expect me to overhear you, Miss Minerva," Battlesby provided smoothly. "I understand completely. But you must not worry yourself into a frazzle over the matter, Miss. You are simply frightened by the situation into which you have gotten yourself by agreeing to aid His Lordship."

"Yes. Yes, that is it exactly. Are you not frightened, Battlesby?"

"Not a pence worth," smiled Battlesby, "for I know quite well who is coming and I depend upon Master Chad's ingenuity to make the whole thing as inconspicuous as possible, especially where Her Ladyship is involved."

"Well, I know who is coming, too. A chit from a brothel. No, that is not fair of me. She is an innocent, Lord Rossland says, and not a cyprian at all."

"And a little boy," nodded Battlesby. "Who, if I guess correctly, will be four years old with black curly hair and tremendous green eyes and will be called Beamer." Battlesby was about to add something else when the knocker sounded below. "I must hurry, Miss," he said moving quickly toward the hall. "That will be His Lordship and I have sent the rest of the staff off for the evening so as to give us some privacy. I will show him up here, shall I?"

"Indeed," Minerva nodded, unconsciously wringing her hands together. Was this not a great mistake? Not only was she endangering Battlesby's position and the rest of her Season, but it now occurred to her that she was allowing one of the most notorious rakehells in all of London to come into her parlor while her aunt was out visiting. If word of it should get out Mina would be well and soundly compromised. No decent gentleman would ever so much as nod to her again.

A magnificent bang jerked her away from her doubts. This was followed by another bang of equal magnitude and that followed yet again by another. Curious, Minerva sped into the corridor and peered down over the balcony railing. What she saw made her laugh. A most endearing young gentleman in boots at least two sizes too large, baggy pantaloons and a remarkably worn nankeen jacket tied with a leather army belt to keep it upon him, was jumping, both feet at the same time, up the staircase. Behind him Lord Rossland, clinging to the banister with one hand, his cane stuffed into one of his boot tops, kept reaching out as he ascended to keep the young turk from plummeting backward after each wobbly landing. And behind Rossland a very pretty young girl, near to invisible beneath a gentleman's greatcoat, was stepping carefully, both her hands extended as though she feared the earl might fall himself and she would be able to catch him. At the very bottom of the staircase Battlesby waited patiently until they should give him room to ascend.

"Ho! Miss Potts!" Rossland called, grinning up at her. "What think you of my army?"

"We are climbin' the Pirhouettes!" shouted the little boy excitedly, spying the lady to whom His Lordship spoke.

"The Pyrenees," corrected Rossland with a wink at Minerva, "so you will understand, Miss Potts, if it takes us a little while to make it to the top."

"Just so long as you do not all make it unceremoniously back to the bottom," rumbled Battlesby, which set all three of the visitors and Minerva to laughing.

When at last he reached her, Rossland loosed his grip upon the banister, plucked his walking stick from his boot and put it to the floor and, leaning forward, bestowed a most chaste kiss upon Minerva's cheek. "You are an angel," he whispered, "to even think of helping me."

"Oh! But I am no angel whatsoever," Mina protested, her hand going to the cheek he'd kissed and touching the spot his lips had touched ever so carefully. "I have been sitting here petrified, worrying about everything and sincerely doubting that I ought to have agreed to any of it."

"No, were you, sweetling? Doubting? Well, we shall put an end to that, shall we not, Beamer?" he glanced at the child who was peeping around the door frame into the front parlor.

"Uncle Chad, they's gingersnaps in there," announced Jaimie agog. "Is they for us?"

"Indeed," assured Battlesby scooping the boy up and taking Mitzie's hand, leading her into the room. "Gingersnaps and lemonade for the both of you."

"And brandy?" Rossland queried hopefully, offering his arm to Minerva. "I have had the devil of an evening so far. Oh, I ought not to have said devil ought I? I *am* sorry, Miss Potts. But I *have* had the devil of an evening so far! I stole these two reprobates away—Beamer in his nightshirt and Mitzie in that atrocious red gown peeking out from beneath the major's coat—and then discovered it is not so easy as I thought to get them new rigs. Especially," he laughed, seeing Mina seated in one of the wing chairs and taking a seat across from her upon the divan. "Especially when one waits until all the shops are closed."

"Close-ed up tight!" giggled Jaimie from where he sat

munching cookies before the hearth with Mitzie on the carpet beside him.

"Right you are, old chum," nodded Rossland accepting a glass of brandy from Battlesby. "Tight. No one about. At least, no one willing to answer our pounding upon their doors. So we had to make do with what we could scavenge, which was fine for Jaimie because a bigger boy lives two doors down from Gaffney, but not one of the women had an extra gown they could spare for Mitzie and she did not wish to be wearing pantaloons."

"I should think not," observed Mina with a pleasant smile for the girl. Could this possibly be the fledgling cyprian? This wisp of a child? The name was the same but certainly there was some mistake. Minerva made sure that she would ask Lord Rossland about it once both children were tucked away.

"Now, Battlesby, sit down, do, and the three of us will discuss what's to be done, eh?" Rossland patted the seat beside him and Battlesby took it, a glass of brandy in his own hand.

"The mite is your nephew," the butler said quietly. "You had best tell Miss that immediately."

"You knew he would be," Rossland grinned at the elderly retainer. "The moment I asked for your assistance I could see you knew it would be Jaimie I brought."

"Aye, my lord. We have been praying daily for you to find the boy, Perkins and Martindale and I. And what a craven I should be if I refused my own assistance."

"Yes, but I hope it will not come to a test of courage, Battlesby, for you or Miss Potts. You see the thing of it is, Miss Potts, that I cannot have it bandied about that Jaimie is here. There cannot be even a hint of the possibility that he is in residence in Green Street."

"But why?" asked Minerva, puzzled. "He is your nephew. Why can you not simply take him home with you and declare to the world that he is not drowned and you have found him?"

"Because—" Rossland took a swallow of the brandy and thought a moment. "Well, not to frighten you, sweetling," he said at last, "but those who took him in the first place will attempt to discover his whereabouts and take him back."

"Uncle Thomas and Aunt Grace," piped up Jaimie around a mouthful of gingersnaps. "I was kidnapped."

"Yes," nodded Rossland at the little boy, "but you did not know it, brat, until I told you and you must not go crowing about it to anyone."

"He won't, Y'r Majesty," offered Mitzie, her soft brown eyes beaming adoringly up at the earl. "I'll see he don't."

"Indeed you will, Mitzie, because that is your job for the moment," Rossland nodded. "And I trust you to do it. And you must both do whatever Mr. Battlesby and Miss Potts tell you as well. We know who Aunt Grace is," he added, turning his attention back to Minerva, "but as to Uncle Thomas," he shrugged expressively. "And Beamer will not be safe until they are both apprehended."

Minerva sat mesmerized as she listened to the tale Rossland spun of murder and kidnapping and spies and counterspies, certain that she had fallen into the pages of a gothic novel. Could all this actually be? Could this gentleman with the sparkling eyes and the tumbling curls and lips that never seemed able to hold a downward tilt for more than one second at a time be telling the truth? Could all of this be going on around her and she all unaware? What a solitary, protected and very well-cushioned person she must be to wander about London without the least inkling of plots and counterplots and counter-counterplots. And what an extraordinary person Lord Rossland must be to be in the very thick of it and not be overwhelmed.

"I think you and Letitia will be perfectly safe once we have carried it off," Rossland concluded confidently. "I already have the letter from your father requesting your aunt to take the two of them in. Battlesby will deliver it to her once you have gotten the children out of the house tomorrow morning."

"But— but how did you reach my father?"

"It is a forgery, sweetling. A gentleman named Neville Terwilliger penned it. Copied the handwriting from some notes your father sent to the Foreign Office a few months back. It probably don't sound a lot like your father, but we made it short, so like as not Letty will be fooled by it. And once we have dressed Jaimie up to look like a parson's son and Mitzie to look like his nursemaid, and you have succeeded in reminding your aunt of poor Mr. Aubury who was your mother's cousin's youngest son or somesuch, why, I doubt anyone will be the least bit suspicious and we will be able to hide the two of them right here beneath everyone's noses."

"Right," nodded Battlesby. " 'Tis only tonight must be gotten through, Miss, without drawing attention to the pair, and I've arranged for that. You must only be certain to be ready by ten o'clock when His Lordship's coach appears. I will see the children smuggled safely inside it and Mrs. Sikes will go along with you for propriety's sake. We will say she has things to buy herself and so will be pleased to relieve your abigail of the duty. My sister, Peggy, is housekeeper here now, my lord," the butler added reassuringly, "and 'tis in her room the young ones will sleep."

"Well, I can certainly advise Aunt Letitia that I have accepted your escort, Lord Rossland, to do some shopping," sighed Minerva, "and approve of Mrs. Sikes accompanying me, but Mitzie cannot go dressed in that—in that—particular creation—or our shopping expedition will be the talk of the town. I shall see if I cannot find her something more appropriate to wear right this moment and a decent nightdress as well."

Minerva stood and hurried away to the safety of the second floor and her chambers. She opened the armoire in her dressing room and stared unseeing into its depths. In a moment her vision blurred with tears. It was too much. To lie to her aunt, to pretend to cousins who did not exist, to bring into her aunt's house a girl from the streets about whom, apparently, no one cared except Lord Rossland and a little boy whose mere existence placed even the earl himself in grave danger. She did not know how she could possibly do it. She was not a wild, flighty sort of young lady like Caro Lamb who did not give a deuce about herself or her reputation. She was a very proper and obedient and compliant person. And she had never—never—lied to anyone.

"Do not, sweetling," murmured a soft voice, and Mina heard

the slight tap of Rossland's cane as he crossed from one carpet onto the other. She was flabbergasted that he should have followed her up into her private chambers. And she would have turned about and admonished him severely for the audacity of such action, but she could not bring herself to face him so long as tears misted her eyes.

And then two strong arms came cautiously around her and The Devil's Delight was whispering in her ear. "Do not cry, sweetling," he whispered huskily. "I can see that you are quite overwhelmed. And I understand completely. I am a brute to have thrown so much upon your shoulders without the least warning. But you need not do any of it, my dearest Miss Potts. You need do nothing at all. I will pack the deucedly dastardly duo up and carry them off to Rossland House and to hell with Gaffney and all his warnings and his rigamarole."

"Oh, but you cannot," murmured Mina with just the tiniest sniff. "I promised to help you, and so I shall. I am a woman of my word and shall not shirk at the keeping of it. These tears are just a—a temporary phenomenon."

"Yes, of course," agreed the earl softly, turning her in his arms to face him. "And I am responsible for every one of them—and after I spoke of giving you prestige and comfort and convenience. What a bouncer that was, eh? All I have managed to do so far is to involve you in scandalous rumors and make a jumble of your life. But this particular jumble I can remove immediately, sweetling. We will be gone at once."

Minerva thought her heart would come to a stop. She had only ever before been in Donald's arms and Lord Rossland's arms had nothing at all of the same feel to them. Lord Rossland's arms were strong and gentle at the same time and she felt carefully, cautiously cradled as though she were a babe. And then he was staring down at her with a most dazed look in those great dark eyes of his. And then he was bending slowly, temptingly, until his lips touched her own. And even as she stood amazed at his audacity, she had not the least urge to deny him. He kissed her softly, his lips whispering against hers like the breeze touching the petals of a rose on a summer's day. And then he kissed away the tears that stood at the corners of her eyes. And then, quite abruptly, he set her away from him and leaned heavily on his cane, smiling down at her. "We shall be off then, sweetling," he said. "But I shall come and take you driving tomorrow—though not so early as ten o'clock. At four perhaps?"

"No," protested Minerva, taking a very deep breath and attempting to overcome the odd feeling that something within her was melting away. She straightened her shoulders and stuck out her stubborn chin. "You shall arrive at ten as you planned, sir, because Jaimie and Mitzie and Mrs. Sikes and I shall be depending upon it. Now, if you will do me the favor to select a gown that will not draw untoward attention to that poor little Mitzie when we go to the shops, I shall go and fetch her something decent in which to sleep."

Nine

Minerva noted that the coachman was without any distinguishing livery and that the town coach was old and worn and bore no crest upon the door, nor was it pulled by any but the most ordinary team.

"I must keep from being remarked upon, sweetling," Rossland explained as his coachman helped Mina to ascend into the vehicle, "or I should quite properly have gotten out and helped you up myself. We are attempting to appear beneath any sort of notice, Luke and I, by making use of this ancient torture chamber. It would be unforgivable of me, I think, to step out and present myself in full view. Peggy, I am pleased to see you again," he added, as Lady Letitia's housekeeper was assisted into the coach as well. "I cannot thank you enough for agreeing to help us."

"And how could I refuse, Your Lordship?" Mrs. Sikes answered with a broad grin.

"Easily, Peggy," smiled Rossland in return, placing an arm about both Mitzie's and Jaimie's shoulders as they sat beside him on the rear-facing seat. "By saying, 'no, Battlesby, not on your life.' "

"No, Battlesby, not on your life!" repeated Jaimie enthusiastically.

"Shhh," hissed Mitzie, "we're s'posed to be like little mice, an' not make a bit o' noise."

"Not a bit o' noise!" proclaimed Jaimie loudly with a most determined shake of his head. "Quiet likes mouses!"

"Apparently quiet does not like this little mouse," chuckled

Rossland, snatching the boy up and placing him on his lap. "Say good morning to Miss Potts, sir, if you please."

"G'mornings," offered Jaimie with a wide grin at Minerva. "We had tea an' cakes for brea'fas', din't we, Mrs. Sikes?"

"Indeed we did, Master Jaimie. And toast and jelly as well."

"An' toasts and jellies as well," echoed the boy. "An' hunnerds of roasted-ed snails."

Minerva, who had been playing nervously with her reticule, ceased to do so at that. "Roasted snails?"

"Yes," nodded Jaimie. "An' a frog with creamy sauce. An' a whole partridge of—"

"Pear trees," inserted Rossland neatly. "He does babble on, Miss Potts. You must forgive him. It runs in the family."

"Babbling?"

"No, having roasted snails, frogs in creamy sauce and partridges of pear trees. My brother, Cam, was always used to have partridges of pear trees for breakfast. I, of course, did no such thing."

"You did not?"

"No, I fancied the frogs in creamy sauce but drew the line at pear trees. I was always the sensible one."

"You?" Minerva exclaimed in surprise, then flushed a bright red as Rossland's eyes sparkled and he laughed outright.

"Yes. Believe it or not, sweetling, I was the sensible one and Cam the proper one. Though there was never a lot to choose between us, I think."

They reached Exeter 'Change in good time despite the rather lowering quality of the team and Rossland, once the horses had been brought to a standstill and Luke opened the door, pressed a small pocketbook into Minerva's hands. "You must be responsible to make all of the purchases, sweetling. I cannot chance to be seen in public with the Beamer just yet. And when you have got both the urchins outfitted, you must wait right inside the entrance. It will be Lord Goodacre comes to fetch you. And Mitzie," he added, placing an arm again around the girl's shoulders and giving her a squeeze, "you must buy whatever Miss Potts thinks fitting for your present position. Very soon you and I will purchase a few more frivolous gowns and your bonnet with the cherries on it."

"Yes, Y'r Eminence," replied the girl with a wide smile. "Anythin' you like."

"A bonnet with cherries on it?" asked Minerva as the little group exited the vehicle and the coach departed.

"Oh, yes, ma'am. His Worship promised me faithfully as I was to have gowns and a bonnet with cherries on it."

"And when did he promise you this?"

"When he was at convincin' me how I din't wanta be workin' for Miz Pimberley. His Gov'norship said as how he'd pay me more 'n she would, an' buy me gowns an' a bonnet with cherries on't."

"I see," murmured Minerva, who did not see at all. What *was* Lord Rossland about promising the child such things as if he were offering her a *carte blanche?* A tiny frown line appeared between Mina's brows. Had he, in fact, been offering Mitzie a *carte blanche?* No, of course not. She shook off the uneasy feeling the thought had given her and taking Jaimie by the hand, set out to survey the shops in search of children's clothing and portmanteaux and whatever else might catch her eye as being necessary to reinforce the fantasy that Jaimie was a parson's son arrived upon a stagecoach from Hertfordshire in the care of Mitzie, his nursemaid.

Major Gaffney, with a smart beaver topping his auburn hair and a double-breasted russet riding coat, buff pantaloons and brightly polished Hessians replacing his usual uniform, leaned a shoulder nonchalantly against one of the central columns at the 'Change and followed Miss Potts's progress into Chapman's Emporium with hooded eyes. He was most uneasy. He could not believe that Rossland had gotten the boy clean away. He expected to discover one of Grace Pimberley's ruffians following stealthily in Miss Potts's wake. But so far the only person following the little crew appeared to be his own man, Terwilliger. And Terwilliger, ever the gentleman, had seen Miss Potts and the little Mitzie and the elderly servant who accompanied them almost overwhelmed with packages, and offered his assistance so that now he was effectively hidden behind a stack of boxes, and what use he would be if someone did attempt to snatch the boy, Gaffney could not imagine. But, that was what one got when one chose the third son of a duke for an assistant. Terwilliger could no more overcome his civility than he could overcome his natural buoyancy.

Gaffney had not the least trouble overcoming either. The son of a reclusive and curmudgeonly old baron who cared little for society, Gaffney had gleaned what he knew of civility from school chums and though he was quite good at it, it was not at all ingrained in him. And he was of a most sober nature besides, seeing always the darkest side of each situation. He saw the darkest side of this one most clearly. If he and Rossland and Terwilliger could not unearth and capture the men hiding in the shadows behind Grace Pimberley and discover what scheme actually lay at the root of their conspiracy, the consequences could prove dire indeed.

He shifted his position to keep the little group of shoppers within sight and wondered, somewhat taken aback. There was no one following them at all that he could see. Apparently no one was taking undue notice of them except Terwilliger and himself. The incredible unlikelihood of it boggled his mind. Rossland had done exactly as he had assured Gaffney he would do. He had somehow misdirected whatever spies had been set upon him and brought the boy and the little Mitzie into Miss Potts's charge without so much as a single watcher in their wake.

Not that he ought to be so terribly surprised. Had not Rossland proven his prowess by dodging the enemy at Talavera and bringing his little band of wounded comrades to safety? *If only I had been in my right mind at the time, I might have learned a great deal then,* thought Gaffney. *I might have learned how such tricks are successfully brought off. As it was, I was in such a daze and in shock most of the time that I learned nothing and must have been a great hindrance to the man besides. I am amazed he did not rake me up one side and* down the other for a raging lunatic and then just abandon me. But I am not dazed or in shock now and I shall learn a thing or two from this particular muddle as well as see Rossland and his nephew safe and the perpetrators of their dilemma soundly dealt with. I vow it!

Rossland's coachman was not at all certain he ought to be doing it and said so with a notable lack of restraint. "Ye've a head full of mush!" growled Luke, handing the ribbons to Rossland and donning the earl's great coat and beaver with considerable surliness. "Drivin' this rig ain't near as easy as drivin' yer curricle! The brake ain't near so good an' the coach a whole lot heavier. Ye won't be able ta manage it wif yer foot, not wif yer leg banged up like it is."

"Then I shall use my hand, Luke."

"Ye ain't that strong," scoffed the coachman. "Even I ain't that strong."

Rossland lay the walking stick on the boards beneath his feet and pulled Luke's cap lower over his brow. "Then I expect I shall run the coach into something, but it will not be the end of the world, Luke. It was an old coach already when my father used it. If I wreck it, it will not be a great loss."

"No," scowled the coachman, "not a'tall till ye consider as how ye might be kilt along wif it an' all them inside as well."

"Then I will not run the coach into anything," grumbled Rossland in exasperation. "I will go slowly and begin braking an entire block before the place I wish to stop. Will that satisfy you, you upstart?"

"Two blocks afore," muttered Luke, his lips beginning an upward twitch.

"Not three? No, do not laugh, Luke, you will spoil your entire harangue. I warn you, I will not take you at all seriously if you laugh."

That set the poor coachman into chuckles and brought a grin to Rossland's face as well.

"Besides, Luke, you will be the only passenger for the first part of the drive. I shall need to stop to pick up Lord Goodacre. If I cannot manage the brake then, we shall know it immediately and only you and I will suffer—you will remember to hold tight to the strap when I slow?"

"Holdin' on to it all the way, I am," grumbled Luke, suppressing the urge to chuckle again. "Yer like ta make a hasty puddin' o' both of us." With that the coachman, looking a good deal like Rossland—his hair being quite as dark and curly, his shoulders of an equal width and his legs almost as long—climbed from the box and into the coach.

"There is another walking stick in there beneath the seat," called Rossland through the trap. "You cannot forget to use it, Luke. They will see right through our hoax if you climb out and stand about talking to Charlie without it."

Luke grunted and fished the stick out, setting it upon the seat beside him.

The team started calmly enough and Rossland directed them out of the cul de sac in which they stood and into the main thoroughfare with a deal of precision. But he was inordinately apprehensive. He knew the brake was going to prove a problem. He had driven this coach before, and even heavier carriages, but he had had two good legs then. And even with two good legs, braking such vehicles had not been an easy matter.

Well, but it made not the least bit of difference because he needed to drive this coach for his plan to work. Luke was to draw the attention of anyone watching to himself and then leave the coach quite in full view of everyone. Whoever might be following would then follow the pseudo-Rossland and give the real Rossland and Lord Goodacre the freedom to collect Miss Potts and her brood without any observation whatsoever, because no one would think to follow the coach once the pseudo-Rossland had exited it. Although no one had apparently thought to follow the old vehicle this morning. But that was because Perkins had spotted the two men lingering outside Rossland House and he and a number of the servants had set up a most diverting ruckus while Rossland and Luke had ducked out through the mews to Captain Sutter's stables.

No one would have expected Rossland to be out and about at nine o'clock in the morning anyway, so the men had probably not been as deadly serious about their jobs as they might have been. But at this hour others might well be on the lookout for the earl and it would be well to give them a sight of him apparently making his careful way in a nondescript vehicle to the place where he had hidden Jaimie. Not that Luke would go anywhere near Green Street. No, they had decided between them to lead whoever might follow to the Duke of Winecoff's residence in Pall Mall where Luke would slink guiltily around to the rear entrance and disappear into the kitchen. Once there, of course, he could cease his pretense at being Rossland, shed the coat and hat and cane, borrow another coat from his friend, Darlington, who was head groom there, and return home in his own persona.

Rossland directed the team cautiously around a pedlar's wagon and between two curricles and spying ahead of him the turnoff into Bond Street, headed the horses into a wide turn to take the corner and began at once to apply pressure on the brake. And he discovered that Luke had been correct. There was no possible way that he could brake the coach with his foot without the pain sending him into a swoon. He shifted the ribbons into his left hand and reached for the brake lever with his right.

Lord Goodacre checked his pocket watch, nodded, and wandered from Jackson's Boxing Saloon onto the flagway just in time to watch in disbelief as the town coach lunged and bounced and swayed and jiggled to a stop. He glanced askance at the driver who did not so much as turn to look down at him. Then Goodacre fished his handkerchief from his pocket and wiped it nervously across his brow.

The coach door swung open, and Luke, walking stick in hand, climbed cautiously down onto the pavement. Several gentlemen exiting Jackson's nodded at him, never noticing his face, which was shaded by Rossland's beaver, but assuming him to be the Earl of Rossland because of his clothing, his cane and the fact that he was in Lord Goodacre's company.

"By Jove, if 'e ain't right," muttered Luke, leaning heavily upon the walking stick. "They's thinkin' I be him on accounta I be wif you, gov'nor."

"Luke," murmured Goodacre hoarsely. "Then who is driving—thunderation!"

"Aye, Yer Lor'ship. It's hisself up there. Yer ta git in wif me, 'e says, as soon as we've stood 'ere long 'nough ta attrack attention. Then we be goin' on ta St. James's an' Mayfair an' finally Pall Mall, where I be goin' ta leave ye."

"But Luke, can he drive this vehicle? I mean, I am not doubting he can handle a team with the best of them but—"

"Well, ye seen 'im stop. Done gooder than what I thought he would. I thought we was goin' ta wind up against a lamppost meself. He ain't got no problem wif the team, 'tis the brake what's hard fer 'im. I reckon we done stood 'ere long 'nough."

Goodacre entered the coach, watched as Luke did so, hampered a bit by the cane, and once they had both settled back against the squabs, gave a knock on the trap door.

"What?" called Rossland, laughing down into Charlie's upturned face. "Do you mean you actually wish me to move this thing forward."

"No, I do not," replied Goodacre with a grin, "but I expect I've no choice in the matter. Whack 'em up, driver. We're off!"

By the time the little odyssey had been completed, Luke deposited before the Winecoff's residence, and the coach driven back to the Exeter 'Change, Lord Goodacre had learned that it was best to hold on to the strap with both hands from the moment the horses began to slow until the coach came at last to a swaying standstill. "Devil a bit if I am not certain you are trying to kill me," he called up through the open trap. "Where am I to meet Miss Potts, Chad?"

"Directly inside the entrance. And hurry, Charlie, because I ain't about to move this rig for anyone—not even if the Prince Regent himself should wish to tie up here. I think I have only one more stop left in me."

Lord Goodacre bounded from the coach and swung energetically up the flagway, entered the mall and discovered Miss Potts and her little band waiting patiently. "Ah, good," he smiled, and then frowned to see a gentleman with them buried beneath a mound of packages. "Who is this?" he asked suspiciously.

"Terwilliger," announced the packages. "And do not even think to give Miss Potts your arm. I cannot possibly make it to the coach behind all these packages without tripping. You shall need to take some."

"Terwilliger? Terwilliger?" Goodacre drawled. "Miss Potts, do we know a Mr. Terwilliger?"

"He is the Marquis of Leland's youngest brother and has been most kind," smiled Minerva. "Will you take some of the packages? Mrs. Sikes and I shall see the children safely to the coach."

Goodacre watched as the little band exited the mall then took a considerable portion of the packages out of Terwilliger's arms and stared at him nonplussed.

"It is perfectly all right," murmured Terwilliger. "I really am Leland's youngest brother and Major Gaffney's personal assistant as well. I have been keeping watch over them."

Goodacre gave a sigh of relief. "For a moment I wondered if all our caution had been for naught," he replied. "But now I think on it, I am certain Rossland mentioned your name. Wait, it was you forged some kind of message."

"Indeed, and I who had to forage for clothes for the boy before we could leave the major's quarters."

"Well, that's all right then. You can bring those packages along to the coach and I shall manage these. You need not think that the coachman is going to climb down from the box and help us stow them, either," he added as an afterthought, "because it is not in the least likely."

"You know," observed Terwilliger as he helped Goodacre stuff the purchases into the boot, "I have heard stories about the Rossland servants. Independent bunch, they say."

"Indeed," nodded Goodacre with a wide grin. "And that bloke up top the most independent of them all. Gets his own way in everything. Treats the man like a lord, Rossland does."

"Yes, well, if he were my father's coachman and ignoring us like this, he should have his walking papers on the spot."

"I am rather certain," replied Goodacre with a sparkle in his eyes, "that that particular coachman will not find himself on the street so long as Rossland is alive. I thank you for your assistance," he added, closing the boot and crossing around to enter the coach. "I expect we shall see one another again, eh?" With that Lord Goodacre climbed inside and pulled the door closed behind him. He reached up and gave the trap a knock. "Home, John," he called, "and be careful, will you not? We have only two straps, which means two of us must share one and we must cling to the tykes to keep them from landing on the floor."

Minerva heard a grunt from the coachman, the trap swung shut, and in a moment they were moving into traffic. "What did you mean, Lord Goodacre, about clinging to the children?"

"I meant we shall have to cling to the children," Goodacre repeated. "Cannot stop without a deal of lunging and bouncing and tilting about. No, it's a fact," he assured Minerva's disbelieving countenance. "Cannot come to a halt without near to tipping over. I know. I have stopped four times so far today."

"Is something wrong with the coach then?"

"No, the driver."

"Oh, my land," sighed Mrs. Sikes, putting an arm around Jaimie's shoulders as he leaned against her very nearly asleep, "ye do not mean 'tis His Lordship driving?"

"Lord Rossland?" asked Minerva, her eyebrows lifting in surprise. "No, it cannot be. Why how can he work the brake on such a heavy vehicle as this—oh my goodness!"

"Yes, exactly, Miss Potts. But not to worry. Chad has not tipped us completely over—not even once—so I think we shall do nicely if we have enough warning."

But they had no warning at all. At the corner of Christchurch Street and Albemarle, a landau ran afoul of a dray which spilled its logs all over the cobbles and sent a Stanhope, two gigs, and a phaeton skittering toward the gutters, forced three curricles into a meeting of wheels, and destroyed a pedlar's wagon and four handcarts. Rossland hauled on the reins and dove for the brake at one and the same time. The horses reared in their traces at the abrupt jerk on their bits; the coach wheels squealed at the sudden and intense contact with the blocks; Jaimie and Mrs. Sikes and Mitzie were whipped back violently against the squabs; Minerva literally flew from her seat to the floor; and Lord Goodacre tumbled down on top of her.

"Oh, I say," moaned Goodacre, disentangling himself from Miss Potts, regaining his seat, and then helping her up beside him. "Are you all right, my dear? He has not killed you?"

"I am fine," spluttered Minerva, attempting to push her bonnet back up on to the top of her head where it belonged and feeling bruised and battered all over. "Mrs. Sikes, Jaimie, Mitzie, you are not injured?"

"Oh, oh," gasped Mrs. Sikes. "All the wind's out of me."

"There's logs everywhere!" cried Mitzie, having raised the isinglass window and stuck her head completely out.

"Ka-whack!" exclaimed Jaimie, rubbing at the back of his head with one hand and beaming happily.

"He is not hurt, is he, Mrs. Sikes?" Minerva asked worriedly.

"No, Miss," Mrs. Sikes assured her feeling the back of the tyke's head. "He were cushioned by the squabs well enough."

"Ka-whack!" Jaimie announced again, and Lord Goodacre laughed at him.

"I cannot believe it," Minerva murmured. "The boy is not a bit upset, or frightened, or—or—anything."

"Obviously gone driving with his uncle before," grinned Goodacre impishly.

At that moment the trap door flew open and a very pale face stared down into the coach. "Charlie? Charlie? Everybody all right in there?"

"Aye, Chad. All's right and tight."

"Are you certain? Miss Potts ain't hurt? Or Mrs. Sikes. Or the children?"

"We all seem to have survived quite nicely," called Minerva, leaning over to look up at him with a composed smile of reassurance. Her smile deserted her on the spot. "What is it? What is wrong?" She had never before seen anyone's eyes so huge and dark as his looked against the pallor of his face. "Oh, you are injured! Come down at once!"

"I have merely wrenched my deuced leg a bit trying to get to the brake, sweetling. But it will take us a while to extricate ourselves from this jumble. I shall have to back 'em, I expect, Charlie," he added as Lord Goodacre leaned into view.

"I am coming up," announced Goodacre.

"No, I can do it, Charlie."

"I am coming up," Goodacre declared again, and in a moment he had descended from the coach and was climbing to the box. "Thunderation," he muttered looking around him. "What a hubble-bubble this is."

"Indeed."

"Give me the reins. You are in no condition to be backing a coach. Not at the moment you are not."

"Well, no, but Charlie, you—ah—how can I say this?"

"You can say I am a mere whipster and have no business attempting to do it, but I shall be forced to darken your day-lights for you if you do."

"Is there any other way I can say it that will prevent your blacking my eyes?"

"No!" growled Goodacre.

"Then I shall say it," Minerva's voice echoed upward through the open trap. "Lord Goodacre, if you are indeed a mere whipster, do not you dare to attempt backing this vehicle! I am coming up," she declared sternly.

"She is coming up?" asked Goodacre with a perplexed scowl upon his cherubic face.

Rossland nodded wearily, the pain in his leg sending jolts of fire through him.

"I *am* coming up," reiterated Minerva now standing upon the cobbles amidst the havoc. "Lord Goodacre, assist Lord Rossland to descend if you please."

"No," protested the earl. "I am the coachman here."

"Not at the moment, m'lad," drawled Goodacre.

"Bring him down, Lord Goodacre," Minerva ordered staring up at the both of them, bonnet askew and hands on her hips, looking a veritable fishmonger's wife. "I shall back the coach."

"Oh, no," groaned Rossland softly.

"Saints preserve us," added Lord Goodacre under his breath.

"Do as I say," insisted Miss Potts with an impatient stamp of her foot. "Lord Rossland cannot be allowed to go on suffering indefinitely. We must remove ourselves from this ruckus and take him home at once!"

Lord Goodacre climbed down first with Rossland's walking stick in hand and waited as his friend tied off the reins and descended painfully to the cobbles. "I shall help Miss Potts to the box, Chad," he declared, "and then help you into the coach."

"I can get inside without help, Charles. Hand me that deuced stick and stay up top with her. But it would be better, I think, if you went to the horses' heads and backed them."

"Yes, just back them over anything or anyone who happens to be behind us," murmured Miss Potts. "You know he cannot see over the coach. It must be done from the box to be done safely. Please, my lord," she added, taking his arm and urging him toward the coach door. "I am a very good whip. My father taught me."

Silently Minerva prayed that the earl would argue no further because he was growing even more pale and anyone but a blind man could see the scalding pain that boiled up into his eyes.

Rossland nodded with a tired sigh and hauled himself up into the coach. Lord Goodacre, at Minerva's insistence, followed. It took a few moments for her to mount to the box in her long skirts, but she had done it a million times before, and did so now without the least fuss. A moment later she had taken the reins and begun the complicated task of backing the vehicle out of the muddle of logs and coaches and around the corner back on to Christchurch Street.

"By Jove, she is doing it!" exclaimed Lord Goodacre, his head, like Mitzie's, stuck out one of the windows. "Whoever would have thought a little lady like that could—?"

"I would have," sighed Rossland, "if I had been thinking clearly. Of course she can do it. Her Aunt Letitia can do it as well. There ain't one of the Potts, male or female, who cannot drive to an inch and never was."

Ten

"So this is your cousin Aubury's child, is he, Minerva?" Lady Letitia stared most interestedly at the properly dressed little boy and his nursemaid as they posed shyly before her in the front hall of Farin House. "Well, he is a pleasant enough looking little chap."

Attempting to hearten the children with a wide smile, Minerva was overcome with relief that her aunt had questioned neither the existence of the fictitious distant cousin, Aubury, nor the necessity of his child's forced excursion to London. And she was relieved as well that somehow, despite the pain in which she had left him at Major Gaffney's chambers in Albemarle Street, Lord Rossland had managed to get these two imps into their new clothes, pack their new luggage and deliver them to the posting inn in time for Lady Letitia's coachman and two footmen to collect them precisely at seven. Really, the man was a wonder. And more wonderful yet, Rossland had managed to introduce both little heads to a bottle of henna along the way, for Jaimie's curls had changed from black to deep auburn, and Mitzie's brown locks had become a light red.

No one who searches for Mitzie or Jaimie will so much as look at these two children twice, Mina thought with a warmth of pride in Lord Rossland's ingenuity. From any distance the searchers will be thoroughly fooled. They will never suspect that these redheads are the children they seek. Why, we need not even fear to take them about town with us. Really, Lord Rossland is the most remarkably devious person!

"I cannot understand why your father could not give us more notice," grumbled Lady Letitia with a sideways glance at her niece. "Though I expect your cousin did not give him much. And certainly Arthur could not be expected to keep such little ones at the manor if he is in the midst of overseeing the planting. Lift up your chin, Miss, if you please, and tell me your name."

Mitzie, looking up shyly, made a tiny curtsy. "Melinda, m'lady," she stated in a hushed voice. "An' this be Joseph."

The names took Minerva by surprise. But then, they could not call themselves Mitzie and Jaimie, she realized. Especially they could not while running tamely about her Aunt Letitia's establishment. Still, Jaimie was such a very little boy. Would he remember to answer to his new name?

"I is Joey," giggled Jaimie, wiggling under Lady Letitia's scrutiny. "An' I is come in a staging coach with six horses an' a fat man."

"Shhh," warned Mitzie solemnly. "Didn't no one ask you about no stagecoach."

"Six horses an' a fat man!" repeated Jaimie enthusiastically thrusting four fingers into the air under Lady Letitia's nose and grinning his most endearing grin.

That grin was fatal. Almost as fatal as his uncle's, Minerva thought as she watched the scowl flee Lady Letitia's face and her aunt kneel before the boy and pull him into a hug.

"And I am certain that you were a good boy on the stagecoach, as well, and minded your Melinda," Lady Letitia commented encouragingly. "And you will be a good boy here and do as you are told, will you not?"

"Uh-huh," replied Jaimie, squirming far enough out of Lady Letitia's grasp to be able to look her squarely in the eyes. "I will be 'ceeding excellent," he announced confidently. "An' I willn't do nothin' I should not. I promises."

"Well, and that is a most excellent promise," smiled Letitia. "And I shall hold you to it, sir. Battlesby, you will see them settled, will you not?" she added, rising. "I believe Mrs. Sikes has given them the blue and the green bedchambers and the sitting room between as well."

"Indeed," intoned Battlesby soberly. "If you will follow me," he drawled and climbed the staircase with shoulders squared and lifted chin. Mitzie followed, tugging Jaimie in her wake.

"Well, I do think your cousin Aubury might have had the good sense to send an older woman with the two of them," sighed Lady Letitia. "Melinda is barely old enough to be without a nursemaid herself. Still, I expect he thought he was doing her a kindness to take her off the parish dole and being a parson, I suppose he could not afford a nanny."

"Indeed," agreed Minerva. "And I am certain Melinda is most competent, Aunt Letitia. Did they not travel all the way to Papa's and then to London without incident?"

Letitia nodded thoughtfully. "A most amazing feat, indeed, for such young ones. Come, Minerva. The Winecoffs' dinner party begins at nine. We must be off at once."

Minerva sat down to dinner with twenty others at the Duchess of Winecoff's table in a gown of Clarence blue satin with an overdress of white silk, its bodice exquisitely embroidered with tiny Clarence blue flowers. Matching embroidery decorated its wide hem and long sleeves. Being a mere Miss Potts, she found herself very near the foot of the table with the Honorable Gerald Davidson to her right and the Reverend Mr. George to her left. She was acquainted with both of these gentlemen and ordinarily would have found their attempts at conversation diverting. They were, after all, considered good catches upon the marriage mart and any young woman who could claim no more than a mere Miss before her name, would have set herself to find them diverting whether they actually were or not. But Minerva's thoughts were not at all focused upon making an acceptable match for herself. They were focused instead upon a particular gentleman with mahogany curls and deep brown eyes and an ebony walking stick with a wolf's head that had diamonds for eyes and which anyone could see he despised most emphatically.

It puzzled the Reverend Mr. George and Mr. Davidson that

Miss Potts constantly required them to repeat themselves. It was as though she did not care to pay them the least attention. This could not, of course, be the case. But her eyes were continually focused upon her plate as though she feared that her helping of *matelote* of eels, or larded guinea fowl, or *peu d'amour* might mysteriously disappear. And she rarely glanced up in either of their directions. Something then was distressing the young woman, and both the gentlemen wished to discover what that something could be. Between them they reached the conclusion that it might well be a particular item upon Miss Potts's plate that absorbed her so completely, for she could not be brought to raise her eyes from the place setting before her.

But the truth was that Minerva had even less awareness of what lay upon her plate than she had of the gentlemen beside her. At the moment her fork was listlessly pushing a small portion of the guinea fowl around in circles while her mind wandered of its own accord off into the night. Where was Lord Rossland at this precise moment? What exactly was he doing? She had hoped that—the Duchess of Winecoff being his godmother—Lord Rossland would be attending this very dinner party, but he was not in attendance. Though he might well have been invited, she told herself, because we are an odd number at table and that is most unusual. Perhaps he has injured his leg more severely than he had liked to admit in my presence and even now is suffering agonies tucked up in his own bed? Or perhaps he and Lord Goodacre and Major Gaffney have gone off in search of the villains who stole poor little Jaimie? Or perhaps, most dreadful of notions, the villains have accosted His Lordship upon his way to this very dinner party and are even now attempting to pry Jaimie's whereabouts from him? The mere thought of that set Minerva's heart to pounding and a shiver of fear sliced down her backbone.

"Is there something wrong with your guinea fowl, Miss Potts?" asked the Reverend Mr. George for the third time, his fine grey eyes studying her with polite but obvious concern. "Would you like me to send it away and procure you something else in its place?"

"What? Oh, no," murmured Minerva, at last spearing a tiny piece of the larded meat and placing it between her lips.

"If you do not care for it," continued the Reverend, "I believe a *boeuf tremblant* is presently coming to table."

Minerva swallowed the guinea fowl and made an effort to smile up at him, but the smile wavered somewhat.

"What is it, Miss Potts? Have you the headache? You have been exceedingly withdrawn since first we sat down."

"Yes, I, no, it is not the headache," responded Minerva with some asperity. "I am—that is—oh, I know I am being the most atrocious dinner partner, but I cannot help myself. There are so many questions buzzing about in my mind."

"What sort of questions?" asked Mr. Davidson, withdrawing his attention from Miss Markham on his right. "I say, Robert," he smiled, "congratulations. You have got Miss Potts to speak to us."

The Reverend Mr. George grinned. "But will she continue to honor us with her attention?" he asked with a lift of an eyebrow. "What questions, Miss Potts, are plaguing you so? Perhaps between Davidson and myself we can provide some answers."

Minerva gazed from one to the other of them and her lips parted to protest that, be they ever so eager, they could never answer a one of them, and then she remembered Lord Rossland's words of the night before. "We know who Aunt Grace is, but as to Uncle Thomas . . ." Could Uncle Thomas be one of the gentlemen even now gathered 'round the Winecoffs' dining table? Yes, Mina thought, with a little nod. He certainly could be. He could be anyone of them. Why, Uncle Thomas might even be the Reverend Mr. George or Mr. Davidson!"

"Miss Potts? Are you gone from us again?"

"Oh! Oh, no, Mr. Davidson! I was just thinking."

"Yes, m'dear, we know that. What you were thinking about is the object of our search," smiled the Reverend Mr. George. "We thought it might be that the food had discouraged you in some way, but since that is not the case, can you not confide in us what has put you into such a brown study? And do not be so cruel as to say you are thinking of Lord Rossland, will you? I do not think I could bear with equanimity the thought that that thatchgallows has possessed your mind even when he is nowhere in sight. Those of us who lost you to Whithall do have some hopes of a second chance for your attentions and are most upset that Lord Rossland might intend to deprive us of that opportunity."

"L-lost me to Lord Whithall? Oh, what a bouncer," responded Minerva with a tiny grin. "You did none of you lose me to Lord Whithall for none of you wished to have me in the first place. You know you were not interested in me at all until it was rumored that Lord Rossland had lost his heart to me."

"Perhaps, Miss Potts," nodded Davidson with a most serious glint in his hazel eyes, "but I find you interesting now, and so does George. Even Kensington speaks of his intentions to get to know you better."

"Well, and I should like to get to know all of you better as well," replied Minerva, hoping she did not sound too very forward but seeing a possibility to gain information which might point Lord Rossland to one gentleman or another as the horrible Uncle Thomas. "Much better."

"Hear! Hear!" exclaimed the Reverend Mr. George softly.

"Well said, Miss Potts," chuckled Davidson. "At last we have got some encouragement to hope in spite of Rossland!"

Grace Pimberley tilted the remainder of the brandy down her throat and frowned at the gentleman seated across the table from her. "And just how was I to know that His bloody Lordship so much as suspected that I had the boy?" she grumbled. "Where would he have come by such a notion? To this moment I cannot imagine how such information could have reached the man."

"Humphf," grumbled the gentleman, sipping at his own brandy.

"Well, for goodness sakes! I run a brothel," protested Grace vigorously, "and Lord Rossland is a notable libertine! I assumed he came for the same reasons as any other libertine. Ought I to have turned him away at the door? What sort of signal would that have sent, I ask you? Why, any number of people's ears would have perked to attention at such a dismissal of him on my part. Imagine the talk once it became known that an abbess who depends upon the Rosslands of the world for her livelihood had nonchalantly dispensed with that particular libertine's business. It was not as though he had caused any trouble at all in the establishment at any other time. Then, I might have had an excuse to refuse him. But I had none."

"Uhmmm," mumbled the gentleman.

"Yes, and besides, the boy was safely locked away. Who would have imagined that The Devil's Delight would go prowling about my house looking for the child? He's a cripple after all and there were five burly men on guard. Someone should have noticed him—have heard him! He could not have gotten all the way to the attic without making some noise upon the staircase. He cannot walk without that stick of his. You know so yourself."

"Well, but he did go prowling about your house, and got to the attic without being heard and discovered the boy," growled the gentleman. "And so now, my dear, though it is not my wish in particular, you are out of business."

"Out of—? I am out of business? But surely—"

"Well, but you cannot think, Grace, that Rossland will allow you to proceed unencumbered as you have done. I am amazed the constables have not taken you up already. Of course, I am equally amazed that our men have not as yet so much as caught sight of the boy or your little cyprian. It is obvious that Rossland has hidden them both away and means to keep them hidden. Which means that he has guessed, of course."

"Has guessed what?"

"Everything, Grace. Everything. What idiots we were to think him ignorant of what was going forward in his family simply because he was so grievously ill for all those early months of his brother's marriage. He brought the girl to England, did he not? Of course, he did. Why he knew everything, and quite likely a great deal of it was his idea. And it was a sad mistake on your part to have been so greedy, too. Had you not attempted to extort money from him, he would have thought the child drowned like everyone else. But now he has guessed all that went forward and he will guess what lies at the bottom of our schemes as well. We will be forced to murder the man."

"Not one of you protested when I sent the first ransom note," mumbled Grace. "And we needed the money. We need all the money we can possibly get our hands upon if we are to succeed. Why should Rossland not be made to support the cause?"

"Because making him support the cause is what brought him in search of us, my dear. And now, of course, we shall not only be forced to recover the boy but to eliminate Rossland as well. And another death in that particular family will arouse a great deal of unwanted speculation I can assure you. No, you have fouled it up royally, m'dear, and so say all of us."

Grace Pimberley sat farther back in her chair and stared at the man wide-eyed as he withdrew a dueling pistol from an inside pocket of his cloak and pointed it in her direction.

"I am sorry, Grace," the gentleman muttered, "but you have become a distinct disadvantage to us at this juncture. Not only does Rossland know your face but he can prove you had the boy in your house. He has taken that little cyprian as a witness to corroborate his statements. And he will not think twice about turning you over to the authorities, Grace, which will put all of us in danger of discovery. I am sorry for it, but the consensus is that you must be swiftly removed from our rolls."

The pistol shot followed immediately upon the completion of that sentence and Grace Pimberley, a most disbelieving look upon her countenance, slumped forward across the table. The gentleman, a slight crease between his brows, set the pistol aside and finished his brandy, savoring every drop. Then he leaned farther back in his chair, stared at Grace's unmoving body, sighed and poured himself another glass of the pleasant liquor.

* * *

"You may answer quite simply, Miss Potts," declared the Duchess of Winecoff as the ladies entered the withdrawing room and she seized Minerva by the elbow, steering her aside from the rest of the company and into a small alcove. "You need not fear being overheard, my dear. Not being overheard is precisely why I have asked Matilda to play the harpsichord for us."

Minerva, looking anxiously about her, could see no help at all nearby the spot where they both stood. The duchess had quite easily managed to set the two of them apart from the rest of the ladies and was holding tightly to her arm.

"I require an answer, Miss Potts," urged the duchess. "And before the gentlemen join us if you please."

"But—but I do not know how to answer you, Your Grace, because I do not know to what you refer."

"Come, Miss Potts, you are not a featherbrain. I refer to the rumors concerning yourself and my nephew, Chadwick. Has that wretch actually lost his heart to you?"

"I have no idea, Your Grace," murmured Minerva uneasily.

"Come, come, girl. Of course you have some idea. Did my godson take you driving in the park? Did he pay you a morning call? Or is it all a hum?"

"Well, yes, he did drive me through Hyde Park," acknowledged Minerva uneasily.

"And the morning call?"

"Yes, he did appear in my Aunt Letitia's parlor for a time, but surely that is nothing extraordinary."

"It is most extraordinary, Miss Potts," declared the duchess with a shake of her greying head. "Most extraordinary indeed. To my knowledge Chadwick has not paid a morning call on anyone since his sixteenth birthday."

Minerva was somewhat taken aback by the slow, upward tilt of the Duchess of Winecoff's lips.

"He may have," sighed that lady with a sudden glistening in her eyes. "He may well have."

"Have what, Your Grace?"

"Lost his heart to you, Miss Potts. The gabblemongers are saying, you know, that you may well become his redemptor."

"Oh. Oh! But—but—they were saying only a few days ago that he had been seen kissing Lady Goodacre upon her door-step."

"Yes, but that means nothing, my dear. Only fools would believe that Mary would play Charles false or that Chadwick would even think to cuckold his best friend. And I am not a fool. Nor are very many of the *ton*, though that is hard to believe at times, I know. It was an interesting bit of gossip, about Chadwick and Mary, but no more than that. No one actually believed it. The rumors that he has lost his heart to you persist, however, and I am greatly tempted to believe them."

"But I have heard that he has stolen a cyprian from a brothel since first he showed an interest in myself," whispered Minerva, blushing. She had not thought, when she had agreed to let the gabblemongers broadcast an arrangement in the offing between herself and Lord Rossland, about the effect such talk might have upon his family. She had not thought of him as even having a family, in fact. "Surely, that rumor has reached your ears as well, Your Grace."

"Yes, but I do not give it the least credit. Making off with little cyprians to appease his own lust is not at all like Chadwick, you see. I expect the young woman begged him to help her escape her fate—that would be more likely. Chadwick is not a villain despite his willingness to let everyone think it of him. He is much more an erratic knight in somewhat tarnished armor, and well I know it."

Minerva smiled. Yes, she thought, that is precisely what he is—a knight in tarnished armor and I wish I had thought to say it, too.

"You agree with me, do you not, Miss?" chuckled the duchess. "I can see you do. And since you would not if you had not had the opportunity to know Chadwick well, I find my hopes for him increasing. He is not at all transparent. His true self has been muffled since first he returned from the war under layers and layers of mystery and misinformation. He has let down his guard in your presence, has he not? Oh," she added with a little wave of her hand, "I believe my heart is about to jump for joy. I have prayed for some pleasant young woman to see through Chadwick's layers of protection for the longest time. And now, when he is most in need, here you are!"

"And here I am as well," whispered a quiet voice in the duchess's ear, which made her jump and spin around into Lord Rossland's waiting arms. He pressed a kiss upon one lightly rouged cheek and with one arm about her waist, turned to grin at Minerva. "Good evening, Miss Potts. I hope I have not interrupted a most important conversation but I could wait no longer to greet Aunt Seraphina."

"Good evening, my lord," replied Mina with a tiny curtsy.

"I apologize, Aunt Seraphina, for not having come in time for dinner. I was called away most unexpectedly. But you did get my message, did you not? And at least I have got here in time to catch the two of you together. Miss Potts is the most devastating and formidable female I have ever met, and a minx to boot. Do you not like her, Aunt?"

"My lord, you ought not—" began Minerva, thinking it most unwise of him to encourage this lady who obviously cared for him to believe in the pretense of their courtship.

"*Do* you like her, Aunt Seraphina?" Rossland persisted, cutting Mina off in midsentence.

"Well, well, yes, Chadwick, I believe I do. But we have only just now gotten an opportunity to converse."

"And I have had the audacity to interrupt. I know. I am a villain. But I have an overwhelming need to steal the girl away, Aunt Seraphina. Surely you will not deny me that opportunity. For once Uncle Henry leads the gentlemen in, I will be obliged to pay him my respects and shall be raked over the coals for having missed dinner and will not have the chance to speak to Miss Potts alone for the rest of the evening. I shall merely take her to the gallery to stare at Uncle Henry's ancestors for a few moments."

"No, you will not," declared the duchess. "You will not go off alone with a young lady in my establishment, I promise you. It is not done, Chadwick. Gentlemen do not wander off unchaperoned with gently bred young ladies. I do wish your father had thought to teach you a bare minimum of manners."

"Then I will sit with her on that atrocious crocodile couch in the corner," he laughed, "where both you and Lady Letitia—and every other lady in the room, for that matter—may keep us well under surveillance. Will that do?"

The duchess nodded her assent and Minerva took the arm Rossland offered and allowed him to lead her away. She noticed that he leaned heavily on his walking stick and the smile he bestowed upon her did not quite reach his eyes. And though she meant to chide him the very first thing about hoaxing his godmother in regard to their relationship, she found she could not. "What is it?" she asked when he had seated himself beside her. "What is wrong, my lord?"

"Wrong? Why nothing at all. What makes you think that there is something wrong, sweetling?"

"I am not blind, my lord. Your lips are smiling but your eyes are not. That, I think, is an indication that something is not quite right with you."

"It is merely that I am weary, sweetling. It has been an exhausting day." Rossland's left eye narrowed just the tiniest bit as he said it, and though Minerva was certain that he must be worn to the bone, she remembered what her aunt had said about his eye and his bouncers and knew immediately that he was lying and that his condition was due to much more than weariness. He had hurt his leg badly and ought to be home in bed and he would not admit it, that was the truth.

"Did the children arrive safely?" he added. "Has your Aunt Letitia accepted that they belong to your fictitious cousin."

"Indeed. And Jaimie, I think, has already won her heart."

"No, has he? Well, and why not. The Beamer has always been a charmer. Grinned at her, did he not?"

"He most certainly did, and assured her that—"

"He would be 'exceeding excellent and would not do nothing he shouldn't.' "

"Yes, how did you—you told him to say that."

"I made him memorize it. I promised him the lady he was going to visit would like him very well if he said it properly. I only wish to warn you to be very careful, sweetling. The children think it all some amusing masquerade. Even Mitzie does not understand the seriousness of it. But it is a dangerous game we are playing. And I could kick myself for having involved you in it, too," he added with a worried frown.

"You, sir, did not involve me," protested Minerva, hoping to ease his distress at least a bit. "I chose to become involved in it and I shall certainly look after both Mitzie and Jaimie with great zeal. I will trust their true identities to no one, believe me. And if one gentleman or another should chance to see them and begin to ask questions—which I do not think will happen because you thought to change the color of their hair and so they do not look at all as they were used to do—if some gentleman should begin to ask questions, I will give his name to you immediately. I have already begun asking questions myself," she added with some pride, "for I am determined to see if I cannot discover who is Jaimie's mysterious Uncle Thomas for you."

It was the strangest thing, Minerva thought, but apparently this piece of information, instead of clearing Lord Rossland's brow added more lines to it. "Do you doubt that I can be of help, sir?" she asked quietly. "I assure you that I can now that I have set my mind to it."

"No, sweetling," Rossland sighed, running his fingers through his perfectly combed locks and sending his curls in all directions. "I do not doubt at all, but you are already helping me immensely by taking Jaimie and providing a place for Mitzie and allowing me to prolong this rumor about—about—our budding relationship. And you might well be in danger should you ask the wrong questions of the wrong gentleman. No, I had much rather you did no such thing. The major and I will find this Uncle Thomas, I promise you. Oh, damn! The gentlemen have finished their port," he added with a tired groan. "I must go and speak with Uncle Henry immediately or he will come stomping over here and cause an horrendous scene. Or worse, he will take it into his head that there is something very wrong with me and be on my doorstep first thing tomorrow morning to demand that I confide in him."

Minerva could not help but notice that it was somewhat of a struggle for Rossland to rise from the couch and that, although he strove not to show it, he was embarrassed at his awkwardness. But once he had got his walking stick firmly planted and gained his feet and acquired the desired degree of steadiness, he took her hand and bowed quite nicely over it.

"I shall call upon you tomorrow if I may, sweetling," he murmured, turning her hand over in his and bestowing a most tender kiss upon the inside of her wrist. "At three. Do manage to be at home, won't you?" And then he crossed the room to join the group of gentlemen who surrounded the Duke of Winecoff.

Eleven

Miss Angelica Deane and her mama swept into Lady Letitia's parlor the following afternoon with the most appalling gossip yet. Not that they wished to cause Minerva distress, of course, for they would never do such a thing if it could be at all avoided. But it could not! Why, people everywhere were speaking of it and Minerva would hear regardless—and was it not much better to hear dreadful news from one's own friends?

"I am certain it has come to your ears by this time," breathed Miss Deane's mama excitedly, "that Lord Rossland has stolen a—a—cyprian. I am sorry, Letitia, but there is no acceptable word for the chit and that is the best I can think to call her. The man just up and stole her right out from under everyone's noses. Indeed, it was not kept secret in the least and was all over town the very morning it happened. Well, worse has come to worst in that matter. Apparently the woman who ran the—place—where that personage worked has now been discovered dead on the banks of the Thames."

"A pistol ball through her heart," added Angelica breathlessly.

"Indeed," her mama nodded, "a pistol ball directly through her heart. And constables were seen to enter Rossland House before nine of the clock this morning."

"Were they?" responded Mina. "Why would they go there?"

"Because Lord Rossland stole the cyprian," declared Angelica Deane's mama. "And it is quite obvious that this Mrs. Pimberley went to confront him and demand the girl back and The Devil's Delight shot her—Mrs. Pimberley, I mean. He would, you know. The man lacks the merest touch of civility. Why, there is not one person among the *ton* doubts that that is exactly what happened."

"Balderdash!" exclaimed Lady Letitia from the depths of her chair. "I am among the *ton*, Sylvia, and I doubt it heartily. Why on earth would Chadwick risk his own neck by shooting the woman when he might just as easily have bought the little jade from her at a good price? Chadwick is rich as Croesus since he inherited."

"But most unstable," provided Angelica's mama hopefully.

"Well, he has got windmills in his head," grumbled Lady Letitia, "but that does not make the man a murderer."

"You forget about his father, and brother and nephew."

"And you forget," glared Lady Letitia, "to whom you speak. I am an old friend of the Brumfield family. I was born upon the land that runs with their own in Hertfordshire. And I have known Chadwick forever. And I am certain that Chadwick never did such a dastardly thing as murder. Besides which, there was absolutely never anything proved against him in the sinking of the *Mary Jane*."

"Oh, Mina, I am so sorry," sighed Miss Deane, managing to totally ignore everything that Lady Letitia had said. "To think that Lord Rossland should lead you on so, when all the while he had lost his heart to a—to a—and then to be so unprincipled as to actually kill someone in order not to lose her!"

"But he did not lose his heart to her until the day before yesterday, I think," Miss Potts murmured. "Which was nearly a fortnight after he had lost his heart to me. And he did tell me, you know, all about Mitzie."

Miss Deane and her mama inhaled abruptly, certain that this quiet, self-possessed attempt to relieve the wretch of responsibility for his actions was nothing more than a precursor to hysteria.

"It occurred, this loss of his heart," continued Mina blandly, "shortly after his illicit affair with Lady Goodacre. In fact, I do think he said it was the very same night that he had kissed Lady Goodacre upon her stoop that he met and abducted the redoubtable Mitzie."

"No, really, Mina," protested Angelica with a great deal of sensitivity. "I do realize that mama and I drew the wrong conclusion in that particular case. But this is different. I have it on the best authority that he stole the girl right off of Lord Langly's arm and then had the gall to spirit her away from that dreadful place before dawn. And when this Mrs. Pimberley came to demand the girl's return last evening, he must have drawn out his pistol and fired it directly at her."

Minerva lifted an eyebrow. "Why, that would explain why Lord Rossland was so late to his godmama's dinner party, would it not? He did not arrive until after the gentlemen were at their port, after all. Imagine! And he did not mention a word of it to me."

Even her Aunt Letitia stared at Minerva, stunned.

"Well, one would think," responded Mina softly to the three slack-jawed faces confronting her, "that Lord Rossland might have had the courtesy to mention to me that he had just murdered an abbess and carried her body down to the Thames and that was why he did not appear at dinner. It could not possibly have slipped his mind. He had just come from the scene of the crime. And we are *friends*. The man confides absolutely everything in me. Of course, he may not have done the grisly deed until after he had left the Winecoffs'. That would explain his failure to tell me what had occurred. But then, that would not have explained his having missed dinner, you see."

"Oh my poor dear!" exclaimed Angelica Deane's mama, rushing to where Mina sat composedly upon the settee and beginning to chafe Minerva's hands. "You unfortunate darling! Letitia, it is too much for her. She is overcome. Her mind has gone all astray. Angelica, have you your smelling salts in your reticule?"

"Phaw!" grunted Lady Letitia, the slackness of her jaw displaced by a stubborn jut of her chin. "Mina is not in the least overcome, are you, girl? She is merely demonstrating what an atrocious Banbury story the whole of this is. Of course the man did not kill this abbess. And Chadwick did not kill his father and brother and nephew either!" Lady Letitia declared as an angry afterthought. "That was gammon from beginning to end! And I will thank you both to leave this premises if you have nothing better to do than to spread lies about Chadwick Brumfield, because I, for one, have had my fill of them!"

"Hear! Hear!" cried Minerva tugging her hands from Lady Deane, and applauding. "And so say I."

"But if it is not true, why would the constables go to Rossland House?" asked Angelica. "Lord Collingsworth saw them himself, just as he saw Lord Rossland take that cyprian from Lord Langly's arm."

"Lord Collingsworth? Oh, my goodness," gasped Minerva. "And he is your favorite beau, Angel! Whatever was he doing in a—for he must have been, you know, to see Lord Rossland take the girl from Lord Langly. Oh, I am so very sorry for you. To think that he should go to such an establishment while everyone knows he is most adamant about pressing his suit with you."

"I—he—" stuttered Angelica.

"And why should Lord Collingsworth be anywhere near Rossland House at such an early hour of the morning?" continued Minerva, wringing her hands. "Oh, Angel, I can only conclude that it was because he, himself, knew something of the woman's death and wished to see if the constables would take action upon some anonymous message he had sent them. Why, perhaps it was even Lord Collingsworth who pulled the trigger and he pointed an anonymous finger at Lord Rossland to keep speculation from himself."

"Alfred would never!" spluttered Angelica. "He must merely have been walking by and—"

"Walking by? Why on earth would he be walking by?" queried Mina. "There is nothing in Mount Street to demand Lord Collingsworth's presence—especially not before nine o'clock in the morning. Why, I would suppose Lord Collingsworth not normally risen from his bed at such an hour."

The horrified look dawning in Angelica's eyes struck Minerva with pity and she ceased abruptly. "I am sorry, Angel. I am being a brute. Do not cry, dearest. Please do not. Certainly Lord Collingsworth would never think to shoot anyone. And as for that place in Bennett Street—most likely he had merely accompanied a friend to that dreadful house and remained only to take a bit of brandy. And it is quite likely that he rose early this morning and decided to take a stroll down Mount Street. He is a most respectable gentleman, Angel, and I am a wretch to tease you. But I wished to point out how easily people may make assumptions and jump to conclusions. And just because it is Lord Rossland they do it to and not your Collingsworth does not make it right—nor any more worthy of your consideration. It is nothing but gossip and you ought to know better than to be spreading it."

"I—The Devil's Delight has been paying you so very much attention of late," stuttered Angelica. "I have been afraid for you. I listen to everything and tell you what I hear because I do not want your heart to break over him."

"Angel," sighed Minerva, going to kneel beside her friend's chair, "I am not like to break my heart over Lord Rossland."

"You are not?"

"Of course not. I am not the least in love with him, Angel. In fact, I have promised myself never to fall in love with any man ever again. I have decided to marry for comfort, prestige, and convenience, and love will have nothing to do with it."

Minerva was quite certain that Angelica and her mama would relate that statement word for word. And sooner or later everyone in the *ton* would have heard of it. And that, she thought, will keep them from thinking me a nodcock for continuing to encourage Lord Rossland, which I must appear to do if he is to have access to his nephew and Mitzie. No one will pity me in the least because he is frightfully rich and titled and the perfect companion for a woman seeking nothing but comfort and prestige and convenience.

The only problem was, Minerva had felt herself weakening in her determination not to fall in love again. The Devil's Delight, quite unintentionally she was certain, had begun to make definite dents in the wall she had hastily built around her heart. Truly, Lord Rossland was the most aggravating man! Any young woman who did allow herself to fall in love with him would be hard pressed to maintain her sanity. Why, she would need to be totally inured to gossip and would be required to trust in him completely and she must never ever doubt that what he did, he did for good reason. And she would need to have the patience of a saint!

It was a mere fifteen minutes after the Deanes' departure that the Marquis of Kensington, his honey blond hair combed with precision, his sea green eyes flashing and his finely sculpted lips adorned by a charming smile, entered Lady Letitia's parlor followed almost immediately by the Reverend Mr. George and the Honorable Mr. Davidson. Each of the gentlemen presented Minerva with a posy and each of them strove with equal might to gain and hold her attention. Never before had such a thing happened to Minerva—three gentlemen at one time, and one of them a marquis! A quick glance in her aunt's direction showed her that that lady was beaming with pride.

Well, gracious, why should she not, Minerva told herself. Until two weeks ago when I had the good fortune to overhear Donald and go rushing off into Lord Rossland's arms, poor Aunt Letty had nothing but an ordinary, unexceptionable and most uninteresting Miss to present to Society. And now, now I am a woman of mystery and well on my way to becoming a complete cipher. And if Lord Rossland should manage to get into any deeper waters, I might well become a romantic legend!

The marquis was murmuring rumors of Rossland's present troubles—being quite discreet, of course, in how he related them—and the other two were joining in from time to time to add what little they could to the story.

"The man is now beyond redemption," announced Kensington with a sardonic smile. "Even if he did not shoot this Mrs. Pimberley—which I cannot truly believe he did—still, to put himself into such a position as to even be suspected!"

"I, myself, cannot imagine what has gotten into the man," added Davidson.

"Whether he is guilty of the murder or not, he has sunk himself completely this time," agreed the Reverend Mr. George with a sad shake of his head.

"Nonsense!" exclaimed Minerva, surprising all of the gentlemen and herself as well. She could feel her color rising even as the marquis's gaze fastened questioningly upon her.

"Nonsense, Miss Potts?" asked the Reverend Mr. George in stunned amazement. "You do not think his reputation ruined?"

"No," parried Minerva, "because he has got no reputation to be ruined."

"True," nodded Mr. Davidson. "There is something to be said for that view."

"Yes, but not much," drawled the marquis. "Really, Miss Potts, what is it makes you defend the villain?"

"I am not defending him," offered Minerva upon whom the marquis's exquisitely tailored morning coat, his pristine neckcloth tied in a perfect Orientale, and glimpses of his black silk waistcoat with hummingbirds embroidered in gold, were having not the least effect. "Lord Rossland had set himself far beyond any defense before I even came to know him. But—"

"But, Miss Potts?" urged the reverend.

"Well, it is just that so many splendid people such as yourselves, gentlemen, find Lord Rossland worth commenting upon and wish to discuss his every move and enjoy the telling of all sorts of tales about him. If he had truly sunk himself beyond notice, I should think none of you would notice him."

The three gentlemen stared at her in silence. Minerva sought hurriedly for a change of topic but, if Battlesby had not just then entered the chamber, she would have come to a complete standstill for she could think of nothing at all to say that did not concern the Earl of Rossland.

"The Earl of Rossland—and friends—" announced Battlesby obviously fighting to keep a most professional and noncommital look upon his countenance.

"Yes, well, you did not need to put it quite so quaintly," drawled the earl as he strolled into the room directly behind the hard-pressed butler. "You might have said, Battlesby, 'the Earl of Rossland and dinner.' "

That was all Battlesby could withstand and he burst into most undignified chuckles, slapped a hand across his mouth to smother them and rushed out into the hall, neatly sidestepping three little ducklings who trailed after Rossland in a straight line. Rossland crossed the room to Lady Letitia. The ducklings waddled, evenly spaced, behind him, quacking happily each step of the way. Rossland possessed himself of Lady Letitia's hand, kissed it gently and stared down at her with a twinkle in his eyes. "Forgive me, Letitia, but I have fallen into a scrape and I have yet to discover a way out of them."

Lady Letitia's lips quivered, her hand trembled, and in a moment she burst into laughter.

"Excellent," drawled Rossland. "I could not guess, you know, since the most unencouraging rumors about me must have reached you by this time, if you would laugh or have me tossed out of your house. I prefer the laughter, let me tell you. Good morning, Miss Potts, Kensington, Davidson, George," he drawled in their direction as he lowered himself into a chair beside Lady Letitia. The ducklings plumped down immediately at his feet. "I have not the least idea how it happened, Letitia," he said, "but these chaps have been following me about since late last evening and nothing I do discourages them. And then I thought—Letitia Potts! I know 'tis Farin now, but I always think of you as Potts. Letitia Potts! I thought. Now she would have the answer. She was always used to be fond of ducks. Let them swim in the fountain on her father's estate. She will know how to detach them from me. And so here I am, seeking your advice. I warn you, I have already proposed turning them each into a neat little pie, but neither my cook nor my housekeeper will consent to do it."

Minerva, diverted, stared mystified at the earl and the little cluster of ducklings at his feet.

"Well, I never!" declared the marquis, exasperated.

"No, neither have I," murmured Davidson.

"I do believe he *has* lost his mind," mused the Reverend Mr. George with a most concerned expression.

"Oh, what very sweet little bits of fluff!" exclaimed Minerva unable to resist longer. She left her chair to cross the room and settle beside the ducklings at Rossland's feet.

"Well, I never!" declared the marquis again.

"Perhaps you ought," sighed Davidson. "That is, if you wish to have Miss Potts settle at your own feet. Do you, Kensington? Mean to have her settle at your feet?"

"I fail to see how that can concern you, Davidson."

"Yes, well, but it does concern me, and George, too. A reverend and an honorable stand small chance against a marquis, Kensington. If you are merely flirting with Miss Potts, you would do the two of us a great favor by withdrawing from the field."

"Indeed," agreed the Reverend Mr. George heartily. "Miss Potts is not your usual type of flirt, Kensington. Go back to the belles and give the likes of us a chance with her why don't you?"

"Because I like her," grumbled Kensington. "She grows prettier day by day and she is definitely not the insipid Miss I thought her when she was used to sit against the wall at Almack's. She has gained a great deal of countenance since first Whithall took her up."

"No, it was when she put Whithall down that she began to gain it," mumbled Davidson. "It is somehow all Rossland's doing."

"You do not for one moment think that Rossland *has* fallen head over heels in love with Miss Potts?" the Reverend Mr. George asked rather dolefully.

"Not a bit of it," Kensington replied. "No gentleman who has lost his heart to a young lady would run off and actually steal a cyprian from her madam. And he would not come sauntering into the lady's parlor afterward, either. And he could never face her having all but been accused of murder."

"Rossland might," sighed the Reverend Mr. George. "There is never any knowing what Rossland might do."

"Yes, well, it does not matter," declared Kensington, "because there is some knowing what Lady Letitia will do. She will send Rossland packing should he propose anything at all serious between himself and Miss Potts. Lady Letitia would not think to accept such a libertine as Rossland for her niece. The Devil's Delight may think to hoodwink Miss Minerva Potts, but Lady Letitia Farin knows he is a born blackguard.''

The three gentlemen, lacking the necessary humility to crawl about on the carpet amidst ducklings in order to procure Miss Potts's attention, bade Miss Potts and Lady Letitia adieu and with misgivings abandoned the field to Rossland and his waterfowl.

"Begin at the beginning, Chadwick," Lady Letitia ordered as the three gentlemen disappeared. "We shall get to the ducklings in time enough. You did not shoot this Pimberley woman. Why do the constables think you did?"

Minerva looked up from the ducklings to see a most unholy light dawn in Rossland's eyes. "And what makes you assume, Letitia, that the constables think I did?"

"Because they appeared at your house before nine o'clock this morning, you ninny," responded the lady impatiently.

"Well, as to that, I cannot explain why anyone would appear at my residence at such an hour and think me to be awake and wandering about. But it was not, I assure you, because they thought me guilty of murder."

"Why, then?" asked Minerva from the floor.

"Apparently Major Gaffney had learned of Mrs. Pimberley's death. He sent them to discover if I had arrived home safely last evening. Though what gives Gaffney the right to send constables to my doorstep for any reason escapes me."

"Gaffney? Major Nicholas Gaffney?" asked Lady Letitia. "Is he not one of the soldiers you rescued at Talavera?"

"I did *not* rescue anyone at Talavera," protested Rossland. "I simply discovered it necessary to save myself and some other fellows came along for the ride. But yes, Letitia, he was one of the fellows came along for the ride. Having heard—I expect everyone has heard by now—that I had stolen some jade from this Mrs. Pimberley, he wished to assure himself that whoever shot her had not shot me as well. Perkins told the constables that I was tucked up safely in my bed and sent them off. Though what gives Gaffney the right to interfere in my life I cannot conceive.''

Minerva gave silent thanks for the major's obvious intention to interfere in Rossland's life until he and Jaimie were safe again and then giggled as a duckling hopped upon her lap.

"Very well, Chadwick," nodded Lady Letitia. "I shall accept that. Now, how did you come by these ducklings?''

"Charity," chuckled the earl, glancing down upon the delightful picture of Miss Potts stroking the fluffy bits at his feet. The bright spring sunlight through the windows had set fire to the young woman's golden curls and they took his breath away. Not that he had never seen golden curls in sunlight before, but these were inexplicably more breathtaking than any others.

"Chadwick! Cease staring at my niece like some halfwit and explain yourself," demanded Lady Letitia.

"Huh? Yes! Well, Charity and Mrs. Dowe went off to the market yesterday morning and they bought eggs."

"Eggs," muttered Lady Letitia.

"Yes, eggs—amongst other things of course. And when they returned home Davenport candled the eggs and informed them that they were useless because they were—you know—occupied." He stopped and glanced mirthfully at Minerva. "At any rate, he could not use them for his baking and so sent Paul off to market to get some others and was about to toss those he had away. But Mrs. Dowe, you see, had the great bad judgment to attempt to explain to Charity what was meant by occupied and the child burst into tears the moment Davenport made to dispose of them. So, they placed the eggs in a little nest near the oven though they were all of them except Charity quite certain that nothing would come of it.''

"And they hatched!" exclaimed Minerva brightly.

"Indeed," drawled Rossland, "at a half-past two this morning, right in the midst of my pilfered pigeon pie and tankard of ale.''

Lady Letitia roared into laughter.

"Well, but I did not have any dinner," bemoaned Rossland. "You know I did not, Letitia. You had all done eating when I arrived at Aunt Seraphina's. And by the time I had gone back home I was starving." Rossland's lips were twitching upward despite his attempt to sound quite put upon and Minerva could not resist giggling at him.

"At any rate, I was sitting quite pleasantly at the kitchen table, everyone else long gone to their beds, when I heard the oddest noises. Little tapping sounds."

"And you went to discover what could be making them," supplied Lady Letitia still laughing, "and discovered the eggs hatching upon the kitchen settle."

"Indeed, and stood and watched as each of the wet-feathered rascals presented himself. And now, unless someone consents to make them into duckling pies, I expect my life will never be the same again."

"It is because you were the first thing they saw when they hatched," Lady Letitia informed him with a twinkle. "They think you are their mama, Chadwick."

"Well, I ain't and I would be much obliged if you would tell them to make Charity their mama instead, Letitia. She was quite woebegone when the blasted birds preferred to follow me about than to play with her upon the scullery floor. I, my-self, was not particularly thrilled about it either."

"Who precisely is Charity?" asked Minerva, curious.

"Charity," sighed Rossland, running his fingers through his hair, "is our junior scullery maid."

"A *junior* scullery maid?" asked Minerva, gathering all the ducklings onto her lap and gazing up with interested blue eyes.

"Well, she ain't a *real* scullery maid, you see. Betsy holds that position. But Mrs. Dowe lets Charity help as best she can."

"I have never heard of such a thing. How did Mrs. Dowe come by her?" Minerva eyed him with a good deal of interest. She could see the mirth literally bubbling behind his eyes and the sparkle of the sunlight upon his mahogany curls made them glint with fire and the whole of him, including the tone of his voice and the tilt of his head, took her breath away.

"Why?" he asked with an impish grin. "Do you need a junior scullery maid, Miss Potts? I will give you Charity. She ain't much good—cannot even scrub the pots because she is very small and might fall in and drown—but she eats like a regular Life Guardsman."

"Chadwick, cease digressing and answer m'niece's question. How did Mrs. Dowe come to hire such an unnecessary little girl?"

"No, now that is most harsh and quite unfair, Letitia. Charity ain't unnecessary. I doubt there is anyone born who is unnecessary. However," Rossland added with a chuckle, "we have not quite divined what it is Charity is necessary for. Perkins found her hiding beneath a bush at the corner of Mount Street crying as though her heart would break. Her mama, it seems, had instructed her to wait right there and not move and then hurried away and never returned. Hid under that bush for two days, Charity did, cold and hungry and as frightened as any little girl could ever be. But nobody so much as noticed her until Perkins came along. Grubby little urchin she was, too, when he carried her in through the kitchen door."

"Did no one attempt to find her mama?" Minerva asked, disbelieving that anyone would abandon a tiny child.

"I found her mama," sighed Rossland. "But she was not in the least interested in having the girl back. Said as how the mite was useless and a burden and worth nothing. So I gave the woman a guinea and went home. She was gin-soaked," he added in explanation. "I expect you do not know about blue ruin, Miss Potts, but it will possess a person until they care for nothing. She's dead now," he muttered with an odd twist to his lips. "Run down in a gutter by a hackney several weeks ago."

"You—you kept in touch with her?"

"Kept my eye on her you could say—in case she *might* want Charity back, you know. Easy enough to keep an eye on her when I was spending a good deal of time in the gutter myself."

Twelve

"But enough about little Charity. It is these wretched waterfowl, Letitia," Rossland grinned, "about whom I require your expertise. I have not the faintest idea what to do with them. From the moment they dried up into the pieces of fluff you see before you, they have done nothing but pester me. I cannot get them to go away. I admit I ought not to have paid them the least bit of attention last evening, but they were all alone in the kitchen, you see, and someone needed to look after them. I could not leave them alone, could I? Think of all the havoc they might have wreaked upon my establishment."

"Do not say, Chadwick," Lady Letitia giggled girlishly, "that you were shatterbrained enough to take the creatures to your chambers."

"All right. I will not say it."

"You did!" laughed Minerva.

"Only to be certain they did not fall off the settle and hurt themselves or make a veritable rat's nest of the kitchen. I made a place for them in the bottom drawer of my armoire. I put in a bowl of water and a bit of grain—"

"Took them under his wing, so to speak," inserted Lady Letitia gleefully.

"Yes," nodded Rossland. "But I was merely attempting to do the right thing by them, Letitia. It was an act of kindness only and now I am become their prisoner. They cannot be made to abandon me. Follow behind me every step I take. I came near to tripping over them attempting to dress, was forced to break my fast amidst quacking and nuzzling and a great deal of pecking at my ankles, and when I climbed into my curricle, they escaped out the door before Perkins could close it and came scurrying into the street attempting to keep pace with my horses and fluttering those little wings—they would have flown if they were old enough, I think. Well, they could not keep pace, of course. But there they were, three ducks in a row, skittering down the middle of Mount Street and quacking away as brave as you please. Caused quite a stir, I tell you! At any moment they might have been crushed beneath a pedlar's cart or attacked by dogs, or—well, who can say? Never expected ducklings to have such bottom. Expected 'em to scatter for home. But they did not, so you can see that I was forced to send my tiger back to collect them."

"And were you forced to lead them into my morning room as well?" asked Lady Letitia.

"Well, no. But it occurred to me that quite likely you had already heard the tale of Mrs. Pimberley and the constables at my door, Letitia, and I thought perhaps the little demons had been heaven sent to divert you from thoughts of tossing me directly back into the street. And they did, too—divert you."

"Indeed."

"Yes, and I thought Miss Potts might find them amusing."

"And I do," smiled Minerva. "But you must know, Lord Rossland, that neither I nor Aunt Letitia believed for a moment that you had murdered Mrs. Pimberley."

"Well, of course you do not believe it," replied the earl. "I trusted entirely in that. But that does not mean that Letitia ain't angry about it, because whether you realize it or not, Miss Potts, your name is like to be dragged through the mud right along with my own if you are seen to go on associating with me. Do you intend to go on associating with me? No one will blame you, you know, if you cut the connection. Even I should not blame you after this Grace Pimberley business."

A militant light appeared in Miss Potts's eyes and Rossland was surprised at it. He had known that she would stand by him so far as Jaimie's safety was concerned, for she had not taken back her offer to give the boy shelter even when he had given her the opportunity to do so. But he had imagined that Mrs. Pimberley's murder would provide Miss Potts with the perfect excuse to dissolve their relationship in the eyes of the Polite World.

"I most certainly intend to continue our association," declared Minerva. "And to Hampshire with those who lift their eyebrows at it."

"But they may do more than lift their eyebrows, sweetling. I think you had best discuss the matter with your Aunt Letitia before you make any final decisions."

"Do you not wish to associate with me further, Your Lordship?" Mina asked with a stubborn tilt to her chin.

"Well, of course I do," replied Rossland glancing sideways at Lady Letitia, "but I cannot think you will thank me for it in the end. The gossipmongers will be proposing all sorts of hideous theories about why you did not abandon the connection."

"Indeed," agreed Lady Letitia with a scowl. "But Mina has already given them grist for the mill by informing that little featherbrain Angelica Deane that she has not the least intention of making a love match and seeks to marry only for her own prestige and comfort and convenience. That will set the gabblers back on their heels. My niece is not afraid of mere words, Chadwick. Minerva is capable of speaking as roundly as any them."

"And you, Letitia? Do you not fear for her reputation—or your own?"

"Ho!" cried Lady Letitia, "as if *you* could possibly destroy a reputation I have been building for more than forty years. I should like to see the day, Chadwick! And I have not the least fear for Minerva. She may do as she wishes in the matter. I, myself, have chosen to believe in you and all you explained to me about your nephew, and I shall make myself available to you regardless of what the *ton* chooses to imagine."

"Birdies!" cried a most excited voice before anyone could say another word. And an absolutely thrilled red-headed four-year-old dashed toward the three ducklings in Minerva's lap. "Birdies!" Jaimie cried again, collapsing onto the floor at Rossland's feet and reaching toward the ducklings.

"I'm right sorry, ma'am," announced Mitzie as she came

nervously into the room. "We was goin' out to the garden to play when Joseph, he heard Your Ladyship's footmen speakin' about birdies and off he ran to look fer 'em. I have been chasin' him from room to room ferever, but he willn't let me catch 'im."

"Joseph," growled Lady Letitia with a frown, but with a very pronounced twinkle in her eye, "have you no manners? Stand up, please, and make your bow to Lord Rossland."

Minerva held her breath as the child rose to his feet and bowed before the earl. Would such a little boy remember to play his part or would her aunt now learn the truth?

"Chadwick, this is Joseph, a distant cousin of Minerva's who has come to visit. Joseph, say how do you do to Lord Rossland."

"Howd'do," grinned Jaimie. "I am Joey."

"Indeed you are," replied Rossland with a wide smile. "And I am pleased to make your acquaintance, Joseph."

"Can I play with the birdies?"

"Indeed you may," chuckled Rossland. "Plop yourself right down where you were and Miss Potts will let you pet them. But you must be very careful because they are very small."

"I am being careful," assured Jaimie.

"Hello," grinned Rossland, leaving the boy under Minerva's watchful eye and directing his attention to Mitzie.

"G'af 'ernoon, Y'r Worship," greeted Mitzie with a grin and a little bob of a curtsy.

"This," offered Lady Letitia, "is Joseph's nursemaid. Though if you ask me, she is child enough to require a nursemaid herself. Off with you, Melinda. You may leave Joey in our charge until Lord Rossland and the ducklings depart. Go to the kitchen and ask cook to give you a glass of milk and a lemon tart."

"Yes, Y'r Majesty," responded Mitzie with another little bob. "Thank you very kindly." And in a moment she was gone.

"Now, as I was saying, Chadwick," began Lady Letitia. "I do realize that—"

"He bited me!" yelled Jaimie excitedly, holding one index finger into the air. "That duckbirdling bited me!" And before Minerva could make a move to stop him, Jaimie seized his uncle's knees and climbed up into his lap. "He bited me," the boy declared holding his finger up before Rossland's eyes and pointing at it with his other hand. "Right there!"

"But he did not harm it," grinned Rossland, making a great show of examining the injured digit. "I should say he muzzled it, is what he did. And muzzling, sir, is not the same as biting."

"It ain't?"

"Oh, no. A thing must have teeth to bite you, Joey, and those poor ducklings have no teeth at all."

"No teeth?"

"Not a one."

"Poor duckbirdlings," sighed Jaimie, scrunching about on his uncle's lap until he could rest his curly head against the earl's shoulder. "How is they gonna eat nothin' without teeths?"

The very next morning Minerva found herself ensconced beside her aunt in a chaise and four pounding along the turnpike with three ducklings in a basket on the banquette facing them.

"I do not recall volunteering my services in this matter," murmured Lady Letitia in a petulant voice. "Do you recall my doing so, Mina?"

"No, ma'am. You did say that Lord Rossland ought to find a place in the country to stow the ducklings, but I do not recall your volunteering either of our services in the matter."

"I did never say we would accompany the wretched things to the country?"

"Not that I recall," smiled Minerva, "though apparently His Lordship took that to be your meaning, for here we are."

"Indeed. And where is Chadwick?"

"Well, the coachman said he had ridden on ahead and would be waiting for us when we arrived, though I cannot imagine why he should do so. Perhaps," grinned Mina, "he thought the ducklings would be better behaved without his presence."

"More likely he could not abide their quacking and fluttering about another moment," observed Lady Letitia, "and he thought it a famous plan to make us their nursemaids. Honestly, Chadwick is a thorough scoundrel!"

"But he has a kind heart."

"Indeed. Did you note how gentle and kind he was with Joseph? If Chadwick were not such an ill-mannered, windmill-headed lout, he would make an excellent father. But who would marry the man as he is?"

"I have no idea," murmured Minerva, turning to stare out of the coach window. Honestly, it was totally unreasonable of her to think it, but *she* would marry him—and marry him exactly as he was, without altering him one smidgeon. And that is why, Mina told herself seriously, I know I must have as many windmills in my head as Lord Rossland is reputed to have in his. With a little shake of her curls, she told herself sternly that she was being totally absurd, that she had known from the very first that her relationship with The Devil's Delight was not to be taken seriously, and that she had best remember what had happened with Lord Whithall and how terrible she had felt and why she had determined never to fall in love again. She had best remember it and remember it well, too, elsewise she was headed for certain disaster. Her heart would be bruised and battered again and this time the whole of it would be her own fault, because to Lord Rossland this was a matter of life and death and his nephew's safety and not at all a matter of courtship and love and marriage.

Lady Letitia and Minerva rode on in silence for a number of miles, only the fluttering and the quacking of the ducklings disturbing their thoughts, and it was not until the chaise left the toll road at Gravesend that Lady Letitia perked up and began to gaze about her. "Why we are bound for Riddle. And I thought Chadwick likely to avoid the place for the rest of his years."

"Why would he do that, Aunt?"

"Because it was at Riddle that his father and brother died—at least, the *Mary Jane* had departed from very near there, and so it is filled with unhappy memories for him."

When they reached Riddle the chaise did not pull up into the huge circle of the front drive but followed a small track off to the east that carried them past the mansion, through more of the park, into and out of a small woods, and at last came to a halt before a cottage where Rossland sat waiting upon the stone steps leading to the front door. He rose instantly and went to lower the coach steps and hand the ladies down.

"Oh, what a snug little cottage!" Mina exclaimed, grasping his hand as she descended and throwing a quick smile up at him.

"It is called Skylark," replied Lady Letitia as she accepted Rossland's hand in turn. "Father and I set out to hunt for it one summer when we came to visit at Riddle. There was not a track to it in those days."

"No, there was never used to be a track. It ain't just as you remember it, Letitia," Rossland mumbled lifting the ducklings out onto the drive. "More than the track has changed. I thought I had best warn you. It is Liza."

"Elizabeth is here?" asked Letitia. "Why I thought you to have sent her to Land's End, or Graymoor. What on earth is she doing here? I know she is in mourning, Chadwick, but at least at the other estates she might have the company of the local squires and their wives to provide her some society. Who is there for the girl to associate with here? She must be lonely beyond belief. Take me to her at once."

"Yes, I will, but she ain't lonely, Letitia. She is—that is to say—she has not been up to, ah, receiving visitors. No, that ain't true. It is just that she—"

"Wicky, Wicky, Wicky, Wicky!" cried an excited feminine voice loudly, totally interrupting the earl's train of thought and causing him to abandon all conversation and turn abruptly toward the sound. In a moment Liza appeared, hurrying around the corner of the cottage with a piece of harness clutched in her hand. "I having found it, Wicky!" She threw herself happily into Rossland's arms, wrapping her arms and the harness about his neck and letting her feet dangle above the ground as he stumbled a bit because of his leg.

Minerva stared at them, her lips parted, her hands clenching just the slightest bit. Rossland's back was to her and the woman almost hidden by his broad shoulders, but she could see very well what was going on. And it is no concern of mine, she told herself, if that woman wishes to throw herself at Lord Rossland in such an unacceptable fashion and hang all over him and kiss him in that most outrageous way. It is not in the least a concern of mine. Though how anyone could behave so disreputably in public! Why Aunt Letitia and I are right here before her! She ought to hang her head in shame! Yes, indeed she ought!

It did occur to Mina that she had come near to kissing the earl in public herself, right in the middle of Hyde Park in fact. But that had been very different. She had not thrown herself upon him with such abandon. And besides, they had not kissed, only come near to doing so.

"Shameless hoyden," chuckled Rossland, attempting to dislodge Liza's grip from around his neck with one hand, while lowering her safely to the ground with the other. "Release me. Our company has arrived just as I said they should. Here is Lady Letitia and her niece, Miss Potts. Liza!" he laughed as he freed himself of her and she immediately jumped back into his arms. "Do try for some propriety!"

"But I have been finding it," protested the woman in a girlishly pouting tone waving the piece of harness before his eyes, "and now you are not wanting it."

"I am wanting it," grinned Rossland, "but not this instant. Now do release me and put your feet firmly upon the ground or I shall climb into that chaise and be gone directly."

Liza kissed his cheek and she did release him—except for one of his hands to which she clung very tightly as she peered around his long, lean body to view her visitors.

Minerva took a very deep breath at her first sight of that lovely face surrounded by a cloud of midnight hair. Her eyes, she thought, are the color of emeralds. And she is so very beautiful!

"Elizabeth, you remember Lady Letitia, I think, and may I present her niece, Miss Minerva Potts," drawled Rossland with suppressed laughter in his voice as he attempted to step away

from Liza and face the other ladies but was foiled in doing so.
"Do behave, Liza, and greet your guests properly. They will
think you a ninny if you persist in peeking at them from around
me."

"That is being Lady Letitia," agreed Liza nodding enthusiastically. "And that is being the niece," she added, pointing at
Minerva. "But who are being they, Wicky?"

"They?" asked Rossland, bestowing a kiss upon the top of
Liza's head and then attempting a quick sidestep in the hope
of being able to turn around. "Oh! Why those are the ducklings who have come to keep you company while I am gone to
town."

"Ooooh!" gasped Liza, clapping her hands and sending
them scattering. "Babies!"

"Yes, m'dear, baby ducks," grinned Rossland as Liza left him
and hurried toward the ducklings. Gathering them into her
arms, she sat down upon the stoop to play with them.
Rossland's gaze went to Minerva and her aunt, and Mina saw
quite clearly a look of defiance in his eyes. He stepped forward,
offered Lady Letitia an arm, and making his way carefully with
his cane around Liza and the ducklings, led both ladies into
the cottage.

No sooner had he seated them comfortably in the long, low
parlor, than Mrs. Beaman appeared with a tea tray overflowing
with freshly baked pastries, bread, and newly churned butter.
"Will you pour, Letitia?" drawled Rossland. "Liza ain't like to
come in for a while yet. I have tied her puppy up in the stable
so it will not frighten the birds. I knew she would wish to play
with them. They will hold her attention for at least a quarter
hour I should imagine."

Lady Letitia, with a solemn nod, did as she was requested.
She poured out in silence, asking only if Rossland wished
cream or sugar and which of the pastries he would prefer.
Minerva, who could think of nothing but the sight of that beautiful woman, well past the first blush of youth, playing like a
child upon the front stoop with three ducklings, passed
Rossland his tea and pastries in silence.

"Well, but it ain't as dreadful as you imagine," mumbled

the earl after a few bites of apple tart and a few sips of tea. "Liza is happy here, Letitia, and there is no one to look askance at her. And Mrs. Beaman and my caretaker, Maitland, are all consideration and kindness where Liza is concerned. They do neither of them mind in the least keeping fond eyes upon her."

"Is she—is she gone completely mad, Chadwick?"

"No, of course not, Letitia. She knows perfectly well who I am and who you are. And she does not run about tearing at her hair and screeching or anything so gothic as that. It is more that she has cloaked herself in childhood somehow. I expect she felt a good deal happier when she was a child—and a deal more protected as well. There has been much too much tragedy in her life of late and she cannot face it coming all at once as it has, so she pretends to be young again."

"And you hid her away here to keep anyone from knowing?" asked Mina hesitantly.

"I had no idea what else to do," Rossland sighed. "I could not parade her about in Society like some dog and pony show, and to send her off to one of the other estates, well, they are so very far from town. I could not simply dash out to see her in Hertfordshire or at Land's End as I do now."

"But Chadwick," groaned Lady Letitia, "a great many people are under the impression that you have exiled Elizabeth to the hinterlands and will not allow her to be seen. They profess that you have done so to keep her from speaking out against your inheriting the title and to prevent her from accusing you of murder."

"Well, but, Skylark Cottage is hardly the hinterlands, Letitia. And Liza ain't never once accused me of harming anyone. And she did not want to stay at Riddle either," he added as an afterthought. "Jaimie was born at Riddle, you know, and it preyed upon her mind that he was not with her."

"Yes, but that is not what people think," replied Lady Letitia in exasperation. "They think you are a villain and a despot and have treated Elizabeth with utter cruelty. It is a great part of the reason you are ostracized, Chadwick!"

"Well, I ain't concerned with *that,*" responded Rossland.

"But—but you and Miss Potts have been so kind, willing to help me and all. And I thought perhaps *someone* ought to know where Liza was just in case anything should happen to me. Not that anything is likely to happen to me," he added with a quick and reassuring glance in Mina's direction. "But I would be obliged, Letitia, did you not mention to anyone about where Liza is unless it is absolutely necessary. Besides, she will be better soon and she will be terribly embarrassed to think anyone knew how she had given way."

"*Is* she going to be better soon?" asked Minerva quietly.

"Indeed. As soon as she has got Jaimie back."

Minerva noticed that the light of defiance in the earl's dark eyes had grown more intense and a most unexpected blaze of pride and compassion burst into being somewhere near her own heart. Why, he was doing everything—giving all—for this lovely lady and daring the two of them to so much as suggest that his efforts might be in vain. This was how much he believed in himself. This was how much he cared for another person—a truly helpless person. And much as she might be uneasy about his relationship with the lady, she could not but admire Rossland's courage and dedication.

"And Liza shall have Jaimie back very shortly," he added, his chin jutting out stubbornly, "and then she will most definitely recover herself and behave just as she ought."

"Did her physician tell you this, Chadwick," asked Lady Letitia, "that returning the boy would cure her?"

Minerva saw Rossland's grip tighten perceptibly on his teacup and she feared for a moment the thing would break in his hand. He caught himself, however, before it did so and set the cup aside. "You know what physicians are, Letitia," he said with visible self-control. "He tossed out a bundle of break-jaw words, peered down his nose at me and trundled off with a gloomy sigh and a shake of his head. But returning Jaimie to her will do the thing. Once she has Jaimie again, she will be just as she was used to be. I am convinced of it."

* * *

It was evening before the chaise and four swept out of the drive at Skylark and began its journey back to London. Its horses well rested, it barreled over the roads toward the turnpike. This time Rossland rode a solitary guard beside it. Minerva watched him in the moonlight, his back straight, his shoulders set. She could almost picture the preoccupied but obstinate look upon his handsome countenance. And for a brief moment her heart felt as if it might fail her. He was so very determined. He was determined to keep the boy safely hidden. He was determined to discover who were the villains in this terrible and inexplicable plot. He was determined to go so far as to risk his very life to return Jaimie safely to this lady. And he was most determined that that action should restore Elizabeth to her senses. He would accept nothing less.

"Is he in love with Elizabeth?" Minerva asked quietly.

"Chadwick? In love with his brother's widow? Without a doubt," replied Lady Letitia. "And would likely have married her himself had he been given any opportunity to do so. Of course, he had no such opportunity. He was exceedingly ill, back from Portugal only three weeks when Cam married the girl by special license. That marriage shocked everyone, you may believe me. Why, no one had so much as heard of Elizabeth! And how she and Cameron came to meet was a source of great speculation. London was abuzz with rumors. No one could so much as put a face to her name. And no one met her either, until almost a year after the wedding, for she and Cameron and the old earl stayed rigidly at Riddle and not one other person was invited to join them."

"How very odd," mused Minerva.

"Indeed. But then, one must remember that Chadwick was gravely ill for a goodly long time and I expect once he was mending, he had no wish for any of his friends to see him limping about like a cripple. And his father and Cameron would most certainly have submitted to his wishes in the matter."

"But when he had adjusted?" urged Minerva. "He goes limping about now and seems not at all mortified by it."

"Oh, by the time he had adjusted to his need for the walking stick and all, Jaimie had been born. The old earl threw the most tremendous party to celebrate the return to health of his son, the birth of the boy, and Cameron's marriage all at one and the same time. It was a magnificent affair, let me tell you, my dear. And I distinctly remember how Chadwick attempted to be so terribly nonchalant throughout it all, for the party continued a good ten days. But when he thought no one noticed, he would look at Elizabeth, and anyone at all interested could see that she took his breath away."

"Oh," murmured Minerva.

"Oh? And in such a tone? Do not tell me, Mina, that you are forming a *tendre* for Chadwick. I agreed to let that scoundrel associate with you as a part of his attempt to recover his nephew and confound the gabblemongers, but I did *not* agree to consider him seriously as an acceptable match. He may not be a libertine precisely, but he has always been a here-and-thereian. And that will not change, my dear. And if his nephew is alive and he does succeed in restoring the boy, he will then become most ineligible indeed, because he will have nothing at all to recommend him—no title, no fortune, no estates. They will all go to his nephew."

"But his father must have left him something, Aunt Letitia. Certainly not everything was entailed. A younger son's portion may not be much, but it is rather more than nothing."

"He will have a place in Shropshire that comes through his great uncle and several investments. He will not be a pauper precisely. But what will support a bachelor in a satisfactory manner will not support a wife and family in any style whatsoever. Of course, Chadwick will likely hold the post of guardian until the boy reaches his majority, but even Chadwick would not use such a position to enrich himself at Elizabeth's and Jaimie's expense. He is not such a slumgum as to do a thing like that!"

"Elizabeth will see he is rewarded in some way."

Lady Letitia made a slight choking sound and turned to stare out at Rossland. "I doubt Liza will ever realize what he has done, Mina. She is quite lost to him and to all of us."

"Oh, no, do not say so, Aunt."

"Well, but someone must say so. It is obvious to me that her physician has said as much. I could read it in Chadwick's eyes, my dear. It is sheer obstinacy on Chadwick's part not to accept it. He willingly ruins himself, Mina, in the eyes of all his peers for a dream most unlikely to come true. The best we can hope is that he saves the child and is not himself harmed too terribly in the effort."

Thirteen

Rossland rode beside the chaise all the way to Green Street where he dismounted and assisted Lady Letitia and Minerva to descend from the vehicle. He escorted them to their front door and waited, his glance combing the street, until they were safely inside Farin House. As far as he could tell, he had only been followed that morning from Rossland House as far as the turnpike, where his shadowman had most likely decided that since he obviously did not have Jaimie with him and had not had the least opportunity to smuggle the boy out of London, it would prove fruitless to follow him farther. No one, apparently, had as yet decided to keep watch over Farin House. That, Rossland thought with a smile, was, of course, because of the obvious impeccability and innocence of Miss Potts. Not a one of these most vile villains, apparently, could bring himself to believe that Miss Potts could be influenced to involve herself in his troubles—or the wretches could not believe that he would choose to involve her in them.

And he had been extremely lucky on another point, too. So far none of the villains had divined the fact that he kept most of his vehicles and teams at Sutter's stables rather than in his own. Luke had gone unnoticed again to fetch the ladies in the chaise and had left London without one rider behind him. Rossland grinned as he mounted Forager, ordered Luke to return the chaise and make his way very carefully home and then turned Forager's head toward Rossland House, musing all the way on the extraordinary blue of Miss Potts's eyes in the lamplight. And he had had the devil of a time to keep his finger from stroking one of those pale, soft cheeks as he bade her good-night upon the doorstep, too, especially when her eyelashes had fluttered shyly beneath his gaze. Not that she *was* shy. Certainly not. She was something very special—a delicious blend of courage and vulnerability.

Rossland nibbled at his lower lip. Five years ago he had thought himself in love with Liza. He knew better now of course. He had at last come to realize that what he had felt for Liza all those years ago had been a soaring admiration combined with deep obligation. But that was not love. Cameron had undertaken to tell him so, too. "If you had not given your word to bring her safely to British soil, Chad," Cameron had pointed out one afternoon at Riddle, "if you had met Liza at Almack's instead of amidst the Pyrenees and had not sworn a blood oath to protect her, you might have commented upon her beauty and sent her a posy or two, but you never would have thought to marry the woman. Which is why," Cam had added with a gleam in his eyes, "I have married her for you. I loved her from the first moment she arrived upon our doorstep, wrinkled and weary and frowning over the jolting you had taken from the rutty roads on the drive from Gravesend."

"Which drive I still cannot remember," sighed Rossland, taking his walking stick in hand and dismounting awkwardly from Forager's back. He handed the gelding's reins to the groom who came running and then he trudged toward the house taking note of a heavy-set gentleman in a dark cloak who lingered in the shadows upon the flagway across the street. That particular gentleman was attempting to appear as though he were not keeping an eye upon the comings and goings at Rossland House, but the earl knew better. The same form, minus the woolen cloak, had been in the same place this morning when he had departed for Skylark.

"You will discover someday that I was right to marry her, too, Chad," Cameron's voice interrupted his observation of the gentleman and echoed authoritatively inside his head. "When at last you meet the woman you truly love, brat, you will know I am not just attempting to placate you at this moment. And when you do discover that particular young lady, I shall jolly well be there beside you, thumping your shoulders and wishing you happy with all my heart."

Except that he was not, thought Rossland despairingly. Cam was not there beside him and never would be again. He would never realize that at last his little brother had discovered a true love of his own. Cam would never share in the joy the mere thought of Miss Potts brought him—nor would his father— and all because someone, somehow, had discovered their secret. "Well, but I will deal with it," he told himself grimly. "With Charlie's help and Gaffney's, I will deal quite nicely with the murdering miscreants who have destroyed my family. And no matter how much they might plead for mercy, I will despatch the lot of them with ruthless impartiality and a smile upon my face."

The earl was well on his way to demolishing the light supper that Davenport had sent up to him, hobbling around his dressing room popping a bit of this and a bit of that into his mouth as Martindale stalked fruitlessly behind attempting to dress him. "Master Chad!" that gentleman exclaimed at last, harassed beyond all endurance. "If you cannot cease pacing about for one moment, how *can* you expect to get yourself one leg at a time into your pantaloons, much less expect me to rig you out in the verimost height of fashion?"

"Well, you needn't rig me out in the verimost height of fashion, Martindale," drawled Rossland, coming to a halt with a suspicious twinkle in his eyes. "I would settle, you know, for somewhere near the middle of fashion. Can you do that while I am pacing about, Trev?"

"No!" declared his stalwart valet. "I cannot get you dressed at all if you do not stand still and cease eating."

"Then I expect I shall have to go naked, for I have not the least intention of ceasing to eat. I will, however," he capitulated in deference to Martindale's sadly plagued look, "cease to roam about the room as I do so. Will that help? Because I expect Charlie will not like to drive me to the club naked. He does have astonishing sensibilities about such things. Trev, do you know what I think?"

"Rarely, my lord," commented Martindale, gazing askance at His Lordship's attempt to balance without his walking stick, pull up his pantaloons with one hand and drink a glass of wine with the other.

"I think," continued the earl, at last setting the glass aside and using two hands on his pantaloons, "that I am seriously in love. Have you ever been seriously in love, Trev?"

"Never."

"Well, I expect it will do me no good to ask you then."

"To ask me what?" inquired Martindale, competently lacing His Lordship's pantaloons while Rossland popped a bit of fine cheddar into his mouth and followed it with a sip of wine.

"To ask you how to go about declaring myself to Miss Potts. She is the most wonderful woman in all the word, Martindale, and I know I ain't near good enough for her. I am a soldier through and through and always in the briars when it comes to Polite Society. And I ain't at all mannerly, even when I set my thoughts to being so. And I cannot cease behaving like a second son, Martindale, even though I am become an earl. But no matter how much I tell myself that I am totally unworthy of her, I wish to marry the girl anyway. I thought at first that she was just another simpering little chit, you know. But she ain't and I am completely captivated by her. And I do think I might stand a chance with her, Martindale. She has not sent me packing as yet, you know, nor she ain't refused me any aid I have asked of her in regard to Jaimie. She is very brave. And—and—frightfully loyal."

"Heaven forbid," mumbled Martindale, his duty to preserve the staff from Miss Potts springing immediately to mind.

"What?" asked Rossland, leaning upon his cane, staring meditatively at two waistcoats and munching on a piece of bologna. "Heaven forbid what?"

"That you should even consider such a dull waistcoat as the white watered silk, my lord," covered Martindale nicely. "If you intend to impress Miss Potts, you would do best to wear the gold with the crimson stars."

"No, do you think so, Trev? It is rather—eccentric."

"No, it is exciting, my lord. Adventurous."

"When I brought it home, you said it was bizarre and un-speakable."

"But you were not then interested in impressing Miss Potts."

"Oh. Well, I ain't interested in impressing her tonight, either. Lord Goodacre and I are bound for The Guards'. Do not I have anything that will make me look depressed?"

"Depressed, my lord?"

"Yes, you know, in despair, ready to blow my brains out."

Martindale stared disbelievingly at his employer. "You wish a waistcoat to convey that, my lord?"

"Asking too much, am I? I thought so. But what would Kemble wear, do you think, to convey such an impression?"

"Black, my lord."

"Plain black?"

"Indeed, my lord. Not just the waistcoat, but black from head to toe—as if he were in mourning, you know. And his hair would go uncombed and his cravat be disheveled. You are not *actually* ready to blow your brains out, are you, my lord?" asked Martindale with a hint of panic in his tone. "N-nothing has happened to little Jaimie or—"

"No, Martindale. The Beamer is fine as fivepence. It is only that I have decided that a gentleman whom everyone thinks has been interrogated by constables about a murder and whom everyone wishes to believe has done that murder and who is spending the remainder of the evening under the eyes of a member of the Foreign Office staff ought to look as though his conscience has been severely pricked and that it has set about driving him to despair. Fitting, I think."

"May I inquire which member of the Foreign Office staff?"

"Gaffney, Martindale. Charles and I have agreed to meet him and discuss what is to be done about Jaimie. I told Gaffney, you see, about the urchin's parentage."

"You did not, my lord!"

"Yes, I did. I thought twice and then I spilled my guts. Gaffney confided in me, you see, that this Mrs. Pimberley was some sort of spy."

"A spy, my lord?"

"Uh-huh, for the French, I think, though Gaffney ain't so certain it is that cut and dried," replied Rossland distractedly, attempting to tie the only black cravat he owned about his throat at what he hoped would be considered a most despairing angle. "Gaffney thinks there's more involved in it than just an attempt against us by the Frenchies. At any rate I thought to myself—if our enemies know about Jaimie, why would it not be a good idea to share the same knowledge with our friends, eh? So I did. I shared our secret with Gaffney, though I made it clear enough that he was bound to keep the whole thing confidential. I thought Gaffney would faint dead away on the spot. That will be Charlie," Rossland added at the sound of the door knocker below. "What think you, Trev? Do I look despairing enough?"

"If I may say so, m'lord, you look absolutely depraved."

"Depraved, despairing, one and the same I should think," mumbled the earl with a final look into the cheval glass. "I ain't got the least idea when I shall be back, Trev, so do not wait up. Oh, and watch through the front window as Goodacre and I leave, will you? There is a rather robust gentleman in a dark cloak pacing the flagway across from our front door. See if he follows us. I noticed I was being dogged on my way through town this morning, though once I hit the turnpike the rider turned back. Of course he would, because anyone could see I had not got Jaimie on the horse with me and I ain't had any time at all to take him off to the country so I would not be going to see him."

"And did no one follow Luke to Lady Farin's, my lord?"

"Luke says not. Says he sneaked out through the mews and over to Sutter's stables and no one noticed him at all."

"That's a piece of good news."

"Why?" asked Rossland, stopping in the midst of slipping into his greatcoat and staring at Martindale.

"Because you've hidden the tyke in Green Street and if they had followed Luke they might well have glimpsed Master Jaimie."

"Damnation! How do you know that Jaimie is in Green Street?"

"I—we—Battlesby, my lord."

The Guards' Club, which had been established through the combined efforts of Prinny and Wellesley for the benefit of those Foot Guards returning from the Peninsula, stood in St. James's Street directly across from White's. Rossland's entrance into it upon Lord Goodacre's arm was met at first with stares of wonder, and moments later by a spontaneous round of applause from those officers and gentlemen present in the front parlor.

Neville Terwilliger glanced curiously toward the major as the applause dwindled and several of the officers arose and stalked forward to shake Rossland's hand.

"I told you how it would be, Terwilliger," grinned Gaffney. "These men do not disdain our devilish lord. They know the man, most of them, better than any of your bucks and dandies and Corinthians ever will. They marched with him down the most harrowing pathways in all the world—pathways littered with bodies and drenched in blood. All of Polite Society might choose to forget the years of Rossland's heroism, but the gentlemen who fought beside him never will."

"He truly was a hero?" Terwilliger asked with wide eyes.

"Indeed. Fought first at Alexandria in '01. Lad of seventeen then and a regular Turk upon the battlefield even at so young an age. Boy was born to soldiering. His father refused to buy him a commission, so he took the King's coin and earned every penny of his wages and more, you may believe me. Worth fourteen men upon the field, his mates always said. And you could count on it that if he stood beside you, you would never fall undefended in battle. I did not meet up with the nodcock until he carried me off the field at Talavera in '09. He had made captain, by then. Promoted in the field time and time again."

"Carried you off the field, sir?"

"Saved my neck, Terwilliger. I would be neatly packed away

underground today if he had chosen to ignore me, I shall tell you that. And there's many a man here would say the same if you should ask. We shall need to extricate him from his fellow soldiers, though, if we are to get anything settled amongst us."

The crowd of men surrounding Rossland and Lord Goodacre had swelled from the first few officers to everyone within reach of the word that Captain Brumfield had finally found his way to the club and Gaffney had the devil of a time even to get close to the pair he sought. In the end he solved his dilemma by simply reaching in, grabbing a fistful of the sleeve of Rossland's coat and giving a yank. The yank set the earl off balance and he stumbled from the midst of his mates directly into Gaffney's waiting arms. Lord Goodacre followed, laughing.

"I have bespoken us one of the back parlors for the evening," Gaffney murmured in Rossland's ear. "We can be private there. But I rather think you shall be forced to have a few drinks with these fellows once we are out in the open again, my dear Captain Brumfield. They will not let you walk out on them without at least that much. You will not particularly mind that, will you?"

"I never thought," muttered the earl, his ears grown red with embarrassment. "I never thought they would take the least notice. Why, by all rights, they ought not even to remember me."

"Not remember you? Are you mad, Rossland? There are men here who would now be lying in unmarked graves if you had not fought beside 'em. They are your mates and will remain your mates no matter how deeply you get into the briars or what the gabblemongers say about you. These gentlemen will believe in you no matter what you are accused of doing."

"Like you," mumbled Rossland with unusual diffidence.

"Like me," confirmed Gaffney, urging him into the parlor that had been reserved for them. "Terwilliger, close the door behind you, lad. Lord Goodacre, there are brandy and glasses on that table. Pour us all some, will you not?"

"Charlie," mumbled Rossland, his ears still burning. "Call him Lord Charlie, Major. It makes him crazy."

"I did not come here to make Lord Goodacre crazy," replied Gaffney, seizing the earl's walking stick and pushing Rossland down into a solid and well-cushioned armchair. "What kind of bizarre rig-out is that you are wearing?"

"He thinks to make people suppose him conscience-stricken and ready to end it all for having shot that Pimberley woman," grinned Lord Goodacre, pouring the brandy and handing snifters of it to the other gentlemen.

"But he did not shoot the Pimberley woman," Gaffney replied, bewildered.

"Well, I know that. But the gabblemongers will have it that he did and that he is on the verge of being arrested for it, too."

"Ho! I should like to see the day," grinned Gaffney. "And do they also expect that Rossland will go quietly to Newgate on the constable's arm, eh?"

"No, they do not!" exclaimed Rossland. "And if the two of you do not cease speaking of me as if I am not here, I shall—"

"What?" asked Gaffney and Lord Goodacre in unison.

"Knock you both in the head and go join the lads."

"Hear, hear," murmured Terwilliger.

"Yes, but why *do* you insist upon providing grist for the rumor mill, Chad?" asked Gaffney, lowering himself into a chair.

"Because he thinks it is funny," declared Goodacre.

"I do not."

"You do. If they ceased to gabble your name about, you would rush to do something to make them start again. You take great pleasure in it."

"Well, it is rather amusing, Charlie," conceded Rossland with a most engaging grin. "It was hilarious, in fact, when the twits would have it that I was seducing Mary behind your back."

"Lord, save me," sighed Gaffney. "I missed that one."

"Well, it was short-lived," explained Goodacre. " 'Twas followed the very next day by his abduction of the little cyprian."

"That is why I missed it," nodded Gaffney. "I was extremely busy that evening. I have gone back to Bennett Street by the way, Rossland, and pilfered the late Grace Pimberley's entire packet of documents. Apparently someone had searched the place for it before me—but I knew where to look. They did not."

"Are you certain?" asked the earl, suddenly serious. "They might easily have substituted false documents to send you off in the wrong direction."

"No. No one had the least idea that the Foreign Office was investigating Mrs. Pimberley, much less that I was inside the house and had discovered her papers. No, the documents are legitimate and several of them are frightening. Terwilliger, hand the packet to His Lordship and let him read what has been going forward. And I'll thank you, Rossland, to keep a rein on your temper. The Foreign Office as well as yourself is involved in this, and the steps to be taken are not up to you alone."

Rossland opened the oilskin-wrapped packet and perused the documents one by one, handing each when he had done with it to Lord Goodacre who read it in turn. Gaffney and Terwilliger merely sipped at their brandies and watched as the faces of both lords grew puzzled, then angry, then totally perplexed. "Well, I know Langly is a dead man," growled Rossland once he had gathered up the documents and replaced them, "but I am damned if I understand at all what their whole plan might be. I thought for the longest time that all anyone would wish to do would be to sell Jaimie to Napoleon, but that ain't it, is it?"

"No," mumbled Gaffney, pouring more brandy all around. "There is a great deal more going on in those documents than an effort to sell the boy to the Eagle would require."

"But what?" queried Lord Goodacre. "Is there some other government involved? It sounds as if another government is involved in the thing. And what is all this talk about Russian peasants and Austria and propaganda decrees and annexation policies?"

"I have not the faintest idea," drawled Gaffney. "Well, no, that is not exactly the truth—I do have some idea but I will need more information before I will feel safe in expressing my opinion. That is why I have made an appointment with Castlereagh for Thursday evening. Lord March and your uncle,

Winecoff, will be in attendance as well, Rossland. I expect amongst the three of them, they will have gathered the details necessary to divine what is going on with your nephew though they probably are not aware of it. I must only prove adept at getting the information out of them."

"Well, you shall need to do it without bringing Jaimie into the thing," Rossland declared. "I willn't have the government involved in my personal affairs and that's a fact."

Gaffney stared at the earl in disbelief. "Keep the lad out of it? But this ruckus is all centered around your nephew, Rossland. It can no longer be considered a personal affair."

"It is a very personal affair and a secret one besides."

"But surely your uncle already knows."

"No. Not a thing. The duke is as much in the dark as the rest of society. Only Charlie and myself and Liza and my staff— and now you and Terwilliger know the truth of it. At least, we are the only ones remaining alive who know the truth."

"And do not forget these villains, Chad. They know," added Goodacre with a frown. "Perhaps it would be best if—"

"No! No one else is to be made privy to it! I took a vow to protect them. A blood oath! And part of protecting them is to keep the thing from becoming common knowledge!"

"Very well," nodded Gaffney, tucking the packet back into his pocket. "Do not work yourself up into an apoplexy, Rossland. I shall refrain from any mention of your nephew on Thursday evening, I assure you. But you must do me a favor in return."

"What sort of favor?"

"You must refrain from murdering Lord Langly until I have spoken with Castlereagh."

"I will try," muttered Rossland, rising.

"You must do more than try, Rossland. You must not murder the man nor so much as force a quarrel upon him until I have got the information we need."

"I will try," grumbled the earl. "That is the best I can say, Gaffney. I will try my damndest not to strangle the man the moment I see him or not to shoot the scoundrel on sight, but

I cannot give you my word on it. I am not so certain I shall succeed in any attempt to restrain myself."

The four gentlemen wandered back into the front parlor where Rossland was immediately pounced upon by a group of soldiers who had been gathering steadily in anticipation of welcoming the captain back into their fold. Within moments wine flowed freely and toasts were offered and drunk one after another after another. Not one of the men who had fought by Rossland's side through the bitterest, grimiest, grimmest war of two centuries was to be denied his opportunity to express his appreciation to a comrade-in-arms whose courage and steadfastness and savvy had saved many of them, their brothers and friends from death time and time again. "To The Devil's Delight!" roared one Lieutenant Bonderly when at last his turn to toast the earl rolled around. "We don't care what the rumormongers say, we know why the devil is delighted with 'im and it has to do with the number of Frogs he sent to Hades!"

By the time every soldier who wished to do so had toasted Rossland, the earl was more than chirping merry. His frustration over Langly had fled. His embarrassment at being the center of attention had fled. All his inhibitions had fled. And his common sense had fled as well. Laughing, Gaffney and Terwilliger tossed Rossland up beside Lord Goodacre on the box of Goodacre's curricle and waved as the two tipsy gentlemen departed for home.

"No," Goodacre chuckled. "I am taking you straight to Rossland House, Chad. I should never forgive myself if I set you down anywhere but on your own front stoop."

"But I do not wish to go home, Charlie. There is something I mean to do, and this is the perfect time to do it."

"You promised not to kill Langly."

"No, it ain't that. It is something—something a deal more important. Stop this blasted coach and put me down."

"It's a curricle not a coach and I am not stopping until I have got you home."

"But you must, Charles. Truly you must. I have—I need— turn here, Charlie, and draw up at the next corner."

Lord Goodacre eyed his passenger speculatively. "That is Green Street," he advised with a hint of curiosity in his voice. "Why should I set you down in Green Street?"

"Because, Charles, I am asking you to do so. And if you willn't do it, I shall jump."

"If you jump, you will kill yourself."

"Yes, and you do not wish to be responsible for such a thing, do you? Your conscience will prick you no end."

"You willn't jump," murmured Lord Goodacre. "You're not so cork-brained as that. No, wait!" he roared as Rossland took his cane in hand and stood up, nearly tipping head first onto the cobbles. "I take it back. You are that cork-brained. Just sit, will you. Sit down! I shall pull up under that light and help you down. But I feel I ought to warn you, Chad. You are outrageously foxed and like to be courting disaster."

"No," grinned Rossland engagingly, regaining his seat. "It ain't disaster I am courting, Charlie. It is someone entirely different."

Fourteen

Minerva paced the length and width of her bedchamber until the small hours of the morning. Her mind was awhirl. Lord Rossland loved a madwoman. Not only loved her, but was willing to die for her. No, he was not willing to die for her, she amended rapidly, because the question of his dying did not come into it. It most certainly did not come into it! But it did, and she knew it did, and the more she protested the fact, the more significant the death of Grace Pimberley became in her mind. "If they would kill one of their own," she mumbled. "If they would kill one of their own, surely Lord Rossland is not safe from them."

Of course none of it made the least bit of sense. Why should kidnappers murder Lord Rossland in order to reclaim the boy? From whom would they extort funds if the earl were dead? From Elizabeth? Well, that would get them absolutely nothing. From the next earl? Who would be the next earl? Did Lord Rossland have an heir? And why would the heir wish to preserve little Jaimie from harm when little Jaimie, should he ever return, would disinherit him? No, that was unfair. Lord Rossland, himself, would not trade Jaimie's life for the earldom and it was unjust to assume that any other member of his family might do so. But the next heir, whoever he might be, was not in love with Elizabeth and so had not as much incentive to save the child as did His Lordship.

"How can he be in love with her?" Minerva sighed into the night. "How can he? She is not even sensible and she acts like a child and she was his brother's wife! He can never marry her.

It is unlawful for him to marry her." But she takes his breath away, Minerva thought then and a tear formed in the corner of her eye. That is exactly what Aunt Letty said. Liza takes his breath away. And I, of course, do not.

Minerva ceased her pacing and sat down sober-faced upon the bed. I have fallen in love with the Earl of Rossland, she admitted sadly to herself. Well, with the person everyone thinks to be the Earl of Rossland, which he is not, because little Jaimie is the true earl. How could I? How could I possibly have done such a thing? I promised myself never to fall in love again! Well, so much for my ability to keep promises!

Minerva, angry tears now streaming down her cheeks, was just about to throw herself upon the bed and beat her fists against the counterpane when the queerest sound broke through her tears. She listened carefully, sniffing. The sound came again.

"W-what was that?" she asked in a confused whisper. The clattering and clacking echoed through her room once more and she turned toward the source of it. Why for goodness sake! Something was spraying against her window. Had it come on to rain? She did not think so. It had not looked at all like rain when Lord Rossland had bid her goodnight at the front door. In fact, a three-quarter moon had been rising without a cloud anywhere in sight. With a disturbed frown gathering between her brows, Minerva secured her wrapper more tightly 'round her, wiped her tears away with her little lace handkerchief and went to discover just what was going on. Cautiously she tugged one of the heavy brocade draperies aside and peeped out into the moonlight. What she saw made her gasp. Quickly she undid the casement latch and pushed her window outward.

"Thank goodness," whispered Rossland, balanced precariously upon a most unsteady tower of pails and buckets and odd scraps of lumber. "I thought I might need to toss pebbles forever."

"Get down at once," hissed Minerva though she could not keep a bit of laughter from her voice. Obviously His Lordship had raided the gardener's shed to build his perch and done a remarkable job of it, but the little piece of architecture wobbled and lurched and tottered threateningly. And how he had ever gotten to the top of it with his walking stick, well! "Get down, my lord! You will break your neck!"

"Undoubtedly," replied the earl, "but I could not throw high enough to reach your casement from the ground."

"You have reached my casement. Now climb down immediately!"

"Yes, I will, but will you come to the back door? I must speak with you, sweetling. Truly I must."

"Yes," agreed Minerva, not thinking anything odd about such a request or the manner in which it was delivered, which she might have done if one of the pails had not at that very moment clumped to the ground endangering Lord Rossland's precarious perch. "*Can* you climb down?" she asked worriedly.

"Well of course I can," answered Rossland disgustedly. "I ain't some namby-pamby fop don't know how to—" The remainder of his sentence was buried beneath the complete collapse of his randomly erected platform. Minerva watched between horror and laughter as his arms flailed, his feet sought purchase, and in a moment he hit the ground with a solid thump.

"Do not move!" she hissed. "Stay right where you are." And with one last glance over her shoulder, she let the drapery fall back into place, took one of her candles, and hurried with it from her chamber. She rushed down the servants' staircase to the ground floor and traversed the ground floor corridor at an amazing speed until she reached the kitchen door. It took a moment to set her candle aside, discover the bolt and throw it open, but then she was out into the moonlight and coming to a halt beside a Rossland who was part groaning, part laughing as he stood leaning heavily upon his walking stick and attempting to brush at the backside of his breeches.

"Good evening, Miss Potts," he said, grinning down at her engagingly. "Very kind of you to come to my assistance. Might we adjourn to your kitchen table, do you think?"

"Are you all right? You have not broken anything?"

"Nothing that I know of, sweetling, though I shall wish for a pillow every time I sit for at least a week." With unthinking ease Rossland's arm went about Minerva's shoulders and he ushered her back toward the kitchen door. "You are cold already, I think," he drawled. "Cannot have you standing about in the night air in such a flimsy wrapper even if it is most fetching."

Fetching, for a certainty, was not the first word that had occurred to Rossland. Alluring, bewitching and seductive had all mounted to his lips, but he had thought better than to voice any of those. Miss Potts was a proper and gently bred young woman and he did not wish to frighten the girl after all.

"I have just now quit the Guards' Club and I think that you and I must have a bit of conversation, sweetling," he added as he tugged open the kitchen door and escorted her through it. "You do not mind if we have a bit of conversation, do you?" He noted the lit candle upon a table near the door and let go Minerva's shoulders to pick it up and light their way.

"No, my lord, I do not mind in the least," Minerva assured him, "but I cannot think what can be so very important that we must come together to converse about it at this hour. It is the middle of the night, my lord."

"No, it is the top of the morning, sweetling, but since I am awake and you are awake—" grinned Rossland placing the candle upon the table and pulling out one of the chairs for her. "Since we are both awake, a bit of plain speech might be in order between us." He settled himself into a chair and reaching across the table, took her hands into his own. "I thank you, Miss Potts, with all my heart, for accompanying the ducklings to Skylark. You were an angel to do it. Yes, and an angel not to look down your nose at Liza, too."

"Wait. How did you know I was awake?" queried Minerva, decidedly aware of the touch of his ungloved hands upon her own but not at all inclined to withdraw them from his grasp. "I might well have been fast asleep. I ought to have been fast asleep."

"Were you?"

"No, but—"

"Well, it does not signify in the least anyway, because I had enough pebbles stuffed into my pockets to keep throwing right up until daybreak. I would have awakened you eventually. I had to see you, Minerva. I could not help myself."

It was the very first time that she had heard her Christian name upon his lips and it sent a tiny shiver through her.

"Minerva? What is it, sweetling? You are exhausted, ain't you? It is unforgivable of me to drag you from your chambers at such an hour, and for no better reason than the opportunity to hold your hands across a kitchen table and speak my mind."

"W-what?"

"Well, I did want to thank you for all you have done and I started to do it, too, did I not? Yes, I did. But that could well have waited until morning. The truth is, sweetling, I hoped if I was brash enough to throw pebbles at your window, you might let me inside and we might at last be alone together and I could say everything I wish to say, though quite probably I will not say any of it exactly right."

"You wanted to be alone with me?" asked Minerva wide-eyed.

"Yes, precisely. I wanted to be alone with you, and hold your hands and kiss you."

"My lord!"

"There, you see. I knew I should not be capable of saying it exactly right. I am making a mull of it, ain't I? But that is only because I am the slightest bit foxed, Minerva. I did not get chirping merry intentionally, mind you. And I had every intention of speaking to you before I took even the very first drink. Martindale will attest to that if you will only ask him. I spoke to him of it before I ever went out. I remember doing so. Distinctly. I could not get you out of my mind, you see, sweetling. Not for all the ride home from Skylark, nor through all the time I spent discussing things with Charlie and Gaffney and Terwilliger, nor through all the toasts I was forced to share with my comrades afterward. Each time I raised my glass, my dearest girl, I could think of no one but you. Even when I slipped getting down off the box of Charlie's curricle at the corner, I did not feel anything at all except the greatest desire to see you again."

"You slipped?"

"Came slam up against a lamppost."

"Gracious," exclaimed Minerva softly, "And you hit your head, did you not? And that is what has brought all this about."

"N-no," replied Rossland in a tone between laughter and exasperation. "I hit my shoulder, you minx. My head is perfectly sound. Now please do cease changing the subject. I am attempting to tell you that I love you, Minerva."

"But you cannot!" Minerva could feel her heart beating wildly while suspended somewhere between Heaven and Hades. "You love Elizabeth, my lord! Oh, you are more than slightly foxed! That is what has brought all this about. Do not say another word, my lord. I know it is Elizabeth you love and not myself. My Aunt Letitia told me as much on our drive home. She said—she said—that Liza takes your breath away and always has done so."

Rossland's dark eyes stared pensively at Minerva's nervously darting blue ones.

"It is true," Minerva insisted. "Why, I could see for myself that she did so. And Aunt Letitia said that even at your brother's wedding she could tell—when you looked at—at—Elizabeth—Aunt Letitia is no fool, my lord. She knows—"

"Indeed," nodded Rossland, grinning. "Your Aunt Letty is correct as usual. Elizabeth does now and always has taken my breath away. But that is neither here nor there, sweetling. A woman may take a man's breath away without his falling in love with her. Letty Lade takes my breath away as well—every time I see her upon a box driving a four-horse-hitch—but I ain't in love with Letty Lade any more than I am with Liza. It is you I am in love with, sweetling."

Rossland stood and made his way carefully around the table. He tugged Minerva gently from her chair and up into his arms and kissed her most tenderly, barely touching his lips to hers. And then, with a sigh, he kissed her again with a fire that set her whole self to burning. And just as she thought she would literally melt from the sheer passion of it, he pulled away. But in an instant his lips were back again, nibbling at her own teasingly. "As I was saying," he whispered in her ear once he had ceased to kiss her and had tucked her safely against his breast. "Liza and Letty both take my breath away, Minerva, but you are the lady who has taken my heart."

He loved her! Lord Rossland loved her! No, *Chadwick* loved her! Minerva could not keep her heart from pounding or her head from spinning or a most unladylike bounce from out her step as she fairly skipped into Drury Lane Theater the following evening upon Lord Kensington's arm. She mounted one side of the elegant double staircase with bright eyes and glowing cheeks and a wide smile for everyone she met. She took her seat appreciatively in the marquis's box and thanked him very prettily for his kindness in inviting her Aunt Letty and herself. She even went so far in her happiness as to pat the back of Kensington's hand. Oh, it had been so romantic—Lord Rossland, his dark eyes seething with passion, declaring over and over that he was not in love with Liza, that he had never truly loved any woman, that his feelings for Minerva were rare and unique and unequaled. And he had kissed her again, too—a most wondrous, melting kiss that had come close to turning Minerva's mind to mush. She was indeed the happiest, most blessed woman in the entire world!

And it did not matter that Lord Rossland would no longer be an earl. He had not mentioned that fact, of course, but when he did she would make it clear to him that his loss of the title would make not the least difference. They would get by. If Aunt Letty was correct about the extent of his competence, why then, she, Minerva, would speak to her father about her dowry. "Papa is not a pauper, after all," she whispered to herself as she scanned the other boxes. "He can well afford to be more generous."

"Eh? What was that, Miss Potts?" Kensington queried beside her. "Who can afford to be more generous?"

"Oh!" she said, one lace-gloved hand going to her lips and her face flushing even more prettily. "I—I—was merely thinking that perhaps Angelica Deane's modiste might have been more generous with the bodice of her gown, my lord. I did not intend to speak aloud. I am so very sorry. Angel is just there, in the third tier of boxes and just to our right. Do you see? And, well, one cannot help but notice that the bodice of her gown is so, so, skimpy."

"Indeed," nodded Kensington. "Who is that with the young lady? Collingsworth, is it not?"

"Yes, my lord," agreed Minerva with a bright smile.

It is that smile, Kensington told himself, that sets my pulses racing. And her vivacity. And her great enthusiasm. And the extraordinary blue of her eyes this evening. "And she will grow out of this predilection of hers for defending Rossland," he mumbled to himself. "He will overstep the bounds sooner or later and she will see him as he truly is."

"Pardon, my lord?" asked Minerva with a most distracted fluttering of her eyelashes. "Who will be him as he truly is?"

"Ah, Mr. Macready, m'dear," sputtered the marquis. "William will portray Hamlet as ought to be done. Well, as I envision the poor, haunted prince to have truly been. Macready is not so stilted and prosy, you know, as Mr. Kemble."

There were five tiers of boxes in Drury Lane Theater and Minerva's gaze roamed excitedly over every one of them. Well, every one she could actually see. She had told Lord Rossland she would be attending this evening and surely, surely, he would be present as well. But she could not discover him anywhere. Perhaps, she thought, he is in the pit. And she leaned forward to look down over the rail at the noisy inhabitants of that notorious section of the theater. Yes, she thought, as a bout of fisticuffs broke out amongst the mayhem at the foot of the stage, that is precisely where Chadwick would choose to be. "In the very thick of it," she murmured, entranced.

"Yes," drawled Kensington, whom a startled Minerva discovered to be leaning over the rail right beside her, his quizzing glass to his eye, "I am growing sick of it as well. Really, there ought to be some way to keep those rapscallions in line. A thorough lack of breeding is what it is."

Minerva, nonplussed that she had spoken her thoughts aloud once again, gave thanks to a merciful God that she had been thoroughly misunderstood and settled back into her chair literally burning with embarrassment.

What a darling, thought Kensington, lowering his glass and settling back himself. *She is so very outspoken at times and yet the very nearness of me at the rail discomposes her. She is a sweet innocent, and so I shall inform my mama. I will brook no interference from that quarter. There is nothing at all that Mama can say that will deter me from pursuing this angel.*

Lady Letitia, having heard not a word either had spoken, noted Minerva's flush and the determined look in the marquis's eyes, and smiled fondly upon them. *Perhaps,* she thought as the play began, *Mina will become a marchioness after all. And I shall have Chadwick Brumfield to thank for it. Who could have guessed?*

Neville Terwilliger held the four matched bays in check with an iron hand. They were fresh and fretting for a run. Had he been an ordinary clerk and not the third son of the Duke of Stafford, he would have been deathly pale and screaming behind a runaway team by this time. But the Duke of Stafford had always been a doting, adoring, and coaching mad father and had seen that all of his sons had been raised to a proper knowledge of horses and teams. There was not a one of his boys, he often boasted, who could not handle a four-horse-hitch of prime goers no matter how sassy they got. Still, the evening was growing chill and an early fog was rolling in and Terwilliger wished mightily that Major Gaffney and Lord Goodacre would hurry. He was getting dashed impatient. "We have got to get to Rossland," he grumbled to himself, "or The Devil's Delight will cease waiting upon our convenience, seek out Langly and force a quarrel upon him."

"That he will, Neville." The voice so near him startled Terwilliger into giving a jerk on the reins. The horses shied. Major Gaffney, halfway up to the box, clutched desperately at the coach top as his feet lurched out from under him. Below him and to his left the door of the drag cracked like a pistol shot

against the side of the vehicle as it was jolted out of Lord Goodacre's grasp. Lord Goodacre, tottering half in and half out of
the drag gave a yelp and clung to the door frame.

"Are you all right, Goodacre?" Gaffney called down once
he had reestablished his footing and gained the box.

"Indeed," replied that gentleman, easing himself down
upon the banquette and pulling the door closed. "Where did
you learn to drive, Terwilliger? Been taking lessons from The
Devil's Delight have you?"

This comment sent puzzled glances between the two gentlemen upon the box but neither was willing to pry the meaning of it out of Lord Goodacre. "Good. We're off then,"
muttered Gaffney. "Spring 'em, Neville. We are to meet
Rossland in Catherine Street at the entrance to Drury Lane
and we dare not be late. I do not trust that nodcock to hold
his peace much longer now he knows who Uncle Thomas is.
And Castlereagh's information along with March's and Winecoff's makes it appear that the plot is thicker and a good deal
more far-reaching than I at first suspected. Astonishing scheme
if I am correct, Neville. And I am correct. I am certain of it.
But if Rossland confronts Langly, he will not come off alive. I
am certain of that as well. While he is taking aim at Lord Langly,
someone else will be taking aim at him."

Minerva had all but given up hope of discovering Lord
Rossland amongst the audience. Her smile dimmed a bit as
she decided that he had most likely not come after all. But
then, he was involved in the most dreadful situation and he
could not forever be setting things aside to reassure her that
she owned his heart. He had said so last night loudly and clearly
and undoubtedly he considered that should provide her ample
proof of his feelings. He was not some dandy, after all, who
had nothing better to do with his life than to stand before his
mirror for hours achieving the height of fashion to impress
her or to wander about beside her quoting poetry and offering
her Spanish coin. He had told her most emphatically last night

that he loved her and she had believed him with all her heart. She should certainly not require any further reassurance.

And that was why she was truly most surprised and delighted when, at the first pause in the performance, only moments after the marquis had gone off to procure the ladies a bit of refreshment, the Earl of Rossland appeared beside her and in all the glory of a golden waistcoat with crimson stars, he bowed over her hand and then slipped into Kensington's empty chair.

"Chadwick, what are you doing here?" croaked Lady Letitia from Minerva's other side. "Scat! Go away at once!"

"I will, Letty," nodded Rossland with that most engaging grin, the one that Mina found irresistible. "I have just come to say how do you do to Miss Potts and yourself."

"No, you have not," declared Lady Letitia with a sniff. "You have come to annoy Kensington and disrupt our evening and set everyone here to chattering."

"I ain't either!" declared Rossland emphatically, his hand possessing itself of Minerva's own well out of Lady Letitia's sight. "I have come to say how do you do and that's all. How do you do, Miss Potts," he said then, softly, with the most saucy and tempestuous glow in his great dark eyes and a mischievous twitching at the corners of his mouth. "How do you do, Letitia," he added, his gaze never leaving Minerva's beaming face. "Are you enjoying the performance?"

"I was," responded Lady Letitia coldly. "Chadwick, if you are not gone from here before Kensington returns I shall push you over the railing the moment he enters this box."

"Oh, Aunt Letty!" exclaimed Minerva, her eyes alight with laughter. "You ought not to say such a terrible thing."

"I must say it," growled that lady. "I cannot help myself."

"No, of course you cannot, Letitia," responded Rossland with a knowing nod of his head. "I do believe you were born to threaten me, Letitia, and I to discover hundreds of ways to make you do it." Rossland's knee came gently up against Minerva's and she thought for a brief moment, as he determinedly prodded her with it, that she was going to burst into giggles, but she controlled herself admirably.

"Do you not like Mr. Macready's interpretation of Hamlet,

my lord?" asked Minerva with a decided twinkle in her eyes. "I find it most entertaining."

"Really?" queried Rossland while his thumb slowly and gently massaged the back of Minerva's hand. "I am afraid I was not actually paying attention to the thing."

"Of course not," scoffed Lady Letitia. "It is because you are a barbarian, Chadwick. You have not the least appreciation for the finer things in life. You did never come here to view the play at all but to carouse in the pit with all the other barbarians."

"Not carouse, Letitia," protested Rossland.

"Carouse. And may I inquire," Lady Letitia added in chilling tones, "what makes you think that I shall allow you to go on holding my niece's hand in that most unfortunate manner?"

The earl's hand, after one last, quick squeeze, found its way into his own lap. "I assure you, Letitia, I was not carousing in the pit at all. I simply wandered in to see could I discover where you were sitting and then some of the lads began quizzing me about Mitzie and I took exception to it and—"

"And who is Mitzie?"

"I am certain you know, Letitia. She is the young woman I stole from Mrs. Pimberley's brothel."

"Chadwick! *Not* in the presence of my niece!"

"What? Not what?"

"A young lady does *not* wish to hear even the mention of such establishments."

"She don't?"

"No, she does not! Oh," scowled Lady Letitia, "how inconsiderate of your mother to have died, Chadwick! *She* would have seen to it that you were raised with at least a modicum of propriety. Cameron never ran about like a wild Indian. He had to toe the line, let me tell you. That is why Cameron had *breeding.*"

Minerva, watching a sudden discomfiture appear upon Rossland's handsome countenance, had all she could do to keep from laughing aloud. "Certainly, Aunt Letitia," she offered quietly, "Lord Rossland has breeding as well."

"None," declared her aunt roundly.

Rossland's mouth opened and closed and opened again. A breathless sputtering emerged from somewhere deep in his throat and then a soft sigh. "Well, perhaps I ain't got breeding precisely, Letitia," he murmured at last, "but I do have—"

"What?" asked Lady Letitia horribly.

"Sensibilities?"

"You? Chadwick, please!"

"Pride?"

"Not a shred of it."

"Well, but—"

"I will tell you what you do have, Chadwick," offered Lady Letitia regally, taking pity upon the gentleman.

"What?"

"You have a good heart. From the moment you began to toddle about, that much was evident—and it is the only reason I allow Minerva to have anything at all to do with you!"

"There you are," sighed a breathless voice from the back of the box. "We expected to find you in front of the theater. Good evening, Lady Letitia, Miss Potts," added Lord Goodacre with a brief bow. "You have no idea how upset Gaffney was when you were not there, Chad. He thought you had gone off to—"

"Is it half-past ten already?" interrupted Rossland with a speaking look. "I am sorry, Charlie. I expect my watch is quite wrong," he added, rising and withdrawing that article from his waistcoat pocket. He gazed at it a moment, then replaced it and took Minerva's hand into his own placing a kiss upon the back of it and then clasping it tightly for a moment.

What in the world? thought Minerva as she felt a piece of paper slide between their two palms. As he released her, the paper slipped into her own hand and she held it silently as Rossland made his farewells to Lady Letitia and then departed with Lord Goodacre.

Fifteen

"But do you have the least idea what the man looks like?" asked Gaffney sitting across from Goodacre and Rossland inside the coach as Terwilliger tooled the team in the direction of St. James's Street.

"None," sighed Rossland. "Unless he looks a great deal like Armand. But that ain't necessarily so because they were merely half-brothers."

"Then Girard did speak of the man?"

"Not often. Once in a while. Are you certain he is in London? How could he be?"

"Came across with one of the free traders I expect," grumbled Gaffney. "At any rate, word is rife that Napoleon's agents are on the lookout for him and that their eyes and ears are currently trained on London. I should never have made the connection, of course, if you had not confided in me about your nephew. Currently our government thinks the Eagle merely in search of a most annoying emigré. But with all I now know added to Castlereagh's information at the Foreign Office—well, it suggests that others are only awaiting this scoundrel's return with your nephew to put their most nefarious plan into action. 'Tis the only explanation for the increased propaganda against Napoleon across the French countryside. Already hordes of French peasants are speaking of General Dumouriez's glorious return."

"Yes, well, he ain't going to return and that's a fact," frowned Rossland.

"Well, but he might, Chad," sighed Goodacre. "Castlereagh says that even King Louis has heard of it and taken heart and

March says the same rumors are strong along the Austrian border."

"That makes not the least a bit of difference, Charlie, because Dumouriez ain't in Austria."

"He is not?" Gaffney's eyebrows nearly flew to the edge of his hairline. "But Austria is precisely where everyone thinks he is. He defected to Austria way back in '93 and there has been no information regarding his movements since. Everyone simply assumed, you know, that he had settled there. Are you certain, Rossland? He is not in Austria?"

"No, he ain't. And do not ask me where he is because I am *not* going to tell you that. I have told you too much already. And as for this great conspiracy of shadowmen you and Charlie have invented, Gaffney, I begin to believe that I am not the only one with windmills in my head. Grace Pimberley and Langly kidnapped Jaimie, possibly with Paul Girard's aid, for someone must have revealed the boy's parentage—though how he came to know of it, I cannot guess. But the rest is balderdash. They planned to bleed me dry and perhaps sell the boy to Napoleon, but that is all."

"No, it is not all," growled Gaffney. "They may have been thinking to hand him over to that madman, but then they came up with an even better plan. A plan to give them unlimited power over the fate of the Continent."

"It is all in your vivid imagination," scoffed Rossland. "Or you are making it up, thinking it will keep me from calling Langly out."

"You cannot call Langly out!" shouted Gaffney in exasperation. "Uncle Thomas or no Uncle Thomas, I will not let you do it!"

"You cannot call Langly out, Chad," protested Goodacre a bit less violently. "He's a bang-up marksman and you are—"

"What, Charlie? I am what? A cripple?"

"No, that is not what I meant, but—"

"I wounded Killibrew neatly, Charlie, and I can outshoot Langly as well, balancing with a walking stick or not. And you, Major, have nothing whatsoever to say about it."

"You meet Langly, Chad, and you will be dead the moment you reach the field if not before," growled Gaffney. "Langly

and Girard have already proved they are murderers and they
will think nothing of murdering you. There will be no duel. If
you should make it as far as the dueling ground alive, Langly
will face you and Girard shoot you in the back. Yes, and shoot
your seconds as well," he added with a scowl at Goodacre, "if
it comes to that."

Rossland's face took on a most absorbed expression in the
flickering light of the street lamps. "So it would help, would
it not, if you knew what Paul Girard looked like?"

"Immensely," sighed Gaffney, relieved to think he had made
his point with Rossland and put all thoughts of duelling out
of that gentleman's mind.

"Then tell Terwilliger to take Charlie home and then direct
his team toward the turnpike."

"Oh, no!" cried Lord Goodacre. "I am not going home and
missing everything!"

"But Charles, you cannot possibly stay out all night. The
rumormongers will have it that you have installed some lady-
bird in a secret love nest and deserted Mary for the chit. And
Mary will be in tears for believing it, too."

"Then I shall stop for a moment and explain that I am off
with you and Gaffney on a secret mission," Lord Goodacre
mused. "And I shall warn her she is not to speak of it no matter
what. That will keep things straight between us. We are going
to Skylark, ain't we?" he asked as an afterthought.

"Yes. It is possible Liza has a miniature there of Armand and
Paul together. It will be rather dated, but it might serve to give
us some idea of the man we seek."

A most beguiled Marquis of Kensington escorted Minerva
and Lady Letitia to their door with a benign smile upon his
handsome face. He bid them good evening and handed them
most charmingly into Battlesby's care.

"Oh, he is definitely captivated by you," whispered Lady
Letitia as the door closed behind him. "You may have yourself
a marquis, I think, if you so desire. Minerva, whatever are you
doing?" she asked distracted from her pleasant expectations
by her niece's fumbling with her reticule.

"I am looking for a note," replied Minerva, searching through the contents of her gold net bag. "It is in here somewhere. I know it is. Oh, good, I have found it."

"A note? From whom? How did you come by it?"

Minerva shrugged her cloak into Battlesby's waiting hands and unfolded the paper Rossland had passed to her. She squinted at it in a most unladylike manner, attempting to read it in the dim light of the hall.

"Minerva, tell me this instant where that paper came from and what it says," demanded Lady Letitia.

"It—it says—I love you," said Mina on a little gasp.

"It says what?"

"I love you," repeated Minerva. "Now why would he write just that? I already know that he loves me."

Battlesby's lips quivered just the tiniest bit as he handed the ladies' cloaks to a waiting footman.

"I expect it is too much to hope that it was Lord Kensington passed you that note," grumbled Lady Letitia grimly.

"I already know that he loves me," Minerva mused tenderly. "Does he think that perhaps I doubt him? No, of course he does not. It is merely an attempt to be romantical."

"It is from that rascal Chadwick, ain't it?" grumped Lady Letitia. "I will thank you, Battlesby, to keep a sober look upon your countenance. I know you are prejudiced in that jackanapes's favor and I do not forever wish to be reminded of it!"

"Yes, madam," intoned Battlesby soberly. "Is there anything further you require this evening?"

"Nothing. Go away!"

"Yes, madam."

Lady Letitia, with a grim visage, shooed Mina ahead of her up the staircase all the way to the second floor. She then followed her niece into her bedchamber, sent the abigail scurrying and plopped down into an armchair beside the vanity. "Be seated if you please, Miss," she instructed, pointing to the vanity bench. "And do cease looking like a moonstruck calf."

"Oh, I am sorry, Aunt Letitia. Do I? Look like a moonstruck calf, I mean? I certainly do not intend to do so."

"Well, you do. That note *is* from Chadwick, is it not?"

"Yes, Aunt Letitia," nodded Minerva. "And I am sorry to

have disturbed you with it, but I could not wait a moment longer to read the thing."

"No, well, is that all it says? I love you?"

"Yes, Aunt."

"And may I ask—have you any feelings for Chadwick at all?"

"Oh, yes, Aunt Letitia. I love him dearly."

"Are you positive, Minerva? You barely know the villain."

"Oh, but I do know him, Aunt, and I have grown most fond of him. Indeed, I have."

"How?" asked Lady Letitia. "Why? You have driven with the wretch only once and our visit to Skylark was certainly not designed to endear him to you. And you have spoken only briefly in public and he visited here only twice—the last time with those confounded ducklings. I cannot see when you have had time to come to love him!"

"Well—well—"

"I can perfectly understand how he might have gained your sympathies, and certainly he is handsome in a rakish sort of way, but falling in love with someone requires much more than that."

"Well, there was a bit more than that," blushed Minerva.

"Tarnation! I should have known! That wretched boy has got you involved in his mischief, has he not? And all the time cajoling me with stories of his little lost nephew and his wish to redeem himself with society! I *will* have his guts for garters the very first thing tomorrow. You see if I don't! You are gone completely mad, Minerva, to let that brat bewitch you. And you were always such a pretty-behaved young lady. You will tell me, Miss, exactly what has been going on. And I will abide no roundaboutation!"

Minerva smoothed the sapphire silk of her gown across her lap and gazed thoughtfully at the tips of her matching slippers. She would need to tell her aunt something. But what? What could she say to explain how she had come to give her heart to the errant earl? She could not possibly tell her Aunt Letty the truth. Or could she?

"Yes," sighed Letitia Farin into the silence. "You may tell me the truth, Mina."

Minerva looked up, startled.

"Anyone of my considerable age knows what it is that you are pondering," offered Lady Letitia in an unusually quiet voice. "But you have never been afraid to trust in me, Mina, curmudgeon though I am, and I will not have you fear to trust in me now. Whatever Chadwick has been doing behind my back, it is best to bring it out into the open at this juncture because a barbarian like Chadwick does not write notes that simply say, I love you, unless he is in very deep waters indeed."

"In deep waters, Aunt?"

"Precisely. A note like that is what the whelp would write, say, before he set out to do something very dangerous from which he might not return."

"Oh, no!"

"Indeed. Chadwick said I love you, Letty, once to me, you know. Just that. And two hours later his papa came searching for him and we looked everywhere for the brat. We discovered him four hours later at the bottom of a gully with his leg broken. He had seen his big brother jump across that gully, you see, and intended to do the same, but he did not quite make it."

"And he said I love you because—"

"Because he knew that he might not make it and he wanted me to know that he did love me, just in case he died."

"But he is not at all a little boy anymore, Aunt Letty," whispered Minerva, a sudden fear gripping her heart.

"Says you," replied her aunt with a shake of her head. "Men always have a bit of a boy lurking within them somewhere. And the boy in Chadwick, my dear, pops out at every opportunity. Very well, Minerva, I have prepared myself for the worst. I have not given up all thoughts of a marchioness in the family or even a wife of a well-to-do vicar—I refer, of course, to the Reverend Mr. George. No, I refuse to abandon my hopes for you, but if Chadwick is in deep waters I will not turn my back upon him. It is most likely that once he comes about I shall rake his hair with a hoe for having the audacity to seek you out behind my back, but for now, I shall control my temper. You must trust me, Mina, and tell me all that has gone on. Because if Chadwick has gone off and put himself in mortal danger, I shall know better what he may be about and how to pull his fat from the fire than you, my dear."

Lord Whithall was not at all pleased as he made his way up Pall Mall toward the Duke of Winecoff's residence. As if it were not maddening enough to have Minerva Potts's name constantly linked to Rossland's by the gossipmongers, now they would be linking her to that ass, Kensington. What on earth had possessed Kensington to make a move on the chit? Oh, he had seen them both clearly enough at Drury Lane making cozy conversation. Yes, and he had seen Rossland wander into the box and wander out again before Kensington should discover him, too. Kensington! Devil take the man! Minerva was a good sight beneath the marquis's touch and he had not the least business to be badgering the girl.

The truth was that Whithall still did not understand what had got Minerva's back up. He had planned a rosy future in that young woman's company and he could not comprehend why the few words she had overheard him speak to Redfield had brought that future crashing down around his ears. "But she will regret it," he whispered to himself, stuffing his hands into his pockets as he strolled. "Once our plan is back in working order and Rossland is got rid of, Miss Minerva Potts will certainly regret having turned me away. I shall be a powerful man soon. More powerful than any earl or marquis, and then won't she come knocking around my door wishing for me to take her back in?" And perhaps I will, he mused. Perhaps I will do just that—though I shall see her punished first for embarrassing me no end by crying off without the least reason.

Mrs. Beaman, wrapped in a warm flannel dressing gown, her nightcap slightly askew, put the kettle on the fire and settled, sighing, into one of the chairs at the kitchen table. She had been amazed to awake to a pounding upon her door in the middle of the night, and somewhat terrified as well. People did not come knocking one up, after all, unless something fearful had happened. But then, of course, she had reminded herself that she now worked for Lord Rossland and that young gentleman did come pounding upon one's door in the middle of the night for the least reason in the world, though he had not done such a thing since she and her lady had abandoned Riddle and taken up residence in Skylark Cottage.

"Have you thought yet, Mrs. Beaman?" asked Rossland in an anxious voice from the doorway. "Might it be somewhere inside Riddle do you think? Or at one of the other houses?"

"No, no, there were only a few miniatures my lady brought with her, my lord, and we packed them all when we came to the cottage," replied Mrs. Beaman quietly. "There is the one of Her Ladyship's mama and papa that sits upon her nightstand and the one of the French gentleman with the dog, and the miniature of Master Jaimie which the master had done for her only last year."

"Yes, but this is of two gentlemen. It is only their faces and shoulders if I remember correctly."

"Oh," said Mrs. Beaman, straightening in her chair. "And one of the gentlemen had a moustache!"

"Yes, that's the one. You do remember."

"I remember, my lord, the moustache, but not where the miniature has gone."

"We have searched through every room, Chad, and cannot find it," offered Lord Goodacre, coming up behind the earl with a branch of candles in hand. "Though we did not go into Elizabeth's room, of course. You do not think we ought to wake her and ask if it is there?"

"No, no, 'tis not in my lady's chamber," mused Mrs. Beaman softly, "unless she has hidden it away amongst her things. But why would she do that?"

"Has she a special box somewhere?" asked Rossland, moving to the table and lowering himself into one of the chairs. "Or a secret drawer in her writing desk?"

"Mary keeps a miniature of her brother in her jewelry box," offered Goodacre, himself taking a seat. "Perhaps we ought to look in Liza's jewelry box."

"We shall have to wait until morning to do that," Rossland

sighed, "because I ain't waking Liza in the middle of the night."

A smile wreathed Mrs. Beaman's face at that. Here came His Lordship pounding upon the front door as if the world were about to end and not thinking once that such a racket might possibly awake anyone but herself. "I suspect, my lord," she said, "that my lady may be awake. I shall go and see, shall I?"

"Would you, Mrs. Beaman?"

"Indeed, my lord. The tea is ready to make, my lord, as soon as the kettle boils. You will do me the favor to set it brewing, will you not?" And with that she hurried off to Liza's chamber.

"Your man Maitland and I have got the team unhitched and tucked up in the stable, Rossland," announced Terwilliger, entering through the kitchen door and stamping the chill from his feet. "We had best rest 'em a space before we head back. Tremendous puppy he has with him in there. Said it belonged to Liza but that it could not remain in the house any longer. Said it broke too much. He also said that you had found it loose upon the street in London. I wonder, Rossland, if you might attempt to find another one? I should pay to have one for myself just like it. Part Irish wolfhound, I think. Wonderful animal. Where is the major? I thought he was with you."

"I thought he was with you," frowned Rossland.

"No. I mean, he was, right enough, but once we got the team unhitched he departed. I, ah, remained behind for a bit to play with the puppy."

"Non! Non! Non!" squealed a high-pitched voice from just beyond the kitchen window interrupting all conversation. Rossland sprang from his chair, grabbed his cane and rushed for the door with Goodacre and Terwilliger close on his heels. The earl snatched at the handle just as the door shot inward with considerable force and a veritable jumble of struggling humanity tumbled in upon him and sent him stumbling back into Goodacre and Terwilliger. All three of those gentlemen crashed noisily and most ungracefully to the hard flagstones of the kitchen floor.

"Non! You are—are—pig!" screamed the voice angrily. *"Arrêtez,* pig!"

Major Gaffney, his arms wrapped tightly around Elizabeth

who pummeled him with extreme vigor, swung both himself and his unwieldy bundle into the kitchen and kicked the door closed behind him. "Enough, you termagant," he chuckled. "I am bruised from head to toe already. You ought to be thanking me, vixen. Why anyone would think you wished to freeze to death out there in nothing but your nightrail."

"Liza," groaned Rossland from the floor, "cease and desist. Major Gaffney is my friend. He ain't going to hurt you."

"Wicky!" cried that lady ecstatically as she spied him tangled amongst the others on the kitchen floor. "Wicky! Wicky! Wicky!"

"Wicky?" laughed Gaffney. "Wicky? I say, what are you doing lounging about on the floor, Wicky? Is it some sort of new game?" And with that he released Liza and offered his hand to the earl. "I saw someone climbing down the trellis at the side of the cottage," he explained, tugging Rossland to his feet. "A more beautiful sight I have never seen, but I did think she ought not to be running about in the middle of the night in nothing but—what she has on at present. Terwilliger, hand me Rossland's stick and do stop milling about on the floor, you and Goodacre both. There is a lady present."

The lady had by this time thrown herself into Rossland's arms. "I think the Jacobins come pounding," she whispered loudly against his chest. "I think this one he is being Jacobin come to feed me to Madame Guillotine. He is not, Wicky?"

"No, he is not, my dear," Rossland assured her as Terwilliger and Goodacre disentangled themselves and achieved an upright position. "It was I pounding upon the door. And all these gentlemen are my friends, Liza."

"Oh! I am not then needing to escape."

"No, not needing to escape," drawled Rossland. "You are quite safe, my dear. Safe as houses."

"My lord! My lord!" cried Mrs. Beaman from the corridor. "She has gone! Her Ladyship is—oh."

"I wonder, Mrs. Beaman," mused Rossland, "if you would be kind enough to return upstairs and fetch Her Ladyship a warm wrapper—and some slippers," he added suddenly aware of Liza's bare feet.

"Indeed," agreed Gaffney who had moved to the fire and

snatched the boiling kettle from it. "You fetch her things, Mrs. Beaman, and I shall brew the tea, eh? Between us we shall warm the little lady up. Terwilliger, add some more wood to the fire. And Lord Goodacre, if you would be pleased to fetch another chair for the table—"

"I sit on Wicky," announced Liza loudly.

"You will sit beside Wicky," grinned Rossland.

"Non, on."

"No, beside."

"Non, between," offered Gaffney with a wide smile. "Between Wicky and the pig."

"Oh, monsieur," whispered Elizabeth, turning in Rossland's arms to stare guilelessly at the major with glorious emerald eyes. "I am most contrite being for calling you the pig. You are not the pig being."

"Then will you sit between myself and Wicky? It would please me no end, madame."

"Oui," nodded the lady grandly. "I will sitting between."

Thomas, Lord Langly joined Whithall in the night shadows behind Winecoff House with a nod and then scratched discreetly upon the kitchen door. It was opened to them almost immediately.

"Here in the kitchen being safe we are," murmured the Duke of Winecoff's chef. "All the staff are having retired for the night. The boy you are at last discovering?"

"No," drawled Langly, taking up a chair at the kitchen table. "We have not seen hide nor hair of the brat nor of that little wench His bloody Lordship stole from Grace either. I cannot at all guess where he might have hidden them. The two are together, I will lay you odds on that, Girard."

"Your men over Rossland House are keeping watch?"

"Indeed, and over this establishment and Lord Goodacre's as well," nodded Whithall. "And I have been making inquiries at the various boardinghouses and hostelries, but there is no word of the boy or the little cyprian. One would think they had fallen off the face of the earth."

"But there are not that many places for him to hide the

child," growled Langly. "We must only give the matter a bit more thought, Whithall. We know Rossland's reputation has come near to ostracizing him from the *ton* and though a number of people tolerate him for the Duchess of Winecoff's sake, he has not many friends who might be counted upon to give him aid. I have dispensed with Grace by the way, Girard, and I have arranged for Rossland to have an accident as well. He will never tell us what he has done with the lad, you know. Not if we were to chop his fingers off one by one. And he is dangerous beyond belief, so it will be better to dispose of him quickly. Several of my men followed him out of Drury Lane this evening and will take the first opportunity to rid us of his interference."

"Oui," nodded the chef. "It will not bring down upon us the suspicions?"

"No. It will appear an accident pure and simple."

"Bon. There can no more mistakes being, *mes amis.* Mistakes are being now a most deadly matter. You must think where at this Rossland have hide the boy. You must think most heartily. And of everywhere you think, you must search. I am clearing at last the way to carry *le petit Jaimie* around the Peninsula and thence to my chateau where remain he shall throughout our negotiations. Dumouriez coming forward will with great haste once word is reaching him of the child's peril."

"And if we cannot discover the child?" asked Whithall.

"Then, *mon ami,* we shall the one person Dumouriez values equally with his grandson steal."

"His daughter," nodded Langly. "But stealing that lady will not be near so simple a matter as it was to seize the boy."

"Non, but it will then have becoming necessity. And Lord Rossland will no longer be one who fights against us. He will being most dead, *non?"*

"I wonder," mused Langly.

"What?"

"It is nothing. But perhaps—rumor has it that The Devil's Delight has been making a cake of himself over Lady Letitia Farin's niece. I wonder if perchance he has convinced the young woman to provide shelter—"

"Never!" exclaimed Whithall. "Not even Rossland would

think to involve such an innocent as Miss Minerva Potts in his scheming. She is not at all the type to be involved in anything untoward. An unassuming, insipid milk-and-water miss, Miss Potts. Biddable, I grant you, but most proper. Why, should Rossland so much as mention to her the merest portion of his troubles, she would faint dead away. I ought to know. I have spent considerable time in the chit's company."

"You are quite probably correct," Langly nodded thoughtfully. "And even if you are not, Rossland no longer has any doubt that his father and brother were murdered to get the boy. And he cannot think that Grace was murdered for any other reason than the losing of him. Even Rossland would think better than to endanger Miss Potts and her aunt with knowledge of his situation when the stakes have grown so very large."

"You are knowing whereat this Miss Potts resides?" asked the chef thoughtfully.

"In Green Street," mumbled Whithall.

"I shall go and pay the young lady a call, shall I?" offered Langly. "Just to set our minds at ease? Yes, that's the ticket. I shall pay a call upon her personally and attempt to draw her out on the subject of Rossland. It will not look at all suspicious, I assure you. Lady Letitia and I are acquaintances of long standing. I shall impose upon that acquaintanceship to gain entrance and then I shall quite pleasantly interrogate Miss Potts upon the subject of the Earl of Rossland."

The Winecoffs' butler, Harrison, his ear against the kitchen door, inhaled deeply and then slipped quietly off down the corridor. Thank heaven, he thought, that I got to worrying over whether or not the rear door had been locked this evening—and thank heaven no one of the footmen remembered locking it. Not that I am terribly surprised, he told himself silently. I did never trust that Frenchie from the very day I hired him. Indeed, if it had not been for Master Chad's soft heart and his wish to help one more of the emigrés, Her Grace would not have requested me to find her a French chef in the first place—but that is neither here nor there. Obviously there is a vile traitor in our midst and we must tend to the matter as soon as possible.

Sixteen

"Perhaps it would be best to inform His Grace," sighed Perkins as he contemplated Harrison's most astonishing news over a tankard of ale at the Coach and Four.

"His Grace has gone off to deal with a situation at the estate in Devonshire," Harrison mumbled. "We do not expect his return for at least a fortnight. I would not have been able to join you here in the middle of the night else."

"It is much more like the beginning of the morning, Harrison. But I am certain that whatever you do on your own time cannot concern the duke," Perkins drawled, leaning back in his chair and yawning.

"I," replied Harrison in a dreadful tone, "am not employed by My Lord Rossland, Mr. Perkins. I do not have 'my own time.'"

"Yes, well, but that's neither here nor there Harrison," declared Battlesby with a shrug of his shoulders. "I do not have my own time either, but it is a certain thing I will not be missed at this hour. My entire household is fast asleep. They spoke of sending the child to the Continent?"

"Yes, and they spoke of murder and arranging an accident, they said, in which Lord Rossland would be killed. And whoever the gentlemen were—and they were gentlemen, I could tell by the manner in which they spoke—they also discussed your Miss Potts, Battlesby. One of them intends to call in Green Street and attempt to discover if the young lady knows anything of Lord Rossland's situation or of the child's whereabouts."

"Damnation," sighed Battlesby. "Well, but now we are fore-warned, we shall simply keep Jaimie out of sight."

"The boy is at Green Street?" Harrison asked, surprised. "I never! Why could Lord Rossland not trust His Grace with the truth of the thing, I ask you! Certainly His Grace would have provided all the assistance His Lordship could possibly require. How dare that rascal involve an innocent young lady—"

"My young lady agreed to involve herself of her own free will," announced Battlesby proudly, "and she will support Lord Rossland to the bitter end."

"Miss Potts?" queried Perkins, somewhat taken aback. "Of her own free will?"

"Indeed Miss Potts. Indeed of her own free will. Lady Letitia has not the least idea that the boy is Rossland's nephew, but Miss Potts knows all. She is head over heels in love with Master Chad, Mr. Perkins, and supports him wholeheartedly."

Perkins's eyes met Martindale's apprehensively. "Surely," Perkins murmured, "you do not approve your young lady thinking to make a match with such a scamp as Master Chad, Mr. Battlesby?"

Battlesby gazed from one to the other of them.

Harrison chuckled.

"I see what it is now," Battlesby pronounced quietly. "I begin to understand."

"Understand what?" asked Perkins in all innocence.

"How Master Chad came to arrive for a morning call in such a state of disarray, for one thing."

"Disarray?" queried Harrison.

"Indeed. Like a lamb to the slaughter Martindale sent him into my lady's drawing room without a collar and with a scarf tied about his neck like a veritable buccaneer."

"No, did you really, Mr. Martindale?" Harrison attempted not to snigger, but failed. "And he actually went?"

"Well, of course he went—came—went—" stuttered Battlesby. "He is in love with Miss Potts and would not let even such a setback in his clothing keep him from her."

"Master Chad is not in love with Miss Potts," declared Perkins vehemently.

"Yes, he is," contradicted Battlesby with great dignity. "The lad is besotted with her."

"Oh, I think not. He cannot possibly be. She is not at all Master Chad's type."

"He does not have a type, Perkins, and well you know it, too," growled Battlesby. "Why even his *chères amies* when he had some were as different from each other as night from day. You and Martindale are attempting to scotch my young lady's romance!"

"Dispense with the romance," interrupted Harrison with a chuckle and a bang of his tankard upon the table. "We have a great deal more pressing problem. What are we to do about these villains, is what I wish to know? I shall keep an eye upon Ebert or Girard, as the gentlemen called him. I expect that is the blighter's true name—Girard."

"And I will be on guard," sighed Battlesby. "Though whom I am to be on guard against I cannot guess—you are quite certain, Mr. Harrison, that he labeled himself an acquaintance of milady?"

"Indeed. An acquaintance of long standing."

"Well, I shall simply be certain that the Beamer is kept well out of sight should any company whatsoever arrive—and I shall warn Miss Potts. Yes, I shall warn the young Miss to be on her guard as well."

"And we shall inform His Lordship of all you have said, Mr. Harrison," declared Mr. Perkins with a glance at Martindale, "as soon as he returns to Mount Street."

"If he returns to Mount Street," sighed Harrison. "I cannot wipe that talk of His Lordship's having an accident from my mind."

"He will return to Mount Street," Martindale replied stolidly. "Those villains may arrange all the accidents they wish, Mr. Harrison, but our Master Chad will not be done in by them. Never! He is a canny one, Master Chad, and equal to any attempts such wretches might think to make upon his life!"

* * *

"If you call me Wicky one more time, Gaffney, I shall bash your head in with this wretched stick," threatened the earl wearily from the front facing seat of the coach.

"All right, Rossland, I shall cease to do so," chuckled Gaffney, his eyes heavy with lack of sleep. "But I do think it a most charming appellation. Give Goodacre a poke why don't you? Perhaps he will turn about and cease snoring."

"I only hope Terwilliger ain't snoring up on the box. By George, the sun is beginning to rise, Major. Apparently we have made a full night of it."

"Indeed. She is a most beautiful woman, your sister-in-law, Rossland. And charming."

"Yes."

"And very brave, I think, to have survived the revolution."

"Exceeding brave."

"And to have been a camp follower—a gently bred lady like that—I swear, Rossland, when you first told me she had been the wife of Armand Girard, I could not believe it. And for them both to have crossed the lines and fought against their own countrymen—when I think how terrible the war is for us—only think of the sorrow it must have caused them."

"It tore their hearts asunder, I assure you. But a man must do what he feels to be right must he not, Major? And his wife, if she loves him, will support him in it. You do not remember Liza at all, do you?"

"Remember Liza?"

"Yes, you featherbrain, remember Liza. She helped me lug you and the others up hill and down dale through the mud and the rain and the artillery fire, dodging in and out of barns and huts and caverns for three full days until we finally reached safety. And when I took those balls in my leg, it was Liza did most of the prodding and tugging and insisting, too. I was all for leaving the lot of you behind—especially yourself."

"You were not," grinned Gaffney.

"Well, perhaps not really, but I was for kicking you in the head from time to time. You kept attempting to be a major, you know, and spouting all sorts of guff about how we were to do this and do that and go here and go there. Giving orders, you were, and arguing with me every step of the way. Out of your mind, of course. I understood that. You had a dreadful head wound. But from time to time I lost all compassion for you, my man, and sincerely wished to apply my boot to your mouth. Liza would not hear of it, of course. 'Monsieur the raving lunatic is being,' she would tell me, 'but he is being, too, most pretty.' ''

"Most pretty?" laughed Gaffney. "Me?"

"It was your hair. She could not get over how red it was."

"I must have been a raving lunatic if I cannot remember such a beautiful woman coming to my aid," drawled Gaffney.

"Well, she looked a bit different then. She was dressed in a castoff uniform and boots. And her hair was cut—very short. I hated to do it, but I could not take the chance that the French would discover us and recognize her immediately. Already word had reached Napoleon that Armand Girard had left the Spanish guerrillas and now fought on the Peninsula with the English and that his wife was beside him. And the Eagle, of course, sent word back to seize them. The Frenchies were watching for them everywhere. I gave Armand my word to smuggle the lady into England the day we intercepted one of the messages alerting the French forces to be on the lookout for the Countess Marie Elizabeth in particular. I was due to be rotated home, you know. I gave Armand my word to take her with me—to England—where she would be safe."

"And she is truly General Dumouriez's daughter?"

"Which is one of the reasons she was almost more important to Napoleon than Armand, yes. You will not mention that to anyone, will you, Gaffney? Castlereagh or March for instance. Charlie knows, but Charlie knew even before Cameron married her."

"I have already given you my word I would not. Though prying the information I needed out of Castlereagh and March and Winecoff without revealing this whole tangled knot took a great deal of finesse, let me tell you."

"I do appreciate it, Gaffney. I could be in a great deal of trouble, you know, for smuggling the lady into England and then providing her a new identity. By the way, I appreciate equally your interest in my father's and my brother's deaths."

Gaffney's eyebrows lifted and his cheeks reddened.

"Mrs. Beaman whispered to me just before we departed that you had been to Skylark before. 'Lookin' to prove there weren't no truth to them nasty rumors,' she said. I knew immediately which nasty rumors she meant. So, now we have a portrait of Paul Girard. A small one, I grant you, and a good many years old. Do you think it will be of any help?"

Gaffney nodded. "It is a good deal better than having nothing at all to go by. Damnation! What does Terwilliger think he's doing?"

The coach lurched drunkenly to the side sending Lord Goodacre plummeting to the floor of the coach and Gaffney and Rossland scrambling for a hold on the straps. It then righted itself and pitched wildly forward as a pistol shot sounded and the horses broke into a headlong run. Rossland struggled to raise the trap and shouted up through it but there was not so much as a grunt from Terwilliger in reply. Holding to the sides of the opening with both hands, Rossland stuck his head up through it. He was back down in seconds. "Something has happened to your man, Major. We are driverless and like to be tipped into a ditch at any moment or dragged to perdition on our sides behind these horses. Charles, are you all right?"

"Mmmm," mumbled Lord Goodacre in reply, attempting to climb back onto the banquette. "What the devil has happened?"

"I have no idea, Charles. We are suddenly driverless and the horses running full-tilt."

"You both hold on tight," growled Gaffney reaching for the door latch. "I shall see can I climb to the box and reach the reins." But no sooner did the Major swing out through the door than another pistol shot exploded into the night and he swung directly back inside, his upper arm awash with blood.

* * *

Minerva, gowned in a morning dress of cherry-striped Georgian cloth, stepped back from the parlor window and let the draperies fall back into place.

"Did you see him, my dear?" asked Lady Letitia. "Is he yet perusing his paper?"

"Yes, Aunt Letitia."

"Well, he must be a dreadfully slow reader then for he has been perusing that paper since nine o'clock this morning when I first noticed him and it is now coming on to eleven." Lady Letitia sat knitting away, her needles clacking, in a scroll-backed chair beside the window. "We are being observed, my dear. Well, at any rate, our door is being observed. Now why do you think that could be? Could it be, perhaps, because Chadwick's nephew has taken up residence here?"

Minerva's mouth rounded into a soundless O as her aunt's eyes met her own.

"Indeed. I have not seen much of Jaimie in his short life, but one cannot help but notice those wonderful emerald eyes—especially when one has just returned from a visit to Elizabeth. Jaimie is the image of his mother. Though it was admirable of Chadwick to attempt to disguise the boy by changing his hair color and quite possibly if the child is merely seen from afar, no one will recognize him. I assume you were privy to this information from the first even though it did not arise last evening when you were telling me the *truth.*"

"I—I—yes, ma'am. But I could not tell you about Jaimie. I—I gave Lord Rossland my word."

"And Battlesby? Is he involved as well?"

"Y-yes, Aunt Letitia. But you must not be angry with him. The child is in grave danger, I believe, and Lord Rossland as well, and it seemed the very least we could do to hide the boy here. Lord Rossland was at point non plus, you see. He had nowhere else to take him."

"And why did you all think that I should be opposed to coming to Chadwick's aid in this matter?"

"We did not, my lady," inserted Battlesby from the doorway. "If I may be permitted a moment of your time?"

"Come in, Battlesby—and explain—or I shall have your head upon a pike."

"His Lordship did not wish to add to the danger, my lady. He thought that the fewest who knew of Master Jaimie's true identity, the safer you and Miss would be. But mostly he feared you would cavil at the little miss, my lady."

"The nursemaid?"

"Indeed. She is the little cyprian, my lady, whom he stole from Bennett Street. It was she led him to Master Jaimie."

"Thunderation!" growled Lady Letitia. "I shall have Chadwick's ears for this, and yours as well, Battlesby!"

"Yes, my lady. But it must wait until later."

"Indeed. We must deal first with that personage across the street who appears so interested in his newspaper."

"He is not our greatest problem, my lady," intoned Battlesby. "If I may be permitted—"

"Yes, yes, continue, Battlesby, and tell us what has happened. For something of import has gone dreadfully awry or you would not be here with such a frown upon your face."

Minerva took a seat and listened intently to Battlesby's story of the gentlemen and the French chef in the Duke of Winecoff's kitchen.

"And does Chadwick know of this?" asked Lady Letitia when her butler had finished his tale.

"No, my lady, I fear he is yet in ignorance. I received a note a few moments ago from Mr. Perkins. His Lordship has not as yet arrived at home."

"Not since last evening?" Minerva queried fearfully.

"No, Miss. His staff has not had sight of him since he set out for Drury Lane."

"And you have no idea who the gentleman might be? The one who proposes to pay us a visit?"

"None at all, my lady."

"Well, well, we must all three of us think upon this most deliberately. And we must be certain to keep young Jaimie out of sight if anyone should call," Lady Letitia murmured, placing her knitting back into her box. "If Chadwick has come to harm—they spoke of his having an accident you said, Battlesby—well it falls upon us to protect the mite then and to see that the remainder of this wretched plot between the gentlemen and the French chef comes to nothing."

By two o'clock Lady Letitia's **parlor held** a number of morning callers, the majority of them gentlemen and all of those gentlemen suspect in Minerva's mind of having embroiled themselves in the plot against Rossland which had been discussed in the Winecoffs' kitchen. The Reverend Mr. George had the great bad luck to proclaim a fondness for French cuisine and thus had drawn a wary and most dour glance from Minerva's splendid blue eyes. He could not for a moment think what he had said to give her a sudden distaste of him and spent the remainder of his visit tasting each of his words before he spoke them.

Mr. Davidson whose uncle, unknown to Minerva, was one of the diplomatic envoys to Russia, revealed a most extraordinary knowledge of the political maneuverings of the war and immediately became suspect. He, in fact, left Green Street scratching his head and wondering why Miss Potts had thrown herself into questioning him so heartily about the war and then stared down her nose at him as though he were a particularly odd specimen only because he had had the goodness to provide her with knowledgeable answers to every question.

The Marquis of Kensington, despite the fact that he had quite admirably brought his mama to make Miss Potts's acquaintance, put himself under immediate suspicion by lamenting the fact that his villa in Spain was likely to remain inaccessible for another year if someone did not do something about the fool fighting on the Continent.

"Why, I had not the least idea that you owned a villa in Spain," replied Minerva to this lament, her eyes suddenly pinned upon the gentleman. "How very interesting." Could it be, she wondered, that this was the precise villa to which the villains had said they intended to take Jaimie? Could the Marquis of Kensington actually be a traitor? Was he here in her parlor hoping for a sight of the boy? After all, she thought, he had not begun to take notice of her until Lord Rossland had taken up her acquaintance. But then neither had Mr. Davidson or the Reverend Mr. George or any number of gentlemen. Why, any of them might well have been in the Winecoffs' kitchen last evening.

Minerva's smile flickered and dimmed and flickered again as she took care to insert herself into each of the discussions going on about the chamber. Even Lord Collingsworth who had accompanied Angelica Deane and her mama to Green Street fell under suspicion though he said not one word about the French. It was the considerable time he spent gazing about the room as if attempting to memorize it that placed him upon the list of suspects. And Viscount Thorpe went down to perdition when he announced blithely to Miss Carmella Deinby that, say what they would about the French, they were still the rulers of the world when it came to fashion. And Mr. Henry Goodsuch made the list when he expounded upon the virtues of a new mare inappropriately named Calais. There was not one gentleman, Minerva became agitatedly aware, who did not place himself under suspicion. And when Lord Langly arrived and was introduced to her quite properly, her ears perked up again seeking to discover what about this gentleman might incur her distrust. She spoke to His Lordship for a full ten minutes on any number of topics. He proved to be most interesting and entertaining and not once did he blunder into any unseemly preoccupation with things French.

"You will forgive me, Miss Potts, for taking up so much of your time," drawled Lord Langly at last, "but I am a very old friend of Lord Rossland's, you know, and he has spoken so glowingly of you that I wished to make your acquaintance for myself. Rossland has so few friends these days that I do think we all ought to make the effort to come to know one another. He has been plagued and harried no end by the gossipmongers. His friends ought to join together to protect him somehow, do not you think? Lord Goodacre agrees with me, though we cannot quite decide how to go about it. It is so very difficult to be an intimate of the Earl of Rossland, is it not?"

"Most difficult," smiled Minerva with a great feeling of relief. This gentleman, surely, was not the one. "A person must be inured to gossip and must trust in His Lordship entirely."

"Indeed, Miss Potts, as I do and I expect you do as well. And your Aunt Letitia has always been the gentleman's friend, has she not?"

Minerva nodded. "Though Aunt Letty does not like to let on to him that it is so. She is forever harassing him about his actions and his manners," she grinned.

"Yes, so Rossland tells me—laughingly of course. He is most fond of your aunt. You do not care for so much company, Miss Potts?" murmured Lord Langly, studying her obvious relief as her visitors began to take their leave.

"Oh, no, it is not that," protested Minerva. "It is only that— that—"

"That what, Miss Potts? Are you expecting Rossland, perhaps, and fear to have him present himself amidst a room filled with his detractors? He will not mind it in the least, I assure you. Lord Rossland is quite immune to the lot of them. I admit I am most surprised that he has not yet put in an appearance."

That innocent remark brought a frown to Minerva's face, reminding her that no one as yet had so much as seen Lord Rossland since last evening. Perhaps she ought to confide that fact to Lord Langly. Perhaps, as an intimate of the earl's, he was privy to information that Lord Rossland's servants were not about the gentleman's whereabouts. Minerva debated the reasonableness of this as she bade the last of her callers farewell. Now would be the time to confide in Lord Langly. There was no one to overhear, no possible spy or villain to take note. And if Lord Langly did know where Lord Rossland had gone last evening, he would surely confide in her and set her mind at rest.

Minerva was just about to broach the subject to His Lordship when a little voice from the doorway made her jump.

"I have got me all dirty an' broked my fingers, too," sobbed Jaimie, hurtling himself toward Minerva's lap. "An' a great ugly giant has stoled Melinda!" The child, tears making great streaks through the dirt upon his face, came to an abrupt stop at Minerva's knees and stared up at Lord Langly.

"Joseph, whatever has happened?" queried Mina, her arms going out to the little boy. But Jaimie did not immediately seek their shelter as she expected. He backed away instead, his big green eyes fastened unblinkingly upon Lord Langly.

"Does you want to kidnapped me again, Uncle Thomas?" asked the child. "My Uncle Chad said I was not to be kidnapped no more or I should be swatted. I cannot never go away with you again. Not never."

Minerva gasped. Across the room, Lady Letitia made to rise from her chair. Langly, chuckling, grabbed the boy and set him upon his knee. "Do not move, Lady Letitia, nor you, Miss Potts, or I shall snap the brat's neck. It is no matter to me if I have a boy or merely his body. Either will do nicely."

"Oh! Oh!" cried Lady Letitia on a little shriek, seizing upon a copy of *Ladies Monthly Museum* and waving it energetically before her face. "Mina, quickly, my salts!"

"Do not you dare, Miss Potts," drawled Langly. "I am not like to fall for such a subterfuge, Letitia. I am well aware, as are most of the *ton,* that it would take the end of the world and more to send you into a swoon. Now, Jaimie, my boy, what is it has happened to your fingers, eh?"

"They are got broked, Uncle Thomas. A great ugly giant stoled Melinda an' I runned to helping her an' I falled on my fingers. And I is not Jaimie. I is pretended to be Joseph. See," the little one added as an afterthought, sticking his grimy hands up before Lord Langly's eyes—so close, in fact, that the gentleman flinched backward.

It was all Minerva required. Rising immediately, she caught up the potted rhododendron that stood beside her chair and bashed Lord Langly in the head with it. Shards of pottery and gobs of damp mulched soil scattered everywhere. Langly slumped down into his seat. Lady Letitia veritably flew to the bellpull to summon assistance. Within moments Battlesby was rushing through the parlor door. He came to a dead stop just inside the threshold.

"Battlesby, it is Lord Langly who kidnapped Jaimie," gasped Miss Potts. "And he was about to do so again."

"It appears he has forfeited that opportunity," murmured Battlesby, approaching the unconscious lord in amazement.

"Is he dead?" asked Lady Letitia eagerly.

"Is he dead?" queried Minerva, scooping Jaimie protectively up into her arms.

"No," replied Battlesby examining the rhododendron's victim. "He is merely knocked senseless, I believe. He will come around."

"Then I shall hit him again," Minerva declared, picking the poor plant up by its stem and brandishing its roots over Lord Langly's head.

"No, no, no, no, sweetling," laughed a most welcome voice and in a moment a disheveled and dirty Lord Rossland was beside her plucking the bedraggled rhododendron from her hand and putting his arms around both herself and Jaimie.

"Chadwick, unhand my niece this instant," growled Lady Letitia. "Of all the audacious, ill-mannered—"

"Where have you been?" Minerva asked, refusing to be unhanded. "You look as though you have been in a mill. We have been terribly worried about you. There is a French chef in your uncle's house who—"

"Yes, sweetling, Perkins told me all about it the moment I reached my door which is why I did not take the time to clean up but turned about and came directly here. There was a ruffian across the street, you know, just waiting for a glimpse of Jaimie. So we gave him one. That is, Battlesby and Mitzie did, while I pounced upon him from behind."

"I did good!" crowed Jaimie just then, his face a veritable blaze of self-satisfaction. "I were ex'lent!"

"Were you?" asked Rossland with a most unholy gleam in his eyes. "Did you remember to cry and tell about the giant and the broken fingers?"

"I 'membered ever'thing! I were outstan'ing!"

"He did not fall down?"

"No, Minerva."

"And Melinda was not stolen by a giant?"

"No, Letitia. I sent her off in care of a footman to see what help she could be to Major Gaffney and Mr. Terwilliger."

"What," glowered Lady Letitia, "has happened to Mr. Terwilliger? He is the third son of the Duke of Stafford, Chadwick, and if he has come to harm by your hand—"

"No such thing, Letitia," smiled Rossland. "Merely fell off the box of our coach. Broken arm, I suspect, though he don't wish to acknowledge the fact. We were waylaid, you see, on our way back from Skylark Cottage this morning. I began to think we should never see London again, let me tell you. The major had his arm clipped by a pistol ball and Terwilliger took a dive from the box when the coach hit a tree limb in the road. He could not see it, of course, the tree limb, I mean. They had shoved it in under a back wheel as we passed. Devil of a good job! Excellent timing, I tell you. I should like to have had those villains beside me on the battlefield. Unfortunately, rather than beside me, they are against me and I shall have the deuce of a time standing against them, I can see that. You are both all right? Battlesby, I thank you for your aid and for informing me of Langly's presence."

"You knew one of them was Lord Langly all along?" asked Lady Letitia awfully.

"Huh?" asked Rossland distractedly.

"The gentlemen in the kitchen—you knew."

"No, no, I am as yet quite uncertain who were the gentlemen in the kitchen, Letitia, but the major and Charlie and Terwilliger and I did deduce from some papers Gaffney stole that Langly was Jaimie's Uncle Thomas. That became excessively clear to us. I was all for calling him out, but everyone else was against it. I may call him out yet," sputtered Rossland, releasing Minerva and Jaimie from his arms and turning to face a groaning, but still unconscious, Langly. "But I expect I had best not do so until we have trapped the rest of the rascals."

"The rest of—" snapped Lady Letitia. "How many kidnappers are there, Chadwick? I should think now that you have this rakeshame, you need only seize the fiend in your Uncle Henry's kitchen and be done with it."

Seventeen

A ray of sunlight played annoyingly across Langly's face and despite his attempts to remain asleep, its persistent assault on his eyes woke him. He muttered and blinked and then blinked again. Inches from his nose the muzzle of a dueling pistol came sharply into focus.

"What the devil?" muttered Langly hoarsely.

"Do not so much as let your nostrils quiver, Lord Langly," warned Minerva in a voice tinged with suppressed excitement. "Lord Rossland has quite lost his mind and will pull the trigger at your slightest movement. I am certain of it. I had to plead long and hard to get him to let you awake before he did away with you. No, do not turn to look at me, please! I cannot bear the thought of it!"

"B-but," stuttered Langly. "B-but—"

The muzzle of the dueling pistol rose the slightest bit and Langly could not help but hear the slight click as the hammer was eased back. "Wait!" Langly entreated, wishing he could see around the muzzle to Rossland, but fearing to move in order to do so. "You cannot possibly, Rossland! You will be a murderer and Miss Potts will bear witness against you!"

"Oh, I think not," replied Rossland calmly. "You will not bear witness against me, will you, Minerva?"

"No, certainly not," murmured Minerva. "Though how I am to convince the constables that Lord Langly came to pay a morning call and brought that dueling pistol along with him in order to clean it, I cannot guess. They will think he expected to find my company dreadfully dull. You intend to shoot him in the head, do you not, my lord?"

"Indeed, Miss Potts. Directly between his shifty little piglet eyes."

"Yes, so I thought. Well then, do you think he ought to be slouched down so? It will make a terrible mess, will it not, and absolutely ruin Aunt Letty's chair. He ought to be sitting up straighter, I think, so that the ball goes into the wall. We can repair the wall less expensively than that particular chair."

"Perhaps you are correct," sighed the earl. "Sit up straight, Langly. Letitia will have my hide if I ruin her chair. Close the door, I think, Miss Potts, and lock it. We cannot have Jaimie come running in and discover his Uncle Thomas with a hole through his dastardly skull."

Langly, the gun barrel urging him on, struggled to gain a straighter position. Oddly enough, though his head ached frightfully, it was not his pain but the wild look about Rossland which he could now see clearly that made him shudder.

The earl, his lips set in a grim line, towered above him with dueling pistol cocked, his mahogany curls in wild disarray, his face unshaven, his neckcloth undone, his clothes begrimed and a most unholy gleam in his eyes.

"R-Rossland, you c-cannot."

"Why not?" asked the earl soberly.

"Well—well—"

"It would not be gentlemanly for one thing," offered Minerva softly as she closed the parlor door and turned the key in the lock. "But then, Lord Langly, you were not at all gentlemanly when you seized Jaimie and threatened to snap his neck."

"You cannot, Rossland!" groaned Langly, his eyes wild with fear as Mina leaned back nonchalantly against the door. "I am not the ringleader of this affair, I assure you. It will do you not the least bit of good to rid yourself of me. The assaults upon you and your nephew will continue and you will be no better off and have become a murderer to boot!"

"I am aware that Paul Girard lurks in my Uncle Henry's

kitchen," scoffed Rossland. "I shall attend to him after I have attended to you."

"Girard is not alone. There are others. And when you are least expecting it you will step out into the street and a strong hand will plunge a knife up between your ribs and your nephew will be gone again."

Minerva gasped.

"Do not spare it a thought, sweetling," Rossland drawled. "It will not happen. I should like to see the day I could not defend myself against some brigand with a knife."

"There will be more than one," muttered Langly. "They will not cease to attack until they have the boy. One day you will be found with your claret spilling into the gutter. If not today then tomorrow or next week or next year. You have not the least idea, Rossland, who stands against you in this."

Minerva, the vision of Lord Rossland with a knife in his ribs coming all too clearly to mind, crossed the carpeting to stand beside that gentleman and put her arm about his waist. "What difference will it make, my lord," she asked Langly then, "if my Lord Rossland were to permit you to live? Could you save him from such a fate?"

"Do not be foolish, my dear," drawled Langly, his confidence increased by the worried crease upon Minerva's brow. "I can give Rossland the names of everyone involved in the thing."

"You would betray your comrades?" asked Rossland, the pistol still aimed steadily at Langly's head.

"Every one of them, Rossland, for a price."

"What price?"

"My life, you fool, and safe passage out of England."

Battlesby came near to jumping out of his skin when Major Gaffney tapped his shoulder. He had been concentrating so intently, his ear pinned against the parlor door, relating each name as Langly uttered it to Lady Letitia who sat at a small table scribbling upon a sheet of vellum, that he had lost all sense of perspective. He had forgotten he stood in the first floor hall in Farin House and indeed even that he was the butler.

"Spying?" whispered the major with a grin.

Battlesby, putting a finger to his lips, nodded. "Le comp del lamar," he mumbled in Lady Letitia's direction.

"Le Comte Delamar," repeated Lady Letitia, scribbling it down. "That is ten, including Lord Langly, Battlesby. There cannot be many more. Do not disturb us now, Major. We are tremendously busy."

"Yes, ma'am," grinned the major, relaxing into one of the straight-backed chairs that lined the corridor.

"Lady Greta Willoughby," murmured Battlesby.

"Devil it! Whoever would have imagined that!" cried Lady Letitia in a hoarse whisper. "Why she is an intimate of the Prince Regent!"

"Mr. Daniel Scoggins who publishes the *Freedomist Press* pamphlets. Him I could see doing it," nodded Battlesby sagely. "And Mrs. Catherine White."

"Who is Mrs. Catherine White?" asked Lady Letitia gloweringly.

"That is just what His Lordship is asking now," Battlesby replied. "Oh, good heavens, she is the wife of a Life Guardsman! Apparently that is all, my lady," Battlesby added after a moment. "They are speaking of booking passage for the fiend to India."

"Which fiend?" asked the major.

"Lord Langly. Minerva and Chadwick have the villain at gunpoint and he has given them a list of all those involved in this hubble-bubble affair," mumbled Lady Letitia staring at her notes. "At least, if he is to be believed, he has done so."

"Miss Potts and Rossland? Have Langly at gunpoint?" Gaffney was out of his chair in a moment. "Open that door," he ordered Battlesby. "Never mind, I shall open it myself."

"You cannot, sir. 'Tis locked from the inside."

"Do not work yourself into a dither, Major," stated Lady Letitia calmly. "Chadwick is not going to shoot the man. I have his word on it. All is a mere charade to dupe that villain into spilling his guts so that we may bring an end to this insanity over Chadwick's nephew." Lady Letitia's eyes glowed with triumph into Gaffney's and then a pistol shot exploded behind the locked door and Minerva screamed.

"Miss Potts, unlock the door," bellowed Gaffney as he sprang forward and pounded against the wood with Battlesby at his elbow and Lady Letitia hurrying forward to join the two men. "Miss Potts, do you hear me? Unlock this door! Hurry, my dear!"

After a long tense moment, a key turned in the lock. All three nearly fell into the room as the door opened inward.

"I beg your pardon, Letitia," drawled the Earl of Rossland from behind the chair in which Langly slouched unmoving.

"Chadwick! You have killed the man! Thunderation, but you are the most outrageous scoundrel! And to think that I trusted you to do no such thing. You gave me your word you would not!"

"No, but I ain't, Letitia."

"You ain't? I mean, you have not killed him?"

"No. Fainted dead away, he did. You did never say that the pistol was loaded, Letitia. I thought sure it was not. We were speaking about booking Langly passage on the India Star, you see, and I was looking at the engravings on the pistol grip—they are most admirably done, Letitia—and I expect I tweaked the trigger. At any rate, the thing went off."

"Why, you ninny," glared Lady Letitia, "would I make you promise not to shoot the man if I intended to give you an unloaded weapon?"

"Well, I wondered that myself," replied the earl with a merry sparkle in his eyes. "But I was not brave enough to ask, Letitia. I was certain you would think me a nodcock."

"You are a nodcock!" exclaimed Lady Letitia.

"Worse, because I have shot a hole in your wall, Letitia, and fairly ruined the wallpaper." Rossland, stepping out from behind the chair in which Langly slouched all unheeding, revealed the extent of the damage and Lady Letitia gasped.

"Yes, I know, Letitia. It is not a pretty sight. But I shall buy you a painting to hang over it, shall I? Then no one will notice it in the least."

"A painting? There?"

"Well, it may be a bit low for a painting—but if it were an enormous painting, the bottom edge of the frame might cover it. Yes, that is exactly what I shall do. Buy you an enormous painting."

Minerva could not believe her ears. Nor could she believe how effortlessly the series of clankers slipped from between Lord Rossland's lips. How can he? she wondered, her eyes quite wide with amazement. And why?

"I am sorry, Letitia," Rossland continued, handing the pistol into her keeping. "Clumsy of me. Major, you cannot think how pleased I am to see you. Battlesby, will you send a footman out to hail a hackney? You will help me rid Letitia's house of this vermin will you not, Major?"

"Indeed," drawled Gaffney, his eyes narrowing, Minerva noted, and his gaze drawn to the earl's shoulder.

"Is you awright?" asked Jaimie in a tiny squeak of a voice as he peered around the door frame. "Is you awright, Uncle Chad?"

"I am fine, Beamer. I thought you were to remain upstairs."

"Yes," nodded Jaimie.

"Well, but you are not upstairs, are you?"

"There was a' splosion an' I were scared."

Minerva scooped the child up into her arms and kissed one very pale cheek. "Everything is fine, Jaimie."

"An' Uncle Chad is not hurted?"

"N-no, your Uncle Chad is not hurt at all," lied Minerva blithely. Gracious heavens, she thought, now he has gotten me to do it. He is not in the least all right and I know so, too. "Why do we not all sit down until the hackney arrives," she suggested, carrying Jaimie over to the sofa beside which his uncle now stood and tugging Lord Rossland down on to it with them. "It has been a most exhausting morning. Did you write down the names, Aunt Letty? Did you get them all?"

"Every one," nodded Letitia, eyeing her niece and Lord

Rossland suspiciously. "Jaimie, now that you know your Uncle Chad is fine, perhaps you ought to go back upstairs and play."

"Why?" asked the boy innocently.

"Because we are going to speak of grown-up things, my dear, and you will be dreadfully bored. Now off with you. And you, Chadwick," she added strolling toward the bellpull, "will tell me again how there comes to be a pistol ball in my wall."

"I have told you, Letitia."

"Yes, and I am not blind. I can see quite clearly that you have told me a whopper."

"You cannot possibly see that," mumbled Rossland in aggravation. "Everyone says that to me. Even Martindale and Perkins have the audacity to say so. How can you see that I have told you a whopper? You cannot possibly."

Minerva recalled quite clearly then the tiny squinting of his left eye as he had spun the Canterbury tale for her aunt and she could not help but giggle the tiniest bit. Would her aunt at long last betray this flagrant sign which had attested to the earl's lack of veracity from childhood? But her aunt's next words proved she was not at all about to betray the secret.

"Lord Langly has more than fainted or he would be recovered by now," stated Lady Letitia matter-of-factly, "and you, sir, are growing more pale with each passing moment."

Lord Rossland sighed wearily. "I am quite certain I cannot account for Langly's lassitude, Letitia. The man will awaken when he feels inclined to do so I expect."

"I want the truth, Chadwick, and I desire to hear it immediately. I am not such a gudgeon as to think for one moment that you actually discharged a pistol in my parlor accidentally."

"Well, I did."

"No, you did not," interjected Minerva.

"Yes, I did. It was most definitely an accident."

"I cannot divine, my lord," breathed Minerva, thoroughly frustrated, "what you hope to gain by keeping the truth from Aunt Letty and Major Gaffney. The truth is, Aunt Letitia, that Lord Rossland turned to speak to me and Lord Langly hoping, I expect, to escape, leaped from the chair with a knife in his hand and hurled himself upon Chadwick's back. Well, the very force of his leap set Chad off balance and though he could not avoid the knife, he did strike at Lord Langly with the butt of the pistol as he fell. And the pistol exploded when it hit Lord Langly's head. And Chadwick is hurt, Aunt Letty! He has been stabbed! His shoulder is right this moment bleeding all over your sofa! I cannot think why he made me help him return Lord Langly to that chair and then pretended that it had never happened. He has even gone so far as to hide the dagger away in his own pocket. I cannot for a moment think why he will not tell you so."

"This is why," grumbled Lord Rossland who had been undressed, bathed, bandaged, shaved, swaddled in one of the late Sir Hugh Farin's nightshirts and tucked firmly between the sheets by Battlesby in Lady Letitia's best guest bedchamber.

Minerva, in a chair beside the bed, giggled.

"Ho! Well you may giggle, sweetling. You are not the object of the lady's good intentions. Any moment now I expect to see a dish of gruel making its way through that doorway."

"What? All by itself? On tiny little legs?"

"No," replied Rossland, his puckered brow clearing and his lips twitching upward. "On a silver tray in some footman's hands, and your Aunt Letitia bustling in behind him glorying in the thought of forcing the dreadful stuff down my throat."

Minerva succumbed to even more giggles as immediately upon Rossland's last word a footman did appear in the doorway with a bowl upon a silver tray and her Aunt Letitia was behind him, urging him forward and waving a silver spoon most gleefully in the air. Battlesby, who had been gazing idly out one of the bedchamber windows, placed a hand over his mouth to stifle a guffaw.

"Enough of this nonsense, Letitia," protested Rossland. "I have more important things to do than to lie about and be cosseted. There's Langly to be looked to for one thing, and my Uncle Henry's French chef for another, and someone must," he added on a smothered chuckle as Lady Letitia sat upon the edge of the bed and directed the footman to set the tray on a table beside her, "someone truly must rescue Miss Potts's rhododendron."

"Balderdash," returned Lady Letitia. "Lord Langly remains utterly senseless and Jem has locked him up with that ruffian you vanquished, the one who was watching over this establishment. The two, I think, are most deserving of each other's company."

"You locked Langly in the cellar, Letitia?"

"Certainly. I intended to send Jem off to fetch a constable, but Major Gaffney protested quite heartily."

"Something to do with the Foreign Office," sighed Rossland. "No, Letitia. Take that spoon away. I am not going to eat any of your gruel. The very thought of it turns my stomach."

"You will eat it, Chadwick. It is good for you."

"I remember. It is the most wretched stuff."

"Nevertheless, you will eat every last bit of it and then you will lie down and go to sleep. I made you well when you broke your leg, remember? And I shall bring you back to health this time as well."

"I shall never forget when I broke my leg," chuckled Rossland. "Why my father thought to deposit me in your father's house instead of carrying me off home—"

The spoon Lady Letitia held, now filled with gruel, slipped expertly between Lord Rossland's lips and the look of insulted innocence on his face sent Minerva into gales of laughter.

"Ours was the closest establishment, Chadwick. You could not be moved further." Lady Letitia dipped the spoon into the bowl again. "And as I did then, so I shall do now, and have you back on your feet in no time," she grinned triumphantly.

"If Lady Letitia and Miss Potts and Mr. Battlesby will excuse us, we may discuss the matter in more detail," sighed Major Gaffney, making himself comfortable in a chair near the head of the bed several hours later.

"If—if we will excuse you?" stammered Minerva disbelievingly. "And do you think we have no interest in the matter, Major?"

"Well, of course Miss Potts, I am aware of your—association—with Rossland. However, you cannot wish to know all of the sordid details."

"Yes, she can too," interrupted Rossland. "In fact, I think they all three wish to know the sordid details. Miss Potts and Lady Letitia and Battlesby have been no end of help to me, Gaffney, and they have every right to know all that is going forward. And now that I know where to discover Paul Girard—"

"You know where Paul Girard is at this moment, Rossland?"

"Indeed. He is presiding over the cooking of dinner in my uncle's kitchen. And as soon as I can convince Letitia to release me from this bed, I have every intention of taking myself over there and putting a period to the scoundrel's existence. Are Langly and the other villain still locked down in Letitia's cellar, or have you made off with them? I cannot think it safe to keep them here, Major. Someone may come searching for them. Langly, by the way, has given us a list of those involved in this debacle, though I cannot vouch for the truth of the names upon it."

"Both of the villains are quite safely hidden away under guard at the Foreign Office for the moment, Rossland. And Lady Letitia has provided me with the list of names. I cannot think Langly was telling the truth, however, because one of the persons mentioned is our own agent and above reproach. But we shall, of course, look into all the others he mentioned."

"I did promise him safe passage to India, Major, in return for the names. Of course, that was before he stabbed me. Now I am rethinking the thing. I mean, it ought to negate our agreement, his attempting to do me in. Or perhaps not. And if the names are not correct, well, that certainly releases me from any promise."

"You shall have plenty of time to ponder it, Chadwick," declared Lady Letitia from a chair near the foot of the bed, "because you are not going anywhere until tomorrow at the very soonest. So said Dr. Macreary and so say I."

"Yes, but Letitia, if Girard is expecting to hear back from Langly, and he does not, why he might very well flee and we shall lose all we have gained."

"You are going nowhere," declared Minerva. "You, sir, have been stabbed in the back."

"In the shoulder," mumbled Rossland.

"In the back of the shoulder then, if you like. But you are chasing no villains until Aunt Letitia and Dr. Macreary say you may. And you, sir," she added, looking across the bed to where the major sat, "are wounded as well. How can either of you hope to defeat this Girard person if he should put up a struggle, when you have one arm in a sling and Lord Rossland's shoulder is swathed in bandages. Men! You are all totally senseless."

"Oh, deuce take it!" exclaimed Gaffney in exasperation. "And Terwilliger's arm is broken so he cannot be of use either."

"I am going this evening to pay a visit upon my Aunt Seraphina," declared Rossland abruptly, "whether anyone approves or not. Truly, sweetling," he added with a most discomposing gaze at Minerva, "it cannot be postponed. Major, does Mitzie stay with Terwilliger?"

"Indeed. She and my batman are looking after him."

"Then it must be you, Letitia."

"What must be me?" asked that lady, a very pronounced frown indicating her intention to deny any compliance with Lord Rossland's plans.

"You must be the one to take Jaimie out to Skylark Cottage. Girard knows that Langly came here this morning and if Girard escapes us, he will most certainly deduce that Langly discovered the boy in Green Street but was discovered himself. He will send his men here for Jaimie so we must move the Beamer to a safer place. Battlesby, you will escort them, will you not?"

The elderly butler nodded soberly. "Myself and my sister

and two of the footmen, my lord. John Coachman, the footmen and I shall carry pistols. I will see to it."

"Yes, good. And you must deliver a message I will write to my caretaker, Battlesby. His name is Maitland. If he is not at Riddle, he will be at the cottage."

"I have not yet consented to this thing," murmured Lady Letitia obstinately. "You nor the major are capable of subduing a madman, which this Mr. Girard must certainly be."

"But you do see the necessity of expediency, Letitia?" queried Rossland.

"Yes, I grant you it would be best to proceed quickly. But why can you not call upon the Bow Street Runners or the Watch?"

"Because, ma'am," sighed the major, "it is a most sensitive and complicated situation and one which the Foreign Office does not wish to become grist for the public mill."

"It is because of Liza," added Rossland, taking Minerva's hand into his own and giving it a reassuring squeeze. "And here we go—off into the sordid details. Liza is the daughter of a most important gentleman, Letitia. A Frenchman. A French General, to be exact, whom these villains hope to force to their will by holding his grandson hostage. If word of their plan for the end of the war on the Continent should reach our allies, panic could very well result."

"It was all done in the effort to order about a French General?" asked Minerva perplexed. "Surely then Lord Langly and these men work for our own cause."

"No, my dear," declared the major, rising and beginning to pace the chamber. "They are madmen with a cause of their own. Elizabeth's father, General Dumouriez, abandoned the Revolution and France years ago—way back in '93. They wish to restore him to it. From the information that has been gathered and from what we can deduce, their plan is to return the general to command and to lead a counter-revolution against Napoleon. Countless numbers of French, Austrian, even Russian soldiers and peasants will swarm to him and march with him. He was a legend, you see, before he defected from the cause. And he is a magnificent soldier still, I should imagine.

He would quite likely defeat that upstart emperor, even without allied assistance. Wellesley and his troops as well as the other allies would become quite unnecessary, because after one or two decisive battles, Dumouriez could very well march straight into Paris and be welcomed as a hero by all those Frenchmen who think that Corsican upstart has gone much too far—and there are a plethora of them who think the upstart has gone too far, you may believe me."

"Yes, but that would be wonderful," insisted Minerva.

"No, it would be terrible," Rossland sighed. "Gaffney thinks that Girard and his cohorts intend for the general to defeat Napoleon and that then they will force him to place their own personally selected people into positions of power, sweetling. The villains wish to control the entire Continent with General Dumouriez as a mere figurehead—a gentleman who will do whatever they tell him in order to keep his grandson alive."

"Well, I never!" pronounced Lady Letitia in most condemning tones. "It must be brought to a halt at once."

"And it will be," nodded Rossland. "This very evening when I have the felicity of presenting to my Aunt Seraphina the woman I intend to marry."

"M-marry?" stuttered Minerva, wondering bemusedly when the gentleman had actually proposed marriage and she accepted.

"M-marry?" stammered Lady Letitia.

"Well, I'll be da-deuced," managed Major Gaffney, his eyes filled with speculation. "Did you by any chance ask this young lady, Chad, to marry you?"

"No, I have not. Not yet. But that ain't neither here nor there, Gaffney, because an approaching marriage is the perfect excuse to burst in upon Aunt Seraphina without warning, which we must do to catch Girard by surprise. If news of our arrival should reach him in the kitchen, he will not at once associate our presence with Langly because he will not be expecting to hear from Langly until much later tonight. But he will already have heard the rumors about Minerva and myself and think only that for once the gossipmongers have got it correct."

"Yes," nodded Lady Letitia. "And since your aunt has already heard the rumors, she will not think it to be anything but a happy exuberance upon your part, Chadwick, to come rushing into her home with Minerva upon your arm."

"Exactly. Uncle Henry is from town, Perkins informed me, so we need not worry that he will be mixed up in the scuffle. And Minerva, you must hold my aunt's attention so she shall not come to any harm. And while you are speaking with her about plans for the wedding, I shall wander off in search of Girard."

"And I?" queried Gaffney with a lift of his eyebrow.

"You, Nick, will fetch Charlie and await my signal in the kitchen garden. I will be certain the door is unlocked. Once I have confirmed that the fellow is Paul Girard, I do think the three of us ought to be able to subdue him."

"My lord, you are wounded," Martindale gasped as he entered Lady Letitia's best guest bedchamber, the change of clothes His Lordship had requested tucked carefully into a portmanteau he carried in one hand.

"Yes, well, but it ain't nothing. A mere prick, Martindale, and I have been coddled and cosseted and made to eat gruel already, so do not dare to harass me about it more. You must only help me to look respectable enough to pop in upon Aunt Seraphina."

"But, my lord—"

"No, Martindale, do not protest. It is a most important visit and cannot be delayed. Miss Potts, Major Gaffney, Lord Goodacre and I are off to capture the spy in my uncle's kitchen. You came in the landau as I asked?"

"Yes, my lord. Luke has hitched the greys to it and is waiting in the street."

"Good. We shall need to hurry, Martindale. Aunt Seraphina dines at nine when Uncle Henry is gone from town and I mean to catch our villain in the midst of preparing the meal when he is most preoccupied."

"I shall accompany you, my lord," offered Martindale bravely. "You will stand in need of support."

"No, Martindale. You must return to Rossland House afoot and warn Perkins and the others to be on guard against any ruffians who might come there in search of Jaimie. I do not know who else we may be dealing with, you see. We may capture my uncle's chef and someone else send word to enter Rossland House in search of the boy. The staff must be prepared to withstand them and capture them if possible."

Martindale's fine grey eyes flashed. "Indeed, my lord. We shall certainly do so."

"I have every confidence in you," nodded Rossland, tying his neckcloth as respectably and simply as possible. "They are worse than kidnappers, Martindale. They are spies and traitors and murderers and must be dealt with severely. I trust in you and Perkins and the rest of the staff to show them no mercy."

"None, Your Lordship."

"No, but you will not kill them, will you, Martindale?"

"Certainly not, my lord, but we shall subdue them adequately, you may be assured of it."

Eighteen

The Duchess of Winecoff welcomed her wayward godson with a hug and a most refined kiss upon the cheek and Miss Potts with a pleasant nod. Once she had seen them seated in the Egyptian room with its puce sofa balanced upon crocodile legs and two chairs with arms which pretended to be copies of the sphinx, and a most intriguing table carved to resemble an upsidedown pyramid, she settled herself upon a most extraordinary couch which was intended to resemble a barge upon the Nile. "To what, my dearest Chadwick, do I owe this most surprising visit?" she queried, smoothing the folds of her Devonshire brown gown across her lap with one slim, long-fingered hand. "And why has Lady Letitia not accompanied Miss Potts? And do you intend, Chadwick, to remain for dinner? It will be on the table in less than an hour."

"No, Aunt Seraphina," Rossland declined with a wide grin. "I assure you I ain't lost so much of my mind as to have invited Miss Potts to dine at your table without ever telling you about it. The truth is that I am so delighted I could not bear to wait another moment to tell you and even though Lady Letitia has gone from town Miss Potts has taken pity upon me and agreed to accompany me here right on the spur of the moment. Truly she is the grandest lady, Aunt Serry! And she is going to marry me!"

"Oh, my goodness sake!" exclaimed the duchess springing from her couch and rushing to take Minerva into her arms. "Oh, my dearest girl! How happy you have made me! I thought never to see the day that Chadwick would find a young woman patient enough to put up with all his starts and vagaries. I did hope, you know, when first we spoke, that you would be the making of him and now you will! His Uncle Henry will be ecstatic!"

Minerva could not help but blush at such enthusiasm. Truly, she had not expected Rossland's announcement to produce so very much excitement in the duchess and she was not at all certain that she cared to encourage the woman in what was apparently a fervent anticipation of events to come. For what will she feel, thought Minerva, when she discovers it is all a sham? It must be wrong of us to do this thing. But then Rossland was interrupting his godmother's exclamations and saying that he was off to his uncle's cellars to select a suitable wine with which to celebrate. "Because Harrison is not at all a connoisseur of wines, Aunt Serry. You know he ain't. But I shall discover something will satisfy all of our palates equally."

"Well, and you must consider your Uncle Henry's palate as well, Chadwick," replied that lady with her arm still snugly about Minerva's waist, "because I am expecting him home at any moment. A message arrived this very morning to expect him. He will be so very happy, Chad, to think that you and Miss Potts have become engaged. He has been most worried about you of late."

Oh dear, thought Minerva, noting Lord Rossland's raised eyebrow and the stubborn jut of his chin as he spun upon his heel and departed the chamber. Now he will need to hurry even more because I am certain he has no intention to involve his uncle in the chef's capture. I do hope it is all over before the duke arrives. And though she still maintained some doubt about the advisability of misleading the duchess in regard to their marriage, Minerva put aside her worry over the Duchess of Winecoff's feelings and set herself to ruthlessly describing Lord Rossland's proposal which had not yet occurred and to discussing the surprise and joy of her impending wedding.

Because capturing that fiend is a good deal more important than anyone's feelings, Minerva told herself. And once we *have* captured him, Lord Rossland and I will explain everything to the duchess and though she will be sad to think that he has not asked me to marry him and so we have deceived her, still she must understand and rejoice that such a dreadful plot has been foiled and little Jaimie is safe at last.

"That is all very nice and romantical I am sure, Miss Potts," declared the duchess at the end of Minerva's description of Lord Rossland upon his knees before her in her Aunt Letitia's rose garden. "But now you must tell me the truth, my dear. What actually is it that has brought Chadwick here at such an hour and without warning?"

"Pardon, Your Grace?"

"My dearest girl," sighed the duchess, "if you do indeed intend to marry Chadwick, which I expect you do or else you would not lend yourself to his schemes as you are doing now, then you must learn the most basic of facts about the rascal. Do you intend to marry my nephew?"

"I—" stuttered Minerva, nonplussed. "Indeed, ma'am. It is just as I have been telling you. We have settled all between us."

"No, you have not settled all between you. I am perfectly confident of that. But do you intend to say yes when at last he does ask you, Miss Potts? He will try his luck sooner or later, that much is most obvious. I have never seen Chadwick so enamored of a young woman in all of his life."

"Yes, Your Grace," murmured Minerva blushing, "I—I am in love with your nephew and would agree to marry him in a moment should he ask me to do so. And I do apologize for—"

"No, no, no, do not bother to apologize, Miss Potts. I know perfectly well how Chadwick may charm a person into doing his will even when it does seem a most unconscionable thing for that person to do. And I ought not to have played along with it at all. But I did think that since he was so determined as to draw you into it, that Chadwick's reasons for wishing me to believe this Canterbury tale are most serious. Are his reasons serious, Miss Potts?"

Minerva nodded.

"Yes, so I thought."

"But, Your Grace, how did you know it was all a Canterbury tale?" Minerva asked in wonder.

"Well, for goodness sake," replied the duchess. "Do you

mean to tell me that Letitia Farin could see you were falling
in love with the scoundrel and did not have the sense to tell
you—"

"—about his eye!" squeaked Minerva and then slapped a
hand across her mouth.

"So, Letitia did tell you. And you forgot. Well, but those of
us who have had to deal with the rascal all his life do never
forget. And it is something his future wife ought to remember
as well, I should think. Do attempt to keep it in mind, my dear,
because no matter how much Chadwick loves you, he is nonetheless prone to telling all sorts of outrageous tales, and I doubt
even marriage will curb that unfortunate tendency. Now, you
will please explain to me, Miss Potts, why my nephew brought
you here and what is your role in this latest plot of his? Come,
Miss Potts, you may confide in me. I am his godmama, his
mama's sister. I care very deeply for Chadwick and always have
done."

Minerva had near to completed her explanation to the
duchess when a most horrendous crash from belowstairs startled both ladies. This was followed by a mighty bellow and then
a number of very odd sounds and more crashes.

"Gracious, that is Henry!" cried the duchess as the bellow
came again. She rose immediately and rushed from the room,
Minerva close on her heels.

"In the kitchen, Your Grace," Minerva cried as the two raced
down the staircase. "Lord Rossland meant to confront the villain in your kitchen."

"Harrison, seize an umbrella from the stand and follow me,"
ordered the duchess as she reached the great hall and plucked
a heavy brass candlestick from the table upon which Rossland's
hat and gloves rested. "Minerva, my dear, arm yourself. It
sounds as though Chadwick has discovered his man and Henry
has walked in upon them. There is a great mill going on in
the kitchen and we must not enter without something useful
in hand. If our chef is indeed the spy Chadwick thinks him,
he will be most dangerous. And apparently the gentlemen have
bungled the thing," she added, sweeping toward the back of
the house as more crashing, a shout, and then a pistol shot

reached their ears. "And why Henry has gone and got himself involved in it, I cannot imagine. He is a good deal too old to run about capturing spies and villains! And Chadwick knows so too and ought to have kept Henry out of it!"

Minerva could see no weapon in sight as she followed the duchess down the long corridor, Harrison marching bravely behind them, umbrella at the ready. The silver épergne was much too cumbersome, the statuettes too small, and the several stately chairs and tables lining the corridor totally impossible. And then, standing just inside the door of the duke's study, the perfect weapon caught her eye and she snatched it up in both hands without missing a step. Other than the fact that the leaves made it rather hard to keep all of the duchess in view at once, the potted rhododendron would prove most efficacious, Minerva thought. After all, a similar pot and its occupant had done the job quite adequately upon Lord Langly.

The kitchen of Winecoff House boiled with activity as the little trio entered. Bodies large and small scurried through a maze of ovens and sinks, cupboards and cubbyholes. "Yer Grace, Yer Grace," squealed a tiny potboy with a great streak of grease across one cheek, dashing toward the duchess and coming to a skidding halt before her, "they has all gone mad! The Frenchie does be whipping about 'im wif a cleaver an' the duke done come in from the stables wif some other gen'lemen an' fired off 'is pistol an' ever'one be runnin' an' screamin' an' throwin' the dishes about and me pots too!"

This speech being punctuated by a piece of Dresden china flying straight over Minerva's head to burst against the doorframe, no one doubted a word the boy had spoken. The Duchess of Winecoff took one long look at the shards of her plate, set the child aside, and marched deeper into the chamber. Minerva followed, her hands tightening upon the heavy pot. At the rear, Harrison raised his umbrella to the combat position.

"Damnation!" roared Major Gaffney's voice, though Minerva could not see him at all as at the moment she was following the duchess through a thick cloud of smoke. Obviously

something in this part of the kitchen had caught fire when the
ruckus began. "Turn loose of him now, Girard!" ordered the
major. "You will not save yourself that way."

"Will not I?" The man who replied chuckled so heinously
that it sent a shiver right up Minerva's spine. "And will you
sacrificing this fool's life, then?"

"Sacrifice?" hissed the duchess coming to an abrupt halt.

"Sacrifice?" gasped Minerva, barely managing to keep
from running over the duchess. They had traversed most of
the maze and were standing just at the far edge of a small
chamber, staring into the main section of the kitchen. Three
bodies lay unmoving upon the stone floor. Minerva squinted
fearfully over the duchess's shoulder, petrified that one of
them might be Lord Rossland, but she recognized none of
them.

"Put that thing down at once!" bellowed another voice.

"Oh, thank goodness," sighed the duchess. "Henry is still
in good form."

Taking very small, careful steps, the duchess, Minerva and
Harrison eased farther into the main room hoping to see all
that was happening without being noticed themselves. What
met their eyes sent Minerva's heart to pounding. Lord Rossland was in the grip of a very large man with curling mustachios, bristling sideburns, and an enormous meat cleaver
which he held none too gently against the earl's throat. "One
step more, and this bloody Lordship is being the next course,"
threatened the burly chef, literally dragging Lord Rossland
backward toward the open door to the kitchen garden.

"Give it up, Girard," grumbled Lord Goodacre from one
corner of the chamber. "You will never get away, you know.
You can hardly go off down the street dragging Rossland along
with that thing at his throat. I expect someone will notice."

"Bah! Walking properly beside me he will until we finding
the hackney. Then he will riding inside all quiet next to me
until I am far from you."

"Chadwick cannot walk properly beside you, Girard, because his cane is over here," growled the duke. "He cannot
walk properly at all without it."

"Then he shall limping along like the crippled dog he be-ing!" shouted the evil chef, his mustachios bristling.

"Well, of all the nerve!" declared Minerva vehemently and charged straight at the dreadful man, the leaves of the rhodo-dendron she carried bouncing and weaving eerily before her.

Girard could not believe his eyes. A most grotesque plant was making its way threateningly toward him. His concentra-tion failed him a moment at the ludicrous sight it presented and Rossland, feeling a slight slackening of the man's grip, shoved against the hand that held the cleaver and strove to spin out of the man's grasp. Girard, thereby distracted from the speedily approaching horror of jouncing, twisting leaves, grabbed at the earl and struggled to bring him back under control. It was all the time Minerva required. She reached the two men, hoisted the plant above her head and brought it cracking down across the Frenchman's brow. Rossland stum-bled aside; the meat cleaver clattered across the stones; and Paul Girard sank to his knees. Minerva angrily raised the plant again and brought the pot down across the back of the French-man's skull. Girard gave a quiet grunt and slipped the rest of the way to the floor.

"Well, I never," declared the duchess. "Harrison, you may sheath your umbrella. Miss Potts has taken on the adversary singlehandedly and felled him nicely. Well done, Miss Potts. You are a veritable demon and certainly a perfect match for The Devil's Delight if I do say so myself."

"Did you hear what that villain called Chadwick, Duchess?" spluttered Minerva, tugging her skirts away from the prone Frenchman and rushing to put loving arms around a most amazed Rossland. "He called him a crippled dog! Of all the nerve! He is the one who is crippled! His mind is thoroughly ugly and disjointed. How dare he! How dare he!"

Lord Goodacre, with a most cherubic smile, winked auda-ciously in the Duke of Winecoff's direction as he set about to assist Gaffney in securing Girard and the other three men stretched out upon the kitchen floor.

"Indeed, Goodacre," chuckled the duke, putting an arm about his duchess's shoulders. "Apparently Miss Potts is just the woman to do the job with my nevvy, ain't she? I did never think to meet another young lady quite so forceful as my Serry. But there, when the need arises, it is met. She will fit into our family very nicely if I do say so myself."

Minerva blushed prettily at his words and Rossland, holding her quite possessively in both arms, chuckled. "She is something special, my sweetling, ain't she, Uncle Henry?"

"Indeed," smiled that gentleman, "and if you have anything at all besides windmills your head, Chadwick, you will not be many days before you go down on your knees and beg the girl to marry you. Gaffney, what is it you intend to do with these villains? I cannot have them cluttering up my kitchen for the remainder of the evening. And who," he added with a teasing glance at his duchess, "is going to save dinner? Some of it is decidedly burned, Serry, and our chef, it appears, is indisposed."

Perkins, having delivered Martindale's warning to the entire staff at Rossland House and having assured himself that all were on guard against the presence of any stranger whatsoever—even the merest pedlar—stepped out into the evening for a breath of air. He stood thoughtfully upon the front stoop looking every inch the perfect butler and pondered the situation. If, indeed, this chef in the Winecoff kitchen were the last of Master Jaimie's kidnappers and if Master Chad and the major succeeded in capturing the villain, then all would be well. The hired ruffians, like the one who even now lingered in the square across the street, would discover themselves unpaid and out of work and wander off in search of other business. But if the chef were not the last remaining member in the affair, then all concerned would be in more danger than before because now the villains would know that Lady Letitia and Miss Potts and Major Gaffney had all involved themselves in the thing and they, as well as Master Chad, would come under harassment. Perkins gazed down at his shoe tops and muttered an expletive to himself, then he looked up and noted a town coach driving slowly past the house. It was a flickering black mirror in the light of the street lamps and Perkins admired it until it turned from sight around the far corner.

Battlesby, Perkins mused, had undertaken to escort Her Ladyship and Master Jaimie to Skylark Cottage and had taken the coachman and the first and second footmen with him. He had taken the housekeeper as well. That meant that only the youngest footman and the maids and the cook remained in Green Street. Certainly they would be most vulnerable to attack if worse came to worst. And if they were to be assaulted, could they not be forced to tell where Her Ladyship had gone and to admit that she had taken a child with her? There must be some way that the Rossland staff could divide themselves between the two residences and thus protect both. The major's residence was out of the question because Perkins had not the least idea where the major's chambers might be. But then he doubted that anyone at the major's chambers was at all aware of this latest start in the affair. No one there would know where Lady Letitia had taken the boy and so could not be coerced into betraying his whereabouts. What he ought to do, he decided, was to take a brief stroll, just to think things over. He stuck his head back in through the front door and informed the first footman that he was off for a walk. "You'll mind the door, James, yes?"

"Indeed, Mr. Perkins."

"And if someone should call, you will say that you have no knowledge of His Lordship's whereabouts and do not expect him back until very late and you will not give anyone entrance."

"No, Mr. Perkins, not even if it should be the Duke of Winecoff, himself."

"Exactly," nodded Perkins and he pulled the door closed behind him and was down the steps in three easy strides. He proceeded at a stately pace down the avenue, reached the far corner and prepared to turn back when the same shining black town coach he had admired from the steps came rolling 'round the corner and proceeded back up the street at a most decorous pace. Perkins's gaze followed it thoughtfully. Was it indeed the same coach? Yes. Perkins could recognize a coach on the instant from the particular alignment of its lamps and the design of its trim and the set of its box. Perkins was a connoisseur of such vehicles. Was the coach slowing as it passed Rossland House? It appeared to do so. Perkins began to stroll back toward his domicile at a more rapid pace. But the coach did not stop before Rossland House. It increased its pace again and rolled on by.

Perkins puzzled over it as he slowed his own pace. Someone lost perhaps? There had been no markings on the doors but that was neither here nor there for a great many of the younger gentlemen neglected to inscribe their crests upon the more modern vehicles. And I did not partake in this exercise to puzzle over a coach, he scolded himself silently. He stroked his chin as he contemplated, then placed his hands behind his back, then stuffed them into his pockets. He was so very deep in thought that he wandered right past Rossland House and on up the avenue to the next corner. Noticing he had done so and realizing he must not prolong this sojourn much longer, he turned back down the street and noticed the same shining black coach coming up the street toward him. Once again he saw it slow as it passed Rossland House. By Jupiter, he thought, I am not blind and I am not stupid either. There is something havey-cavey about that coach. His long legs carried him rapidly toward the house. The coach must pass right by him and he would be brazen as a hussy and stare straight into its windows. But when the coach and Perkins came up beside each other he discovered that the shades in the vehicle were lowered and no one to be seen. He glanced back over his shoulder hoping to recognize the coachman, but he had not the slightest recollection of having met the driver before, nor was he acknowledged by that man.

For a long while after he had returned to his post, Perkins stood quietly beside the long window on the left of the front doors and gazed out into the street. The coach passed the house ten more times in one half hour. "James," Perkins called to the first footman at the end of that time, "I am going out again and taking Mr. Martindale with me. We shall return as quickly as possible. You would do best, I think, to lock up the house tight and answer to no one."

The sole occupant of the town coach raised the shade and stared out into the night. His world-weary grey eyes fastened upon the two men descending the steps of Rossland House. With the head of a walking stick he tapped against the trap.

"Aye, Yer Lor'ship, what be ye wantin'," responded the driver lifting the door.

"Follow the two who have just exited the house. Keep well behind them. Pull over if you must to wait upon them, but do not lose them for a moment."

"Aye, Yer Lor'ship. Easy enough done."

Minerva could very plainly see that Lord Rossland's leg gave him enormous pain. It was the way he sat so silently next to her upon the very edge of the crocodile sofa. And his shoulder must hurt a great deal too, she thought, glancing quickly up at him and then away. He is so very pale! He ought not to have scuffled with that villain in the kitchen.

The fact that he raised a snifter of brandy to his lips and drained it quite efficiently and that his eyes, turned hard and angry, never left the huge man bound quite competently into a wing chair near the hearth, warned her, however, that worried about Lord Rossland though she might be, this was not the time to urge him to retire from the scene.

"You are being the fool, Rossland," mumbled Paul Girard, struggling against his bonds. "Do you think I alone am wishing to seize the boy? Powers greater than I are involved, I assure you."

"Be still," hissed Major Gaffney from behind Girard's chair. "We already have a list of your greater powers. Langly was more than pleased to provide us with one."

"Bah! Langly! He small fish being in this most enormous of ponds. He does not knowing all. Not even I am knowing all. And a liar he being besides. This I assure you."

"Enough," muttered the duke from the Nile sofa where he

sat with an arm around his intrepid wife. "The Guard will be here shortly and you will be well-served for your part in this infamy, I promise you. Silent though it must be kept, you will meet just punishment, Girard, and Langly and the rest of your men with you."

"And the boy still not safe will be," scoffed Girard. "This I promise, monsieur."

"Who else?" asked Rossland in a tone so savage that Minerva would never have recognized that voice for his own.

"Oh, many others, *mon ami.*"

"I ain't your friend, you unnatural cur, and do not call me so. Armand would rise from his grave if he could, and strike you dead on the spot for all you have done."

"But he cannot, eh, *mon ami?* And so for him you must do this killing. You have the nerve to be killing me, Rossland?"

Minerva leaped from the couch as the brandy glass shattered in Rossland's hand. He took her arm and tugged her back down beside him on the instant. Lord Goodacre who had been standing just behind the sofa brought out his handkerchief and offered it to the earl who coolly picked several slivers of glass from his hand before wrapping it in the square of muslin.

"Your carpet is safe, Aunt Seraphina," he murmured. "The glass was empty at least and I seem only to have sprinkled a bit of blood on my inexpressibles. No, Girard, I'll not be the one to kill you. For Jaimie's sake, I will not. Because you are his uncle, though it gives me great pain to admit that fact. Tell me, do you not care one bit that it is upon your own nephew's back you planned to rise to power?"

"His nephew?" breathed Minerva softly. "He is Elizabeth's brother? But surely you said her father's name was Dumouriez."

"*Oui*, mademoiselle," Girard replied with a smirk. "And her husband's name Armand Girard, le Comte d'Iberval, my most misguided and overzealous half-brother. So overzealous as to thinking himself must sacrifice all to stand against the revolution. And so he dies, does he not, Rossland, forgotten and alone upon some piece of foreign soil?"

"He died at Talavera," whispered Rossland. "And he was

not alone and he will never be forgotten. And Liza was anticipating Jaimie then. They both might easily have perished there as well."

"Ah, but how sad that would have being, no? I should have no such important nephew, no such wonderful hand to play, no marvelous bargain to be making."

"Elizabeth was a widow and in the family way when she married Cameron?" asked the duchess aghast. "No one said a word!"

"Jaimie is not Cameron's son?" the duke queried, frowning.

"This child le Comte d'Iberval, son of Armand and Marie Elizabeth," replied Girard smugly. "Already she increasing when they join with the *Anglais* in Portugal. This secret Armand entrusts to myself in letter which is coming tattered to my hand three years after my brother's death. Great searching it takes to discover where Marie and the child having gone. These Rosslands are steal my nephew and pretend him to be their own."

"To keep him safe. He was born at Riddle. After Cameron and Liza married. Cameron was his stepfather, Girard, and I merely a step-uncle. You are his only true uncle. You are the only one shares his blood. Which makes it even more despicable that you should use him in such a way," growled Rossland. "How could you choose to use the young Count d'Iberval as a pawn in your own quest for power? Armand was correct to fear for the safety of Liza and her unborn child, but he thought most incorrectly that you could be trusted. His hopes, I am sure, were that you would restore the child to his own lands and titles should you both survive the war. We all would gladly have helped you to do so. But now—"

Minerva was certain she could not be following the conversation correctly. Jaimie was not the son of Lord Rossland's elder brother? He was the son of Elizabeth and a French aristocrat? But then—but then—"Chadwick, you are truly the Earl of Rossland!" she exclaimed on a tiny shriek and immediately clapped a hand over her mouth and reddened considerably.

Rossland, his eyes most suddenly regaining their mirth-filled sparkle, grinned engagingly down at her and took her hand into his own. "For better or for worse, sweetling, I am. Although I am quite certain that Uncle Henry's hopes are now totally destroyed. You were hoping, were you not, Uncle Henry, that Jaimie would grow up to be the earl—a proper and responsible earl—an earl of whom you could be proud?"

"I am proud of you, my boy," grumbled the duke, embarrassed. "There is not a gentleman worth his salt has proved himself more brave and honorable than you have done over and over again since first you took the king's coin like a wretched commoner. And even if you are not accustomed to standing upon ceremony and playing propriety, there is not a man can say you have shirked your responsibility. And as for your present reputation—"

"Which is in shreds," inserted the duchess neatly. "And not like to improve without a good deal of effort—"

"—I am certain that neither your aunt nor I nor anyone who loves you shall ever hold that against you, Chadwick, and to Hades with the rest of the world. You do agree, do you not, Miss Potts?" the duke added, gazing at her through slightly hooded eyes, a smile twitching his lips upward. "You will not hold his present reputation against him?"

"Oh, never!" declared Minerva emphatically, ignoring the disgusted grunt which emanated from Paul Girard. "It is all nothing but a sham in any event—his present reputation. He came by it because he was searching in the most horrendous places for word of Jaimie, you see."

"Indeed," nodded the Duke of Winecoff knowingly. "I do see, my dear. I see everything most clearly," and he sent the most outrageous wink in his nephew's direction.

Nineteen

Once Major Gaffney's men had arrived and taken Girard and his cronies into their custody, Lord Rossland took Lord Goodacre up in his landau and dropped him at his home and then directed Luke to proceed at a stately pace to Green Street and the Farin residence. "I am sorry, sweetling, to have involved you in all of this nonsense," he mumbled beside Minerva on the banquette. "It was unconscionable of me—but you seemed the perfect answer to my dilemma at the time."

"I was exactly the person you needed," replied Minerva with a degree of smugness.

"Indeed. A beautiful, intelligent and formidable woman—especially formidable when in possession of potted rhododendrons. I will remember not to keep any of those particular potted specimens around the house."

"You will—? Whatever does that mean?"

"It means, Miss Potts, that I do not treasure the thought of my countess hitting me over the head with a rhododendron if I should happen to arouse her ire from time to time. You will be my countess, will you not, sweetling, once I have wheedled your Aunt Letty into bestowing her blessings upon us? Your father, I think, will have no objection if only you tell him you wish for the union. You do wish for the union?"

"Oh, yes," sighed Minerva growing rather misty-eyed beneath the night sky.

"Good, because I love you more than life itself, Minerva, and I do not think I could survive without you. I almost did not survive without you in my uncle's kitchen, you know, but that is not in the least what I mean. I mean—well—that I love you, sweetling, and that my life would not be worth living without you. Are you certain?" he added then with a most engaging wink. "Are you quite certain you will marry me? Even if I should prove to be less prestigious, comfortable and convenient than I mean to be? Because I most probably will, you know."

"I must have been mad," sighed Minerva, gazing wistfully up at him. "I must have been truly mad to have determined upon such a dreadful ideal."

"No, not mad, sweetling, merely sad and disappointed and frightened." His great dark eyes sparkled in the light from the coach lamps and his mahogany curls rioted over his brow as his lips came ever so slowly down to caress her own. And then the landau lurched to a sudden stop, the two bumped noses and Luke cursed loudly and roundly.

"Devil pulled out right in front of me," grouched Luke. "Ought to learn to drive, he ought. Got 'imself a four-horse-hitch an' don't know how to handle even one horse at a time!"

"Chadwick!" cried Minerva, rubbing at her stinging nose. "Aunt Letty's house is afire!"

"Oh, the devil!" muttered Rossland, his gaze following her own. A tower of heavy black smoke was indeed rising into the air from the back of the building. "Luke, spread the alarm," he shouted, setting Minerva aside and springing from the landau only to stumble and haul himself up short by clinging to the side of the vehicle. "I forgot," he mumbled, embarrassed. "Hand me my walking stick, please, Minerva."

Minerva, with quiet determination, plucked the cane from the floor of the carriage and climbed out of the vehicle herself. "I shall give it to you, Chadwick," she said, "but you are not going inside alone."

"Go, Luke, go!" bellowed the earl at his coachman. "Roust the fire brigade! I must go in, Minerva. There is no one at all to be seen, so it is very likely that your Aunt Letty's servants have not yet been roused by the smell of the smoke. I cannot let them burn to death," he muttered, seizing his cane from her hands and hurrying with it toward the front door.

Minerva kept pace with him easily and she was somewhat astounded to discover the front door ajar. "Perhaps they are all safely out," she offered, pushing the door wider.

"No, someone is yelling. Can you not hear?" Rossland entered the hall and looked around him attempting to identify from where the now clearly distinguishable shouts came. "It sounds very much like Martindale," he muttered. "How could that be? And there is no smoke here, Minerva. Whatever is afire is at the rear of the building only. Martindale?" he bellowed then at the top of his lungs. "Where are you?"

"Master Chad? In the kitchen!" called another voice.

"Perkins? What the devil is going on?" frowned Rossland, taking the arm Minerva offered him without hesitation.

The sight they saw when they arrived in the Farin kitchen was discomposing to say the least. Perkins and Martindale sat tied to chairs at the table and just behind them black smoke bellowed into the chamber through an open window and tongues of flame licked in around the kitchen door.

"The staff is locked in the still room," Perkins announced as Rossland fumbled to untie him. "He left Martindale and I out here as a message to you, my lord. He said that we would be the first to be burnt to crisps, but that the others might well escape. And that was as it should be, because you deserved all the grief with which he could provide you."

"Who?" Rossland asked angrily, freeing Perkins and moving on to Martindale as Minerva rushed off to unlock the still room door. "Who did this thing? What is it burning out there? Where the devil is that fire brigade?"

The gentleman in the shining black town coach settled back against the squabs as the four prime bays made their way through the throng of vehicles along St. James's Street toward the toll road. That had been a near one. A moment longer inside the house and whoever had been inside the landau would have been upon him. It was too bad actually. The unexpected appearance of the landau would mean that the fire would be doused before it could do any real damage to the building, much less to Rossland's interfering servants. And how kind it had been of them to interfere and lead him directly to the last place the boy had been, too. And he had been equally lucky that the terrified little fireboy had overheard Lady Farin's destination and had blurted it out quickly when threatened.

But the fire, the fire would be a total loss now, though it had given him a most satisfied feeling at the moment he had set the thing. And perhaps it would do some damage—enough to pay Lady Letitia back for having thrown him out of her house.

Ah, but that wretch, Rossland, was a cool one, he thought then. Not one of them had so much as suspected that The Devil's Delight could be so completely devoid of principles as to involve such innocents as Lady Letitia and Minerva Potts in his schemes and maneuverings.

And to think of that insipid little miss, Minerva Potts, actually consenting to help Rossland! To think of her agreeing to stow the boy at Farin House beneath their very noses! It came near to boggling his mind. But then, to think of Rossland having brought the Countess d'Iberval to England already increasing and disguised as an English foot soldier and to think of Rossland's brother marrying the woman and letting on that the child was his own, was mind-boggling as well.

And if Girard had not had that letter from his half-brother mentioning Rossland's promise to see the countess and her unborn child safely to England, well, not even Napoleon himself would have thought to seek them on British soil. Indeed, no one in the *ton* had even suspected the extensive deviousness of the Brumfields. Everyone had simply accepted that Cameron's marriage and the child's birth had all been kept private because of Chadwick's illness. No word had so much as reached the gossipmongers that the child had been born well before the requisite nine months. "No," the gentleman sighed, "the secret was so well kept that no one need ever have known the boy was not Cameron's heir. And everyone at Riddle, servants and masters alike, were in on it, too!"

The gentleman sighed again and gazed out into the night.

They had reached the toll road and his driver had sprung the team as instructed. He would stop in Gravesend to hire some ruffians before he went on to Riddle. He had a number of acquaintances in Gravesend who would acquire for him precisely the type of lowlifes he needed. He wondered for a moment what had become of Langly and the man they had stationed outside the Farin residence to keep an eye upon Rossland when he visited there, but then, Langly was a fool and there was no telling in the least what had got into his head.

Visions of triumph raced through the gentleman's mind. Girard and the others would be ecstatic to learn that the child had been retrieved. And because of his success where even Girard had failed, he would be appointed to a far greater position of power in the new regime than he had at first expected. Whether that position would be on the Continent or here in England, he cared not. But most certainly the plan would have failed without him and the others would be exceedingly grateful.

He would not use the men he collected at Gravesend, of course, unless it should prove necessary. The fact of the matter was that he did not think he would actually require their services. After all, it was Letitia Farin had been put in charge of the child, and of course, only Minerva was with her. And he had not the least doubt that he would be able to twist both those ladies to his will once he had presented them with a few farradiddles. He set his mind to composing an acceptable story. Something involving Rossland's death and his dying wish, he thought with a sly smile. That would make things interesting.

Liza stared bewildered at Jaimie as he came running toward her across the parlor.

"Mama! Mama! I am come to see you! Uncle Chad has sended me! Mama?" The excitement in the little voice faltered as he came to a halt before the lovely woman who shared his wide green eyes. He stared up at her with a most perplexed frown. "Mama? Ain't you 'ceeding happy to see me?"

Lady Letitia, entering the room just behind the youngster, held her breath. She had not thought. She had been so very worried about protecting the boy and getting him safely to Skylark, she had not given one thought as to how Liza would receive the child.

Elizabeth looked at the boy as if she had never seen him before.

"It was Chadwick's idea to dye his hair," muttered Lady Letitia roughly, stripping off her gloves and shrugging out of her cape. "He thought 'twould keep Jaimie from being recognized."

"Wicky?" asked Liza wonderingly.

"Yes, Wicky. He has spent the last three months searching for this little scapegrace of yours. Found him, too."

"Mama?" interrupted Jaimie, tugging at Liza's gown. "Ain't you glad to see me? I have been kidnapped."

Elizabeth, in response to his tugging, knelt down before him and the boy threw his arms around her neck and hugged her mightily. He then bestowed a most enthusiastic kiss upon her cheek and looked up at her expectantly.

Lady Letitia handed her bonnet and cape and gloves into Mrs. Beaman's hands. So, she thought with a most sinking feeling, Chadwick was wrong and I was correct. Liza does not at all realize that the boy is her own. "Come, Elizabeth," growled Lady Letitia, "it is Jaimie. Welcome your son properly, my dear, or he will think you do not know him."

"Jaimie?" Liza's great green eyes looked up at Lady Letitia and then back at the tiny gentleman who stood eagerly before her. "You are being Jaimie," she murmured to the child, "and I am being Liza. And I a puppy having. Playing with him we shall, *non?* His name is being Wicky."

A sigh behind her made Lady Letitia turn.

"I knew how it would be," murmured Mrs. Beaman sorrowfully. "But His Lordship was so determined that restoring the child to her would restore her mind. And I did hope. Oh, ma'am, I did so hope against all I knew to be sensible."

"Well, there is nothing to be done about it now," Lady Letitia sputtered. "Bring tea, Mrs. Beaman, if you will. And I am certain the tyke is hungry. I shall keep watch over the both of them. Only tell Battlesby where that confounded puppy is to be found and he shall fetch it for them to play with."

"And they did not recognize the bounder?" asked Gaffney, from the rear-facing seat of the Goodacres' traveling coach beside Lord Goodacre and Rossland.

"He wore a half-mask," Minerva provided. "And he so frightened Jebby, our fireboy, that the poor tyke cried out that Aunt Letty had gone off with the boy to a place called Skylark." Minerva and Lady Goodacre both occupied the banquette across from the gentlemen. "I am so very sorry, Chadwick, but Jebby is such a little boy. He did not at all understand what he had done."

"Well, at least your Aunt Letty's house did not burn to the ground," offered Lady Goodacre consolingly. "And no one was truly harmed. And you did have the good sense to come and fetch Charlie's coach and team. They will carry us much more speedily to Riddle than the landau and a single horse would have done."

"I still cannot believe you wished to come, Mary," drawled Rossland. "This is not the sort of escapade you ought to be involved in, you know. It is like to be dangerous."

"And who would stand propriety for Miss Potts if I did not come?" asked Lady Goodacre with a stubborn jut of her chin. "Truly, Chad, you have not the least idea how her reputation would sink should word get out that she had accompanied three gentlemen, unchaperoned, all the way to Skylark Cottage."

"Well, I rather thought she would *not* accompany us," sighed Rossland, "but she would not hear of remaining at home, anymore than she would hear of my going on without Charlie and Gaffney to lend me support."

"And rightly so," nodded Lord Goodacre. "No telling what awaits us at Skylark."

"Though why," mused Gaffney, "this latest villain should set fire to Lady Farin's house, I cannot conceive. He could not know that we had captured Langly and Girard. Not so soon he could not have known. No, and he could not have known that you and Miss Potts were on your way to Farin House either. And the servants were all safely tucked away and not like to cry for the Watch until it would have been much too late to catch the man, so why should he wish to set the house afire?"

"Perhaps he thought to pay Lady Farin back for some supposed slight or other. If we knew who it was, we would likely know why he set the blaze. And he has got an hour's start on us because of it," the earl added, a weary despair working its way into his tone despite his effort to avoid it. "An hour's start—merely because we had to put out that damnable fire."

Minerva leaned forward and reached across the space between them to take Rossland's hands into her own. "We will not be too late, Chadwick. Aunt Letitia and Battlesby will not so easily surrender Jaimie. And there is your caretaker as well. You did send a message to warn him, did you not?"

"Indeed. And I trust implicitly in Maitland's ability to organize the servants and stand off a ruffian or two. But it is Liza, you see. She does not need to be involved in any more nonsense, sweetling. Now she has got Jaimie back, she does not need to think that someone is attempting to take him away again. There is no telling what that might do to her."

Lady Letitia could not believe her ears as Battlesby announced the visitor. "Lord Whithall, what are you doing here?" she asked gruffly as that gentleman entered the parlor.

"May I be seated, my lady?" drawled Whithall as a great hairy puppy came to sniff at his feet and two sets of wide green eyes stared up at him from the carpet before the hearth. "My, what a pleasant scene. This, I think, must be Elizabeth and this young man—"

"I am Jaimie," contributed that lad, jumping to his feet and going to bow before the visitor. "And this is my mama. Only we is pretending she ain't my mama right now because mamas ain't s'posed to sit on the floor an' play with puppies."

"Oh." Whithall lowered himself into an ancient wing chair, dismissing the child with a nod of his head. "Well, I must say I never imagined, Lady Letitia, that you knew the least thing about all of Lord Rossland's troubles, much less that he had placed you and Miss Potts right into the midst of them. I am virtually astounded to discover you here. I thought at first that surely Rossland's mutterings were the product of a fevered brain."

"Chadwick's mutterings?" asked Lady Letitia with a glare. "And what, may I ask, do you know of Chadwick, Donald? And why should he be muttering anything at all within your hearing?"

"Yes, well, that is the sad part of the whole affair, my lady. You see, Lord Rossland has had a most unfortunate accident and I have come to fetch yourself and Miss Potts and the boy to him as quickly as possible."

One of Lady Letitia's finely drawn eyebrows lifted. "Chadwick told you that he had sent Mina and I here to Skylark in charge of his nephew?"

"Indeed, my lady. Lord Rossland has been attacked in the street by brigands, a knife shoved up under his ribs, and though in great pain, he begged that someone come fetch you and Miss Potts to him, and Elizabeth and the boy as well."

Battlesby, who had been standing silently in the doorway, was off like a shot at those words, darting out the front door of the cottage and around to the far side.

Lady Letitia, taking note of her butler's hurried departure over Whithall's shoulder, placed a most troubled look upon her face and began to wring her hands.

"Who is you?" asked Jaimie, staring at the gentleman. "I told who I is. Now you is s'posed to say who is you."

"Sturdy little chap, is he not?" smiled Whithall, giving the auburn curls a pat. "I am a friend of your uncle's, my lad."

"Rossland sent you to fetch us all?" queried Lady Letitia again. "He is badly injured then?"

"Oh, quite," replied Whithall. "Knocking at death's door. May not last the night. And dreadfully worried about the lot of you, if I may say so. Requested Goodacre to fetch you, but Goodacre would not leave Rossland's side, you know. So here am I, come to escort you back to London."

"Very well, Donald," nodded Lady Letitia with the merest tear in her voice. "Minerva is presently upstairs unpacking. I shall go and tell her to repack and we shall be ready in a matter of a few moments. Are you certain that Chadwick wishes for Liza and Jaimie to come as well?"

"He was most explicit," nodded Whithall, rising as she rose and then lowering himself back into the chair.

"Jaimie, come with me at once," urged Lady Letitia waving the child toward her. "And bring your mama. We must pack for the both of you as well. There is brandy on the cricket table by the window, Donald," she added, as Jaimie ran to take his mama's hand and tug her after him. "Please make yourself at home. We shall hurry, I assure you."

"Wicky, come," called Liza as her son tugged her from the room and down the hallway. The big puppy scurried after them. Lady Letitia led the little party up the front stairs and then as stealthily as possible, led them back down the back stairs.

"Mrs. Beaman," she hissed as they entered the kitchen, "take the boy and Elizabeth and hide quickly. Mrs. Sikes, you will help her to look after them. There is a gentleman here wishes to do them harm. I shall hold him at bay as long as is possible, but you must hurry and hide these two where they will not be found."

"There are men on watch at the edge of the woods, my lady," announced Battlesby, entering the back door. "And some along the track from Riddle. We shall have a fight of it, I fear."

"Ah, but we have the advantage, Battlesby," Lady Letitia smiled. "That oaf, Whithall, does not at all suspect that we know him for the villain he is. He assumes Minerva is with us. And lucky we are he made that assumption or else I should never have guessed. Even a dying Chadwick would not be such a nodcock as to send anyone to Skylark in search of Minerva when Minerva had accompanied him to the Duke of Wine-coff's residence."

"Indeed, my lady. I knew as well, the very moment he said Miss Minerva's name, that he had not come at Lord Rossland's bidding. I have warned Mr. Maitland and the others in the stables. Mr. Maitland, I believe, has established a plan with the servants remaining at Riddle for just such an occurrence. They will be here to assist us shortly."

"So, Mrs. Beaman, you shall take Jaimie and Liza and Mrs. Sikes to a place of safety. Where?" asked Lady Letitia.

"There is only the stable, my lady, if there are watchers in the wood."

"To the stable then. And I shall return to the parlor and occupy Lord Whithall's attention. Battlesby, have you Sir Hugh's pistol still? John Coachman will be required by Mr. Maitland, I assume, and our footmen as well if there are a number of ruffians."

"Indeed, madam, and so I told them," nodded that stalwart butler. "But I have Sir Hugh's pistol right here and I shall remain just outside the parlor door with it."

Lord Goodacre's traveling coach thundered into the drive at Riddle to find the house ablaze with lights, the front entrance standing wide open and the staff a remarkably horrible and dwindling army of spectre-like creatures marching determinedly off across the fields to the west with torches blazing.

"What the devil?" hissed Major Gaffney, gazing along with the rest of the occupants from the coach windows.

"I expect the villain has arrived at Skylark," mumbled Rossland. "That parade of torch-lit demons is most likely Maitland's doing. And there must be more than just our one man— quite likely a considerable number of them—or Maitland would not have gone to such an extreme."

"Straight down the track to the cottage?" asked Lord Good-acre.

"And speedily," nodded Rossland. "No telling, but from the look of it there may well be a whole contingent of villains lying in wait for us. Maitland is not one to waste his resources. The staff are marching toward the woods that front the Thames, but there may be ruffians along the track to the cottage as well. It will not occur to Maitland to attack those along the track until he has cleared the way for Jaimie's and Liza's retreat to the river. He don't know we are coming, you see."

"I am going up on the box," mumbled the major withdrawing a pistol from inside the sling on his arm. "The coachman has enough to do to hold the horses to the track at a dead run in this darkness. He shall be glad of a guard beside him to watch his back, believe me."

"Sweetling, it would be best, I think, if you and Mary remained here," announced Rossland as the major exited the coach and climbed awkwardly up beside the driver. "Charlie and I would both feel a good deal better knowing the two of you were out of harm's way."

"Not on your life, my lord," replied Mina, her lips set in a stubborn line. "You proposed marriage to me in case you do not remember and I had the good grace to accept. Therefore, wherever thou goest—"

Rossland could not help but grin. "Still, there is like to be some sort of battle, Minerva, and shooting."

"Yes, I know. And that is precisely why Mary and I shall sit upon the floor where we are less likely to be shot," declared Mina, suiting her actions to her words.

"Charlie, move your big feet," Lady Goodacre ordered as she followed Minerva's lead. "Oh, my gown will never recover from this experience. I shall need to buy a new one, Charles. No, do not frown down at me so. Miss Potts is not the only one who will not send her gentleman off into battle and wait around behind for news of him. Besides, we may contrive to be of some assistance. One never knows about such things. We can at the very least reload your pistols for you should you require it. I know very well how to do that. Are the powder and balls still in the case beneath your seat?"

"Yes, m'dear," Lord Goodacre replied and took one of his dueling pistols from the side pocket that always held them.

Lord Rossland, who had stopped to procure his own set of pistols from Rossland House, uncased them as well. Then the two gentlemen rearranged themselves, taking seats at opposite windows as the coach moved forward. In moments they were hurtling down the track at a spanking pace.

The first of the pistol cracks came as a great surprise to the young ladies huddled upon the floor of the coach. They had thought to have been prepared for them, but they were not and both jumped at the sudden popping sounds. They jumped even more at the roar of Rossland's pistol as it echoed and re-echoed within the confines of the coach. "So, we are correct," Rossland muttered. "There is a contingent of ruffians along the track. Sweetling," he asked, his mahogany curls tossing wildly in the wind as he passed his empty pistol down into Minerva's hand, "you will be careful, will you not? You *do know* how to reload a pistol? I shall never forgive myself if you should shoot yourself with my own popper."

Minerva's hand came up to take the emptied weapon from him as he aimed the second of his set. "I am not a mere schoolroom Miss, Chadwick," she sputtered. "I can load a pistol just as competently as I can drive a coach. My papa believed it good form for a young lady to be able to take care of herself in all situations."

"Oh, well then," mumbled Lord Goodacre, firing his own weapon. "And we know how well she can drive a coach, Chad. Not to worry about her. She'll do. Here you go my pet," he added. "I have every confidence in you, Mary, to do the thing properly and quickly, eh?"

Mary, her cheeks flushed with excitement, took the emptied weapon her husband thrust down at her and began reloading it as Charlie had taught her to do at their country home in Sussex.

Twenty

Inside Skylark, Whithall fidgeted impatiently, tugging his watch from his waistcoat pocket over and over again and frowning down at it in displeasure. He had downed one glass of brandy and was sipping sparingly at his second. He paused for a moment with the glass partway to his lips. He thought he heard a cry and a number of odd noises. He set himself to listen more attentively, to catch the sound again.

"I cannot imagine what is taking Mina so very long," growled Lady Letitia, who had also heard the noises. "I do believe, Donald, that Mina is flustered by the mere thought of your presence," she continued, hoping to draw Whithall's attention from whatever battle might be going forward in the field beyond the cottage where it stretched into the woods along the Thames. "Do you know, Donald, I do not think even to this day that Minerva has quite got over you. You were her very first love, you know. That, I think, is what makes her linger over the packing. She fears to come down and meet you face to face again.

"Of course, she must contrive to pack something for Elizabeth as well, but that cannot take an inordinate amount of time. I do so wish she would hurry. I cannot bear the thought of Chadwick dying all alone with only Lord Goodacre to support him. I have known Chadwick since he was in leading strings, you know, and though he may be deserving of a great deal of adversity, he most certainly does not deserve to die like that.

"Do you know, Donald, I believe that Mina was quite wrong

to have spoken to you the way she did that day. Now that I think on it, it was most uncalled for. But then, she is young and romantical and her dreams of love were crushed by over-hearing your reality. It is so sad, really, your misunderstanding."

"Misunderstanding?" grumbled Whithall. "Misunderstanding? I thought I was a cawker and a cur, Lady Letitia." Whithall scowled, his attention withdrawn from the odd noises by bitter thoughts of the indignity he had suffered at this lady's order. "You had me tossed from your house! Told me never to darken your doorway again! Is that how you handle a misunderstanding?"

"Tossed? Oh, never, Donald. Battlesby is much too old and too tired to have tossed such a large gentleman as yourself. But I do think I was a bit too harsh on you at that. It is the whole idea of marriage, really, for a gentleman to find himself a pliable Miss who will regard him with respect and give him heirs and keep herself quite out of his way in the country."

"Exactly!" nodded Whithall. "Exactly! And what Miss Minerva Potts found to be so scathingly angry about, simply because she had overheard me speaking the truth of the matter to Redfield—" Whithall did not finish the sentence. He thought he heard in the distance more odd noises and even farther off, the faint pounding of horses' hooves. "Demme, Lady Letitia," he frowned, downing the last of his brandy, "what is taking Minerva so very long? We must be away as quickly as possible. Rossland is like to be dead before we ever leave this place."

"Only be patient a moment longer, Donald," Lady Letitia was quick to respond. "In a moment we will hear the three of them upon the staircase, I assure you."

Three quick pops, like distant gunfire, reached Whithall's ears just as clearly as they reached Lady Letitia's, but that lady strove to ignore them completely.

"What was that?" Whithall mumbled to himself. "It sounded very much like—"

The sound of gunfire came again, this time much closer to the cottage and accompanied by the near and unmistakable

pounding of hooves along the narrow track from Riddle.
Whithall spun to his feet and seizing Lady Letitia by the wrist
yanked her to her feet as well. "Run upstairs and fetch them
all down into the hall immediately," he ordered. "Hurry!"
And he gave the little lady a most violent shove toward the
doorway.

"Why, Donald," droned Lady Letitia, ignoring his words,
rubbing at her wrist and staring implacably up at him, "whatever has come over you? Anyone would think you had run
mad."

"That was gunfire, my lady," sputtered Whithall, "and a
coach approaches rapidly. The villains who attacked Rossland
have followed me, I am certain of it!"

"Oh, I rather think not," replied Lady Letitia calmly. "I
rather think it is Chadwick in the coach, Donald, and you who
are the villain. Because Chadwick will have followed you, you
know, once he twigged to the fact that you are one of the
conspirators. And though Lord Langly did not betray you as
he should have done, I am certain that, faced with Chadwick's
wrath, your friend Mr. Girard was most free with your name."

"Girard? Girard? What do you know of Girard? Get the
dowager countess and Minerva and the boy at once!" Whithall
exclaimed, tugging a small pistol from inside his coat and
pointing it at the lady. "I will have them, Letitia. Immediately."

"I think not, sir," replied Battlesby stepping into the parlor
entrance, one of the late Sir Hugh's dueling pistols pointing
steadily at Whithall. "Your game is up, you see. Step away from
the bounder quickly, my lady," he urged then, but a mere
second too late as Whithall pulled Lady Letitia before him and
pointed the tiny pistol at her heart.

"Stand away, fool," Whithall roared. "Clear the door and
toss that popper to the floor. Lady Letitia and I are leaving this
place. You may keep the others for now. I have no more time
to wait upon them. Only inform Rossland that if he wishes
Lady Letitia's return he may advise me of it by placing a subtle
advertisement in the *Times*. I shall be pleased to exchange the
old bat for the boy at his convenience."

"Old bat indeed!" exclaimed Lady Letitia indignantly,

bringing the heel of her walking boot soundly down upon Whithall's instep and jabbing a sharp elbow into his ribs. "Of all the nerve! I shall part your hair with a kitchen knife, you great oaf!" And then she kicked him in the shin for good measure.

Whithall all but lost hold of his pistol. He did lose hold of Lady Letitia who threw herself energetically to the side. The pistol in Battlesby's hand fired and a wound erupted in Whithall's shoulder spewing blood. Surprised, but undaunted, Whithall took steady aim at the butler and cocked the hammer.

"Non!" Liza, an iron hoe in hand, burst into the room through the long casement windows behind him. "Pig!" she cried shrilly amidst a great deal of barking and bouncing from the puppy who accompanied her. And in a flurry of passion, before Whithall could so much as turn completely around to face her, she began to beat him violently about the head and shoulders. "Jacobin pig!" she shrieked, following each word with a whack of the hoe. "Papa saying Jaimie belonging to me! You be not my Jaimie stealing!"

The pistol flew from Whithall's grasp. He dodged away, his hands raised to cover his face, attempting to duck the next swing and the next. And then quite suddenly, the hoe came crashing down with a tremendous force at just the proper angle upon his skull and he noted with astonishing clarity the fierce, blazing emerald eyes that glared at him as he slipped toward the floor and the gigantic puppy's bared teeth that sank into his thigh, and then he groaned and slipped into unconsciousness.

Minerva gave only the tiniest of shrieks as the coach whipped to the right, shuddered madly and then toppled on to its side. The frightened, plunging horses dragged the vehicle a few feet further along the ditch before they were forced by the lack of wheels and the weight of their load to cease a forward progress though they continued to struggle and plunge amidst the traces. Below Mina, Lady Goodacre moaned, and atop her Lord Goodacre and Rossland muttered somewhat dazedly.

"Minerva, sweetling, are you all right?" asked Rossland worriedly. "Do not move, my girl. Not yet. Lie very still. We shall have you out in a moment, I promise you."

"Mary, Mary, dearest, do not you move either," Lord Goodacre mumbled. "No, Chad, do not you go kicking at that door. You will set your leg back three years doing that. I shall do the kicking. There, I have got the door wide now, Mary. We shall be off of you directly. Can you climb out, Chad?"

A distinct groan answered this question as Rossland pulled himself, stabbed shoulder, bad leg and all upward through the opening. In another moment he was helping Charlie out and then they both were tugging Minerva and Mary upward into the night.

It was very dark, for the coach lamps had gone out and clouds covered the moon and the stars. And it was ominously silent as well, Minerva noted with a shudder, as Rossland and Goodacre lowered her to the ground behind the wrecked vehicle and then lowered Mary gently down next to her. Not the slightest breeze whispered through the leaves or through the long grass beside the track. No birds called. No animals scurried about in the underbrush near them. Even the horses had ceased to plunge and whinny and now stood stock still in their tangled harness. It was a great shock after the rattling and creaking and wheezing of the jouncing coach and the exploding cracks of gunfire, that silence.

And then Rossland was beside Minerva, taking her into his arms and tugging her down to huddle behind the overturned vehicle and whispering in her ear. "Are you all right, sweetling? Are you certain? You have not broken anything?"

Minerva shook her head.

"Thank God," whispered Rossland, holding her tightly against him and kissing her softly and most tenderly upon the ear. "I shall never forgive myself for drawing you into this debacle."

"You did not draw me into it," breathed Minerva, leaning her head back against his broad chest and looking upward at his most stubborn chin. "I chose to join you of my own free will and I do not regret a moment of it. I would do exactly the same thing again. Why is everything so very quiet, Chadwick? And where are Major Gaffney and the coachman?"

"I don't know, my sweet girl. I expect the major and the coachman jumped as we hit the ditch. And I expect it is so quiet because our attackers are deciding how best to approach us. They cannot know that both Charlie and I have lost our weapons. But you are not to worry, sweetling. Even if Gaffney and the coachman have broken their necks and cannot come to our aid, I shall not let anyone harm you. Not while I have a breath of life in me. I love you, sweetling. Remember that will you not? By gawd, but I shall tear those villains apart with my bare hands if I must. I ain't called The Devil's Delight for nothing. Just think how delighted the Devil will be to have those villains with him in hell this very night and for all eternity. Shhh, someone comes."

And indeed, Minerva could hear footsteps approaching through the long grass on the far side of the coach. And then there were whispers. Muttered words reached her ears and gruff, heavy voices, though she could not make out what was said. And in another moment, Rossland leaned down and kissed her passionately on the lips and then moved awkwardly but quickly to the front of the coach and crept carefully across the traces. And Lord Goodacre, giving Mary one last kiss, nodded at Rossland and hurried in a crouch to the rear, leaving Mary and Minerva to huddle together behind the broadest part of the coach in the dark, frightening night.

The silence came again in a great and overwhelming wave that set both ladies to shuddering. And then, abruptly, Rossland bellowed an oath loud and strong into that silence, dispelling the unnerving hush and Lord Goodacre roared an oath just as loudly and strongly directly after him and both gentlemen flung themselves out into the darkness on the other side of the vehicle. Pistol shots again exploded, the stench of gunpowder filling the air, followed by a great hue and cry and the thudding of fists into flesh and the scuffling of feet amidst twigs and gravel. Gasps and cracks and groans and muttered expletives rained down all around them, some of the groans recognizably Rossland's and Goodacre's as Minerva, urged on by fear for the earl's life, dug about and around her searching for anything that might serve as a weapon. She was determined to join in this nightmare battle that she could hear but could not see. It might well be Chadwick's final battle, she thought, frantically seizing a rock in one hand and Rossland's ebony walking stick with the wolf's head top in the other. It might well be Chadwick's final battle, but he will not die alone on the field with no one to support him except Lord Goodacre. He will not! And gaining her feet, Minerva hurried as swiftly as she could, her skirts swirling around her, to the front of the coach. Carefully, she negotiated the broken traces behind the nervous horses and then with a cry born of love and fury she flung herself into the midst of the dancing, gibbering shadows that fought grimly and determinedly on the far side of the coach.

Lady Goodacre, with a solid piece of trim from the side of the coach in both hands, was not far behind. She, too, was determined to stand beside the gentleman she loved and though her heart beat wildly and tears blurred her vision as much as the darkness itself, she ran from the back of the ve-hicle to the spot where she thought Charlie still stood, fighting valiantly though surrounded by ruffians. With all the power she could muster, Mary swung the heavy oak board at one then another of the shadow figures, hitting shoulders and heads and thighs and knees. "Charles," she gasped, overcoming tears and trepidation to provide him all the support of which she was capable, even the support of her voice. "Charles, my darling, I am beside you. Fight on, Charlie, do. We shall rout them! We shall!"

Minerva's rock crashed down upon a great heaving shoulder because she could not reach as high as the villain's head. And that gone, she swung Rossland's cane with as much strength as fear and determination and adrenaline could produce. Left, she swung, and right, and around in circles, the fierce wolf's head biting into uncovered skin, cracking solidly against bone, increasing the groans and the cries of the battle. And then at

last the clouds were moving above them, being scattered by
the wind, and as the shrouded moon flickered into full light
Minerva saw through tear-filled eyes that Rossland's leg had
betrayed him and he had been felled. He had taken two
wretched hulks of humanity down with him, but he lay near
helpless upon the ground and was being kicked and pummeled by three other men above him. She watched him struggle wildly to regain his feet, but he could not. There was no
break in the beating to give him the least opportunity to get
his injured leg under him.

With a banshee-like cry Minerva rushed into the group of
men who towered over Rossland. Great hands clutched at her.
She tore free of them, the sound of her ripping gown never
reaching her ears. She swung the walking stick again and again,
beating the villains away, sending them dodging back, distract-
ing them from the earl. "Well done, Chadwick!" she cried as
she saw him at last struggle upward from the ground. "Well
done, my love. Now we shall take them, you and I and Mary
and Charlie! Now we shall show them what honest English
men and women are made of!"

"And I showing what an honest Frenchman being made of
too!" came a great bellow from down the track, and Minerva
became aware, most suddenly, of torches blazing and feet
pounding toward her. With a great clamor and cry, Rossland's
servants, led by an elderly gentleman with bushy muttonchops
and greying hair entered the fray, pouncing upon the ruffians
from Gravesend with enormous enthusiasm and cudgels
swinging.

Major Nicholas Gaffney fought his way determinedly into
consciousness. Somewhere very near to where he lay upon the
damp, cold ground the sound of fighting called to him. For a
very long moment he was certain he lay upon the battlefield
at Talavera, but the more he struggled to sift through the
noises assaulting his ears, the more he began to doubt the
truth of that. No, this fighting had not at all the correct sound

to it. There was no great belching and trembling of cannon for one thing. And though the sweaty fear of horses and the stench of gunpowder tickled at his nostrils, still he could hear no long guns firing. There were whacking noises and grunts and groans and cries of renewed attack, but all of it close and low and muffled. And there was most definitely the cracking of fists against jaws, he was certain of it. But there was not the barest clashing of sword against sword as there ought to have been.

His head ached fiercely though he kept his eyes tightly closed and when he attempted to achieve a sitting position all the dark world around him tilted and swayed and a blinding pain erupted behind his brow. He reclined again immediately. His ears were wrong then. He did lie upon the field at Talavera, must lie upon the field at Talavera, for that pain and dizziness were exactly what had forced him back into unconsciousness the first time he had attempted to rise after the barrage of cannon had sent his Challenger tumbling to the ground beneath him. He raised his hand to his brow and felt the blood flowing and sighed.

"Non," whispered a little voice somewhere above him. And a small hand caught at his own and placed it back down upon his chest. "The blood I am fixing," said the voice, and then he felt a pad of cloth placed upon his brow, his head very tenderly lifted and something being tied in place to hold the pad in position. "Papa and Wicky be not needing your oh so brave self right now. Papa and Wicky be winning."

The major opened his eyes. Pain burst and popped and shivered behind them. Still, he was determined and struggled through the torment to peer up at the person who spoke. Shimmering in the moonlight above him was the most beautiful face he had ever seen—the face of an angel. He blinked. The angel smiled down at him. "Almost over this most tiny battle is being," the angel whispered encouragingly. "Do not being afraid. I am not letting you to die. For Papa only to come and helping us I am waiting. Wicky he is helping now."

Major Nicholas Gaffney blinked and blinked again. The angel's face became that of a young soldier, then that of a thoroughly lovely woman, then that of an angel again. This was not the first time he had seen that face. He had seen that face often and always, always, it was accompanied by the deep and unrelenting pain in his head. Surely he was at Talavera!

"Who? Who are you?" he asked hoarsely, and the clear, smooth brow above him puckered. Then the sweet lower lip stuck out just the tiniest bit in a heavenly pout.

"I am thinking I am being Cameron now," whispered the angel in a most disturbing tone. "But not having the trousers and the jacket as is being proper am I. *Oui*, I am Cameron being because I cannot being Marie Elizabeth if there are fighting and armies. So saying my Wicky most explicitly. And you are being my most beautiful soldier. I am remembering you most well. Wicky is saying always we must not let you die. You are being a 'ceptional good man. Most especially I am not to letting you be dead."

"Cameron?" mumbled Gaffney, closing his eyes to ease the pain for a moment. "Marie Elizabeth? Thunderation!" he rasped, jolting upright and then gasping from the pain. He grimaced and groaned and then set his agony aside and stared around him in the moonlight. All confusion with Talavera fled as he caught sight of the overturned coach almost fifty feet behind Elizabeth. It was surrounded by torches and shadows bobbed and weaved and danced like spectres in their unsteady flare.

"Rossland," he mumbled, swiping at his brow with the back of his hand, knocking the hastily made bandage askew, and abruptly realizing that he only had one useful hand, that his other arm was still cradled in a sling. "Damnation, they have got Rossland and Goodacre surrounded. I must get to them."

"Non," replied Liza. "Is being papa's torches you see. Papa and his friends go running to save Wicky. Wicky and I are following, but Wicky is not stopping to fight. Wicky is sniffing and finding you and the other gentleman instead."

This explanation bounced in uncertain circles around Gaffney's brain, until a movement in the moonlight to his left betrayed the presence of a most ungainly puppy being shoved gently aside by Lord Goodacre's coachman as he rose groggily from the ground and stumbled dizzily toward them.

"Wicky," Gaffney muttered then. "That wretched puppy's name is Wicky?"

"*Oui,*" nodded the angelic Liza. "After my Wicky I am calling him. It being right I do so. Helping me to saving Jaimie and saving you he is doing. Being most brave and resourceful and curly he is, just like my Wicky. Mine Jaimie is," she announced then with pride and confidence. "My papa telling me this. This boy is being my Jaimie who is not being at all dead and I am not to letting the Jacobin pigs have him. I am not letting the Jacobin pigs having you, either," she added with a fierce scowl upon her beautiful heart-shaped face. "I am not letting them having you because Wicky would being most unhappy and perhaps crying even. And because," she added on a soft breath, "I am remembering that I am liking you very much."

"Cowards!" Minerva shouted as the ruffians who had attacked the occupants of the coach turned and fled before the onslaught of the newly arrived forces. "Poltroons! Recreants! Twits!"

"Ssshhh," chuckled a voice in her ear and a pair of strong arms wrapped possessively around her. "Hush, sweetling. We want them to run—all the way to Gravesend at the least. Do not be challenging them to return by despising their masculinity. May I have it, do you think?"

"Have what?" asked Minerva, settling adoringly into the great bear hug in which she was so tenderly wrapped. "Oh, Chadwick, I have never been so very angry in all my life. How dare they to attack you so? How dare they?"

"They were well paid to do it, I imagine, sweetling," Rossland murmured, nibbling at one of Minerva's ears. "Will you give it to me now? It will be a most horrendous hike for me to Skylark without it. Though I do admit that it proved to be even more destructive in your hands than the rhododendrons and perhaps ought to belong to you as a part of the spoils of war."

"Oh!" exclaimed Minerva. "Your walking stick!"

"Indeed," laughed Rossland, "my walking stick. I would ask if you were all right, sweetling, but even such a gudgeon as I can see that you are in top form at the moment. I doubt you will so much as feel the worst of your bruises for an hour or more. I have never seen you look so alive and invigorated as you do at this very moment."

Minerva turned in his arms to stare up at him in the moonlight. His face was as pale as ever she had seen it and great dark splotches covered his chin and his cheekbones. Blood flowed freely from a deep cut near his lip and a gash on his brow. And he seemed not quite as tall as he had always done, because he tilted down at her as though he could not quite hold himself erect. But, oh, he was the most beautiful man in the world, and she buried her face against his chest and hugged him with all the strength and energy that still pulsated through her—hugged him in thanksgiving for his continued existence and hugged him in joy at the knowledge that this courageous, honorable gentleman loved her and that she, indeed, loved him with all her heart.

In moments Lord Goodacre, with Mary tucked neatly and protectively beneath his arm, both of them looking quite as alive and invigorated as Minerva felt, appeared beside them. "The general has found Gaffney and m'coachman," Goodacre offered, and then leaned down and bestowed a soft kiss upon the top of Mary's head. "They were thrown a good fifty feet or more from the box. Gaffney hit a rock and split his skull, but John will do nicely once his dizziness disappears."

"The major is not dead?" Rossland gasped.

"No, no, broke his skull, Chad, not his neck. And Elizabeth has him well in hand, I understand. Your servants are helping him to the cottage. Appears there was some sort of confrontation at Skylark just as we suspected there would be. But the gentleman responsible for it, the general says, has been soundly defeated. I say, Rossland," mumbled Lord Goodacre shyly as he took the earl's cane from Minerva's hand and placed it into Rossland's, "have you ever seen the like of these two rapscallions of ours?"

"Never," grinned Rossland, starting toward the cottage with one arm firmly about Minerva's shoulders. "Two fire-breathing harridans we have got us, Charlie. Most certainly two of the most courageous and formidable and terrifying ladies in all of England. We shall need to be on our best behaviors forever now we know how dreadfully well they fight. Met the enemy blow for blow and sent him staggering backward. I have never been so very amazed or so very proud of any of my mates in all my life."

"The general?" Minerva queried, flushing prettily at so great a compliment though none could see she did so in the night. "You referred to a general, Lord Goodacre? Which general is it you speak of? And where did he come from? Are there troops stationed at Gravesend then who came to assist us? I saw only what I thought to be grooms and footmen."

"He means my caretaker, Maitland, sweetling," Rossland informed her, giving her shoulders a squeeze. "Maitland is my very own private general. But I doubt he will appear to help us make our ways to Skylark, not if he is involved in helping Liza with Major Gaffney, so we had best start off without him."

Twenty-one

"I am merely telling her that the gentleman in the parlor comes her boy to steal," explained Rossland's caretaker as he applied a slab of raw beef to one of Lord Goodacre's eyes—the one that was rapidly swelling closed. "And then I am handing her a hoe and assisting Wicky the dog and herself in through the casement window."

"You did not fear for her life?" asked Major Gaffney resting his aching head, competently swathed in bandages, against the high back of the chair into which he'd settled.

"*Non,*" chuckled Maitland with a shake of his greying head. "Already are the most formidable Lady Letitia and the stalwart Battlesby discomposing this Whithall. My Marie, the final touch she must add only. She is knowing well what we do to Jacobin pigs wishing to steal little boys. Most especially her little boy, which I am telling her Jaimie is."

Maitland's wide green eyes bestowed a good-humored gaze upon Major Gaffney as that gentleman stared amazedly up at him. "Your Marie?" the major whispered hoarsely.

"Mine Jaimie is being," declared Liza emphatically from where she sat upon the carpeting beside the major's chair with Jaimie asleep in her lap. Gaffney's fingers played gently, unconsciously, through her thick, dark hair.

Rossland's eyes, though battered about the edges, sparkled with mirth in the major's direction. "And now Whithall is quite competently thrust up and under guard in the stables. Well, and that's a good night's work. What is it, Gaffney?" he asked with a grin, his arm tightening about Minerva, who had snuggled in beside him upon a wide wing chair. "You look thoroughly dazed."

Major Gaffney's lips parted to speak, but before he could utter so much as one syllable, Rossland's caretaker shrugged and laughed and went to remove the major's fingers from Liza's frizzled curls. "She is being not the dog, Major. A lady my Marie is being and not to be petted by any gentleman without he expressing a most serious intent to her papa."

Gaffney flushed like a schoolroom Miss and removed his fingers from her hair.

"And of the ladies speaking," continued the caretaker, "never I am seeing such magnificent ladies, Chadwick, as the Lady Letitia and the Lady Goodacre and your Miss Potts. I am thinking is only my Marie being so brave in all the world and here are three also of the bravest sitting in our own parlor."

"Indeed," agreed Rossland, bestowing a kiss upon Minerva's head as she rested it cozily upon his uninjured shoulder much as Mary rested hers upon Lord Goodacre's shoulder where they lounged upon the small settee.

"We would have sooner coming to your aid, Chadwick," continued Maitland, handing the bruised and battered but remarkably wide-eyed Major Gaffney a snifter of cognac while stepping carefully over Wicky who nestled at his feet. "We would have sooner coming, but I am thinking to rout those along the woodland first in case we escaping to the Thames must be. We driving them off, Chadwick, with a show of force so heinous that we fire only few shots. Which is *bon*, no? Because is only I am having the long gun. Is Lady Letitia's footmen and coachman pistols only fire."

"Yes," nodded Rossland, "but the sight of all of you marching so fearlessly amidst those blazing torches was horrifying enough to give even me pause."

"And your staff did have a most horrible variety of lethal implements upon their shoulders," offered Lady Goodacre, tenderly stroking her husband's cheek. "It is no wonder that those ruffians fled when your servants fell upon them, Chad."

"I should have fled," agreed Lord Goodacre, "had I not realized that they were on our side when they finally came."

"Continue your tale, Maitland," urged the earl. "You routed those along the woodland and you sent Liza to provide the final blow to Whithall. And then—"

"And then hearing the great crash of your coach we are coming as quickly as is possible," provided Maitland as Mrs. Beaman and Battlesby arrived with trays of cold meats and cheeses and bread and butter and he helped them to offer refreshments to the roomful of weary warriors. "But being most naughty is my Marie and running after us to helping her papa. Still, she is being most brave and is finding her beautiful soldier and keeping him safe, so there is no harm for her.

"These ladies are being all remarkable are they not?" he added with a most admiring look at Lady Letitia, so admiring, in fact, that that lady flushed and wiggled quite perceptibly under his gaze. "My Marie, and the incredible Lady Goodacre, and the so courageous Miss Potts, and the most intrepid and admirable and beautiful Lady Letitia! Such a fine woman, the Lady Letitia," Maitland declared and shook his greying mane and cocked a bushy eyebrow most seductively in Lady Letitia's direction. "Such a tigress she is being and so verimost drenched in courage! I have always desiring such a woman as this."

"Ah, a conquest now begins, I think," grinned Rossland. "Am I not correct, Maitland?"

"*Oui,*" nodded the bright-eyed and enthusiastic caretaker.

"Well, you most certainly shall have my assistance in the affair. It is the very least I can do. Though the last of our secrets shall need to be disclosed if you are to have any respectable opportunity for success in the matter."

"What matter?" queried Minerva softly, tugging at Rossland's undone cravat. "What in the world are you speaking of?"

"Bah, it is not the secret no longer," declared Maitland with a shrug of his broad shoulders. "All here are knowing now that I am Marie's papa being. I am saying so myself. You are hearing me and they are hearing me."

"Yes, I expect they have heard the words, but Gaffney, for one, cannot believe it. I can see from the look in his eyes. And if I do not introduce you properly to Letitia she will have nothing to do with you, you know, because I have told her only the tiniest bit of our secret and aside from being a most formidable and intrepid woman, she is a very high-stickler."

Minerva giggled at Rossland's description of her Aunt Letty and at the most provocative gleam that fired in Maitland's eyes, and Rossland tickled her cheek with one long, slim finger.

"My dearest Letitia," he continued after blowing once in Minerva's ear, "may I have the great pleasure to present to you General Charles François Dumouriez, who is, as you may have determined, Liza's papa and Jaimie's grandpapa. He is a Frenchman, of course, and a most brilliant soldier and he has generously been acting as caretaker of Riddle in my absence. Well, actually, he has been acting as a number of things at Riddle for the past three years, ever since my father and Cameron smuggled him across the channel on the *Mary Jane*."

"Smuggled him across the channel on the *Mary Jane*?" bellowed Gaffney and immediately placed a hand to his head at the pain that flashed behind his eyes. "Smuggled him across the channel on the *Mary Jane*?" he asked again more softly. "Are all of the gentlemen in your family mad, Rossland?"

"Yes," declared Lady Letitia roundly. "Every single one of them. But Chadwick is the very worst."

"Well, but, he is Liza's papa, Letitia," Rossland pleaded with a distinct twinkle in his eyes. "And he needed our assistance or he should never have been able to come to England."

"*Oui,*" nodded the general. "And coming I wish to be with my Marie and my Jaimie."

"Exactly," agreed Rossland. "But we could not let on who he was, Gaffney, and simply request the government to allow him entrance any more than we could acknowledge Liza's heritage, because we were not at all certain that Napoleon would not send agents into England to destroy them both. He did send agents into Austria to seek the general, Letitia. But that is of no particular interest at the moment, I expect, because all I mean to say is that the general is indeed the general and quite an eligible match, let me tell you."

"A match?" sputtered Lady Letitia. "An eligible match? And

what has that to say to anything? Chadwick, have your wits deserted you completely?"

"Minerva, my sweetling," drawled Rossland, ignoring the lady's protest ruthlessly as he bestowed a kiss upon the top of Mina's most disheveled golden curls, "have you told your Aunt Letitia that we are to be married?"

"N-not yet."

"We are going to be married, Letitia, your niece and I. I have asked her and she has said yes."

"Well, I should hope so," Lady Letitia pronounced with some asperity. "Else I should be forced to have her papa call you out for sitting there with her practically in your lap. Though how you will support her, I cannot imagine. Well, but I expect something must be worked out because you have positively compromised the gel. I shall speak to Arthur about it. Perhaps he will see his way to increasing Minerva's dowry. Or perhaps I shall be able to provide her with an income. But now that Jaimie has been returned, he is the Earl of Rossland and you are back again to being a mere second son with nothing to recommend you, Chadwick. And though the general may be an eligible match for someone, you are not."

"Wrong, Letitia. I have considerable to recommend me because Jaimie ain't the Earl of Rossland, I am. Jaimie is le Comte d'Iberval. He is Armand Girard's son, not Cam's. I shall explain it all to you later. I only mention it in support of the general's apparent new cause, to prove his most considerable respectability—it is considered respectable, I think, to be the grandpapa of a French count—because I know the general will require all the ammunition he can get in his approaching battle."

"In support of—? His approaching battle?"

"In Dumouriez's new cause supporting," chuckled the general as he stooped to pluck Jaimie from his mother's lap and carried him to the sofa where he settled with the boy in his arms beside Lady Letitia. "Wake up, my little one," he whispered in the child's ear, "and see who is being here with you."

Jaimie's wide green eyes fluttered open, his hands reached

up to go about the elderly gentleman's neck. "Grampapa," he smiled on a yawn, "I missed you."

"Grandpapa," breathed Major Gaffney then, still clearly astounded. His hazel eyes glowed in the firelight as his gaze roamed from Maitland to Jaimie to Elizabeth who now rested her head comfortably against his knees. "It is all true then. To think of it! The whole affair is mind-boggling! And never a word of it reached our office. Castlereagh will be utterly astounded!"

Rossland sighed. "I do hope, major, that you can refrain from informing Castlereagh until we are assured of the general's safety. Even the band of villains who thought to plague us, and imagine themselves so very intelligent and powerful, have not the least idea that General Dumouriez resides in England and we should like to keep it that way for a while longer."

"Yes, well, I quite understand that," nodded the major.

"But you will agree, Gaffney, that Lady Letitia cannot be thoroughly and appropriately wooed by a mere caretaker," added Rossland. "So we shall need to think of something more appropriate to make the general. Perhaps a foreign diplomat? Because the general is determined to woo the lady—even I can see that. And you, Gaffney, now that I think on it, had best watch yourself very carefully. You are entwining your fingers in Liza's curls again and Liza's papa will begin to take note and will be forced to call you to account for it."

"Marie's papa already have been noticing," chuckled General Dumouriez, one large hand abandoning its hold upon Jaimie to reach out and pat Lady Letitia's knee. Lady Letitia started at such an audacious action and slapped his hand away. But then she blushed quite prettily and looked up to study the craggy French face and the emerald eyes that smiled down at her.

"Yes," murmured the general. "Be pleased to be study me well, most wonderful lady." And with a cock of an eyebrow and a most seductive pursing of his lips he brought another, most beguiling flush to Lady Letitia's cheeks. "Marie, come away from that gentleman," ordered the general, never taking his eyes from the lady beside him.

"*Non,* Papa," responded Liza emphatically. "This most beautiful gentleman I am liking very much. I am remember him. He is in the fighting with my dear Armand. Me and Wicky are saving him. Then he is disappearing—poof—and I am marry Cam. I am loving Cam, so is being all right. But now Cam is being dead, Papa, and the pretty soldier is return. I am keeping him, Papa."

"She is keeping me, Papa," grinned Major Gaffney.

"But Elizabeth is not well," protested Lady Letitia.

A thick but very gentle finger applied itself tenderly to Lady Letitia's lips. "Shhh, most wonderful lady," murmured the general. "Already my Marie is knowing Jaimie belonging to her and is accepting. Soon again she will being herself."

"Yes, but she is not herself as yet," replied Lady Letitia with a formidable scowl. "And we do not know Major Gaffney at all well. And in England, my dear general, a gentleman does not sit about stroking a young lady's hair unless there is an understanding between them."

"Poof!" laughed the general, snapping his fingers in the air. "Dumouriez saying there is be the understanding between them. My Marie is keeping him and he is keeping my Marie and I, most formidable of women, am keeping you!"

"Well, of all the audacious old libertines!" declared Lady Letitia, struggling to sink a winsome smile beneath a scowl.

"He has been taking lessons from Chad," snickered Lord Goodacre giving Mary's earlobe a gentle tug. "Audaciousness lessons. Audaciousness does creep over one when one spends too much time in Rossland's company."

"I do think, sweetling," Rossland murmured in Minerva's ear, "that they have all become lunatics. Somehow we have set a most demented cupid loose upon the world, you and I. What say you?"

"Oh, most assuredly," giggled Minerva softly. "But they are delightful lunatics to be sure. The cupid who spurs them on, Chad, must be applauded. His aim of the arrow is capricious but most cheeky. Will Aunt Letitia allow the general to woo her do you think? I do hope she will. She has been so very lonely since Uncle Hugh passed away."

"She will have no choice in the matter, sweetling," whispered Rossland in reply. "The general will woo her say yea or say nay. And if I could devise to win such a heart as your own, why the general, who has much more experience at such things than I ever dreamed of having, will certainly contrive to win your Aunt Letitia's heart."

"Oh, I do hope so," sighed Minerva. "Only think how very happy Aunt Letty will be to have a husband again."

"Yes," Rossland smiled, "and a nephew-in-law within reach whose ears she can box at the slightest provocation. She will be in high fettle with two of us to chase about and terrorize, believe you me, for the general will not deny her the pleasure of it any more than I have ever done."

"And Lord Goodacre and Mary will never doubt each other's love again," sighed Minerva. "It is so romantic how she rushed to his aid. It will be his shoulder Mary cries upon from now on and not yours, Chadwick, ever again."

"No, and if all goes well, the major and Liza will make a match of it too and I shall not need to worry about either Liza or Jaimie."

"Most certainly not," agreed Minerva, thinking how wonderful it felt to be so well wrapped in her Chadwick's strong arms.

"I will only need to worry about you, sweetling. And that will be delightful," Rossland announced with his widest and most endearing grin. He then punctuated his statement with a tender kiss upon her brow which jumped to her nose and lower to her waiting lips where it turned much less tender and much more passionate as Minerva returned it with great enthusiasm. "Now," he chuckled breathlessly as their lips parted, "there is only one more hurdle to be got over and we shall all live most happily ever after."

"What hurdle is that?" asked Minerva, her blue eyes widening. "I cannot think of a one."

"Perkins," sighed Rossland dramatically, though his lips twitched upward. "Perkins and Martindale and the rest of my staff in town. They are afraid you will prove to be a high-stickler like your Aunt Letitia and usurp their power and return them to an equal footing with other people's servants. I have known it from the moment Martindale assured me that my gold waistcoat with the crimson stars was adventurous and that you would be mad for it. They have been plotting, I think, to make you spurn me."

"Why, I never!" gasped Minerva.

"No, do not frown, sweetling. You have not the least idea how intimidating the thought of having a woman like your Aunt Letty for a mistress is to them. Perkins and Martindale have known your Aunt Letitia since she was a schoolroom Miss and she has always been most demanding. I cannot for the life of me guess what stratagems even now bubble and boil and brew in Mount Street. But we shall need to seize the fire from under them, you and I, and cool them down to nothing. Though I have not the least idea how to go about it."

Angelica Deane swirled into Farin House, breezed right under Battlesby's nose and fairly flew up the staircase to the back parlor with her mama puffing and heaving and rustling right on her heels. "You will not believe it!" she cried excitedly, spying Mina upon the striped settee and rushing directly to her. "Oh, Mina, my poor darling, you will never believe what has happened! Word of it is all over London!"

"Everywhere, simply everywhere," nodded her mama in agreement, lowering herself to a lyre-backed chair beside Lady Letitia. "One cannot walk down Bond Street without hearing it spoken of. It is even the topic of conversation at Hatchard's. Good morning, Letitia. I do hope your house did not suffer too much damage from that terrible fire the other night. I did come to see if I could be of any assistance, but I was advised you were from town. Was it something in the kitchen burnt?"

The rush up the staircase had brought a distinct breathlessness to Angelica Deane's mama's voice and a hot red flush to her cheeks and she paused to wave her chicken-skin fan most violently before her face. But before Lady Letitia could speak so much as a word in answer to her query, Angelica's excited voice filled the gap. "Lord Rossland's nephew has been found alive!" trilled that young lady. "But he is not Lord Rossland's nephew at all!"

"He is not?" asked Mina, making her eyes into great circles of wonderment while attempting to keep from giggling. "But who is he then?"

"He is—he is—oh, my dearest Mina, I would give anything at all not to have to tell you this, because even if you do not love The Devil's Delight, still you have been much in his company and have grown fond of him, I think."

"Yes," nodded Minerva innocently, "I expect I have grown rather fond of Lord Rossland."

"Yes, so I thought," sighed Miss Deane, "and that is precisely why you must know what everyone is saying—because it would be such a tremendous shock for you to hear it on the street or at someone's drawing room."

"Angel, do get on with it," prodded Minerva with a tiny chuckle disguised as a gasp. "What are they saying?"

"That Lord Rossland's nephew is actually his—his own—"

"Love child," fluted Miss Deane's mama into the pregnant pause. "They are saying that The Devil's Delight seduced Elizabeth from under her papa's very roof, ran off with her, put the poor woman in the family way and then refused to marry the gel!"

"They are saying Lord Rossland's elder brother married her to avert a prime scandal," chimed in Angelica with great enthusiasm. "But that is not at all the worst of it!"

"It is not?" Minerva asked, struggling to keep from bursting into laughter.

"Oh, no! Because it turns out that Elizabeth does not hold a British title at all—she is Prussian! The daughter of a Prussian Prince!"

"Oh, good gracious," responded Minerva, putting a hand to her mouth in feigned amazement.

"Yes, and the boy was discovered wandering near the shore after the *Mary Jane* foundered by hirelings that his own grandpapa had sent to England to search for him. And once the prince—Prince Vladimir Androkov he is called—had the child, he set about to discover where The Devil's Delight had hidden Elizabeth as well and—and—"

"And what, Angel?" Minerva prodded.

"And Lord Langly and Lord Whithall helped his highness to discover her at Riddle. But when they went to fetch her, Lord Rossland was there and there was the most terrible fight. Lord Langly and Lord Whithall and the prince's hirelings beat The Devil's Delight to within an inch of his life!"

"Oh, I cannot believe it," Minerva mumbled.

"But it is true!" protested Angelica. "At this very moment Lord Rossland is confined to his bed and both Lord Langly and Lord Whithall have departed upon a ship to the Americas because The Devil's Delight has sworn his revenge upon them, you see. He has vowed to kill them both the very instant he has recovered enough to stand!"

Minerva's hand clapped over her mouth again. Tears started to her eyes. And then Battlesby appeared in the doorway with Lord Rossland and General Dumouriez directly upon his heels. And Lady Letitia, with eyes that twinkled mischievously, had the effrontery to blurt out, "Why, I believe it is Prince Androkov and his victim arrived even as we speak!" And Minerva could control herself no longer and burst out into uncontrollable whoops and guffaws and giggles, tears streaming down her cheeks.

"Oh! Oh!" gasped Angelica's mama, fluttering her fan spastically.

Miss Deane simply stared toward the doorway with jaw dropped and eyes wide.

In a moment Rossland, his much battered countenance thoroughly bemused, was kneeling before Minerva, offering her his handkerchief, his lips twitching upward. "What is it, sweetling?" he asked softly, though not so soft that Angelica Deane did not hear. "What has sent you over the edge?"

"You—" gasped Minerva on an indrawn breath. "You—"

"I what, Minerva? I cannot possibly be responsible. I have done nothing but enter the room."

"You, sir, are a rake and a scoundrel and you ought to be

ashamed to show your face in this house!" declared Angelica roundly and then gulped.

"N-no," laughed Mina with a shake of her head. "N-no." Attempting most forcefully to control her laughter, Minerva put her hands upon Rossland's shoulders and looked him squarely in the eyes. "You s-seduced Liza and g-got her with child and m-married her off to your br-brother!" she managed on strangled laughter. "And—and her papa beat you to with-within an inch of your l-life!"

"No, really?" asked Rossland innocently, his eyes sparkling with mirth.

Minerva nodded, her curls bouncing gaily.

"Devil take it but the gabblemongers have managed to get it all wrong again! I tell you, sweetling, there is not a one of them can carry a straight tale about me even when I have invented the tale myself. Why that ain't in the least what I told Perkins and Martindale to pass around. Is it the servants you think cannot get it aright or their masters and mistresses? Miss Deane," he said then, turning to look up into Angelica's awe-filled eyes, "does the rumor at least mention that Liza's papa is a French aristocrat who emigrated to Russia at the first rumblings of the revolution?"

"N-no!" laughed Lady Letitia from across the room, tugging at General Dumouriez's sleeve gleefully and urging him into a chair beside her. "He is a Prussian Prince named Androkov!"

"Moi?" asked the General, his green eyes crinkling with mirth. "But my most dear lady, I cannot the Prussian speaking."

"You cannot the English speaking either," grinned Rossland, giving Minerva's knee a pat and regaining his feet. "Imagine, Letitia," he threw over his shoulder, "you are being courted by Prussian Royalty!"

"Courted!" gasped Miss Deane's mama, staring around Lady Letitia to the foreign gentleman. "Letitia?"

"To this marvelous lady I am losing my heart," nodded the general. "I am her courting until she being my wife."

"Oh! Oh!" gasped Miss Deane's mama.

"Yes, but I have quite ceased to court Miss Potts," announced Rossland to the room in general.

"You have?" Angelica queried, staring up at him.

"Indeed. I have decided to marry her instead. And you, Miss Deane, because you are Minerva's very best friend, have the first chance at that tidbit because the announcement will not be in the papers until the end of the week. Miss Potts has agreed to become the Countess of Rossland and I have agreed to provide her with prestige, comfort and convenience. Well, whichever and as much of the three as I can manage at any rate. You will be certain to get the thing straight, will you not, Miss Deane? Because I have been informed that you are to be Minerva's witness and it would be most unkind of you to spread an incorrect rumor about her. I am the one she has agreed to marry, not the Tzar of Russia or some Prussian Prince or an Italian Count, just me."

"Indeed, Angel," grinned Minerva, giving that young lady's hand a happy pat. "I am to marry Chadwick Leonardo Brumfield, the Earl of Rossland, and no one else. Will you do me the honor to stand up with me? It is to be at St. Paul's and Lord Goodacre is to be Chadwick's witness and my papa is coming all the way to London to escort me up the aisle."

"Yes, but at this particular moment I have come to escort you to Rossland House, sweetling."

"Not on your life, Chadwick," declared Lady Letitia. "Mina is not your wife as yet and she will not enter a bachelor's establishment. You would know such a thing is totally unacceptable if anyone had bothered to raise you with the least sense of decency and decorum."

"Not even if we take Battlesby with us—and—and—Miss Potts's abigail?"

"Minerva does not have an abigail," sniffed Lady Letitia. "She shares my Amy."

"No, you are wrong there, Letitia, because I have hired Miss Potts an abigail."

"You have what?"

"He is hiring already for Miss Potts the abigail," reiterated the general. "It has costing him a most dreadful expedition amongst the shops."

"An expedition amongst the shops?" Lady Letitia's very confused gaze met Minerva's most curious one. Angelica Deane's ears literally perked up in anticipation. Angelica Deane's mama ceased to fan herself and leaned eagerly forward in her chair.

"What has the hiring of an abigail to do with visiting the shops?" queried Lady Letitia. "Chadwick, what does this mean?"

"Only that I have been to every fashionable emporium and haberdasher's in London, Letitia, in search of a bonnet with cherries upon it. Found the right one, too. The chit is happy as a clam, you may believe me."

"Oh!" cried Minerva, jumping up and throwing her arms most disgracefully around Lord Rossland's neck. "Mitzie is to be my abigail!"

"Yes, if you will have her. She does not know the first thing about how to go on, mind you, but I thought perhaps you might teach her, sweetling."

"Of course I shall teach her and she will do admirably, I promise you."

"Mitzie?" murmured Miss Deane thoughtfully. "Mama, was not that the very name of the little, ah—"

"Good heavens, Letitia!" exclaimed Miss Deane's mama, rising from her chair in agitation. "The man proposes to turn his stolen cyprian into your niece's abigail! I have never heard such a disgraceful proposal in all my life."

"Bosh," responded Lady Letitia with a grin playing about her lips. "I have heard much more disgraceful proposals. But Mina still cannot accompany you, Chadwick, unless you provide me with a most excellent reason for this most exceptional outing."

"Well," sighed Rossland, one arm quite blatantly around Minerva's waist, "it ain't exactly my idea, Letitia. It is Perkins and Martindale and Mrs. Dowe and Davenport and all the rest of them. The, ah, Prussian Prince here, has been regaling them with tales of Minerva's courage and all she did to aid me at Skylark, and they wish to cry peace."

"Cry peace? I had not the least idea that there was a war."

"Yes, well, there were the beginnings of one, but they are now inclined to reconsider their stance in the matter. Only, they wish to interview Miss Potts in reference to certain points."

"Interview Miss Potts!" cried Angelica Deane's mama at the same moment that Minerva burst again into laughter. "Well, I never heard the like! Of all the unmitigated gall! A gentleman is expected to rule his servants, Lord Rossland, not to be ruled by them. How dare they! Have you no pride whatsoever?"

"None," grinned Rossland. "I know that for a fact because Lady Letitia has told me so time and time again. Oh, and I believe little Charity has a request to make of Miss Potts as well and she will not be quite so intimidated, you know, if she is allowed to speak before Mina is my countess."

"Your junior scullery maid?" asked Lady Letitia bestowing a glowering look upon the general, who took note of it and removed his hand from her knee.

"Uh-huh."

"What is it Charity wishes of me?" Minerva queried, nestling comfortably in the crook of Rossland's arm.

"Well, I have not heard her entire speech—she has made up a speech and was practicing it word by word when I departed the house, you see. But the gist of it is, sweetling, that Charity wishes to go to the penny school to learn to read and write."

"Oh, but that is wonderful! She can do so, can she not, Chadwick?"

"Most certainly if you approve, though she will be the very youngest scholar there—it is held in Lady Glendening's back parlor every Tuesday and Thursday afternoon. Lady Glendening's housekeeper is one of the teachers and my first footman, James, is another. But there is more to Charity's request," chuckled Rossland, bestowing a kiss in front of everyone upon the tip of Minerva's nose. "Charity wishes to, ah, have her ducklings back."

"Have her ducklings back?"

"Well, I have told her that those precise ducklings are no longer available—because I do not want them traipsing around behind me everywhere I go—but she has agreed to settle for new ducklings who will love to follow her instead of me and has devised a most particular plan for caring for them—it involves the sinking of a great pot into what remains of my back yard to make a pool for them to swim in—"

"Oh, dear," grinned Minerva. "And I expect that if I am seen to discourage such an undertaking, your staff will think me most unfeeling."

"Not at all, sweetling. There is not a one of my staff but Mitzie thinks it at all a good idea—which is why I think you ought to allow Charity to do it. Perkins and Martindale and the rest have had their ways in most things for an amazingly long time, you know. And since I know you are not about to tear down their quarters or dispute their precious three entire free days a month or demand that I remain in the country nine months out of every year—well, you really ought to do something contrary."

"I ought?"

"Um-hmmm, just to show that you are the lady of the manor and not to be ruled by their every whim."

Lady Letitia could resist no longer and burst into chuckles. "This is it, Chadwick? This is the extent of your power over your staff? You hide behind Mina's skirts and get her to discipline them with ducklings?"

"Yes," nodded Rossland gazing most innocently in Lady Letitia's direction. "Besides, Letitia, I think I liked the little fellows. I think I should like to have some of them swimming about in a great pot outside my kitchen door. And just think of the speculation and conclusions such a situation will raise amongst the gabblemongers. Why they will be able to dine out for weeks upon it. And what a wonderful laugh it will provide us when Miss Deane and her mama hear the rumors and come to tell us why I have put them there. You will come, will you not, Miss Deane, and see that Mina hears every word of what is said?"